THE WOMAN IN THE CLOSET

BOOKS BY KENNETH J. HARVEY

The Woman in the Closet

The Flesh So Close

Everyone Hates a Beauty Queen

The Great Misogynist

Nine-tenths Unseen

Kill the Poets

Stalkers

The Hole That Must Be Filled

Brud

Directions for an Opened Body

THE WOMAN
a mystery
IN THE CLOSET

KENNETH J. HARVEY

A Midnight Original Mystery
THE MERCURY PRESS

The publisher gratefully acknowledges the financial assistance of the Canada Council for the Arts and the Ontario Arts Council. The publisher further acknowledges the support of the Department of Canadian Heritage through the BPIDP.

Cover design by Gordon Robertson
Edited by Beverley Daurio
Composition and page design by Task

Printed and bound in Canada by Metropole Litho
Printed on acid-free paper
First Edition
1 2 3 4 5 02 01 00 99 98

Canadian Cataloguing in Publication

Harvey, Kenneth J. (Kenneth Joseph), 1962-
The woman in the closet
(A midnight original murder mystery)
ISBN 1-55128-065-5
I. Title. II. Series.
PS8565.A6785W65 1998 C813'.54 C98-932202-5
PR9199.3.H37W65 1998

Represented in Canada by the Literary Press Group
Distributed in Canada by General Distribution Services

The Mercury Press
Toronto, Ontario, CANADA M6P 2A7

For Beverley Daurio,

in appreciation of her unwavering faith

ACKNOWLEDGEMENTS

The expertise of various individuals helped me greatly in completing this project. I would like to thank the following for giving freely and generously of their time and specialized knowledge: Jerry Russell, Head of Security at Newfoundland Telephone; also at Newfoundland Telephone: Jack O'Keefe and Emily Strong. Numerous members of the Royal Newfoundland Constabulary helped without reservation. Among them were: Chief L.P. Power, Constable Karl Piercey, and those in the Central Investigative Division (CID): Inspector Bob Shanahan, Lieutenant Ab Singleton.

A special thanks must be extended to Sergeant John House of the Criminal Behaviour Analysis Unit for his innovative knowledge of Investigative Psychology. His patience, generous cooperation and mental astuteness made my research all the more enjoyable and intriguing.

THE WOMAN IN THE CLOSET

PART ONE: DIALLING

PROLOGUE

The teenager stretched up on her tiptoes, her sneakers pressing hard against the narrow concrete walkway at the rear of the suburban bungalow. It was difficult to get a clear view of what was going on. Straining, her leg muscles quivering with pressure, she could just barely see in through the window. The scarlet curtains were drawn in the bedroom, but in the middle— where the two drapes met— a thin slit gave her a view of the paralysing, red-shadowed scene. Two women lay on the bed. One of them was completely still; the other was pleading desperately behind her gag. A man in a uniform was standing above them, holding a gun, pointing it at the dead woman and speaking to the other, commanding her. Then, without further gesture or explanation, the man fled the room, the bedroom door slamming shut, the sound vibrating in the clapboard against the teenager's chest. The teenager watched the woman roll from the bed, her struggling hands bound behind her back, her fingers quivering, scrambling to open the drawer in the nighttable, her fingertips reaching in and delicately, awkwardly attempting to lift out a pair of scissors that dropped back in. Her face shrieking silently, her features contorting as she tried again, digging hysterically.

The sound of the back screen door creaking open. The man standing there as the girl flinched away from her view through the thin red slit, dropping back down onto the soles of her sneakers. The man called her name, in a harsh hushed tone as he came toward her. A firm hand clasped her shoulder, leading her toward the back door, leading her into the house as she gasped to catch her panicky breath.

ONE

Yvonne endured the line-up at Consumer's Distributing. She hated line-ups, hated having to wait. Anticipation wore her down. She needed something; she wanted it. Birthdays. Christmas. Presents. What was the point of wrapping up presents? Why couldn't the gift just be given over without all the bells and whistles? It was going to be opened anyway. Why torture someone with: "Guess what it is? No, just *guess.*"

Glancing back toward the store fronting that led out into the mall, Yvonne considered leaving. If she didn't need the caller ID so desperately she would take off. But the phone calls were beginning to resemble the exact pattern from her past. And she craved to find out who was trying to drive her crazy. This time. There was no end to it. She shook her head in disgust and leaned ahead to have a look up the line. No movement. The calls could not be coming from the same person who had made them so many years ago. That was impossible. But she needed to know who was taunting her, and she needed to be certain.

Yvonne shifted on her feet. She glanced at her watch, although she vaguely remembered doing so about thirty seconds before. Still 3:00 p.m., peak shopping time at the Village Mall. Three p.m. on a Saturday. Three p.m. any day was peak time for consumers to be out and about. She had learned this invaluable piece of information while working for Terri Lawton, her exceedingly efficient, ball-breaking boss at Eastern Trade Shows. The crowds always became unbearable on the convention centre floor around that time of day, the line-ups at the registration desks snaking down the wide luxurious foyer of the Delta Convention Centre.

Three p.m. and she still had to visit the liquor store. She had barely made her 2:00 appointment to have her hair trimmed, just a half inch snipped off to even up the ends of her long coal-black hair. What was it about Saturdays? They were supposed to be holidays, but ended up being as busy as any work day, with a seemingly endless string of shops to visit, chores to do.

She scanned the mental list: pick up a bottle of merlot for Terri Lawton to celebrate the success of the upcoming Canadian Police Chiefs' Annual Convention and Trade Show, which reminded her (that sinking feeling, the weakness in the backs of her knees) should she contact the police or not? Those aggravating telephone calls were starting to become more than just a nuisance. The person had not said a word yet, not a word. But that was only a matter of time, Yvonne realized, delving back to the memories of the calls that had tormented her teenaged years.

No, she told herself, I'm not interested in delving. She stopped herself from remembering. What was done was done. Her psychiatrist, Dr. Healey, continued to insist as much. The past— forget it. It was just a bunch of abstractions. She glanced at her watch, tapped the facing with her brownish-red fingernail, then brought it to her ear to hear that it was ticking. Still no movement on the line. She scanned the shelves behind the counter. Electronic goods at cheap prices. Telephones, answering machines, caller IDs....

She'd take care of the calls herself. If there was one thing she wouldn't be doing it was running to the police for every little thing that happened in her life. That's right, she told herself, clenching her jaw tighter. I can look after myself. Have up to this point. Here I am. My own place, my own car, a good job. Who did that for me? No one, except me.

A bottle of wine, she reminded herself, shifting her thoughts back on track. If the show wasn't a success— and Terri Lawton rarely touched anything that did not prosper— then Yvonne would drink the wine herself. Best to get a good bottle of Australian red, a Wolf Blass, great value for the dollar, Terri had told Yvonne. A fine bottle of wine; that way, if the show flopped, then Yvonne would keep the bottle for herself; the rewards of failure would be sweet for her.

After popping home for messages, she'd scoot over to Ideal Charms to pick out a new outfit for the show. A sexy yet classic dress for opening day. That was the tradition. She'd bought a new dress, a cotton spring number with short sleeves and a blue floral design for the last show— ComputerWorld. That had been her first exhibition with Terri. The show had been a great success and so— in Yvonne's Irish superstitious ways— she had declared that the buying of a new dress had been responsible for the show's good fortune. And why not, she told herself. I bend over backwards to please those exhibitors, everything short of giving them blow jobs.

Tilting slightly to her right, she peered forward, counting out the people leading up to the young man at the computer register who was checking in customers, keying in their orders and then summoning the next person on line. Five, six, seven ahead of her. She straightened and flicked the gleaming length of her black hair back over her shoulder, her attractive features hardening in distraction as one of the clerks laid a large box with a photo of an infant's car seat on the counter and called out, "Mr. Davies." Her shockingly white skin seemed even whiter beneath the fluorescent lights, her deep brownish-red lipstick glistening lusciously on her full lips, her long thin brows so black above her wide hazel eyes.

Yvonne felt the anticipation tightening in her stomach. Maybe I don't really want to know who's calling. Maybe I should just get my number changed. She teetered on the verge of stepping out of line, leaving, but the air conditioning was soothing against her bare arms and legs. She had been wearing t-shirts and shorts for the past three days. A heatwave held St. John's in its grip. Stifling temperatures of 31 Celsius. North America's oldest city, usually so temperate in the summer, a mixture of sunny days and grey foggy ones, was burning hot in the streets. The outdoors was like an airless oven. How much to get my apartment air-conditioned? She made a mental note to ask her landlord, Mr. Prouse. Heat troubled her greatly. The mere thought of it made her sweat. Plus, she hated being around people while under bright lights. Something about this unnerved her, unsettled her stomach. She thought that she might be sick. Too many people. But she steadied herself, clutched onto her patience. She imagined her apartment, the telephone sitting on her desk, ringing. Once she discovered the number of whoever was pestering her, she would call back, have a little fun of her own, scare the hell out of whoever was responsible for toying with her. I can play the game just as well. I'll show them. The wave of nausea creeping through her stomach worsened. She imagined herself in the mall bathroom, on her knees, emptying her stomach into the toilet bowl. She heard a shrill ringing in her ears, as insistent as the drilling of a telephone. She was going to be sick. A cool sweat broke loose on her skin, chilling her arms and legs, dampening her forehead.

"Fuck," she mumbled, louder than intended, so that the elderly woman in front of her glanced back with a suspicious look, briskly eyeing Yvonne up and down. The woman then tilted her head in an impatient manner, as if trying to tell Yvonne something, as if party to the tension mounting in her head, the woman's old face so accusing. "You," she said, pointing her wrinkled ring-clad finger toward the smiling clerk standing so accommodatingly behind the counter. "You. It's your turn."

The apartment door was locked. Deadbolt plus standard household lock—Mastercraft or Stanley. The man traced the keyholes with his gloved finger, then raised the Entry-2000 from his pocket. It was shaped like a handgun, but with a shorter, thicker barrel that measured two inches in diameter. Setting it against the deadbolt keyhole, flush to the metal, the man held the device steadily in place and listened to make certain no one was near in the upstairs hallway. Only the faint sound of a television playing. He tightened his grip on the Entry-2000. He had named it himself. The word "Entry" had such resonance in this day and age.

He tautly pulled the trigger, his hand reverberating with a jolt as the tight springs released, as the thin resilient slivers of metal were propelled into the keyhole, fitting the contours of the slot. Pressing the lock switch on the device, he then carefully revolved it, as if turning a key, and the deadbolt was smoothly withdrawn.

Again, he paused to listen before pressing the retraction switch on the Entry-2000, extracting the slivers of metal with a resounding click. Glancing toward the main entranceway— no more than ten feet away— of the old Victorian house, he saw through the frosted glass in the porch door that no one was near. No shadows cast from approaching figures. He would hear them coming in the main door first, pausing in the vestibule to either buzz someone into the refurbished four-apartment house or to unlock the inside door. For that matter, he would hear them coming up the walk. The house was set back sufficiently from the tree-lined street to provide plenty of warning.

Positioning the Entry-2000 against the lower lock in the centre of the doorknob, he repeated the procedure. Without looking over his shoulder to study the apartment door directly behind him, he slipped the apparatus away into his pocket and turned the knob.

The initial sensation of the door letting go to his touch never failed to thrill him. Moving into someone else's apartment was like stepping into the guts of a mute machine, lifting away the lid to view what made the machine tick, so quietly.

Opening the door, he caught the perfumy fragrance in the air; every house and apartment had its own unique smell that alerted him, revealed certain minuscule workings. He stepped in and carefully, without glancing back (never give the impression that you are entering a place where you are not meant to be), shut the door behind him.

The first thing he noticed was the telephone on the desk by the window. The flashing tiny red light on the answering machine, the basic white rectangular model with no bells and whistles, only the message and the beep and the red light, flashing. Real dinosaur technology. Probably bought at Canadian Tire. But women were generally like that. Nothing too complicated when it came to technology. As long as the basic function was performed they desired no knowledge of how the contraption was structured, the electronic components that sparked within. Women were more concerned with image, the surface. Style, and the prettiness of design. The colour.

This was how the man saw things, in relation to Yvonne, anyway. He was quite familiar with her anxious nature, her demanding ways, her superficial strength, masking the devastating toll the past had exacted.

He glanced at the clock on the wall, imagined its guts, the notched wheels and springs, the batteries slowly, obligingly releasing their charge, a faultless current. The clock was made of thick ceramics and featured a colourfully painted cow and chicken raised on the surface, a pig and a horse as well.

The time was 3:15 p.m. The safe time. The time when people would most likely be out, working, shopping or picking up the kids from school.

He did not bother touching her items, shied away from opening cupboards and drawers. He was not interested in familiarizing himself with the way she might be living. He knew that it was all a lie. She had not changed that much.

Reaching into the pocket of his suit jacket, he extracted the XLR-40 and moved through each room, holding the square three-inch transmitter in his hand. It failed to vibrate, informing him that no hidden electronic bugs had been set in place prior to his visit.

Glancing up at the hallway ceiling, he scanned ahead until sighting a smoke detector just outside the kitchen entranceway. He pulled a chair from the kitchen table, briskly uncapped the smoke-detector cover and reached into his pocket to lift out the 3.7 mm. pinhole lens. It was one-inch square, larger than a quarter, and fit neatly behind the clear cap of the guide light on the detector. He hooked the wires to the 9 volt battery already present. Snapping the cover shut, he thought of other measures. There was no detector in the bedroom. He would have to deal with that room later.

Video taken care of as best he could manage, considering the circumstances, he set his mind on audio.

Standard places of concealment for microphones. Out of the way areas. The kitchen: behind the dusty refrigerator (the bugging device coupled with a static reducer to eliminate the hum of the cooling system). The living room: the wooden framing beneath the couch. The bedroom: looped to one of the centre springs in the bottom of the bed. The bathroom: beneath the sink in the vanity, secured with a thin strip of silver duct tape, up around the drain pipe.

Crouching by the vanity, he opened the doors and smirked at the twisted arrangement of pipes and drains. All these hidden particulars, stuck away, buried. No one interested in seeing the systems that permitted life to function in an efficient trouble-free manner.

Awkwardly leaning in, he carefully ran his hands over the copper pipes, sensing their coolness, then checked the black plastic ABS pipes for leaks and found that they were in a competent state of repair. One thing he did not need was a plumber snooping around.

The microphones would give him faultless audio. They were intensely sensitive, with a bottom range of -104 dB, ensuring him the luxury of picking up even the most intimate whispers.

He made a point of not looking at Yvonne's belongings before leaving. Treading straight toward the door, he glanced at the clock and saw that it was 3:28. He smiled at the expediency of the task performed. Those who had trained him would be quite proud. No, he doubted that. They would be pleased with his efficiency but not with the nature of his invasion or the means by which he produced the end result. Not any more. Times had changed. His people no longer thought that way.

Recalling the final thing he had come for, he hurried back into the bathroom and searched out several long black hairs. There was one swirled beside the silver taps of the sink, another four stuck to the tub. He placed the strands in a plastic baggie, then stepped into the bedroom and discovered several more around her pillow and in the sheets. The couch offered him numerous hairs, all lost down between its cushions. He zipped up the baggie. A done deed.

Listening with his ear against the door, he heard the main door shutting and his heart roused him, speeding steadily, his eyes shooting toward the clothes closet to the left of the door. Always somewhere to hide, always places of concealment where people kept their hidden things, out of view.

He held himself perfectly still as the footsteps passed, moving toward the stairway and up to one of the apartments on the second floor of the big old house. He sensed the thud of the apartment door closing upstairs, the sound travelling through the structure of drywall and lumber, the sound rattling the copper pipes in an almost imperceptible way, the sound vibrating through the lengths of 110 and 220 volt electrical wire that snaked within the walls.

He opened the door to see that the carpeted hallway was empty. It was easy after that. Stepping out, he shut the door. A man in a hallway, looking perfectly in place. Nothing abnormal about that. A visitor, or a tenant. He would seem as if he belonged.

Outside, with the afternoon sun pressing fiercely hot and brilliant on his face, he was paused by the arid quality of the air. At once, he began sweating, the droplets rising on his scalp. He stepped down from the threshold and glanced at the number beside the door— 64. 64 LeMarchant Road. Numbers told him so much. He would be lost without them. He was just about to stroll up the short walk that led out to the street when he caught sight of Yvonne in the corners of his eyes. She was standing at the side of the house, in the shade of a maple tree, studying the colourful flowerbeds, no doubt after having parked her red Escort in the small tenant lot in the back.

"Hi," she said, looking straight at him, offering a friendly smile. She was holding a bag with something square inside, more than likely a box, its hard edges straining against the white plastic. The man smiled and nodded, moving on quickly, not wanting the human feel of her. That would only complicate matters. He erased the fit length of her body, the warm sensation of her smile, the crinkling at the corners of her eyes, the rise of her pronounced cheekbones, the faint invitation in her wide hazel eyes. He dismissed the pale delicateness of her skin, the fine sleekness of her hair. He chased all of her charms from his mind. They were of no use to him. Absolutely no use.

TWO

The narrow closet was dark, masking the two still eyes that stared straight into blackness. Judy Cramer had been dead for seven hours and eighteen minutes, a numb cool body with a grimacing expression fixed permanently on her masculine face.

Seven hours and eighteen minutes before, she had been sweating, naked, masturbating on her bed while someone stood over her, watching, her senses shockingly alive.

Now, her skin was dry. She did not feel the earwig zigging across her greenish toes. She did not perceive the sleeve of her favourite white cotton dress resting irritatingly close to her cheek. She drew no breath in the closed space where she had been dragged and stuffed.

The previous night, Judy had welcomed her visitor, had been led into the bedroom. The couple had undressed, the visitor instructing Judy to lie on the bed and open her legs, touch herself. Her body becoming aroused, twitching and swaying, painstakingly nearing climax. The visitor had been speaking, giving instruction, but then had abruptly lifted the telephone receiver from its cradle beside the bed, as if it had rung.

The visitor had pretended to listen, giving a mock surprised reaction. The visitor had said, "It's for you," and then leapt onto Judy, playfully guiding the receiver into her opened mouth, making her suck it, pushing it an inch deeper while Judy's eyes registered bewilderment and discomfort, then forcing it down the tight enclosure of Judy's throat until she retched and squirmed, startled, frightened by how her jaw ached. She was finding it impossible to breathe.

Then— in one swift movement— the visitor had reached over, ripped the telephone wire from the wall and wrapped one end around Judy's hands, the other around her neck. The telephone receiver was yanked out of Judy's raw throat, making a sucking popping sound. In a mounting frenzy, Judy kicked and gagged, her lips swelling while the visitor sucked them a bruised purple, and the surge of Judy's life gradually dwindled to a mute flicker. The last sensation she had felt was something hard and cold being forced between her legs. Then she had died.

The next morning, when the closet door was pulled open by Judy Cramer's ex-husband, he was shocked and horrified by the sight of her opened mouth, her protruding tongue, curled and hard, her bruised face and purple breasts tightly bound with telephone wire.

Taking one step back, Judy Cramer's ex-husband saw that her thighs were splotched with blackish-red blood. A curve of sculpted plastic protruded from between her legs, and from the receiver's listening piece hung the coiled length of cord— as if something inconceivable had been born and snipped free to survive on its own.

Mrs. Kieley watched out the front window of her upstairs apartment in the old Victorian house at 64 LeMarchant Road. From the second storey, she had a sweeping view of the old narrow streets sloping toward downtown, the colourful row houses huddled together— their flat, slightly slanted roofs and small windows. Off to the east, out of her field of vision, stood the huge elegant Victorian mansions of Circular Road and King's Bridge Road, where the merchants had lived— the Crosbies, Ayres, Bowrings and other powerful families of their sort— and then north, running back into the land, the suburbs of the seventies, the strip malls, burger franchises and the newer modern divisions that continued to be constructed.

Mrs. Kieley rocked in her chair. She stared down over the hill, past the clutter of row houses— burnt orange, turquoise, robin's-egg blue— toward level ground that skirted the harbour, where several modern buildings poked up through the lines of squat historic properties. At the foot of the steep hill stood the chunky grey building that housed city hall and all its "foolish municipal politicians," as Mrs. Kieley called them, "special-ed politicians." To the right of that— the Delta Hotel Complex. Mrs. Kieley had been there to lunch with her son. Fine service, but the food wasn't all that hot; nothing to write home about.

Water Street— the main commercial area— lay just a few streets over, nearer the water, its attached rows of merchant buildings lining both sides of the street. Downtown certainly had gone downhill since when she was a child, shopping in all the fancy stores, being treated like royalty. Bowring Brothers, London, New York and Paris— all gone now, driven out of business by the monstrous malls across town. She missed that special attention from the clerks, everyone knowing everyone else. She recalled the old cash payment system, the money set in a container and run along the ceiling through a system of thin cables. It was a joy to watch it scoot toward the cashier's office, then whisking back as the change was delivered. Such thrilling magic!

Scanning the waterfront, Mrs. Kieley caught sight of a red and white Coast Guard ship tied up across the harbour, beneath the ragged granite of the White Hills. And another ship with FISH PATROL printed on its side in red letters. She enjoyed this view immensely after those bland years in the St. Agnes Home with no view other than of the parking lot and a narrow grassy path with a few stark benches set here and there.

She drew her gaze back to the street beneath her window, beyond the concrete walk leading in to the house. Gregory, her police sergeant son, would be arriving home soon from work, and she looked forward to his talk of the latest news on the murder of that woman down on Prescott Street. They had found her this morning. The reporters on the two local channels, CBC and NTV, had said it was believed the victim had been found in the nude. A sex murder!

Just the sort of thing Gregory had tried to escape by leaving Toronto, transferring to the Yukon, and then back to Newfoundland. Mrs. Kieley worried for him. He seemed under a great deal of pressure lately. He had changed so much, working on all those horrible cases. Then his move to the Yukon. All those years in the St. Agnes Home and not a word from Gregory. Maybe that's why he was so set on having her live with him now, to make up for his neglect. Of course, she forgave him, but there was still the pang of hurt that wouldn't go away when her thoughts drew up the past.

Rocking in her chair, she pledged not to pry into his work. It only seemed to aggravate him. She would mention it briefly, and if he seemed apprehensive, then she'd broach another topic. No doubt, he'd been assigned to the case.

Gregory Kieley had moved to Toronto when he was a young man, leaving his mother back in St. John's living on her own— until she had fallen and broken her hip. No one to look after her. No family left living in St. John's. While up along, Gregory had managed to get his dream— a job with the RCMP. But a few years on the force and he had stopped talking about work completely, vowing— it seemed— to keep all the speculation and information about the murders he was trying to solve out of his personal life. It was interfering too much, he once confessed (a rare confession, so unlike him), with relationships. Was that what had caused the break-up with his wife, Donna? The morbidity of his work? Gregory wouldn't talk about Donna with his mother. Another subject that was taboo.

Sixteen years stationed in Toronto had made him a different person, quieter, more reserved, changed him so much so that— at the age of thirty-eight— he gladly accepted the position back in St. John's, Newfoundland, after he'd received the memo circulated from RCMP headquarters.

Gregory had telephoned his mother at St. Agnes to inform her of the news. She'd sensed a muffled enthusiasm in the announcement. "I'm coming home," he had said.

She was overjoyed when he told her that they would be living together. He planned to rent a comfortable apartment for them. He would be working fewer hours in St. John's. After all, it was a quiet enough city, only 170,000 people, a quaint place with its small-town warmth.

Mrs. Kieley appreciated living in the centre of town. She was only a few blocks from the Basilica, not that she could ever visit, her knees bothered her too greatly, and her hip still gave her trouble, but it was nice knowing that she was close by. She felt at home in the refined surroundings on LeMarchant Road, took comfort in the shadings of the mature golden and red maple trees. Her apartment was close to two hospitals, St. Clares and the Grace General, as well as having a choice of video and convenience stores just around the corner on Cookstown Road.

Mrs. Kieley continued rocking, watching out the bay window and sipping her afternoon tea from a rose-patterned china cup that she lifted from the wooden serving tray beside her. The tea was tepid, but bearable. Holding her cup in her lap with both hands, she glanced around the living room, then took a bite from her toast, the orange Robertson's marmalade thickly spooned on. She was still somewhat amazed by her move to this new place; the high ceilings and the ornate trimmings instilled in her a feeling of belonging, of affinity with the ways of her youth.

The place was classy. Only three other tenants in the house and plenty of room in each unit. She had met all the other tenants when she moved in. Mr. Prouse, the handsome sixtyish landlord, had made a point of taking her around, leading her in a gentlemanly fashion to each apartment door. There was the attractive young businesswoman, Yvonne something or other. She was very sweet, and offered her assistance should Mrs. Kieley need anything.

"Sarah," Mrs. Kieley had insisted, touching the young woman's hand. "Please, first names, we're neighbours."

Mrs. Kieley had dressed up for the visit, wearing a loose grey house dress, matching grey bauble earrings and a grey bauble necklace. She wanted to show the other tenants that she fitted nicely with the refined look of the neighbourhood. After all, these houses had once belonged to the fishing merchants in Newfoundland, the upper class that ruled the island. It was up to her to not tarnish their image.

Mr. Prouse had fawned over Yvonne, watching her with a special look. No doubt, he was taken by her. When they were through visiting with Yvonne, Mr. Prouse complimented Mrs. Kieley on her looks, a twinkle in his ice-blue eyes. She knew that look. The man was a real charmer, nodding and bowing as they made their way along the introductions.

Across from Yvonne's apartment was Mr. Prouse's own apartment. "I'm here, right on the premises, just in case you need anything at all," Mr. Prouse had said, tapping his door with his fingers as they passed.

Mrs. Kieley liked the idea of the landlord living on the premises. He could keep an eye on things. No noise. Mrs. Kieley despised noise, especially at night when she was trying to catch a bit of sleep. It was so difficult to sleep these days.

"I'm poisoned by the noise," she would often say at the St. Agnes Home, because there was always some disturbance going on, the other patients calling out or the nurses milling about the corridors.

Guiding her upstairs to meet the tenant in the apartment across from hers, Mr. Prouse apologized about the climb, but the apartment on the second floor was all that was available and they would move her downstairs if Yvonne Unwin decided to leave. He would give her his apartment, but it was required under Section 669 of the Landlord and Tenants Act that the landlord reside on the bottom floor of the building in which he lived.

Mrs. Kieley gave a moment's thought to this piece of information as she climbed the stairs. He must be telling the truth. Unless he was trying to romance Yvonne. She wouldn't put it past him.

On the top level, they paused by the doorway across from Mrs. Kieley's. "Mr. Brett," Mr. Prouse whispered carefully. "Very temperamental," he said, scrunching up his face. "Artist. I saw his picture in the paper once. But a nice young man." Mr. Brett would not answer the door at first. He roughly called out, "Yeah?" but then turned polite once he heard who it was (which— of course— was perfectly understandable considering there had been no buzz on his intercom security system to announce their arrival). Mr. Brett was a young unshaven man with dark hair, decked out completely in black: t-shirt and jeans, running shoes and a string of thin black rawhide tied around his wrist. His features struck Mrs. Kieley; the sharp angles and the deep brown of his eyes gave him a predatory look. He was eating a wedge of canteloupe, slicing out pieces with a steak knife and stabbing the orange fruit with the tip before popping it into his mouth. He smiled at Mrs. Kieley in a dark menacing way that young male artists favoured. The boy had charisma, but he was suspicious-looking, too, as if he was trying to hide something.

Standing in young Mr. Brett's doorway, Mrs. Kieley had caught a glimpse of paintings hanging on the walls. Smears of black with pink in them. The pink resembled something, but it would be too pornographic to believe that what she was seeing was accurate. It would be a scandal. She wished she had taken her glasses for a better look. Other paintings had what appeared to be yellow eyes staring out from the darkness.

Mrs. Kieley recalled the young artist's menacing smile as she laid her cup of tea on the table beside her rocking chair. The smile had been so youthful and self-assured, cocky. The boy was capable of anything.

Taking another neat bite of cold toast, she faced the window and saw a taxi pull into the paved drive that led around back to the small gravel parking lot. It stopped within her sight and her son leaned his tall body out from the passenger seat, raising his hand in thanks to the driver.

He was home, finally. Now, she could learn the latest about that strange murder. She wouldn't pry. But hopefully Gregory was in the mood to talk.

Yvonne slid the caller-ID machine out and tossed the small white box onto the forest-green velour couch. The couch and its matching armchair were both brand spanking new. She was renting to buy. Most of the furniture in her apartment— the new table— with the pine top and milk-blue wooden legs— and pine chairs in the kitchen, the double bed with its wrought-iron headboard and the pine bedroom set— were rented. Even the big black stereo television, the video recorder and the CD unit were being paid on. She could buy them in a few years, if she still cared to keep them. The only item of any value that she owned was the huge Navajo rug that covered most of the living room's hardwood floors. She had been surprised to find it at Walmart.

Slipping the clear protective plastic off the caller-ID module, she lifted the fitted styrofoam from the top. "Another toy," she said, feeling somewhat like a child at Christmas, a hint of the magic, only there was no cool draft to complement the thrill of the season. The apartment was humid, sticky, the air stale and heavy. She had stripped down to her mauve bra and bikini panties as soon as she stepped into her apartment, finding any excess clothing a gross irritation in the merciless heat. She grabbed up the white box to find the coiled cords in their own clear plastic bags.

Setting the contraption next to her phone, she pulled out the chair at her desk, the wood clammy against the backs of her legs. She opened the instruction booklet and began reading.

As her eyes skimmed over the attachment diagram, matching jacks with jacks, the telephone rang. She could not get it all in fast enough, her eyes skimming the words for immediate understanding.

"Shit!" She raised the device and, fumbling with the chords, plugged one end into the back of the caller ID and then... what?... the other end into the wall jack, so she'd have to disconnect the caller and then connect the telephone plug into the back of the machine.

The telephone continued ringing. Her stomach turned over. She clamped her lips tighter.

If I pull the plug, she reasoned, then the caller will think he was disconnected and call back. She reached down and pinched the jack's tiny lever, tugged it loose. The telephone died. She quickly replaced it with the plug from the caller ID and shoved the line from the telephone into the receiving jack in the back of the caller ID. Heart beating soundly, she paused, staring at the digital display, waiting for it to reveal the number the moment the telephone sounded its first ring.

A smile grew on Mrs. Kieley's lips as she braced both hands against the arms of the rocker and pushed herself up. Groaning, her knees were troubling her; the arthritis seeming to have worsened since her move to the apartment. Was it the stairs? The hardwood floors with no rugs? They looked nice, sure enough, but they were hard as the top of Christ's head. That, she told herself, and my weight. If only I could lose a few pounds. She went out of the living room, down the windowless hallway toward the back of the house and into the kitchen. At the oak counter, she stuck her fingers into the bag of jube-jubes, fingered out a red one and popped it into her mouth.

"Diet tomorrow," she assured herself, fishing out a black jube-jube, her favourite. "No excuses." She pushed the bag back toward the off-white teabag tin next to the bigger tin marked Sugar and then the largest one with Flour in raised letters across its front. She glanced at her high-blood-pressure pills, wondering if she had taken them after lunch. Her buzzer sounded and she waddled out into the living room just in time to hear her son announce himself in a formal manner that made her feel very proud.

"Hello, Gregory," she said through the speaker, sputtering slightly, out of breath, her heart pounding from the exertion.

"Forgot my key."

"Come in, my love." And she pushed the button to permit his entry.

No more than ten seconds later, she heard his tap-tap-tap on the door and opened it. She hugged him warmly and stretched up on her tiptoes to kiss both his cheeks, holding his face in her soft hands to look at his features. He was a tall man with straight brown hair combed neatly in place. He was handsome in a rough way. A man hardened by what he had seen and been through, his shy grey eyes unwilling to meet hers.

"How you doing?" he asked, briefly glancing at her.

"You get up here so fast," she commented, ignoring his obvious discomfort with her open display of affection. "And not even out of breath."

Gregory smiled, his eyes sad, dipping down at the ends. He tossed a newspaper on the table beside the door, then flung his suit jacket down on top of it. He was wearing a white shirt, the top button fastened even in the heat, a navy blue and white striped tie perfectly in place. He had not even allowed himself to roll up his sleeves. The sharp creases in his navy blue trousers were there because he had ironed them himself.

"Why don't you take off that tie?" Mrs. Kieley asked, reaching to pull it off. She had it in her grip before Gregory could protest.

"I'll iron it." She held it crumpled in her hands and started toward the hallway at the other end of the living room. "I don't know why you won't let me iron your clothes, or wash them. You want a nice cup of tea?"

"Sure." Gregory followed his mother into the kitchen, a man in absolutely no hurry, arriving at his leisure. He watched as his mother filled the kettle, holding the tie in one hand as if having completely forgotten about it. He leaned back against the counter and folded his arms, stared at the white linoleum.

"I think I'll just have a glass of water," he decided. "They say it's the best thing for weather like this."

Watching him, Mrs. Kieley's heart sank. He seemed so dejected, so concerned, preoccupied. "Don't be foolish," she said, shooing him back with a wave of her hand. "Have a nice cup of tea." She patted her soft silver hair with her palm, fluffing it, making certain she looked presentable.

"You sit down, Mom," his voice was low, measured. "Relax."

"No." She held out her arm. "I like doing this. You just be quiet. Respect your old mother."

A dull protest registered in his eyes, "You know I don't like you using the stove. I worry."

"How's work?" she asked, ignoring his displeased tone as she twisted off the cold water tap.

Gregory frowned and glanced away, toward the small window at the corner of the kitchen that gave a partial view of the long narrow back yard with its huge trees, neatly clipped grass and flower beds— tended to by Mr. Prouse— surrounding the edges of the wooden fence and skirting the narrow tenant parking lot. Gregory sighed evenly, "I don't know."

"Of course you do." She gave him an encouraging smile as she set the kettle down on the stove and switched on the wrong burner. She sat at the small round table beside the stove, the neck-tie crumpled in her hand.

Gregory went over to the stove and slid the kettle onto the burner that had turned bright orange. "You want tea?"

"What're you doing?" his mother asked, but she did not wait for an answer. "Leave that alone."

Gregory raised his hand, a slow gesture of surrender.

"It'll boil. Just leave it."

"I'm backing away," he said, hands still raised, wondering what he would do with her, if he could bring himself to putting her out of her misery.

His mother smiled, "Now, tell me about your day. What about that woman who was killed? I saw it on the news."

Gregory settled in the chair across from her. He glanced back at the cupboard doors. Again, he regarded his mother, leaned with his elbows on the wooden table-top. His hands joined in one big fist beneath his solid chin.

"What's the latest?" she asked.

"Not much."

"You want some tea?" his mother asked. "I'll put the kettle on."

"It's on, Mom," he said plainly, without the slightest strain of impatience, watching the table-top.

The kettle whistled and Mrs. Kieley rose from her chair. "That was fast," she said, whisking cups down from the cupboard. "That's a fine new stove."

"A few things that might add up," Gregory offered vaguely.

"What?"

"Hair samples."

"That DNA thing, like that black guy... OG?"

"OJ. Yeah, that's it." He frowned morosely. "Just like OJ."

"And you'll have a better idea who it is?"

He gave her a tired smile, picked up a napkin from the slotted tray with the daisies printed on its sides and tried to fan himself with it. "Let's not talk about this. It'll just upset your dreams."

"Don't be foolish," said Mrs. Kieley, turning to give him an exasperated look.

"I'll try," Gregory said under his breath. "Not to be foolish."

Mrs. Kieley blew her large nose in his tie, then tucked it away up her sleeve. "Come rest."

She stepped over and sat at the table. After a moment of watching her son, admiring his face, his "perfect complexion" as she would often refer to it, she asked, "It's too hot for tea, isn't it?"

"Yes, definitely," Gregory said.

"You need someone to look after you." Mrs. Kieley nodded.

"Don't we all." He turned in his seat, stared at the refrigerator door as if thinking of something he might want inside. He studied the magnets shaped like bananas and oranges. The one he had sent her from Toronto: #1 Mom.

"That young woman from downstairs." Mrs. Kieley leaned as far across the table as her girth would allow and whispered, "Her name's Sheevon. No, Eve... Yvonne. She lives right under us, you know?" She peeked at the floor.

"Is that so." Gregory took a careful sip from his water.

"You must've seen her coming and going."

"The ghostly-looking one."

"She's so delicate. Pleasant, too. And she's a working woman. That's important. Security."

"Come on, Mom."

"I'll give her a call and set you guys up." She winked at her son.

"Don't you dare."

"Yes, I'm going to." She chuckled, her large bosom rocking. "I'm going to, Gregory. I'm your mother." She laughed freely, her mouth open, tears in her eyes. She dabbed them away with her son's tie and took in a deep breath, "Oh, Blessed Virgin," she said, delighted by Gregory's fierce, indignant expression.

"I'm going to lie down," Gregory said, standing from his chair, the humour more of an irritant than a distraction, with his mother's imminent death so close to him, so near at hand. "This heat is too much."

"I'll call and set up the time," his mother teased, her fits of laughter continuing as Gregory stepped down the hallway, into his room, and shut the door.

Yvonne waited, watching the display window of the caller ID.

"Ring," she said, her legs flinching as the muscles in her limbs tightened, then began trembling immediately.

The drilling of the telephone was like a punch to her chest. She waited, her heart jerking, her eyes fixed on the digital display. The words: UNKNOWN NAME, UNKNOWN NUMBER silently appeared like strange magic.

She snatched up the receiver. This was way too much. She was about to shout that she was having the call traced, but that might scare off the caller. She didn't want to do that. It was important to find out who it was, what he wanted. It could be her father, calling to hear her voice. Even though she had warned him about calling. No communication with her. She had warned him.

"Hello, sweetheart," the first taunting words, a woman's voice. Yvonne's limbs shivered more fiercely in the clammy heat, the hard plastic of the receiver pressing intrudingly into the flesh surrounding her ear.

"Who is...?" her voice faltered, a contracting whisper, closing in on itself, her boldness erased.

"Don't you recognize me, honey?" The woman's voice with its masculine undercurrent. The way she should sound. The disturbing way a woman like her should sound.

Yvonne shook her head, knowing the voice, knowing the voice so intimately that tears gushed from her eyes. The voice from the calls.

All those telephone calls. "It's Mommy, Yvonne. Remember what I have for you. Remember where you came from."

"No." Yvonne slammed down the receiver in violent denial. Her eyes hurt, strained by a chaotic tension. She rubbed them savagely, smearing the tears away. Repulsed, she shoved the receiver off its hook.

The man heard the sound of the receiver being knocked off its cradle. He smiled at the electronic continuance. The telephone was only the instigator. Marconi had no idea of the can of worms he was opening when he sent out that first signal, and how appropriate, the man thought, for all of this to be playing out under the shadow of Signal Hill, Cabot Tower set high on its majestic hill of impenetrable rock, towering above the city. Cabot Tower, where Marconi had transmitted his first wireless message all those years ago.

He grinned at the irony. Yvonne Unwin back in St. John's, back to her roots to make the connection, to find family, to discover the true value of family.

The telephone was the first spark of entry, the violation, like a microscopic pinprick, and the seed of a transmitter dropped in, the implant generating tiny roots that eventually grew larger, enormous, piercing the collective psyche, then branching out in record speed, searching for other life, other connections, uncontainable, the radio, a telephone or two in every home, a television, the penetration into each and every household and— remarkably— the people allowing the entry, permitting the electronic rape of their precious households and families.

The invasive microwaves like tendrils, industrious and growing vigorously, pulsing through the airwaves, cellulars, satellites, probing deeper into the core, into the soul, to electrify and listlessly displace the concept of human intimacy. The electronic invasion of self.

"No, no, no..." Yvonne's scratchy whisper in his headset, in his ears, so close to him, believing she was alone. Never alone. Footsteps hurrying out of the living room and down the hallway.

The man flicked the #7 switch, converting the circuits, bringing him right into the bathroom, right there with Yvonne, the sound so pristine as she dropped to her knees, vomiting and gasping, weeping helplessly between each violent retch.

THREE

A brisk walk was how she usually dealt with anxiety, but that was impossible in this heat. She had left the apartment with this strategy in mind, striding beneath the huge golden maples, chestnut and dogberry trees on LeMarchant road. At least they offered some shade, a hint of relief. She passed Caul's Funeral Home on her right, pausing at the walk lights at the intersection of LeMarchant and Prince of Wales Street, watching the cars, staring at the drivers, expecting to see her mother cruising past, a ghoulish smile on her face as she pressed her greenish-white palms against the window, smearing the glass with decay.

The walk light flashed. She paced ahead, glancing at the old three-storey Victorian houses with their elaborate trimmings and huge windows. They were set back in the shade. Soon, she was drifting into what she called "the doctor zone," the immense houses converted into doctors' offices. She slowed as she approached Doctor Healey's entrance, thinking for some obscure reason that he might be in there, watching out his window. She didn't want him to see her hurrying by. What would he think?

"God," she swiped at her forehead with the back of her bare arm, the skin wet and slippery. She could feel the sweat running down the backs of her legs. She glanced at her hands, sheening.

It was close to suppertime. It should be cooling off by now, she told herself.

But it wasn't. She peeked back at Doctor Healey's window, believing she saw the parting of a curtain, a thin slit where the drapes met. Was he watching her? He was the only one who knew about her past, her file having been transferred down from Toronto when she moved. Doctor Fisher had recommended Doctor Healey with great enthusiasm. Healey had even given Yvonne his home telephone number, something Fisher had never done. What did that mean? Was he interested in her in more than a professional way? He was a yuppie, Yvonne warned herself. He thinks too much. Everything meant something to him. Not the sort of man to get involved with. She preferred the dangerous sort, the foreboding. That artist guy in her building. They'd passed each other a few times and had exchanged knowing smiles. Something about him that she really took to. Thinking of him now, she felt the twinge between her legs. Nothing of this sort for Dr. Healey. She stared at his window until she almost lost sight of it. But in that fleeting moment, she could have sworn she saw the curtain fall back into place.

Mr. Prouse bent and slid the video player back in its place beneath the long coffee table flush against the peach-coloured wall. He had carried it from the spare bedroom where his work table was set up. Electronics was his hobby, one of many hobbies he had dabbled in over the years. He had become interested in electronics years ago, while working in public relations for the telephone company. His mind carried him back and a thought struck him. The name, Unwin. Wasn't there a woman named Unwin working in his department just before he retired? He wondered if the woman might be related to Yvonne.

"Hm," he pondered, connecting the cable wire and the patch cord to their corresponding "in" and "out" slots in the back and then plugging in the VCR. He loved tinkering with electronics. He'd taken the video recorder apart to adjust the tracking pins. They were constantly slipping, plus—while the metal covering was off— he'd decided it was just as well to clean the heads with a Freon-soaked Q-tip.

"That should do it," he assured himself, giving the video recorder a final shove to set it in place.

Standing, he lifted one of his favourite videotapes from where it lay on a bookshelf beside the coffee table and bent again to slide it into the slot. The machine swallowed the tape hungrily. He reached for the buttons on the fan where it was set on top of the television and switched it up from Low to Medium.

The whirring sound was comforting, the cool air turning fuller against his face as the wire-shrouded blade pivoted across his body and then toward the window at the front of the house.

Backing away from the television, he glanced at the Monet prints framed on the wall, the soft pinks, greens and purples of the flowers. He glimpsed behind himself at the recliner before sitting back and lifting his cool glass of Southern Comfort. The first sip was satisfyingly cold and sweet. He made a sound of extravagant pleasure and raised the remote control, hit the button to bring the television to life, waited for the image to strengthen— a commercial for an allergy remedy— and then pressed the "play" button on the remote.

His eyes watched intently as the picture flashed on in mid-scene. Two women were seated at a patio table, talking with each other. Their acting was not believable at all, but they were very attractive women, both of them blondes, and dressed in bathing suits cut low in the front.

"Where are the women like that?" Mr. Prouse asked himself, chuckling. "Boy, oh, boy!" His mind flashed on his neighbour— Yvonne Unwin. She was pretty close to being beautiful (although not a blonde and not petite) and she was right across the hall. The chances of them getting together were fairly good. He'd seen that sort of thing in all sorts of TV sit-coms. Neighbours always dated. He'd have to romance her, buy flowers, that sort of thing. Play the game and mind his p's and q's. Women these days were really touchy. And he understood why. It was about time they got their due in the world. He had no argument against equality. He just wanted women to act like women. Men were men and women were women. Simple biology. But as far as equality went, he had no problem with it. Equal pay for equal work? Definitely. A stop to sexual harassment? No question. Women were just as smart as men? Agreed. But they were still women and shouldn't forget their feminine side.

The two women on the television screen were talking about men; the older one was consoling the younger. It seemed the younger one had been dumped. The older one offered her hand across the wrought-iron veranda table, fingers entwining. A hand raised to slip through the young one's hair. Soon, they were standing, comforting each other, a sparkling swimming pool in the background. The taller older one led the younger one by the hand toward the blue edge of the pool.

Pausing there, the taller woman carefully kissed the shorter one, an innocent kiss on the cheek. "Are you still my baby?" the taller one asked. She was the aggressive, dominating one. The short one was innocent, unsuspecting, shy. She turned her eyes away and said awkwardly, "This isn't right, Mother."

"Boy, oh, boy!" Mr. Prouse took a sip of his drink, the glass beaded with droplets of moisture beneath his fingers, the cubes jingling mutely.

In a matter of moments, the taller woman had slipped the straps of the younger one's swimsuit down away from her shoulders. Mr. Prouse raised the remote control and hit the pause button, the image— the taller woman's slightly opened mouth being lowered to a small perky breast— freezing, sharply and with perfect clarity.

He slowly shook his head in appreciation, admiring the minute distance of the cherry-red lips from the stiff nipple. "Beautiful," he whispered, entranced. "That's just gorgeous." Taking another sip of Southern Comfort, he continued shaking his head in utter amazement.

Yvonne's mind was torturing her. She found it difficult to think in this heat, her thoughts languid and weighty. Plus, she had a headache, a dense throbbing one. She stepped off the curb, waiting for a gap in the sparse traffic, then crossed the asphalt, watched Healey's window again as she went back the way she had come, swiping at her thick black brows to prevent the sweat from running into and stinging her eyes. At least there was ice at her apartment. She would strip down when she got home and fill a towel with ice, run it over her body. A popsicle, that's what she wanted. A cherry or pineapple popsicle. She would kill for one.

Increasing her pace, she returned to the apartment and went straight to the refrigerator to dig out a cherry popsicle. With a solid whack, she broke it in half on the edge of the counter and tore open the wrapper, shoving the other half away. Sucking on it, she returned to the living room and checked the caller ID on the desk. Why wasn't it working? Why didn't it know who was calling her?

By the front closet, she slipped off her damp, slate-blue canvas shoes and glanced at herself in the full-length mirror bolted behind the front door. It was there that she always checked herself before going out. It was there that she studied her body, pinching the flesh around her slim waist, disgusted by the unshakable idea that she was too fat. Her straight black bang was matted to her forehead. There was a dark line of perspiration at the neck of her slate-blue t-shirt, but her white shorts looked fine. She clamped the popsicle between her lips as she used both hands to pull down her shorts, sensing an immediate brief coolness taunting her thighs, a coolness that was still slightly warm but vaguely refreshing all the same. She bit off a piece of the popsicle and then pulled off her t-shirt, using one hand at a time.

She stood there, completely naked, staring at her sweat-glossed flushed face. This heat, she told herself, averting her own eyes, turning for the couch, trying to deflect her thoughts from the idea of going into the bathroom and taking the box of laxatives from the cabinet above the sink. She hadn't touched them in twelve days. Dr. Healey had said he was proud of her. And that mattered. His words of encouragement mattered to her.

Yvonne flopped down on the couch, one hand holding the popsicle stick, the other lifting the instruction booklet for the caller ID, seeing a boxed portion of text right on the first page that she had overlooked. She read: *It is required that the owner subscribe to a telephone caller-ID service in order for the machine to function.*

"You're kidding," she said. "I bought the machine." She threw the instruction booklet onto the Navajo rug and tossed her legs over the edge of the couch, sitting up, her skin shimmering with sweat. It was too hot to lie still. "God, you're kidding." She glared at the machine, standing and snatching it up with one hand, her pale cheeks flushing redder. She thought of throwing it, but held back, her fingertips turning white as her grip tightened against the dark grey plastic casing.

Who was calling, trying to trick her? It couldn't be her mother. That was impossible. Or was it? She pictured her fingers sinking into the throat of the caller, or was it her own throat? Fingers sinking in there. That voice! She coughed and closed her eyes, then opened them, unnerving herself.

She reset the machine on the desk and turned away, headed for the bathroom, dropped the remainder of her popsicle in the sink and stood— dazed— watching it melting, the pinkish fluid dripping down the drain. She needed a sedative; Dr. Healey had warned her about becoming over-excited. Remember your mother, he had warned her, knowing he had made a mistake. She had seen it in the doctor's eyes. It was too soon in their relationship to bring all of that up directly. She could not get the words out of her head, "Remember your mother."

She opened the cabinet, dipping her eyes toward the sink, avoiding her reflection, her face so much resembling her mother's. She glanced up at the cabinet's shallow white shelving and reached for the box of laxatives, but then changed her mind, instead taking hold of the brown plastic bottle of Corium. She stared at the childproof top. Childproof, as if to protect someone.

Her temples were throbbing. Pounding. She wondered if the sound was real.

Pausing, shifting her concentration from within, gradually hearing, listening outside herself, she discerned the sound of a knock on the door.

No preliminary sound of the buzzer from the porch. She alerted herself, waiting. Who was it? How did they get in?

Another knock.

"Yes," she called out prematurely, a startled quality to her voice as she stepped from the bathroom, almost bolting down the hallway, hurrying into the living room as if rushing face-first into a nightmare, pill bottle still in hand, pills gently clicking against each other.

"Yes?" she called again.

"It's Zack. Brett."

Yvonne approached the door, but stopped herself from opening it, facing her reflection in the mirror, standing naked inches from the source of the voice. "Yes."

"I have something for you."

Why weren't there eyeholes installed in the doors? St. John's was hardly the crime capital of the world or anything, it wasn't Toronto or New York, but there was crime all the same.

"Slip it under the door," she detected a playful tone in her voice. Why so playful?

"Too big to slip under the door."

She almost giggled at his reply. Naked and giggling. She felt relieved, the heat leaving her body, a calmness. The nausea dissipating. She glanced at the pill bottle, popped the top off and swallowed back two pills without water. She opened the closet door and stuffed the recapped bottle into the pocket of her black plastic raglan. The pills would help. They would make it easier between her and her visitor.

"Gimme a second," she called out, rifling through the clothes. Her emotions were raging, torrents of indecision rushing against unsteady waves of mounting self-assurance. She wanted no one near her and yet someone just to hold her, hold onto her, desperately. Her fingers slid over the black plastic raglan. She thought of putting it on. It would feel cool against her skin. For a few moments, anyway. Nothing underneath. What would Zack the artist think of that?

She felt edgier, uneasy. Not the time to be getting involved in a new relationship.

"Hang on," she said, almost to herself. "I'm naked." But what was the appropriate time? Always something going on in her life. Things interfering with any relationship. They were so difficult to hold onto. To control. Control, that's all. Keep things level, even, uneventful. But enticing. Use the body, always use the body first, then the mind later, but not too much of the mind at first. The mind takes over later.

She fingered a red windbreaker, a thin, vaguely transparent short piece of almost nothing. She yanked it off the hanger and put it on, glanced at herself in the mirror, the hint of her full breasts behind the shimmery nylon, the double fold of fabric along the bottom just barely concealing her pubis. Her long black hair against the red. After all, Zack Brett was an artist. This would dazzle him. The image. The first intimate image. The recollection of it. It was everything. Memory. It was all there was. Nothing was ever seen or felt until it sat in memory.

Mrs. Kieley watched the television news with the volume turned up extra loud. The report on the murder was the same as what she had seen earlier that day. They didn't mention the hair samples, though. She smiled at this knowledge, basking in her privileged information.

A few moments ago, she had felt the faint resonance of someone knocking on Yvonne Unwin's door directly below her. The young lady had a visitor. Maybe it was that young artist from across the hall. His door had opened and closed a few moments before that. Love in the air. The heat making people restless. She thought of Mr. Prouse, his charming smile. Maybe she'd drop by for a visit later, or tomorrow morning. She could use the companionship. That was one thing about the St. Agnes Home— she had always had someone to talk to, but everyone was just sitting around waiting to die. She still had a few good years in her. And she'd like to have a man. What was the matter with that? All the old women in the nursing home, pining for their husbands, giving up after their husbands died. She would have no part of that. She had loved Peter, but he was dead fifteen years now and she wouldn't live in the past.

Shutting down the volume with the remote control, she wondered what Mr. Prouse was doing, if he— like her— could use a little company.

"Okay," Yvonne called, clicking the solid deadbolt and unlocking the knob. Opening the door, she saw Zack Brett's dark hair and black wrap-around sunglasses. From the nose down, his face and body were blocked by a large canvas, a nude of a female with glowing white skin and long black hair. Scarlet red veins were mapped over her entire body. In the place of her brain, a huge yellow moon glowed inside her head. An ocean pulsed at her feet that the veins were all growing towards, connecting with, powering the waves. A blue sky gleamed above her raven black hair. Yvonne's jaw slowly slackened. A few stunned moments later, she said, "Wow," in a hushed, enthralled whisper.

"It's a present," Zack said, smiling with shut lips, smug, cynical.

"I don't..." Yvonne scanned the painting. "I just... I mean, wow! It's beautiful."

"It's yours," he said, smiling in a way that changed his face completely, the sinister facade dismissed by a boyish grin. "You can have it for a slice of bread and a glass of water. A prisoner's rations. I've escaped from the studio. A free man."

"Bring it in," she said, stepping aside, allowing him entry. "It's huge," she enthused, extending her hand to help, but then pulling it back, not wanting to touch the paint, wondering if it was still wet.

"Where to hang it?" he wondered, resting it against the wall beside the full-length mirror. He turned to face her. Yanking off his sunglasses, he gave her a wink, his eyelids artfully dusted with faint blue eye shadow.

The living room was finally selected as the fitting place to hang the painting. Yvonne had suggested the bedroom, but Zack preferred it in the living room, perhaps so it could be viewed by the greatest number of visitors. The large canvas was intrusive to Yvonne, not really matching her decor, but a gift was a gift and— besides— she admired it a great deal. It was real art. And it looked so much like her. The resemblance was disturbing, watching herself in that way, the body revealed, her body matching her own. How had Zack guessed the shape of her breasts?

"She'll keep an eye on you," Zack told her as he sipped from the glass of red wine Yvonne had offered. He was sweating from the labour of hanging the painting, his face sheening. Yvonne was sitting on the hardwood floor at the edge of the huge multi-coloured Navajo rug, her back against the wall, the windbreaker stuck to her skin, her eyes on the painting. She held her glass between her raised knees and smiled up at Zack who stood over her, glancing across the knickknacks on the ledge of the hand-carved oak mantelpiece. He noticed two small photographs set in ornate dark grey metal frames. One captured a picture of a man in a police uniform, the other a photograph of a woman who resembled Yvonne. The woman was wearing Bohemian clothes, black slacks, black turtleneck. If it wasn't for the cars frozen in motion on the street behind her, dating the photograph, the woman could be living now, dressed as she was, the attire still fashionable in certain artistic circles.

Yvonne took a leisurely sip of wine, savouring the taste. She had popped the bottle of Wolf Blass that she'd bought for Terri Lawton. She could easily get another tomorrow.

"This is nice stuff," Zack said, glancing at the glass. "Smooth. No sting." He stared down at Yvonne, his gaze shifting across her bare lustrous legs.

"I don't know that I like being watched over," Yvonne said, feeling a trickle of sweat run down her left thigh. She could not take her eyes off the painting. Its colours were luscious, almost luminous, colours she could not readily name. He had obviously mixed them himself. "Am I wrong, or does she sort of have my features?"

"Sort of." Zack scrunched his brows together and pursed his lips in mock analysis. "Eef you vill notice ze fair skin," he said, imitating a French accent. He extended his hand. "Ze prominent, how you say, cheek'a'bone. Ze hazel eyes that see you in your soul." He kissed his fingers and tossed them toward the painting, "Oooow. Magnifique!"

Yvonne laughed and shook her head, "You're crazy."

"No doubt about it. How about the body?"

"What?"

"How'd I do?"

"Don't be so fresh," she said, blushing.

"Now, there's a classic movie line," he teased, drinking from his glass. "Haven't heard that one in a while."

"The body's fine," she whispered.

"All from brief memory."

"It's kind of disturbing." She looked at him, confused, as if attempting to recognize who he might be. She stared at his eyelids, the eye shadow, the black clothes like the sort her mother used to wear. She saw his face metamorphose into a woman's, his black hair lengthen, lipstick brighten on his lips...

"Admiration or violation," Yvonne said in a voice so far away that it made Zack gulp down the remainder of his wine, anticipating something unpleasant.

"What?" he asked, shifting back toward Yvonne. He raised the bottle from the mantelpiece ledge— where his host had laid it before sitting on the floor—

and poured himself another. Then he swiped at the space above his top lip with the back of his arm.

"Something I read once." Yvonne braced her palm against the wall and stood when Zack tilted the bottle toward her, stood nearer to him than intended, her damp palm having almost slipped. She caught her balance.

"I'm okay," she said.

"Admiration or violation? Art, you mean?" He filled her glass, then settled on the floor with his back against the cream-coloured wall, careful not to allow his eyes to peek up her windbreaker. Yvonne dropped back down to the spot from where she had risen. She stared at Zack's profile, saw a drop of sweat running from his temple down his cheek before he smeared it away with two fingers. He was regarding the painting with peculiar admiration, a hint of distaste tainting the sentiment. She studied his eyelids, wanted to touch one of them to see if that actually was eye shadow on his lids.

Unwilling to hold the thought any longer, she asked outright, "Is that eye shadow?"

Zack smiled without regarding her, a slow menacing smile.

"Do you like it?" he asked.

"I don't know." She reached out and gently dabbed at his eyelid with the tip of her index finger.

"I find that women love it," he admitted.

"Women?" She studied faint traces of powder on her fingertips.

"Once," he said, his eyes focusing on her, intensely, "for Hallowe'en I dressed up as a woman. It was a party at university. The women loved it. I couldn't believe my luck. They were all over me, admiring my dress, my make-up. I could've seduced any of them."

"But you didn't?" Yvonne said, restrained humour in her voice. "Being so honourable and all."

Zack laughed suggestively. "I wouldn't do a thing like that." He glanced at Yvonne's red windbreaker, the timing just right.

"No, I suppose not," she said, feeling his dark gaze on her body, feeling herself going moist at his ominous scrutiny.

Zack watched her face and then stood abruptly. "I better get going." He finished his wine and laid the glass on the mantelpiece.

"Oh." The announcement had been unexpected, harshly out of line with how she believed things were going, as if something had suddenly taken a turn for the worse, without her realizing it. She stood, but her disappointment added an obvious awkwardness to her gestures. "Well." She nodded toward the painting, "Thanks." She reached behind her soaked neck, gathered the length of her hair and tied it in a loose knot.

"Oh, you're welcome." Turning away, without meeting her eyes, he opened the apartment door. "I'll see you, I guess." He merely glanced at her feet as he moved over the threshold. "Thanks for the wine."

"Okay." She stepped nearer, but Zack shut the door. Yvonne stood behind it, seeing herself in the mirror, watching herself. "What's the matter with you?" she accused herself. "You're fat, that's what's the matter." Frustratedly spinning away, she noticed Zack's sunglasses on the pine coffee table. She snatched them up, raced for the door and flung it open, about to call out. But she stopped herself. The quietness of the hallway, the bold imposing sight of the landlord's door directly across the hall, prevented her from shouting. She decided it would be best to hold onto them. It would give her an excuse to visit him tomorrow.

She shut the door and faced her reflection again. "Fat," she whispered, watching her lips move. She laid the sunglasses on the mantelpiece beside the small bronze Pelerin Foundation Arts Award that belonged to her mother and hurried into the bathroom, snatching the box of laxatives from the shelf and pushing all twelve pills through their flimsy protective sheet of silver foil. Mercilessly swallowing them without thought, she shivered and felt gooseflesh rise to her skin.

She was too fired up to sleep now, even though she should be storing up her energy for the move-in day of the trade show— the busiest day— and it was only two days away. Early Monday morning. She'd have to get up extra early. She wouldn't be able to sleep tomorrow night in anticipation of waking. And now tonight was shot.

Despite her disappointment at Zack's early departure, her excitement lingered. The painting was quite a declaration, she assured herself. Zack must be obsessed with her to create such a work. She knew all about obsession. And to find a man who seemed equally as capable of such strong emotions was fabulous! But why had he backed away when things were going so well? Artists were so temperamental. Temperamental. Her mother. No. She blocked the thought, found it easier to do so with the lull of sedatives in her veins. The combination of pills and wine instated a numbing drugged-up throb in her groin, a want of anything to please her, absolutely anything. Her cheeks burned with the heat of sexual imaginings. The sweaty slippery texture of her skin added to her horniness. The heatwave was the perfect sort of weather for depraved sex, for hands and tongues gliding over wet arms, chests, legs...

Pulling on a pair of red shorts, she left the red windbreaker on, decided to go for a walk, to feel the night air against her skin. The nylon of the windbreaker would hold the coolness if there was any stirring. Her breasts were almost visible through the fabric. She would walk the street, unzipping the windbreaker, coaxing the zipper lower and lower as she strolled, watching the cars passing. She wanted to show them. She wanted them to see. She wanted so desperately to show them her breasts, cup her hands beneath the symmetrical weight of each breast and give them a playful jiggle, pinch her nipples until they were rock hard.

Stepping out of her apartment, she locked the deadbolt, her thoughts on Zack, on his eyes, his blue dusted lids. It really did work, just as he'd explained. It excited her in a carnally forbidden way.

FOUR

It was 2:41 a.m. according to the glow of Sergeant Gregory Kieley's digital watch. He had paused in the narrow hallway to make certain he knew the exact hour and minute. Satisfied, he continued on. The first thing he noticed as he neared the bedroom at the end of the hallway was the red tint. Crossing the threshold, he caught a faint whiff of smoke lagging in the clammy stifling air. Someone had tossed a red t-shirt over the lamp in the corner of the cramped bedroom. The fabric was singed. He went over beside the unmade double bed and pulled the plug. Lifting a pen from his pocket, he used it to flick on the light switch, sparking the overhead bulb. He studied the lamp again, then read the time on the clock-radio. Two-forty-five a.m. He noticed an open magazine on the bed, pornographic images of two women engaged in sex. A strap-on dildo rested against the far pillow, pointing up, as if positioned that way.

Scanning the bedroom walls, Kieley regarded the brown badly installed panelling. Someone had attempted to do the place up, but had used cheap labour or done it themselves. The stuccoed ceiling was marked with rust-coloured water stains. He noticed that the closet door was slightly ajar. Expectantly stepping toward it, he cautiously opened the edge with the tip of his shoe.

The naked woman's body did not startle him. It was just where he'd expected;

in the closet like the first victim. What caught his attention was the woman's long, jet black hair, very similar to Judy Cramer's hair.

Kieley studied the woman's bulging inquisitive eyes, her webbed brow and swollen lips. He frowned at the sight of her bound veined breasts and— scanning lower— numbly shook his head when his eyes fell across where the telephone receiver had been plunged deep between her legs. Sighing, he forced his thoughts to switch back on procedural track. The first thing to do was check the thermostat. Recording the temperature of the room was imperative in order to determine the time of death.

Glancing across the room, he could not find a thermostat, went out to the living room, discovered it on the wall beside the television, and made note of the temperature. Then he returned to his examination of the body.

Of course he had immediately noticed the thin mark grooved along the throat. A ligature strangulation. He crouched in front of the woman's legs, acutely aware of the dangling cord, and searched around her naked feet, spotting the coil of grey telephone wire. It was just as useless to him as the one used in the first strangling. Fingerprints could not be lifted. Reaching out, he gently touched the foot. It was still warm, only about one degree off normal body temperature, barely noticeable. One and a half to two degrees lost per hour for the first twelve hours. And what was it after that? He searched through his memory. Ten to twelve hours before the body feels cold to the touch. But what was the heat loss after twelve hours? He couldn't recall, shook off the thought and stared up.

Body number two.

There would be a massive effort now. The local police, the Royal Newfoundland Constabulary, would set up a task force in the morning. Chief Rowe and his deputies would meet with the head of the Major Crime Unit and Lieutenant Johnston and they would put together a team. Forty or fifty men. Sergeant Uriah Cooper would take over the case. No doubt about that. The investigative psychologist— the doctor— from the Constabulary's Criminal Investigation Division. "Doctor Sergeant" was how those on the force jokingly referred to him.

The locals didn't know it, and they mightn't ever, but the case belonged to the RCMP. Kieley was relieved that he wouldn't have to endure Cooper's idiosyncrasies. He had heard plenty about Cooper. He was only a young man, thirty-four, thirty-five, a strange fellow, into all sorts of peculiar procedures. Always telling bizarre stories about things no one else would ever think about.

Exotic places and people. Different ways of putting two and two together. A quirky surreal sense of humour. Was a Buddhist or something like that. A vegetarian.

The Constabulary would assign a number of crime analysts. The whole show. This case would be the biggest thing that St. John's had ever seen. The reporters at the local rag of a newspaper— *The Evening Telegram*— would have a field day. They'd finally get their big-city murder story. They'd be delighted. Sales would soar. Nothing like a series of murders to get people interested in the news. If the angle on the murders was accurate, and he knew that it was (this victim was a lesbian just like Judy Cramer), then this would be a first. Not only a first for the historic town of St. John's, Newfoundland, but for anywhere in the world.

Kieley glanced at the woman's hands. They should be bagged to protect possible evidence lodged between her fingers or under her nails; the locals would do that once they arrived. One of them had already been here, following the suspect, no doubt— *his* suspect. The local had entered the premises after his suspect left. But then the local had left as well. No sirens. No coroners or ident officers. Standing, Kieley studied the width and depth of the indentation along the woman's throat, delicately tracing the swelling with the tip of his finger.

He took his time studying the naked length of the body. A shell with a stopped heart. No signs of a struggle. The victim had allowed the murderer into her apartment. He was certain of it. Lack of evidence was the only problem, making the charge stick. You practically had to witness the murder yourself to ensure a conviction. Even if you had a signed confession it wasn't enough. There had to be corroborating evidence. And in the meantime, the person who had done this would continue to kill other innocent women.

Focusing out of his thoughts, he discovered that he was staring straight at the dead woman's face and that she was staring straight at him with that startled overblown expression that defeated most strangulation victims. He observed how her lips were slightly parted, the hint of a tongue, the shy tip out, like a cat's.

He walked out of the bedroom, into the narrow hallway, and was in the living room, a small eight-by-eight box that was the front room in most of these old row houses. It was a questionable area of town. Hard cases, hard luck stories— drunks and single mothers. He heard a man shouting in the connected house, a man threatening someone, a monstrous brutal shout, "Bitch," and the yelping shriek of a woman that reminded him of a dog being beaten.

He crossed the cluttered living room and stepped close to the wall. Standing beside a cheaply framed print of a wilderness lake, he listened to the accusations, then he went to the front doorway and pulled it open. The street was virtually deserted, seeming ever more desolate in the inescapable heat. A few car wrecks further up the narrow road. The row houses ran off in both directions across from him.

He paused there, wondering. What was the right thing to do in this situation? Deciding, he stepped from the doorway and shut the door behind him. He took a few steps toward the neighbour's door and knocked loudly, then again, until a small woman answered. The door was only opened a crack, the dark oppressive behind her. Kieley was not permitted a complete view.

"I'm Sergeant Kieley." He patiently flashed his badge. "We were notified about a disturbance."

The opening of the door narrowed. No response.

"Is your husband home?"

"No."

"I'd like to speak with him."

"Who the fuck is that?" A roar from the back of the house, the scraping of chair legs against flooring.

The woman opened the door slightly, giving in, the sound of her husband's voice jarring her, her hands trembling, losing their hold on the knob.

"Can I come in?" He needed the invitation. It must be by the book, just in case there was a court challenge. Everything by the book. He wanted the invitation, then provocation, and anything was possible.

The woman nodded.

"Is that a yes?"

"Yes," she whispered groggily.

Kieley stepped in. He glanced at the woman's face, seeing the fresh red scrapes as if from a ring, the welts, the lips swollen excessively out of shape at the corner of her mouth. An abrasion making her lick there.

Sensing his breath deepening, growing hotter, harsher, he stepped toward the rear of the house. He found the man standing beside a veneer-covered kitchen table with metal legs. He wasn't wearing a shirt. He was skinny and wiry, one hand holding a beer bottle, his hair with no particular style, sticking up in the back, the small room clouded with grey-blue cigarette smoke.

"What're you doing?" the man asked loudly, peering at Kieley. "My house..."

"I'm a police officer," he indicated, having to hold himself from rushing for the man. "We had a call about a disturbance."

"Nothing here." The man stared at the beer bottle, his expression defiant, unchanged. He slowly sat in his chair, his eyes unsteady.

Kieley glanced behind at the woman hiding in the shadows of the dim hallway. "You have a friend close by?"

The woman gave no response.

"Any children in the house?"

She shook her head.

"No fucking children," the man barked.

"No," she said, the man moving in his chair. When Kieley looked that way, he saw the man's eyes searching down the hallway, hearing the sound of the woman and meanly wanting to silence her.

"You go on, now," Kieley said to the woman. "Go to a friend's house for the night."

"She's not..." the man raised his voice.

"Go on. Gather some things."

The woman stayed where she was, staring, profoundly uncertain, whimpering. Then she turned and raced up the stairs. Kieley watched the man in silence, the man ignoring him, taking a drink from the bottle.

Kieley heard the woman come down the stairs and begin to go out, but pause in the doorway. "Don't hurt him," she said, in a voice so low and frightened it chilled Kieley to the bone.

The door shut.

"I just wanted to ask you a few questions," Kieley quietly informed the man.

"No one invited you," the man grumbled.

"Your wife did."

The man stared at the small refrigerator in the corner. He took another swallow of beer and kept watching the refrigerator.

"Have you abused your wife in any way?"

"No."

Kieley stepped near, stood inches from the man so that the man's eyes flinched.

"Do I have to ask again?" Kieley enquired plainly.

"I don't have to," the man tried raising his voice but it was a failed attempt at brashness.

"Does your wife fear you?"

"She deserved it. Always bitching. Fuckin'—"

"Have you harmed your wife—"

"She's a fuckin' bitch." The man looked up at the officer, the hint of humour in his eyes. "She's a bitch. You know. She likes it." He laughed in a way that tightened the sickening knot in Kieley's stomach.

"Is that so?"

"Fucking right," the man snickered, scanning Kieley's emotionless face.

"I think you should hit me."

"Bullshit."

"No, let's be reasonable. I'm about the same size to you as you are to your wife. So let's say I'm you and you're your wife."

"Fucking crazy." The man stared at the refrigerator, scoffing out a nervous laugh.

"In case you didn't understand. I'll put it in baby talk for you. I'm big, you're small. You're big, your wife's small."

The man took another swallow of beer and smirked nervously, defiantly.

It was the smirk that did it, with its knowledge of the man's rights and everything the man could get away with, that broke Kieley, made him rush forward and shove over the man's chair so that the man crashed against the wall, harming his shoulder in some way because he winced and grabbed for it the second he landed.

"Call *me* a bitch now." Kieley kicked the man in his stomach and he crippled into an embryo-shaped ball. Kneeling down, Kieley raised his fist, tightened the muscles in his arm and shoulder, clenching together all his might to punch the man repeatedly in the face until the man was whimpering, grunting and grunting with each smack that brought him nearer to silence.

Once he was done, Kieley stood and went to the sink. He carefully washed his hands, taking his time to scrub his fingernails, and then glanced at the man on the floor. Should he call an ambulance? The man needed medical attention. Blood thickly pooled along the linoleum so that Kieley had to move his right shoe out of its path.

What was the right thing to do?

The man wasn't moving. In this case, Kieley decided, that was a good thing. Right or wrong didn't matter. It was simply— undeniably— a good, clean, fine thing. The man should be dead. Not the woman next door.

The heat made sleep an impossibility. Even though her window was open, the Venetian blind raised to accommodate the gap, the screen positioned in place, all windows in the house open, not the slightest breeze reached her. Her anxious thoughts would not lull. Move-in day for the Police Chiefs' Trade Show was only the day after tomorrow, bright and early Monday morning, and she was mentally working through the schedule she had arranged over the past two weeks, how she had called all the exhibitors to fit them into time slots, juggled different companies so that all could be accommodated according to their business duties.

Yvonne rolled over in her bed. Sighing at her frustration and the merciless heat, she decided that sleep was *completely* out of the question. She could not distract herself from going over the move-in schedule. She stared at the ceiling, not wanting to close her eyes, not willing to allow her mind to reel back through the years. Those telephone calls had affected her. These things were always that way. You never knew when you were under severe stress. It was invisible, undetectable. It just existed, like some kind of toxic gas that infiltrated your body and mind.

Kicking the sheet away from her sweaty feet, she stood and moved to the window to try for a breath of fresh air. She had attempted to buy a fan when she was in the mall but they were sold out at every store. No one had been expecting this kind of heatwave. It was so out of place for St. John's. Twisting the rod on the blinds, she watched the slats open to a view of the street. It was deserted, the lamplight filtering down through the huge maple trees that framed her view of the front yard. It was a calming sight. And she needed to be calmed, always needing to be calmed. She hated this state of agitation, of being perpetually on edge.

She glanced behind at the dim space of her room, her mind alert with insomnia. She stared into the darkness, then peeked at her closet door.

Twirling the rod, shutting the blinds, she whispered, "Stop it." She was spooking herself. She was thinking of taking a few more pills when she heard a rustling outside her window, footsteps coming along the side of the house. No, not footsteps. It was probably just a cat. There were countless cats in the neighbourhood. Everyone had them to keep the mice at bay.

She bent one of the blinds up to peer out, and flinched back, her fingers rattling the slat. Mr. Prouse, the landlord, was standing there in front of her window box, watching in through the screen, undoubtedly seeing her naked mid-section through the mesh. She shifted away from the window into the shadows of her room, not wanting him to know. But there was no avoiding it. He had seen her, seen her naked mid-section, was so close that his lips could have easily pressed across the petals in the flower box to kiss her skin.

She remained out of view, heard him walking away from her window, listened to the sounds of his body shifting. She had caught a glance of something in his hand, a tube of some sort, about nine or ten inches long, that he was raising toward the window and shaking into the flowers. He quietly went in the front door and made no sound moving further into the house.

Yvonne leaned toward the window and twirled open the blinds completely, realizing that she was giving anyone who passed on the street a clear view of her entire naked body. She shifted her feet slightly away from each other, craving a breeze, some sort of distraction that might relieve her of her mind for a few moments. Watching through the blinds, she observed the street again. A taxi passed, the passenger's head facing the driver.

"Look at me," she whispered, and— as if by magic— the passenger turned his head to catch a glimpse of her. His eyes, the way he watched her, discharged a thrill through her body, weakening her knees and neck muscles. She shut her eyes, buoyed by the delight of her exhibitionism, and then glanced back at the empty bed, heard the dull ringing of her telephone out in her living room, her eyes deceiving her, her eyes convincing her that she had not risen from the bed at all. A young woman with long black hair lay face down on the sheets. A young woman with young white unblemished skin.

Hesitantly, Yvonne stepped toward the bed, her fingers slowly straightening as she reached for the young woman's shoulder. She bent slightly, breathlessly, pausing, uncertain. A fragrance in the room. An odour of roses and lavender, her own fear changing the smell of her perfume. The sweat. The scent of another feminine body. Yvonne remained rigid as the young woman's head turned against the pillow, revealing her own face plainly looking up at her.

"Yvonne, is that you?" one of them asked.

PART TWO:

AND RINGING AND RINGING...

ONE

The second body, identified from possessions in her apartment as Mary Hood, had been taken to the morgue under strict police escort and promptly locked in the steel casket.

Sergeant Uriah Cooper, PhD, BSc, full-fledged police officer, plus investigative psychologist with the Criminal Investigation Division of the Royal Newfoundland Constabulary, received the call Sunday morning at 8:00 a.m., and was informed of the unfortunate existence of a second body. The theme was identical. Mary Hood had been strangled with telephone wire, a telephone receiver violently inserted in her vagina. They had discovered another sampling of long black hairs that did not match with the victim's. They had discovered lesbian pornography and a strap-on sex toy. A task force was being established and Cooper was needed at Fort Townshend to devote all of his attention to working out a psychological profile of the killer.

Cooper hung up the Mickey Mouse telephone, a birthday gift from Natasha to boldly highlight Uriah's love of cartoons. It was part gift and part joke. Natasha loved joking with him, barbing him. Setting the mouse's arm back on the hook, he glanced at Natasha, her youthful profile against the pillow, a length of short blonde hair on an angle across her cheek. She could sleep through anything. He, on the other hand, would awake at the sound of a feather dropping in the bedroom. Besides, he hated sleep, considered it a waste of time, still marvelled at how his body just shut itself down. His mind called up a legend he had once read about a warrior who stayed awake all night, sitting with his spear, anticipating the beast called sleep creeping up on him. The warrior would glance around, attentively, but soon grew tired, and then the beast would leap upon him. Each night, it was the same. He could never catch nor kill the beast called sleep.

Cooper slept no more than six hours a night, and got off on the wired feeling it left him with, everything slightly hyper-real, his mind startlingly awake to minute details.

Reaching for his small wire-rimmed glasses, he hooked them on his ears, then ran a hand over his crew-cut hair, admiring the feel of the short bristles. It was a fresh cut. Natasha liked it that way, loved running her fingers through the soft uniformity. His black moustache and goatee were itchy. He scratched vigorously, making a ferocious wheezing sound. Fresh out of bed and he was already sweating. The sickly heat made growing facial hair a great discomfort. "You will never get the princess," he cackled to himself. "Never." He imagined a dead body. Sleeping Beauty. If only he had the magical kiss.

Before dressing, he moved down the hallway of his suburban bungalow and stood in the kitchen in his underwear. His mind called out for caffeine to sustain the mental sharpness. Sometimes his mind was so sharp, his thoughts so focused and concentrated on one single idea, that he was totally unaware of what his body was doing. Some mornings he would set the kettle in the refrigerator or place the milk in the dishwasher, while his mind explored a thought so expansive it was wholly distracting, a thought that he eventually got lost in, having no idea what he had been thinking about in the first place. Other times, the residue from dreams had not completely detached from him. He believed that dreams sometimes coated a person, like skin; you had to shed them, like a snake moulting, a colourful skin coming away, left for the other predators, the ones without imaginations, to gobble up and shit out.

There were a few beer bottles on the counter. He hated that, seeing them there on a Sunday morning. It meant that Saturday was over. The teenager-life-style look of them. They reminded him of university days. Natasha was still in university, working on her thesis. Special Education. Cooper liked that university feel of having books and ideas constantly around him, of discussions that expanded in countless directions. It made him feel like a kid, still learning, always learning and fascinated at the possibilities of everything around him. As long as you were still learning, you'd always be a kid.

At thirty-four, he refused to "grow up," as people often said. "Grow where?" he'd ask. He was quite familiar with all the psychological interpretations related to those who "refused to grow up." Failure to successfully negotiate childhood (he really hadn't), loss of a parent (he had lost both of them in a car accident, but he had survived, fought so hard to survive, but now felt the need to control Natasha because of that loss, the intense need to keep her near, to protect her, so that no harm would come), misguided in adolescent love, (he had loved so many girls with such crippling passion that he was sensitized to the most subtle female expressions, loved their faces, their movements, loved them, adored them all). And so on and so on. All of the very finest psychological crap, he told himself. Primo stuff, really. He'd sorted through it and applied what he could to himself, then had gone about his business.

He filled the kettle, and plugged it in, flicked the switch. "Who's the most stable person in the world?" he asked himself. "And why am I?" he mused, grabbing up the beer bottles and sliding them into their case in the back porch. The porch was cooler than the kitchen, an earthy chill rising up from the concrete floor of the basement, his refuge in the heat. He and Natasha would go down there, where they had set up the inflatable camping mattress on the floor, and lie naked in each other's arms, bathing in the coolness and marvelling at the gooseflesh texture of their skin.

Cooper glanced through the porch window at a view of his back yard, heard the hum of a lawn mower. Some anal-retentive out mowing his lawn so early on a Sunday morning. No regard for others, no view outside their own heads. Self-consumed. The neighbour mowed his lawn at least three times a week. What was the point of that? Cooper wanted to open the door, climb the shallow grade of his back yard, step toward the fence and call the guy over, ask him what he was doing. Give the guy some therapy. Lawn-mower therapy.

"Is it a thing about lawn mowers? Or is it the noise obsession, exerting your power, your blade-spinning sputtering roar over the sleeping helpless? What is it? I just need to know, friend, because I'm fucking interested, see? So fucking interested in the workings of mankind. Mankind, man." And he would grab the neighbour by his t-shirt, doing his best James Cagney, and apply a little aggression therapy. Or maybe pull on his caped-crusader outfit. Punch. Smack. Bang. Boomph. Same Bat-time. Same Bat-channel.

Covering his ears with his palms, he sang the lyrics from an early Bowie tune, "Hey, I'm a dude, man. All the young dudes," and surveyed the spruce trees he had planted along the edges of the fence. They had grown quite a bit over the three years since he'd moved in. He appreciated spruce trees for their stunted durability, so indicative of the Newfoundland landscape, the internal mapping that he felt, that made him feel so out of place anywhere else in the world except here, in his home. His home. He liked the sound of it.

Back in the kitchen, he glanced at the calendar, saw that the mortgage payment was marked due in a few days. He filled a glass with water, drank it down, then filled it again. Two glasses of water in the morning. Like oiling the engine. It helped the system work more efficiently. Kept the skin moist, the image in good shape to freely glide through the world. Slick, baby. Primed.

Watching the back yard through the window above the sink, he thought ahead to the morgue. It was a great day for having a few friends over on the patio. Great day for a barbecue. Ten or twenty cold brews. Another real scorcher! The morgue. The body. He imagined the flesh, the curves and slopes of the dead body. He imagined himself cruising in a tiny dune buggy over the thighs and hips, sinking in the soft belly, getting stuck, one of the wheels caught in the belly button, needing a tow truck. A toe truck, he laughed to himself. He downed the rest of his water, set the glass in the sink, then tore off a paper napkin from the roll, swiped at his forehead and eyebrows.

The kettle boiled and clicked off. He turned away from the window and saw the note stuck on the fridge in Natasha's handwriting: "Good morning, lover." She'd gone to bed after him, had been up playing Nintendo, hooked on the game Zelda, taking to it immediately because of the strategies that needed solving. He thought it was a good one, too. Lots of maps and puzzles to be worked through. Beneath the greeting, Natasha had written, "Made it into the ice palace. Ha, ha. Suffer (not really). XXXOOO — Natasha."

If the guys at the station only knew he was into video games, they'd never leave him alone. The way it was now, it was all bad enough, being teased because of the doctor that had been added after his name. A cop first. A psychologist second. Why was it that people teased those with higher education? He pondered while cutting a whole-wheat English muffin in half and popping it in the toaster. Waiting, humming, staring at the silver side of the toaster, how it warped the objects in the room; he moved his hand closer to the reflection, then pulled it back, moved it closer, pulled it back. When the muffin popped, he buttered it and added blueberry jam. Another glass of water. Then a cup of tea. He was considering fasting for a few days. If he was really going to get into this case, then a week-long fast would greatly assist him, hone his senses, inflate tiny details in such a way that he could practically step into them, walk around, look closely at the cracks and seams that held everything together. A three-dimensional video game where he sniffed at the grain of things.

He was staring at the English muffin. Raising it to his nostrils, he savoured the odour and then carried it to the garbage tin in the back porch and tossed it away.

Just as well to start now, he told himself, heading for the bedroom to retrieve his orange shirt and brown cotton pants. Pulling them on, he glanced at his watch: 9:17. He searched through the clutter on top of his dresser and found the western tie, shaped like a cow's skull. Fitting it around his neck, he slid the cow head up tight to his throat, then glanced at himself in the mirror.

"You," he demanded of himself, pointing an accusing finger. "You're one fried-chicken-eating, scum-sucking, varmint-humping bad man."

Natasha grumbled sweetly, tossing in the sheets. He went over and leaned close to her, kissed her smooth cheek, his heart growing lighter at the delicacy of her perfect image.

"Lucky fucker," he whispered to himself, savouring her sleeping form. "Me. Not you. You got the shit end of the stick in this relationship, princess."

He glanced at his watch again: 9:23. Constable Pendegast, that middle-aged steroid-pumped macho man who thought he was a cop out of *NYPD Blue*, would be waiting for Cooper at the morgue. He could make it by quarter to ten. There was no hurry. Let Pendegast wait, telling tough-guy stories to the pathologist or spewing out the latest lesbian jokes that were being passed around at the station. They could both pretend they were in a movie, acting out parts in the latest big-screen thriller, going over their lines.

The body wouldn't get any deader. He carefully tugged the sheet further away from Natasha's bare shoulder, stared at it, then kissed her on the smooth slope, smelling her, sniffing louder and licking her, drooling and making lecherous grunting and panting sounds until he saw the smile gently curve on Natasha's lips.

Sundays had that limbo feel to them. Sometimes they were nice, a long-needed pause, but other times they went so slowly they could be hell. Yvonne sat on her couch, reading a magazine, having just come from the bathroom. The release. The unburdening. The laxatives were working. This early in the morning and she was already coated in sweat, every inch of her slippery to the touch. She was restless and in a state of exhaustion, and the words she was reading simply would not register. She read them over and over again, while a music video played low on the television in the background, the image of a black-haired woman running in slow-motion through the desert as if being pursued, a woman with an attitude wailing about a lost love. Her mind snagged on a memory of Zack, and she was aroused momentarily by an erotic twinge. She hoped to see him later that evening. She wondered what he was doing, pictured him standing before a canvas, intensely dabbing at an image, another portrait of Yvonne. There was comfort in the thought and she found herself calming, welcoming the thought of a man admiring her compulsively.

Staring at the TV, she felt the watery sensation in her bowels. She was drained from her nightmares of the previous night. Whenever she awoke in panicky fear, the tumultuous energy and the shock emptied her body, robbed it of all energy. And the nightmares had been bad; a bloody orgy of grotesques groping across her skin, leaving their sickly trail as they made their way to fit between her legs.

To distract herself, Yvonne imagined a trip to Bowring Park. Feed the swans and ducks and simply watch the people moving around in the heat. She'd been there only once since moving back to St. John's. But she had remembered the swans from her childhood, her mother feeding them, having such great regard for the graceful quality of the swans. But a sadness as well. A strange sad expression on her mother's face. Yvonne remembered staring up at it from that childhood angle.

In the car, Yvonne pulled her hands back from the hot steering wheel and immediately rolled down the two front windows. She switched on Q Radio—the oldies channel. Hits from the seventies. She was overcome with nostalgia when the tin whistle intro from "One Tin Soldier" sounded. She turned up the tune and sang along: "Listen children to a story..."

Yvonne slipped on her sunglasses and sped up as she continued west on Water Street, passing the turn-off on her left, a short bridge over the shipyard, connecting to a long road that wound through the barrens, leading to Cape Spear, the old lighthouse. The winds were always extremely violent out there—the most easterly point in North America. Wind always attracted her, the roar of the waves on the jagged brown cliffs, watching the waves pounding the shore below, the fizzle of the water withdrawing, the mist hanging in the air, the powerful draw and release of the water.

Water Street connected with Waterford Bridge Road. She slowed to admire the beautiful houses she had always longed to own, the sprawling grounds and huge trees, the expensive cars parked beneath the tree shade framing ambling driveways. The graveyard appeared on her right, ancient grey or white marble tombstones lurking beside her. Her mother had loved that graveyard, had often taken Yvonne in there to search out dates and interesting names and read biblical quotes that were etched on the old slabs. It was a picture-perfect graveyard with its immense trees and dilapidated stones. Her mother searched out inspiration there, discovering some sort of grim tragic pleasure or classic intrigue among the calm of decease.

Crowds pleased him greatly. Enclosing him, they seemed to steady his conviction. People never suspected that they were being followed in a crowd.

Bowring Park on a Sunday. The man glanced up at the flag staff featuring the four flags; the white, red, blue and golden arrow of the Newfoundland flag, the red and white Canadian, the predominantly red Union Jack with a few blue stripes, and the City of St. John's flag, featuring the city's shield set against a white background. The paved incline heading down toward the swan pond was long and gradual, pulling at the back of his calves, making him sweat even more. On either side of the incline, narrow paths led off in various directions, wooden bridges constructed of tree limbs along those paths crossed over the Waterford Bridge River, and large statues were hidden in the woods, placed there as mysterious locations for children to discover. At the end of the incline, the man spotted Yvonne Unwin stepping into a circle of trees to admire the Peter Pan statue.

She was taking a trip down memory lane. That could be helpful. The man didn't bother to turn away when she glanced his way. He kept walking.

Moving from the tree shade out into the sun, he could feel more sweat rising on his scalp beneath his baseball cap. The full thrust of the sun was on his face, tightening his skin, making it sweat and drying it almost at the same time. He imagined clasping a hand over her mouth. That look in her eyes, at first shock, and then relaxing, every muscle in her body easing with dark acceptance. Yes, she would like that. She enjoyed those games. But there were too many witnesses.

His heart beat a fraction faster when he thought he might be interested in her in more than a professional way. He would not allow himself to explore these possibilities. He could be at Yvonne's apartment right now, installing other devices, shifting articles around in her apartment so that she might think she was losing her mind. He could be tending to wiring her bedroom, but that would come. He had already devised a plan that would take care of that, give him the view of her sleeping form, when she was most vulnerable.

Last night, he had heard her grunting and moaning with nightmares, the startled gasp as she awoke. But he needed to see her face. He wanted to see her terrified as she snapped from her dream. He wanted to see her suffer for what she had done to him.

Yvonne pulled the cellophane bag from the back pocket of her shorts. She had taken along two heels of bread to tear up and toss to the swans. The bread was squat and warm. Crouched before the water, she tore away pieces and flicked them toward the ducks that rushed for the bread. The swans were further out, nearer their island in the centre of the pond.

A toddler caught sight of Yvonne's actions and hobbled close, watching the bread leave her hand and land in the water. The toddler held its tiny arm out as if to grab the bread in mid-air when it was flung. Yvonne smiled. The toddler was a girl, she surmised. The pink outfit, the faces of boys and girls so alike at that age. One so much like the other. She stared at the girl's face, uncertain. The colours the baby wore were pink and white and there was a pink bow in her hair but her face was peculiarly masculine. Yvonne glanced for the toddler's mother to see that no woman stood near. She searched around, turned to look back on the bench and was jolted by terror when she saw her own mother sitting there, watching with a grim expression, her arm extended, pointing toward the swans that were coming from the island, drifting through the water in a trail as if beckoned to shore. Yvonne had stopped breathing. The air has emptied of sound and oxygen. She struggled to pull air into her lungs. Her mother wore a white blouse, the outline of a black lace bra perfectly obvious beneath the material. Cupping her palms, her mother placed them against her breasts and smiled, the moist inside lines of her top and bottom lips turned grey, her tongue mottled grey as she showed it to Yvonne. Her mother raised her legs in the manner of a contortionist, drawing them up by the sides of her head, the short skirt she was wearing hiking higher, revealing that she was not wearing panties. Delicately, she sucked on her finger, soundly wetting it, then lowered it between her legs to eagerly slip it in. She forced more fingers inside. Then— as her expression turned from seduction to surprise— her entire hand was lost between her legs, her wrist, the lower length of her arm, her upper arm, the action accelerating until— spine bent at an impossible angle— her shoulder was tugged in, the side of her head, then her head, sucked in as if by the force of a monstrous vacuum.

And her mother disappeared.

Something was touching Yvonne's fingers, nipping at her fingertips like hard thin skin. She flinched spasmodically and turned to see that the swans had come ashore. They were nipping at the bread dangling from her fingers. Huge birds with black beaks and small sinister eyes. Her bowels went watery. She needed to go to the bathroom. Dropping the bread, she turned away, hurried from the scene, brushing past a man in a baseball cap who intently watched her face. Yvonne barely saw him as a blur, her mind still gripped by the harrowingly erotic images of her mother and then the swans tasting her fingers.

TWO

Sergeant Cooper always avoided looking the victim in the face. Depending on his frame of mind, his imagination might lead him in directions he wished to avoid. He might burst out laughing. He had done so in his first pathology class at Memorial. While other students were turning white, looking away or rushing unsteadily to leave the examination theatre, Cooper was trying to hold the laughter in. His professor had assured him that laughter was perfectly natural in disturbing situations. Nervous energy. Cooper had excused himself and gone to the bathroom, giggling crazily. The fit had lasted several minutes.

And besides, he often told himself, I'm seeking specific information on the body and so should focus only on those exact parts. The worst scenarios were when he was called to a murder scene, a body in the woods for months and he had to study the remaining bulk, discern something from the mess of green flesh, liquefied body tissue, stirring insects and rotted fabric. He would focus on components, fractions, parts, not look directly at what it was he was actually bent over, take it one detail at a time, shut his mind off from elaborating visions while he officiated over the inspection of biological decay.

Constable Pendegast was waiting for Cooper outside the morgue in the basement of the Health Sciences Complex. Pendegast had his suit jacket off and hung over his shoulder, his sleeves rolled up, standing there leaned against a wall as if posing for a snap. Without fail, Pendegast was dressed in blue pin-striped suits and white shirts, blue ties. It was standard for him, a muscular man who worked out, believed in the traditional image of a police force, his blonde hair neatly clipped in what Cooper liked to refer to as the disco-do, high on the top and close on the sides. Pendegast had all the classic mannerisms and behaviours of a textbook misogynist.

"The expert's here," Pendegast said, loudly snapping his spearmint chewing gum and giving Cooper the once-over. "Where you been?"

"Thinking."

"Can't you think and walk? How about chewing gum at the same time?"

"Walk, think and chew gum? Hmm." Cooper flipped up the sunshades clipped to his glasses, moved toward the morgue's swinging doors, and pushed them open, muttering, "Can't say I've ever had the pleasure of being party to such a complex cacophony of cognition, Mighty Man."

Pendegast snickered, waited a moment to scan the room. The pathologist sat on a stool toward the far corner, ignoring them. Pendegast glanced at the steel casket. Carrying the snide tone, he said, "Got another dead lesbo."

"So they say."

"Nice shirt," Pendegast said. He tossed his suit jacket onto one of the stools positioned before the ledge that skirted three of the walls; the other wall was a grid of steel doors.

"Thanks," Cooper said, pretending it was a genuine compliment. "My dead Mom bought it for me at the Sweet Everafter Mall." He stepped nearer the locked steel casket, shoved his hands deep into the pockets of his brown pants and twiddled his fingers expectantly. "It was a Christmas present, wrapped in Muslim linen."

Pendegast stared in silence, then gave his gum a solid chew.

"The key?" Cooper asked.

"Gave it to our friend." Pendegast nodded toward the pathologist still seated on the stool across the room, filling in a form. The pathologist, Doctor Rahri, hadn't looked up yet, and this irked Cooper. Manners, he told himself. What's the matter with people? Is Rahri so preoccupied as to not notice someone entering a room? No, he's just ignorant, attempting to show importance. The whole stance implied— "I'm much too busy and preoccupied with my mighty all-powerful job to be distracted from it for a second by the worthless likes of you. When I'm done, I'll look up and pretend I didn't hear you coming in. I'll act surprised, or not. Business as usual."

Cooper and Pendegast stood side by side, silently waiting for Doctor Rahri to join them. This was the part Cooper hated. Waiting. Waiting in this particular room. He felt slightly faint, overheated, the smell of hospitals spooking him, shifting him into a surreal place where everything was deceptively scrubbed clean of death. And Pendegast's presence— so near him— disturbed him even further, the carefree cop. All of this meaning nothing to Pendegast, just images with no depth. He was in his forties, had at least ten years on Cooper, but was still a constable, having failed in his attempts to gain promotion. Cooper regarded him as a big dumb dog, or a hairy oafish caricature of the R. Crumb variety. You could fit Pendegast into the skin of any perverse male cartoon figure. Most of the officers on the force viewed him as a fool, yet occasionally he had the capacity to surprise everyone. He had solved a few cases, as if by accident. Or they had almost solved themselves, and he had just happened to be in the right place at the right time to suggest something, out of the blue.

"Another one." Pendegast snorted, staring at the casket. "This is the real deal."

Doctor Rahri stepped off his stool. Cooper watched the man's face register nothing. No surprise. "Hey," said Cooper. "Morning."

"Good morning," Rahri said plainly, stepping near to unlock the casket and lift the lid.

Pendegast smiled when he saw that the body was naked, a leering smile that he checked, then glanced at Cooper to discover that the doctor sergeant was watching him.

Cooper and Pendegast helped Rahri lift the body from the steel casket. Cooper paid close attention as the bags were removed from the head and hands. In the corner of his eyes, he could see Pendegast, his eyes fixed on the dead woman's breasts.

"Hey," Cooper said to him. "Ever fuck a dead woman?"

"What?" Pendegast asked, shocked. "What's your problem?" He sounded almost Italian, an impersonation of something he had seen on television.

"You look like you want to fuck her. When we're through here maybe you can climb on for a ride."

"Don't be so fucking sick," Pendegast said with disgust.

Cooper waited while the pathologist— ignoring their conversation completely— weighed and measured the body.

"Man, it's always so fucking chilly in here." Pendegast declared, shivering and putting his jacket on again while Cooper's eyes darted over the body several times. He touched the woman's fingers and— as usual— was alarmed, astonished by the numbness, the emptiness that stabbed him at his mortal core. Pendegast's eyes lingered here and there as the pathologist collected vaginal and rectal swabs. "A strangulation, most certain," Rahri indicated. "Here we have obvious ligature markings." Rahri plotted the markings on a pre-printed diagram of the human body.

"Like Rent-a-Wreck," Pendegast joked, pointing at the form. "Circling the dents and scratches." Cooper and the pathologist gave him a cool look.

Thumbing back the eyelids, Rahri noted the redness of the conjunctivae, blood spots on the membrane connecting the inner eyelid to the eyeball. "Caused by haemorrhaging from choking," he explained evenly, without glancing away from his work. "The great force. It pops the vessels."

Cooper watched while the Y-shaped incision was made, the flesh opened like a hidden mystery, a carnival of mucousy colour, the body fluids collected and labelled. Blood. Urine. Cerebro-spinal. Stomach contents. Intestinal contents. Samples of liver. Vitreous humour...

When they were through, Cooper nodded thanks to Rahri. "I would say it's been a pleasure, but that'd be a profound over-statement."

He made a point of smiling goodbye then turned from the room, chilled to the bone. The dissection, the sights and sounds of flesh and bone coming apart by razor and saw, made him feel strangely whole, peculiarly alive, touched by the absurdity of his own life, the blood coursing through his veins. Too absurd to even consider. He shook off the thought, focusing on images of Natasha, always images of Natasha to clear his thoughts when they turned troubling. His brain as a blob, slithering up through the grill of a sewer cover to find light and beauty. Natasha. He wished that she were ten feet tall. He wished that he could suck his thumb and snuggle in her arms while she stroked him.

"Fucking ignorant towel-head," said Pendegast, tossing a look back toward the morgue door.

"What?"

"That Doctor Punjab. They're all fucking ignorant."

Cooper shook his head, vaguely queasy. He had a metallic taste in his mouth, felt as if he was fading into the whiteness. He took several deep breaths, flipped his sunshades down.

"Want to grab a bite?" Pendegast asked, passing beneath the row of panel lights in the bright corridor. "Cafeteria's just upstairs."

"No."

"You okay, Doctor Sergeant?"

Cooper stared at Pendegast, further disoriented by the man's outlandish nature.

"Bite to eat." Pendegast laughed and slapped the button at the elevator.

"No, I'm fasting."

"Voodoo, huh? Doing you a lot of good."

"What?"

"You look a little pale. Maybe fasting's not such a good idea."

"Clears the head."

"Don't be so fucking sensitive all your life. You'll be crying on me soon."

Cooper sniffed, "Boo hoo," and took a stick of lip balm from his pocket, drew it over his dry lips. Pendegast watched Cooper's movements, then the glossy sheen of the lips. He snorted, "Nice lipstick," while shifting his eyes to stare at the glowing elevator button.

"Piece of information for you, Pendegast," Cooper said, having had enough, his mind racing with a litany of retorts. "Did you know that the most aggressive men are usually the ones most uncertain of their sexual identity?"

"Yeah?" Pendegast snapped his gum. "Is that so?"

"It's a certified fact, Jack."

"That's a fact I'll have to remember."

"Not only that. Misogynists are generally latent homosexuals. You might want to keep that in mind."

The elevator doors slid open.

"You saying I'm a misogynist?" Pendegast stepped on, looking down at Cooper, who pressed the button for the main lobby, not saying another word.

"What're you smiling at?" Pendegast asked, his tone not demanding but wanting to share the joke, as if it was about someone else.

"I was thinking how much fun I'd have working up a psychological profile on you." That was enough. No more, he warned himself. He didn't bother looking at Pendegast. He didn't have to. He knew exactly how he was being watched. After all, poor old Peckerhead Pendegast had such a limited selection of emotional responses to choose from.

At home, Yvonne threw herself onto the couch, distracting herself with images of Zack, his want of her, his preoccupation with her. That painting. She shifted toward the other end of the couch so she could have a view of the painting. It really was fabulous. The veins in the body, the moon in the head. She was waiting for the night to come so she could return his sunglasses. That would occupy her night anyway, keep her thoughts from fretting over move-in day for the Police Chiefs' Convention. She should go into the office and do a little work, make certain she was prepared, but she didn't want to move. The heat was making her super lazy.

She'd like to see Zack now. How mad would he be with her if she interrupted him? He had told her that he worked when it was daytime, in the morning when the light was strong. That was when her mother had worked.

Her mother. What was it with her mother all of a sudden? Again, she shifted on the couch, rose and turned the other way to face the television. She pointed the remote and pressed "on." A religious service in a fancy church, a nature program on another channel, reruns of *All in the Family, The Beverley Hillbillies*, an info-mercial with smiling, overly enthusiastic people with all the answers readily at hand. She wished that one of the talk shows was on. She learned so much from them, took comfort in sharing the grief of the guests, took solace from the ones who were worse off than her. Screwed up beyond belief. Nothing like her. They were so far gone.

Switching back to MuchMusic, she watched a k.d. lang video. "Miss Chatelaine." k.d. dressed up in her frilly dress, trying to be glamorous. It was supposed to be a joke, Yvonne guessed. She raised one leg and studied the length of it, ran her hands over the fronts of her thighs, checking them for smoothness, her palm coming away damp. She wiped it on the front of the couch.

She had taken the phone off the hook. It was useless to have it ringing. The ID service couldn't be hooked up until tomorrow, Monday, when everyone at the telephone company returned to work, so she had no way of finding out who was tormenting her before then. She thought of calling her Aunt Muriel, who worked in marketing for the telephone company, but she doubted that anything could be done on Sunday. And anyway, she did not want Aunt Muriel thinking she was desperate. That would only encourage the woman to come around. And if there was one thing she didn't need it was her mother's sister poking her nose into her affairs. Muriel seemed nice enough, but what was she really like? She and Yvonne's mother were made from the same flesh and blood.

Unsatisfied with the music video, she snatched a fashion magazine from the coffee table and flipped through it. She studied a photograph of a buxom blonde wearing an evening gown. The woman was so slim. Yvonne believed that the woman was exactly as she wanted to be. Exactly. How could she possibly be slimmer or more beautiful? She tore out the photograph and laid it on the carpet, rolled over on her side to look down at it. She felt her heart beating faster, the sweat increasing, her skin slippery, her thighs moist against each other.

"Now, *you're* beautiful," she said to the image, wiping her brow with a dish towel she'd taken from the kitchen earlier. "You're so perfect and beautiful."

The image was sharp. High resolution— 525 lines. Peerless low-light performance. Linear electronic iris that operated faultlessly. Top-of-the-line equipment.

The man watched Yvonne lying on the couch reading a magazine. He had heard when she first took the phone off the hook. The steady shrill beeping sound that soon abated. The thought that such a simple act would stop his intrusion was preposterous. He could make the telephone ring regardless, if he chose to, charge the wire with fifty volts. It was simply a matter of sending a pulse through her phone line. The flicking of a switch.

The man watched the electronic image of Yvonne as she tore a page from the magazine and laid it on the floor.

"Now, *you're* beautiful," she whispered, wiping her brow with a dish towel. "You're so perfect and beautiful." Rolling onto her back, she shut her eyes.

The man watched as her right hand moved down over her belly, her left leg shifting slightly, bending at the knee, her hand disappearing beneath the waist-line of her panties. The man heard her slow, steady breath turn deeper, complicated, drawing in on itself. Yvonne's index finger rubbing, bending at the knuckle.

The man waited for the sounds of muttering. It was a definite pattern. Even masturbation played itself out in patterns. Yvonne whispered the specific words, the commands, her body twitching in response to her own fingers, her hips lifting slightly as her body became more aroused, the mounting pleasure tightening her muscles until the orgasmic spasms hit, seizing her body as her spine arced.

Rigid, she gradually, gracefully relaxed, her eyes remaining shut. A few minutes later, her breathing slowed, became indistinguishable. She had dozed off, satiated, calmed by the voiding of her imagination.

THREE

Mrs. Kieley was in the kitchen baking date squares. Gregory knew because he had been out to check on them several times. He could smell the odour drifting into his room. Standing from his desk, he left his diagrams for a moment. Pulling back his shoulders to relieve the strain, he yawned, then turned for the door and went out.

In the kitchen, his mother was wearing her apron, and a bandanna around her hair. She had just slid the cookie sheet of date squares out of the oven and was softly patting them with the tip of her oven mitt.

"Date squares done?" Gregory asked.

Mrs. Kieley started slightly, darting a look at him. "Merciful God," she said, "I didn't hear you." She glanced him up and down, noticing his swollen hand immediately. She pulled off her oven mitts, came over to him and took his hand in both her soft wrinkled hands.

"What happened?"

"Work."

"You're not a common ditch digger." She led him into the light over by the window at the back of the house, and lifted his hand toward her squinting eyes. She raised her glasses from where they hung around her neck, and slipped them on, dabbing the bruise here and there.

"It's okay." He tried pulling away, but she held onto it until she was satisfied it did not require medical attention. "It's nothing," he insisted.

His mother looked him in the eyes. "Be careful," she said, as if she somehow knew what he was doing, what he had done to the wife-beater the night before.

"Sure." He avoided her eyes, turned away to get breakfast.

"I'm going to run these down to Mr. Prouse," she said.

"Mr. Prouse. The landlord?"

"I'll keep some for you. Because you love them," she said in a cheery singsong.

Gregory turned and looked at his mother, his stern face taking on a gentle quality that was generally kept well concealed. He smiled self-consciously. "I see. You and Mr. Prouse."

"Just a few date crumbles." She briskly left the room. A few minutes later, she was back in the kitchen, stale White Shoulders clouding the air in a sickening way, the perfume unsettling Gregory's stomach.

"I cut them for you," Gregory indicated, his manner newly withdrawn as he laid down the knife, stared at its keen edge.

"Thanks." She arranged the date squares on a china plate, giving little attention to her son, and then anxiously left the room again, platter in hand.

"Good luck," Gregory quietly called, trying to humour her, adding, "cradle robber." He pulled his thoughts away from the wife-abuser he had beaten. How wrong that had been, he told himself; then his mind shifted back to his mother. Something about her intended visit with Mr. Prouse was bothering him. What was it? The stairs. He went out to the living room to see his mother fussing with her hair in front of the mirror by the door.

"I'll give you a hand with those stairs," he said as she picked up the platter of date squares from the knickknack table.

"No, I can manage," she said, leaning away from the hand he offered. "I might be eighty-one but I'm not feeble, you know."

"Your knees."

"I can manage."

"You be careful with that Mr. Prouse," Gregory warned. "He's the playboy bachelor type."

"I can take care of myself," Mrs. Kieley assured him with a brimming youthful smile. Staring at the shut apartment door, squinting, she then glanced at Gregory who jaunted for the door and pulled it open. His mother paused, her soft face powdered, her eyelids smeared with blue eye shadow, her lipstick a soft pink, to ask with schoolgirl excitement, "How do I look?"

Back at the office, Cooper switched on his computer terminal, logged in, and brought up the digitized mapping system. The colourful world map flashed on his screen. He selected the country and then clicked the mouse, selected the province—Newfoundland, clicked, then the city—St. John's, clicked. The field narrowing. He typed in Gower Street and set the radius at half a kilometre. One tap of the mouse and the street map appeared. He selected the search function for previous offenders and clicked. All prior offenders in the area lit up, grey rectangles appearing, marking the corresponding addresses.

Murderers usually moved in familiar areas, locations they were comfortable with, knowing the ways out, the ways in, the hiding places, the safe areas. This system pinpointed those most likely to be operating in the area. He had established the program himself, having learned of its existence while studying at Oxford University in England. It was flawlessly efficient and cut through the sloppier method of having to search through the CPI computer and narrow down names in a manual, time-consuming way.

He was jotting down notes on his pad when the telephone rang. He picked it up, his mind racing ahead to who it could be, either Natasha or a fellow officer. It was Sunday. Maybe another murder. That was possible.

"Sergeant Uriah Cooper." His pen began doodling immediately, drawing circles and marking X's in the centres, circling and circling the X's, then drawing mouse ears on them, nasty snarls, big teeth...

"The famous Doctor Sergeant Cooper?" the female voice slyly proposed.

"Yes?"

"When I watch them gasp for breath," the voice said, "it makes me so wet. It makes me come. You're still sitting there. Why? Haven't you read the file?"

Cooper's hand froze, the doodlings abruptly halted. He reached for the mini-recorder on his desk, pressed the "record" button and immediately attached the suction wire to the earpiece.

"What file?" he muttered.

"The case file. The one I sent you. The one that details my death."

"I haven't seen a file."

"Oh, don't play with me, Cooper."

"I'm not playing."

"Well, then, I'll give you a little clue, because mysteries are just so delicious."

"Of course, they *can* be." He was squinting without realizing it. There was something behind the voice that he could not pin down. An electronic shadow.

"Two bodies. Yummy lesbian bitches."

They hadn't released the information relating to the sexual preferences of the murder victims, so Cooper assumed there was some degree of authenticity in the call.

"Set your digitized mapping system on LeMarchant Road. Hurry, if you can. I can't control who's dead next." The line clicked off.

Words lingering in his mind, Cooper hung up, played back the tape and was relieved to discover that he had captured the voice. The electronic shadow was present. His ears rarely deceived him. He would have a psycho-linguistic analysis run on the voice to determine what region it was from, the dialect, the slight inflections of speech that would narrow the location of the caller's birthplace. He'd also have a digital breakdown performed on the voice, to see if what he believed could be confirmed.

He called Lieutenant Johnston's number while he punched in LeMarchant Road, hit a radius that would give him the full length of the street, and watched the grey squares light up as Johnston answered. Cooper informed the lieutenant of the call.

"I should hear that tape," said Johnston. "Bring it over."

"Sure." Anxiously hanging up, Cooper did a quick scan of the names on LeMarchant Road, delighted to be able to test his new toy. He passed through several petty criminals, and concentrated on the more obsessive crimes. One immediately struck him. A grey rectangle at 64 LeMarchant Road.

Lawrence Timothy Prouse. Convicted. Stalking. He wrote down the name and address, knowing there would be others. He'd finish the search after he brought the tape over to Johnston, but for now he'd send an officer to Lawrence Prouse's place. Get the ball rolling. He picked up the phone to call Communications, to have a car dispatched to 64 LeMarchant Road. But then decided against it. Lost in thought, he slowly reset the receiver on its cradle. He'd go over himself instead. He trusted no one to bring back the details that he could only see if he were there.

He stood back from his desk and snatched up the tape, made a motion to lurch toward the door, but held himself in check long enough to say, "Super-shrink to the rescue." Charging ahead, he glanced at his bulletproof vest, hung on the stark coat tree by the bulletin board. He never wore it. After all, super-shrink was capable of psychoanalyzing bullets to a dead stop in mid-air. Hot, aggressive bits of metal so fiercely set on harming people. What was at the root of such behaviour? A terrible childhood in the bullet factory, forged from the abuses of fire. He continued this line of reasoning as he left his office in the sub-building alongside the main station. Flipping down his clip-on shades, he glanced around with mock, severe suspicion, while clutching the tape recorder tightly in his hand. He felt that he should be smoking a cigarette and speedy intro music should be playing in the background. He hummed the theme from Hawaii Five-O while purposefully stepping across the parking lot, in beat with the punchy music.

Mrs. Kieley extended the glass plate of date squares as soon as Mr. Prouse opened the door. Lawrence Prouse smiled and offered a gentlemanly bow, opening the door to his second-favourite tenant.

"What's that you have there?" he asked, giving a welcoming sweep of his arm and shifting aside, allowing room for her entry.

"Date squares," Mrs. Kieley cheerily announced. Stepping in, she glanced around the apartment, obviously extremely pleased with herself. "The colour is lovely. So fresh," she said to him, referring to the shade of peach the walls were painted. "The white mouldings really show off the colour."

"Do you like Monet?" he congenially asked, shutting the door, but not before peeking at Yvonne Unwin's apartment across the hall.

"Very nice," said Mrs. Kieley, studying the wavery pastel watercolours tastefully framed.

"I just love flowers."

"Yes, your gardens around the grounds are grand!"

Noticing the plate still in Mrs. Kieley's hand, Mr. Prouse leaned forward, "I'll take that for you." Mrs. Kieley gave a distracted but obliging smile, allowing the transfer.

"Come out into the kitchen," he said, nodding his way toward the wide archway across the living room that led into the hallway. Taking a right turn, he moved toward the kitchen door halfway down the hall. He paused to let Mrs. Kieley pass, to place a gentle hand on the woman's back as a friendly means of guiding her into the kitchen.

"The kitchen used to be the dining room," he said, crossing the threshold. "There was a set of double sliding doors right where that refrigerator is. It had to be covered up. I tried to work around it, but..."

"You must have spent a great deal of money refurbishing the house."

"Oh," Mr. Prouse exclaimed as he laid the date squares on the table. "Don't talk about money. I don't even want to think about the money I sank into this place."

"It must be wonderful, though, owning such a historic house."

"As they say, it's the bank that owns it. I'm just renting from them. I have a few other properties around town as well. Mortgaged to the hilt."

"Really?" Mrs. Kieley took an appreciative look at a vase of flowers in the centre of the white kitchen table. She recognized the pansies and the daisies and the tiger lilies, but there were other smaller flowers she could not identify. She glanced at the walls while Mr. Prouse went about preparing plates and boiling water for the teapot. Again, artwork featuring flowers was hung on each wall. "It's a nice bright kitchen."

Mr. Prouse glanced back, "Thank you. Please, sit down." He dropped two teabags into the yellow round ceramic pot and turned to lift placemats— featuring huge sunflowers— from the drawer. He laid the placemats in place and set the plates down, each with a date square in the centre, then helped Mrs. Kieley with her chair.

"This is such a pleasant surprise," he said.

Mrs. Kieley settled in the seat offered her. Once Mr. Prouse made certain she was sitting comfortably, he returned to the stove and poured the boiling water into the pot.

"I get so few visitors."

Mrs. Kieley smiled and arranged a napkin on the lap of her cream-coloured house dress. Then she fluffed her hair and checked the string of cream-coloured baubles at her neck.

"There you go." The teapot was set in the centre of the table, a quilted floral-patterned tea cozy fitted over it.

Mr. Prouse sat. "It's so very nice to see you. For you to be thinking of me. Date squares. I love them." He patted her hand.

Mrs. Kieley blushed, the colour brightening beneath her face powder.

"You look ravishing."

"Thank you." Mrs. Kieley shyly averted her eyes. It had been a while since she had done such a thing, but it came so naturally.

"I was thinking about you just last night," he said, straightening his napkin in his lap. "This heat. Do you have a fan up there?"

"Yes, but I don't mind the heat."

"No? I wear silk." He fingered his shirt. "It helps a great deal. To keep cool."

"I'm perfectly fine."

"I thought so. You seem like a woman who can look after herself." He nibbled from his date square. "Mmm. Delicious. My mother was just like that. Looked after herself, I mean."

Mrs. Kieley was slightly dejected by the mention of his mother. She didn't want to be viewed in a motherly way.

Mr. Prouse waited a moment, his eyes on the tea cozy, thinking of other things, distant. He caught himself and shook his head, "Sorry, was I drifting? It's so difficult to sleep in this heat."

"That's perfectly all right." Mrs. Kieley checked her bauble necklace again, praying that she would not start sweating and ruin her make-up. She thought about having a cup of tea. Hot fluids cooled down the body.

"What was I saying?" He tilted his head slightly, and smiled charmingly.

"I believe you were talking about your mother."

"Yes." Again, Mr. Prouse became distant. He lifted the cozy from the pot and spoke evenly. "She died a few years ago. This was her favourite of all the properties she owned. She adored all things old and quaint."

Mrs. Kieley held her china cup while he poured.

"Milk."

"No, thank you." She raised the cup to her lips.

"That was her favourite cup," Mr. Prouse said, staring at the faded rose on the side of the china. "Her very favourite." His eyes shifted to Mrs. Kieley's and again there was a detached quality about them, a longing that seemed so sad and pitiful. Mr. Prouse watched how the rim of the cup touched Mrs. Kieley's lips. "I'd like to show you something," he said, standing from his chair, "photographs of..."

There was a buzz from the living room. The intercom system.

"I'm not expecting anyone," he said. He went out and Mrs. Kieley heard him speaking, but she could not make out the words. When he returned, he said, "I have a visitor. More visitors. Can you imagine! All of a sudden everyone's here."

Mrs. Kieley smiled and blinked, fluttering her eyelashes.

Mr. Prouse sighed, "I'm so sorry, but the visit is of a private nature. Perhaps you could drop down tonight, and we could finish..."

"Oh, certainly." Mrs. Kieley stood, straining to push herself up.

"I'm terribly sorry about this..." Mr. Prouse moved quickly to assist her, "I was enjoying our visit," then just as briskly led her through the living room, all the while attempting to remain polite. Opening the door, he wished her goodbye, but then felt obliged to help her up the stairs.

"Don't forget about tonight," he reminded her. "Our little rendezvous." Delivered safely to her door, Mrs. Kieley watched her new male friend hurry downstairs.

Mr. Prouse returned to his apartment and buzzed the police officers in. He was greatly concerned that he had waited too long. They might think he was stalling, hiding something. And he didn't need attention from the police. He didn't need that. He was being so good.

Mrs. Kieley entered the apartment in a chipper mood.

"That was quick," Gregory said, glancing up from the Sunday paper.

"We had a nice talk," Mrs. Kieley said, slightly out of breath.

"You shouldn't be going up and down those stairs."

"Don't be foolish. You're just jealous."

"Especially in this heat."

Mrs. Kieley plunked down in her rocker, sighing. "Get me a drink of root beer will you, Gregory?"

"Sure." Kieley went to the kitchen and returned with the root beer in a glass filled to the brim with ice.

Mrs. Kieley drank, gulping with enjoyment. "Oh, that's some fine."

"So, what's this Mr. Prouse really like?" Gregory asked, folding shut the newspaper and laying it on the couch beside him.

"A nice talk." Mrs. Kieley held the glass in her lap and shut her eyes, rocking slowly.

"You talked."

"About things. He likes flowers. We were about to have a nice cup of tea and some of my date crumbles."

"But?"

"He had visitors."

"Who?"

"Don't be so nosey, Gregory." She opened her eyes to look at him, gave a little laugh. "You're always so suspicious of people."

"It's my job, Mom."

"You've got to learn to relax a little. That time in the Yukon really robbed you of your sense of humour. You used to enjoy a laugh."

Kieley glanced toward the window, his expression souring. "Yeah. Well, things aren't that funny sometimes."

Mrs. Kieley peeked at him. The Yukon was a lie. Every time it was mentioned, he looked away from her. A dead giveaway. She knew her son so well. She was his mother, so why wouldn't he tell her about the Yukon?

FOUR

Yvonne discontentedly passed the late afternoon fitting together a jigsaw puzzle, an expansive photograph of a scenic countryside. While struggling with the pieces, she listened to a Melissa Etheridge CD, singing along with the booming words: "Am I the only one who'll walk across the fire for you." She loved that song. She really got into it. The beat and the singing had an intensely passionate feel to it, an indisputable sincerity.

At suppertime, she ate a slice of toast with peanut butter (the old standby) and raspberry jam, and a glass of banana-strawberry juice that cooled her throat. A great Sunday dinner, she scolded herself. But it was a small enough quantity of food to hold down. She didn't feel the need to go into the bathroom and purge herself.

At 7:15 she left her apartment, avoiding her reflection in the mirror. Heading up the stairs, she heard Zack's apartment door close and then saw him wandering down the stairs, coming toward her, his dark eyes cast down, not paying attention, lost in his thoughts. A few more slow steps and he caught sight of Yvonne.

Zack smiled, slowly, genuinely delighted to see her, relieved and then mildly pleased with himself, a hint of arrogance changing the expression, ruining it.

"Hi," Yvonne raised his sunglasses. "I was just coming up."

"I was working," he said, distantly, gazing at her eyes. "You found them."

"Yeah, they were on the mantelpiece."

Zack stared, the smile fading.

"Are you okay?"

"Yeah, I'm... just a little gone. Been working. I'm in it. Then I'm torn out of it."

"The painting?" She shifted over, leaning against the stairwell wall.

"Yeah. Working... I'm off somewhere else and when I stop it's like I'm tossed outta that place. It takes a while to get readjusted to where I am."

Yvonne glanced back at her door. "You need a glass of wine. There's that bottle that needs serious finishing."

Zack smiled warmly. But the warmth was unable to draw him out of the frigid pit he seemed stuck in, the lingering subconscious severity. He reinforced his smile and nodded. "Yeah, I could use a drink, or twenty."

After returning from visiting with Lawrence Prouse, Cooper sat at his desk and carefully wrote out the facts on his lined notepad. Prouse was like some sort of bizarre playboy from a 1960s movie. Flowers and pastels and frilly shirts. If Cooper had to cast him in a cartoon, Prouse would be a cross between Mr. Magoo and Fritz the Cat. Cooper chuckled to himself and sketched Mr. Magoo's round head with cat's ears and a tongue lolling hungrily on his chin. Then he drew a curvaceous female cat. He glanced toward his door to see that no one was entering, then dotted the nipples, feeling like a schoolboy. He tore the sheet off and crumpled it up, tossed it toward the wastebasket. Prouse could not be responsible for the murders. The man lacked the customary background for such behaviour, though Pendegast had notions of Prouse being a perverted mastermind.

Prouse had a background of stalking. Had been charged, Pendegast insisted. "He's already come up against the strong arm of the law. We should haul him down to the station for further interrogation."

"For an interview," Cooper had corrected him.

"Let's bring him in. I got a hunch."

They had sat in the car behind the house on 64 LeMarchant Road, the sun beginning to drop over the line of row houses beyond the yard, orange tinting the blue sky, drawing warm shadows across the city.

Cooper smelled the strong body odour of Pendegast so near him across the seat: some cheap cologne and sweat, a floral stench that hung heavy in the closed humid air of the car.

"That Prouse is a sick bastard. I can smell it."

"Yeah. What's it smell like?" Cooper looked away from his view of the sky through the windshield and frowned at Pendegast. "Strands of long black hair at both scenes," Cooper offered.

"Maybe he was wearing a wig. We didn't check for a wig. Maybe he's one of those freaks who dresses up in women's clothing."

"It wasn't wig hair."

"There's nothing back from the lab yet. You don't know. The hairs could've been planted."

"Sure, that's possible," Cooper agreed, trying his best to be reasonable.

"Let's go back in." Pendegast's hand darted for the door handle, every muscle tensed. "Mess the fucker up."

"You're joking, right?"

Giving a hard laugh, Pendegast reached into his pocket for a packet of cigarettes. Taking one out, he clamped it between his teeth. "Relax, baby. It's cool."

Cooper stared, baffled. "I really don't think it's necessary to 'mess the fucker up.'"

"No? Tell me why."

"The voice on the phone belonged to a female."

"Voice changer." Pendegast snatched the cigarette out of his mouth and pointed it at Cooper. "Get with the times."

"Yeah," he whispered. "I'm with them. I'm way with them."

"A concerned citizen with a tip." Pendegast whisked out his zippo and flipped the lid with his palm, then spun the tiny wheel. He cupped his hand around the flame, even though they were in a car, and puffed noisily, blowing smoke through his nostrils.

"No, something more than that," Cooper said, rolling down his window.

"Yeah." Pendegast took a harsh draw from his cigarette, his eyes squinting. Again, he pointed at Cooper with the cigarette between two fingers. "I say we keep an eye on him. That's for sure."

"I agree." Cooper had to suppress the smile that tickled his lips. He started the engine to distract himself. He was beginning to find Pendegast amusing, shifting from agitation to satirical introspection. But then an idea came to him. "That's a good job for you."

"All right." Pendegast said, triumphantly shaking both fists. "Drop me off at the station. I'll get my wheels and head back here."

"I'll do just that."

"We'll see who's guilty here," Pendegast laughed. "Mark my fucking words, Doctor Sergeant. I know where this one's heading. Those dyke bitches. They're gonna keep turning up dead."

Back at his desk, Cooper glanced at the bulletin board directly in front of him. Newspaper clippings of recent cases he had solved were neatly displayed there. He wrote down the words "black hairs," the sentence: "I can't control who's dead next." Did that mean the owner of the voice couldn't control the person who was actually doing the killing? Or was it a case of split personality? Jekyll and Hyde. A woman killer? By the look of the ligature marks on Mary Hood and the victim before her, Judy Cramer, it appeared they had been choked by a female. But it was easy enough for a man to exert the right amount of force to make it appear that he was weaker.

Very little information on such cases. If the victims were— indeed— lesbians, as things seemed to indicate, then this would be a breakthrough case for him. His mind flashed on headlines. Media from all over the world would fly in to St. John's to cover the case. There'd be a frenzy of reporters that he'd have to deal with. There'd be book deals and movie negotiations. He'd heard about such offers from his instructor at Oxford University. Richard Higgins had received numerous offers relating to the sensational cases he had handled. There was even a TV series based on him over there in the UK.

Cooper sighed, scratching his palm. The thought of wealth teased him. It would be a true test. Scruples and integrity. They'd be hard to hold onto. He vowed to make certain it wouldn't come to that. He grinned, held the grin as if standing before a camera. He adjusted his glasses and fussed with his crewcut. Keen to the stillness of his office, he realized he was alone in the annex. He glanced out his window and saw that it was late, shadows almost stretched fully across the parking lot that divided him from the firehall. A yellow fire truck was parked in front of one of the big open doors. Firemen in slate-blue shirts and black pants were washing it.

This case was something most police officers would kill for. He felt ill at ease in a soul-shaking way, almost fearful of the disruption that was surely forthcoming. He thought of birds and animals that could sense an approaching storm and milled about restlessly from the energy divined from the air.

Cooper focused back on the computer screen, the names on LeMarchant Road that he was searching through. There were a couple of others of interest, but no one with the violent background required of the person carrying out these murders. Your average person just didn't kill another person. In most cases, the murderer usually had a long record of previous violent offenses. Assault, at the very least.

Cooper cleared his thoughts with a glance out the window. The firemen were still washing the yellow truck. It was well after suppertime. He checked his watch: 8:20. He had called Natasha and explained that he would be home shortly. She informed him that she was making curried chicken and chick peas with wild rice.

"Your favourite," she had said.

He didn't have the heart to tell her he was fasting. That was the end of that. He couldn't disappoint her. He'd have to eat and then start again tomorrow, try from there.

"I'm starving," he had admitted, his stomach grumbling at the thought of the meal. "I'll be late."

"And Black Forest cake for dessert."

"Stop now. You're gonna make me cream my jeans."

"Don't be a saucy boy. And retro, too. See you soon." She hung up.

Cooper stared at his note pad, circled the word "cunt." A woman caller. The tape was with Don Thistle, one of the crime analysts, who was breaking it down, performing a digitized tone spread. Cooper wondered how he was doing, and decided to drop over to the main station across the parking lot before heading home for supper, check out what Don could see in the delineated composition of the voice.

Yvonne was pleasantly surprised to find Zack so receptive. He was most definitely in a sexual mood, a completely different person from the one who had been in her apartment the previous night. Every movement of his body, every look that he gave her after stepping into her apartment was dripping with innuendo.

"I'm working on another surprise for you," he said mischievously. "Very realistic and you're in it. Deep in it."

"Another one." Yvonne was sitting on the couch, one elbow up against the arm rest, her hand holding a glass of wine. She took a sip, quizzically watching Zack over the rim as he stepped near. She was unsure of his new behaviour, his drastic change in disposition. "You're quite taken with me," Yvonne smiled, brimming with the energy of a kindred spirit. They seemed so natural together, as if they had known each other for centuries. "What's the surprise?"

"I can't say," he whispered, leaning down, his face nearing hers, impulsively kissing her lips, warmly, tenderly but with obvious passion, that delicious combination that aroused, not touching her, taking his time with the kiss. Goosebumps rising on her skin.

"Mmmm," Yvonne opened her eyes as Zack drew away. "You're a little warmer tonight."

"The heat of creation, baby. Art. It boils my blood."

Yvonne searched his eyelids, "No eye shadow tonight?"

"You liked that?" Zack said, a hint of intimidation in his voice. "I thought you might."

Yvonne gave a light secretive laugh and then peeked back at the painting. The canvas was so large, it loomed in the corner of her vision. No way of escaping it.

"You just close your eyes and see me?" she asked.

"Yes." He took a casual glance at the painting.

"Why isn't this scary?" she asked him. "I should be scared of you. Someone out of the blue, delivering paintings." She laid her wine on the coffee table and stood, about to wander from the room. "You want some cheese?"

Zack grabbed her wrist, holding tightly. "Because it's genuine."

"You could be crazy," she laughed nervously, slowly backing away. "Insane. Psychotic."

"I am." He was smiling in a way that matched her amusement exactly, his eyes quickly exploring hers, seeing the fear, the uncertainty. He yanked her toward him and kissed her again, still keeping his hands off of her body, making certain their bodies didn't touch. He even released his grip on her wrist.

"Where do you draw the line?" she asked, retreating from the kiss, the heat of him. "Between what's genuine and not?"

"I don't know." He shrugged off the question and turned away to scan the items on the mantelpiece. "We've got brains, right? We should know the difference." A calculated sip of his wine.

"I was... going somewhere."

"Cheese," he said, pointing at the photographs. "Who're these people?"

"My mom and dad."

"Yeah, hmm. Your mom looks just like you." He glanced at Yvonne to see that she had turned to pick up her wine glass. She stepped toward the mantelpiece, not looking at the photographs, then sat on the floor, shyly dropping away from him. Zack sat beside her and let his head tilt back against the wall. He turned his face to watch her. "You were getting cheese."

"I don't want any," she said. "This is where we were last night."

"The action spliced together. Montage. Collage. Parts of me snipped over you."

"How close does a person have to get?" Yvonne held her glass with both hands as if warming it. "So that obsessive admiration isn't violation."

"This close." His eyes, seeming to probe so deeply into her, tugging on her heart and groin, his sharp features and the way he tried so hard to be cruel.

"No, seriously."

"You think that's violation?" As if commanding an army, he raised his hand toward the huge painting.

"No."

"Why?"

"Because it's art."

"Art's excusable. Anything done in the name of art."

Watching his face, she wondered what he believed in. After all, wasn't he an artist? Shouldn't he be defending art? "It's just beautiful," she said.

"Thanks. How about objectification? Don't you think that painting makes an object of you?"

"It couldn't—"

"Of course it does. It's an object and you're part of it."

Yvonne took a wet sip of wine, swishing it around in her cheeks, savouring the oaky flavour. Then she swallowed, surprised at the noise it made. She almost laughed. She was drinking quickly. The heat made her thirsty. A dangerous thing.

"That's what beauty should become," he languidly explained, as if his own words were drugging him, slipping him into a trance. "Objectified. That way it exists beyond the human shell. Great original art gives eternal life to a very original woman."

"Oh, that's touching," she said, smirking. "So, I'm an original?"

"And deserving."

"What makes me deserving? Beauty? Charm? Wit?"

Zack stirred his wine with his index finger, making a tiny whirlpool, watching down into it. "From a romantic point of view, yes. Beauty. Beauty defies the ages."

"So does pornography."

"Sure, but pornography's vulgar."

"What about vulgar art?" She reached for the bottle beside his feet. Raising it, she topped up her glass, then glanced at his. It was half empty.

"You want?"

"Sure, thanks."

When she was done, she reset the bottle between them.

Zack watched her, intently. "Vulgar art that captures a woman's beauty? Is that what you mean?"

"Right, a nude, like a gross nude. No, not even that. An ugly woman captured grossly that's like some kind of..." She searched for the proper words, watching his eyes as if plumbing the mood in him, "...screwed-up beauty."

"Wounded beauty. I don't know."

"Is that just as special? Is that objectification in the name of some kind of derelict beauty, or is it degradation?"

"Man, this is getting way too deep for me. You gotta go to art school to get answers like that."

"You mean I'm too smart for you." Yvonne smirked and drained her glass. "I like this wine," she said, "it's cheap and it's good."

"An excellent combo." He studied her lips, her nose, her chin, her eyes. She was— indeed— beautiful, but didn't seem to know it, to realize it, and this made her beauty shine even brighter. "Intimacy's a really fucked up thing these days."

"Yeah." The way she said it was saucy, a challenge. She reached behind her head, brushing the sweat from the back of her neck, and gathered the length of her black hair, hung it over her right shoulder.

"You can't look at a woman without having the cops at your door."

"You're looking at me. And not in an innocent way, I might add, sugar pie."

"Want me to call 911?"

"I think you're out of your mind." She turned away from him, but remained seated, searching the CD rack. She slowly spun it and selected a case, inserted the disk and pressed the play button. The music jumped to life, a scratchy guitar unevenly cranking out notes.

"Romeo Void," she said above the music, "a band long gone."

"Never say never." Zack smiled, familiar with the lyrics. He practically had to shout: "One-hit wonder. The lead singer got really fat."

I'd like you better if we slept together, Oh, I'd like you better if we slept together. The music was careening, swirling, inciting. Yvonne was prompted to her feet. She stood and reached down, took Zack's hand, pulled him up with surprising vigour.

Leaning close to his ear, she said, "Gimme another one of those kisses."

Zack kissed her, his hands delicately holding her cheeks, his fingers longingly in her hair.

"Your kisses make me wet," she whispered, her voice a little girl's shiver.

Lips close to her ear, "Good."

"I want you to fuck me," she said through gritted teeth, pressing her body into his. "Violate me. Objectify me."

"Severe admiration," Zack said, his hungry smile mirroring hers. He set his hand between her legs, gripping the material of her black shorts.

Yvonne shoved her groin against his hand, then rammed him back against the wall, "Do me," she called out above the music. "Severely."

The monitor was aglow with the image of Zack Brett savagely thrusting into Yvonne. She grunted wildly, her hands held back against the couch cushions, her fingertips prying into the fabric as Zack pounded harder, then grabbed beneath her arms and pulled her body up on an angle, slid underneath and rolled her on top of him. She worked just as savagely, swiping her black hair out of her face and groaning as she kissed him with her mouth fully open, sucking his tongue.

"Fuck me," she commanded, pounding up and down. "Deeper, oh, fuck me."

The image played to an empty room, the red "record" light on the video laser aglow beneath the monitor featuring the live performance. The staticky sounds of Yvonne's groans and pleas spilling out from the headset laid at rest on the console.

There was a knock on the door. Spent and panting with her head against Zack's shoulder, she climbed off him and plopped back onto the other end of the couch, sensing the damp film that coated her skin. Breathing deeply, she closed her eyes and swiped her hair away from her sweaty flushed face. "Fuck, that was good!"

The first knock had been low, tentative, unconvincing, but this one came with slightly more conviction.

Opening her eyes, she peered over at the door.

"Cops," Zack whispered, humorously. "Gotta be the cops. Morality squad."

Yvonne stood, bending for her shorts, uncoiling them from her panties, allowing Zack a view of her smooth glistening buttocks. Tossing the panties behind the couch, she stepped into the shorts, then went to retrieve her black t-shirt and pulled it over her head.

"Ignore it," Zack said.

"Why?"

"It's obvious, isn't it?" He sat up, holding his hands out by his sides, indicating that he was naked.

"Get dressed," she said, nibbling on the corner of her lip.

"Yes, sir. My little Nazi she-wolf."

The knock again.

"Yes," Yvonne blurted out.

"Hello," a muddled voice she did not recognize.

"Who is it?"

"Larry Prouse, the landlord."

"Uh, oh." Exasperated, Yvonne turned to Zack and put a finger to her lips. "Shhh," she said.

Zack shrugged, "I'm not saying anything."

Soundlessly moving toward the door, she carefully opened it a crack.

"Hi." Mr. Prouse stood in the doorway, his hands hidden behind his back.

"Hi..." Yvonne swiped at her forehead with the back of her bare arm then wiped the arm on her shorts.

"The heat is punishing," he said, his eyes taking in her red face, then flicking over her shoulder as if expecting an invitation. When he realized one was not forthcoming, he thrust a bouquet of flowers from behind his back. "Flowers," he explained.

"Gee." She glanced over at Zack, saw that he was hopping to pull on his heavy black denims. How could he wear those, she thought, her mind racing. All image. Artists! Jesus, why did they all dress the same! The fragrant, vaguely bitter smell of flowers reached her, the bouquet held so close to her face, her senses shocked to life, alerted by the manic sexual escapade. Her nerves were tingling. She needed a glass of wine, a tranquillizer, something to calm her down. She was fired up, did not understand what the landlord wanted. Romance? What? Was he pathetic, or sweet? She couldn't decide.

"Have you company?" Mr. Prouse asked innocently, scanning her cheeks.

"Oh, yeah." She peeked back at Zack to see him bent over, fully dressed in black, lacing up his black boots.

"I just thought you'd appreciate them," Mr. Prouse said. "They're from the garden." He pointed toward the front of the house.

"Yes," she said. "Thank you, they're beautiful. I was just admiring them yesterday." She studied her landlord's face, his expression vaguely embarrassed.

"Thank you," she said again, too prettily for her liking, too candy-coated. She usually despised those sugary displays that most women engaged in. And now she found herself playing the part for him.

"Oh, you're more than welcome."

She gave him a cute smile. "That's really nice."

Mr. Prouse's eyes shifted as Zack stepped in beside Yvonne. At first, Prouse was obviously disappointed, but he adjusted his mood, smirking in recognition.

"Zack," he said, pointing above his head.

"From above. Heaven," Zack nodded. "I'm Yvonne's new guardian angel. Sent down to keep her out of trouble."

Yvonne laughed abruptly, and Mr. Prouse did the same, obviously relieved to have the awkwardness defused.

"Thanks for the flowers," she said.

"You're quite welcome." He smiled with his lips pressed together. "See you two later."

Yvonne raised the flowers, saluting him.

Mr. Prouse opened his door and stepped in, not looking back when he shut it.

"Fucking flowers," Zack laughed, "right in the middle of all that sexual chaos. How ironic."

"Shhh," Yvonne chastised, briskly shutting her door. "Now there's genuine admiration. The old-fashioned kind."

"Ohhh, you want me to buy you flowers," he teased, "and a nice house with a picket fence. We could raise chickens. I mean children. And throw dinner parties for all our stupid friends. It's the road to numbness, destruction, spiritual carnage, soulless materialism."

"Flowers?"

"Yeah, flowers. Flowers and then dancing and before you know it you'll be smoking cigarettes and turning into an alcoholic, knocked up in some woman's shelter with four kids biting at your ankles, wishing you'd never accepted those flowers."

"Get lost." She shoved him aside and stepped toward the kitchen. "You and your morals."

"I'm an artist," he said, laughing, catching his balance and following after her. "I'm full of morals. Morality's my pet worm that I like to drag around on a leash. Little tiny collar."

Yvonne gave a slight laugh and shake of her head. "I think it's touching." Dipping her head forward, nose close to the petals, she breathed in their entrancing fragrance.

"A bit of tenderness and beauty intruding upon mean old animal fuck lust."

"Yeah." Yvonne opened the drawer and lifted out a pair of scissors. Staring at the open blades, her hand froze, began trembling. She dropped the scissors back into the drawer.

Zack had been watching her hand, drawn by her silence, "What's the matter?"

"Nothing."

"Your hand's shaking."

"Shut up."

"What?"

She turned to him, anger burning in her eyes, "I said shut up."

Bewildered, Zack wondered if she was joking. She threw the flowers onto the counter.

"Why don't you go now." She braced her hands against the counter top, stared out her kitchen window, a view of the back yard in almost total darkness.

"What'd I do?"

"Just fuck off."

Zack kept his distance. He watched her tense shoulders, insult glazing his eyes. Without a word, he turned away and left the kitchen. Moments later, Yvonne heard her apartment door slamming shut. Immediately, she snatched for the drawer handle, yanked it open and reached in to grab the scissors. Opening the blades, she pulled up her t-shirt and pressed the silver edge against her left nipple, pushing it. "Do it," she whispered, threateningly, sensing the pain, the exquisite pain that would assist her in forgetting. "Do it." Sensing that the sharpness would soon slice her, she tossed the scissors down and raced out into the living room, facing the mirror. Abruptly she slapped her face, the sting prompting tears to her eyes.

"Stupid," slapping again, harder, "ugly," another bitter sting, "no good..."

Don Thistle was replaying the tape when Cooper entered the bright crime analysis lab. He glanced at Cooper, his concentration unchanged while he gave a blunt obligatory nod.

Cooper squinted at the brightness. He cast an irritated glance up at the fluorescent lights. He despised them. They hurt his eyes, made everything too bright, too clear. He wished that the world could be lived under candlelight. That orange-shadowed glow would slow things down. Bright light made people behave in a frantic way. It incited them. And get rid of cars while they were at it. Machinery of any sort. Walk with your legs and work with your hands. As a matter of fact, while they were cleaning shop, get rid of people, too. They were a fucking nuisance. Leave only animals. He imagined himself as a dove. No, a rat. Wet from the sewers with mottled fur and nasty breath.

"You get a breakdown?" Cooper asked, suppressing the urge to gnash his teeth.

"I'm not certain about the dialect," Thistle remarked, immediately giving out the information, not one for being cordial. He was a red-haired man with glasses and an uneven pasty complexion that hadn't seen daylight in quite a while. "We'll have to call someone in from the university. Linguistics."

"Who's there?"

"Paddock."

"Right. What about the actual voice?"

"No doubt it's a voice changer. Probably a YU 198, or something a step up. Something more complicated. It's authentic beyond anything I've heard before. Listen." He played the tape, the female voice sounding from the small twin speakers. Adjusting a sliding lever on the audio panel, the voice became deeper. "I'm lifting off the pitch shadowing. It's from another voice. Two combined. Laid over each other. A woman's over a man's."

Cooper heard the voice transform, metamorphose. He pictured a woman's face turning into a man's. A science-fiction flick. Wavering lights. Flashing laboratory columns. A lightning storm. A cackle from the evil professor and his hump-backed, wart-faced, smelly-toed assistant.

"Which is the real one?"

"Both of them."

"No, which is electronic?"

"There's a double shadow on the female. The initial electronic shadow of recording and then the second shadow through the telephone. There's only one shadow on the male voice, as if it came through the telephone only."

"So, it's a man's?"

"Seems that way."

"So, someone recorded a woman's voice..."

"That's right—"

"Digitized it..."

Thistle shut his eyes, nodded encouragingly, delighted to be in the company of someone who understood his trade.

"And then put their voice behind it to say whatever?"

"Exactly." Thistle opened his eyes, rewound the tape, played it again. The female voice electronically separated. "Neither voice is from Newfoundland. As far as I can tell. But Paddock would know for certain."

"Give him a call."

"It's Sunday."

"Can we find out where he lives?"

"Sure."

"That's great. Thanks, Don." Cooper turned to leave. "This is exciting stuff. All good stuff."

"Listen," Thistle called out.

Cooper paused to face him.

"This is something else, isn't it?"

"Yeah, the genuine article."

"Any ideas?"

"A few. But nothing worth a pinch of atomic shit."

"It's like something out of a movie." Thistle grinned at the idea.

Cooper snorted mildly. "Could be." He turned to leave, but paused again, remembering a detail of Thistle's life, always necessary to ask something personal, to show that you cared. "How's your daughter, Emily?"

"Oh, great. She just turned seven, going into grade two in September."

"She's a real sweetheart."

"Thanks. I know." Thistle's eyes brightened for a moment. "This heat is pretty intense, hey?"

"You wouldn't know it in here." Cooper smiled compassionately. "The air conditioning."

"It's something else."

"Yeah." An interesting term— "something else." It wasn't itself. It was something else.

"I'll track Paddock down."

"Thanks. I'll be home." Cooper left the analysis office and weaved through the carpeted corridors of the CID headquarters, moving out into the subdued lighting in the second floor walkway that overlooked the reception area. He felt his muscles relaxing, the lighting calming him. He caught sight of Pendegast entering the main doors on the first floor, and he stopped in his tracks, leaned back slightly, peeked out to see him continuing on into the offices beneath him.

"Man," Cooper mumbled. "I can't handle him now."

Natasha had the table arranged in a romantic setting when Cooper arrived home: candlelight, paisley fabric napkins in ring holders, shimmering silverware that had belonged to his Nan, dead years ago. "What's the celebration?"

"Seven months today."

"Seven months?" he said under his breath, then louder, "Whoops!" He smacked his forehead in a clownish way, almost knocking his glasses off. "Stupid me," he said, leaving his glasses askew until she looked at him.

"I don't expect you to remember," she said, not the slightest hint of sarcasm in her voice. "I know how preoccupied you are. The mind's only capable of so much, right?" She glanced up from the salad she was tossing in a large cobalt blue pottery bowl. "Fix your glasses, fool."

"You're a saint," he said, realigning his glasses. He stepped into the kitchen and wrapped his arms around her waist, blew on the back of her neck and then kissed the spot where she liked.

"Mmmm. That's nice." She tilted her head for a moment, a gesture of calm, then glanced at the stove. She stepped out of his arms, swiped at her forehead with the oven mitt before opening the oven door. "How's work?"

"Oh, insane and confusing."

Natasha brightly laughed it off.

"You playing video today?"

"Who me?" She raised her eyebrows innocently as she turned with the pot in her hands.

"You get into that fucking castle yet?"

"Nope." She laid the casserole on the counter.

"Want me to do anything?"

"Get out of the kitchen. Go sit down. Have a beer."

"Good idea. Cooking in this heat, hey." He grabbed a beer from the fridge, the bottle so cold and invigorating against his hand, and sat at the dining-room table, watching Natasha through the archway that gave a view of the kitchen. She moved toward the fridge, opened it and bent in, her white ribbed t-shirt hugging her small breasts, her baggy grey shorts sexy in their own way.

"Those are my shorts, aren't they?" He pulled at the back of his shirt, stuck to his skin.

"Yeah."

"I want them back." The air in the house was so heavy. The window was slid open and through it came the sound of a bird chirping, then the sight of two small birds swooping past.

"Later."

"No, now." He thought he caught the whiff of a breeze, but it seemed to be only his imagination.

"Don't be a jerk all your life."

"You can see right through that t-shirt, you know," he said.

"Stop it." She gave him a sideways glance, smiling as she squinted, searching the inside of the fridge.

"Put on your glasses."

"I can see." She reached in and took out the cellophane-covered dish of cranberry sauce, raised it. "See?"

"I don't need that with curried chicken," he said.

She looked at him, this time her expression not so forgiving.

"Whoops again!" He raised a hand. "Okay, I'll just shut up now."

While they were eating supper Natasha enquired about the case. Cooper did not protest but neatly, patiently explained the facts that he had gathered up to this point.

"So, you think it might be a lesbian killer," Natasha commented. "That's a different twist."

"Like I said, I don't know if that's the case or not." Cooper made a mental note to call Higgins at Oxford University and pick his brain. He looked at his watch: 7:18. It was approximately quarter to eleven in England. Too late. And Sunday. He could call Higgins at home, but it wasn't that important. He was silent, staring ahead, chewing slowly. "Probably revenge of some sort." He continued staring, his eyes fixed on a photograph of his parents hung on the wall, his focus shifting.

"What're you thinking about?" Natasha asked, lifting a mouthful of salad lightly coated with lemon honey dressing into her mouth.

"Sorry, I'm fading again." He sipped his beer. "England. I was thinking of calling about background on similar cases."

"Oh."

"This is great," he said, giving attention to the food. "Mmmm. Absolutely fabulous."

Natasha took a mouthful of beer, swallowed it while watching him. "Are you finished?" She glanced at his plate.

"I suppose."

"Good, then let's go to bed." Natasha's voice was so sweet that Cooper's insides seemed to soften and warm at once. He watched her, his eyes glossing.

Natasha stood from the table and walked off, glancing back over her shoulder to make certain that Cooper was following.

"What about the cake?" he asked.

"I am the cake," Natasha replied.

In bed, they lay still and softly kissed, lightly touching one another.

"You're so beautiful," Cooper said to her as he ran his fingers through the damp blonde hair at both sides of her head, brushing it back away from her face so he could watch her features, feel the pure loving power of what her eyes were doing to him.

Sitting up, Natasha pulled off her t-shirt, then lay back down and raised her backside to scoot down her shorts.

Cooper analyzed her naked body, his mind flashing on Mary Hood, her dead body on the silver table in the morgue, the slight straight dent along her throat, the Y-shaped incision and the cutting and sawing. The taking apart.

"I love you," Natasha whispered.

"I love you, too." He took his time kissing her, his fingers skimming along her skin, sensing the faultless texture, the silence in the room so luscious, the light through the orange curtains deepening the tender mood.

His beeper went off.

"Shit," Natasha said quietly.

"Sorry." He shut it off, watched her face tentatively. "Now, who do you suppose that could be?"

"Two guesses." She searched his features. "Go on. Bug off."

"I'll just be a second."

Not wanting to further defile the loving scene with talk of murder, he ignored the phone beside the bed and made the call from the spare room. He heard from Thistle that Paddock had determined that the female voice was— in fact— from Newfoundland. The digitized voice had faint traces of a Newfoundland accent. The owner of that voice had been away for quite some time. However, the male voice could not be pinned as easily. His words were spoken carefully. Paddock had surmised that the man had some connection with Newfoundland, but he couldn't be definite.

Cooper thanked Thistle for his help. Hanging up, he went back into the bedroom to find that Natasha had left the bed. He saw her standing by the window, naked, with the dim orange-shadowed light brushing her skin.

Stepping up behind her, his mind again flashed on an image of the dead woman, Mary Hood, her cool flesh beneath his hands as he examined her, her skin coming apart, her organs revealed in a wash of glistening red, beige and purple that swelled in his brain. When he touched Natasha, he was relieved to sense her wholeness and warmth. He slid his hands around her waist, then up over her smooth belly, higher to cup her breasts, feeling her nipples softly stiffen against the crevices of his palms.

FIVE

It was Monday morning and Kieley was pondering the murders as he ate his breakfast at Van Gogh's on Duckworth Street. Nibbling his partridgeberry muffin, he savoured the sweetness of the cake mingled with the tart taste of the fresh purplish-red berries that burst in his mouth. Taking a sip of hot coffee to wash it down, he wondered when the pieces would fall into place.

"We're working day and night," was all Kieley could tell anyone who asked, even his mother. He was often tempted to go into a detailed description of the process, the bureaucracy involved in police work these days, how easy it was to have your evidence challenged by the crown prosecutor, the need to keep certain information to oneself when others— close to him— might be suspected. The necessity to maintain strict continuity with all evidence. One slight slip-up and it was all over.

Kieley took another bite of his partridgeberry muffin. The air was steeped in the rich odour of expensive coffee beans brewing. He became aware of the smell as he watched the people pass along Duckworth Street. Van Gogh's was a popular place because of its large front windows, its stools and ledges flush to the glass, its well-spaced tables and uncluttered floor area. Kieley made a point of sitting at one of the stools by the window. He considered it his perpetual duty to watch people pass by. He'd study their faces, wondering what crimes they had committed.

This exact type of guessing game was one of his preoccupations on Queen Street West when he lived and worked in Toronto. He didn't look much like a cop. His smooth complexion and well-bred features coupled with his neatly combed brown hair, neatly pressed shirt, tie and suit, his exaggeratedly upright appearance, gave him the look of a lawyer or a doctor.

It was a comment he often got from people: "You don't look like a cop. Act like one. Think like one." What was an undercover RCMP officer supposed to look like? The only feature that people agreed fitting of the stereotype was his height of six-foot-one. Watching out windows like this one in Toronto, fresh from his supposed stay in the Yukon, he had seen the accused pass right before his eyes. The accused he knew from years ago. The exact one who had slipped through the system and been responsible for all the trouble in his life, his fall from grace.

The sighting had been an unbelievable stroke of luck. Kieley had hurried out of the Queen Street coffee shop, briskly stepping after the killer, following until determining a home address and later discovering that a move was being planned. A move to St. John's, Newfoundland, Kieley's home town...

Kieley stopped himself from thinking, turned on his stool to clear those thoughts away with a sweeping glance at the occupants in the coffee shop.

They were a funky mix. Half-asleep artsy types roused too early to deal with the real world, mixed with sensitive hip business people and the occasional suit and tie pretender, occupying a table because the place was fashionable. The same sort of crew that frequented such places in any city.

He glanced at his watch, 8:45, his teeth paining from the caffeine buzz. He finished the last bite of his muffin and left the coffee shop, stepping out into the dead heat. He glanced at the concrete war memorial across the street, the harbour visible down the incline beyond that, the shimmering water. Grungy teenagers were skateboarding lazily across the memorial's wide concrete foundation. They wore torn lumberjack shirts and jeans with the knees ripped open. A few of them sported rolled up woollen hats in the unreasonable heat of the summer morning. They looked like kids in Toronto, or anywhere in North America.

Traffic passed without interruption. The occasional body said hello to another in passing, the salutations crisp as a bell in the still air. A quaint, quiet city, attempting to preserve its architecture. That was the difference from other cities. The buildings. People set up heritage foundations to ensure that the face of the place wouldn't be torn away and made the same as every other downtown area. The facade would be maintained, seemingly different, but the people were the same everywhere, operating with the same thoughts. People caring less and less about what happened in the world. Caring less and less...

His mind flashed on an image of the man he'd beaten two nights ago, the man's surprised face. Kieley wondered if the man's attitude had changed since the confrontation. He doubted it. He wondered if the man had called Constabulary headquarters to complain. The man had no idea who he was. Maybe the man was even dead. The thought crossed Kieley's mind, but failed to cause the slightest rise of concern.

The sun was sweltering on his face. He tried to admire his own sense of stillness, of peacefulness, everyone passing around him, the workings of the world completely external to his sense of internalness. All actions performed for or against him.

He watched the details of the people's faces, the features that made them all so utterly different. He was intrigued by the expressions, the shapes of faces, lips, eyes, noses, and the varying styles of hair that lent people their distinct identity. He stared toward their chests, imagined their heartbeats pumping at custom speeds, blood racing through the miles of veins and arteries as they walked. He was fascinated by the movements of bodies coming and going so freely without faltering, their individual guilt not impeding their progress in the slightest. Each of them guilty of countless small crimes, but moving without detection.

All there to be explored, he told himself, watching a young woman pass in a matching peach-coloured summer skirt and jacket. He could follow any of them, ask them questions concerning their pasts, manipulate their words, detain them with his badge. The possibilities were endless. The walking talking bodies and then the force exerted and a dead vessel of flesh. Instantaneous. Alive, then dead. He recalled the body of the woman he had found in the closet two nights ago. Mary Hood. The people on this street were walking around, carrying out their whims, and where was the dead woman now? Shut down. Empty. Not a missing soul, simply the machinery disconnected. The presence wiped out. Eradicated.

He wandered off, toward the ghost car he had finally been able to pick up, a five-year-old Toyota (who would ever suspect such a car?), inadvertently following the woman in the peach suit, glancing up at the disc-shaped sign for Fred's Records, its windows plastered with promotional posters for upcoming musical events, then Livyer's, an antique store, its facing recently remodelled and painted to blend with the colourful historic look of the street. His eyes took in all details, pretending himself to be an admirer, an explorer, perhaps a tourist, glancing in the window of Pollyanna Gallery, his gaze briefly skimming over the collectibles and artwork before continuing to follow the woman, to see if she would notice him.

It was a game he often played, seeing how close he could get to these perfect strangers, what sort of contact could be made in his mind's eye without them knowing. He waited beside the woman at the crossroads where Duckworth met Prescott Street, which rose on an almost impossible incline from the downtown area. Kieley tried to keep his eyes off the woman. Instead, he studied the traffic officer, the "meter maid" as he liked to call the men who went around checking meters, most of them thinking they were cops, cowboys, big mirror shades and that slow ambling walk. A sorry lot. Eunuch policemen.

Waiting for the traffic officer to give them the signal to cross, Kieley stared down at the sidewalk, catching sight of the woman's white nylons, admiring her slim legs, the fit of her white shoes.

"Okay, cross—" the call from the traffic guard.

Kieley allowed the woman to get slightly ahead by pausing to admire the artwork painted on two concrete walls about eight feet high, a set of wide stairs dividing them. On each of the walls a large eye was painted against a black background, an advertisement for a play at the LSPU Hall, just up over the concrete steps that led to Victoria Street, a hall that was once a congregation place for the fishermen's union and now housed artistic productions.

Kieley glanced to his left, seeing the woman fifteen feet ahead. He started after her, gaining as she slowed to glance at a newly opened restaurant across the street. A low-key bistro of some sort, a simple wooden plaque announcing its name.

The downtown lock-up was a block ahead on the opposite side of the street. The huge stone structure with its peaked towers was once police headquarters and now housed the Supreme Court courtrooms, its interior walls constructed of dark rich wooden panels. All hand-crafted from a time when precision and attention to detail were valued. A time when people had nothing better to do than toil over minute details, a leisurely time before technology, before civilization gradually advanced, picked up its pace to a trot, then burst ahead, accelerating to the point where society and technology blurred into a world obsessed with dizzying speed and efficiency.

The woman walked a few more steps and turned to enter a doorway. Approaching the building, Kieley read the brass plate beside the entranceway, his eyes skimming over the engraved letters. A law office. By this simple procedure he had determined where the woman worked. It was that easy. A beginning that could set the foundation for future activities. Valuable knowledge to be built upon. People rarely knew that they were being followed.

Dismissing the game, he turned back to retrace his steps, heading in the direction from where he had come. He recalled seeing a pay phone in one of the restaurants up around the coffee shop. He needed to make a call, to verify the whereabouts of the suspect. Then there were related matters that needed tending to. And— of course— the Police Chiefs' Convention was taking place at the Delta. The officers always received invitations to such functions and were encouraged to attend, to keep abreast of the latest advancements in the field. He'd make his calls and then take a run to the Delta, just about half a kilometre west. He envisioned the tall hotel tower next to the squat grey structure of City Hall. He'd run into all sorts at the convention. Maybe even people from Toronto he hadn't seen in years.

Far behind him, the door to the law firm opened and the woman in the peach-coloured suit stuck her head out, watching him walk off, shaking her head in disbelief.

Yvonne was faced with a miniature crisis. Arriving at the Delta Convention Centre at 6:45 a.m., wired from lack of sleep and invigorated by the cool relief of the air-conditioning system, she discovered that the loading doors beyond the exhibit area were chained and padlocked shut. And, of course, no one on the premises had a key. Caught in a slight spell of panic, she had felt the scene take on a dream-like quality.

The trucks were already lined up in the loading area, having parked there the night before. Fortunately, only one exhibitor had arrived on the trade show floor, but unfortunately for Yvonne, he was an obsessive-compulsive type (who else would be up at this hour?), a sales manager from FibroTech, a mainland company, who happened to be staying in the hotel, a man who obviously was an insomniac and hyper as hell. He was friendly enough, wishing her a cheery good morning while he helped himself to the coffee from the metal urn on the trolley Yvonne had arranged to be wheeled in for the exhibitors. Pouring his cup, he glanced at her, trying very carefully not to spill a drop on the white cloth.

"Our truck's first in line," he informed her. "My crew's out there." He waved a hand toward the rear of the building.

"Just be a few minutes," Yvonne stalled, smiling and handing him a floor plan before wandering off to the reception desk to have someone paged who might be able to unlock the chain. She had to get things moving or this would turn into a nightmare.

If things did not work out shortly, the man would turn snarky in a matter of half an hour. Yvonne knew his type all too well. Not only that, if the door was not opened soon her complete move-in schedule would be thrown off and Terri Lawton would be severely pissed off. Move-in was the most important day of the show. It set the mood for the fair. Exhibitors had to be kept happy or that unfavourable tone would prevail through the coming days. Even if the trade show was mildly successful and the exhibitors were kept happy, then it was a success, but if it was mildly successful and the exhibitors were generally displeased with the service, then that could kill a show. All of this had been explained to her— in explicit detail— by Terri Lawton.

The woman at the Delta reception desk was polite and attentive, but displayed almost too much of a good thing, too many smiles, too many reassurances, so that Yvonne became irritated by the shallow intentions.

"I've just paged the banquet manager," the woman confirmed, returning from a back room beyond the front desk. "He'll meet you on the convention floor. He's calling the head of security at home."

"The head of security is the only one with a key to the lock?"

"I think so." The smile, and more words spoken through that saccharin expression. "He lives close by."

"Thanks," Yvonne smiled politely and hurried off, seeing the national sales manager from FibroTech coming toward her, a coffee cup in his hands, his eyes straight on her.

"How's it going?" he asked with a businessman's jocularity. "We going to get our stuff in today?" He laughed, but it was tinged with unpleasant promise.

"No problem." She smiled as she passed, calling, "Just getting the doors open."

"Great," the sales manager said, his tone hopeful as he turned to have a good hard look at the back of her, the way her body moved beneath her dress, as Yvonne briskly strode off.

The man had caught sight of Yvonne through the Delta's floor-to-ceiling windows before entering through the automatic doors. He stood in the lobby, the air conditioning bathing his face and hands as he watched Yvonne hurry down the wide foyer toward the convention centre's double doors. He waited until she had passed into the exhibit area before turning for the brass elevators. There was no need to check in. He could access the room of his choice in any hotel. Even the latest electronic card key systems were no trouble to bypass.

Hitching the strap of his overnight bag up on his shoulder, he stepped into the elevator's mirrored compartment with its brass trimmings and chose a floor toward the top. The top floors were usually less occupied than the bottom ones. Guests preferred to keep close to the ground. A general fear of heights. The hotel management also preferred to fill the bottom floors first, to keep the housekeeping staff contained in one area.

Stepping off at the fifteenth floor, he lifted the HeatWave Sentry (an appropriate name considering the current weather predicament) from the pocket of his suit jacket and raised it, thumbing the grey tab forward and watching the green light shift on.

Discreetly, he aimed the device at the rooms while he passed, the green light shifting over to yellow on the first two rooms. Occupied. The microwave scanner picked up the massive heat output of bodies, either at rest or awake. The first two occupants were awake, thus the yellow light, greater heat exerted when awake. If they had been sleeping then the blue light on the HeatWave Sentry would have lazily blinked on. He had added a progressive fade option which made the blue light appear in a lethargic way in order to give the feel of sleeping. It was a nice touch.

The third room was unoccupied, the light remaining green. He clicked off the Sentry and slid it back into his pocket, laid down his overnight bag and reached back for his wallet, extracted the card key, its surface blistered with a multitude of microchips capable of reading and decoding any hotel card entry system. He slid the plastic card into the slot and clipped the wires to the hot plates at its end, then switched on the mini battery pack in his pocket, watched the brass door handle. The green light flash on. Green always for "go," a standard in any industry.

Twisting the handle, he opened the door, then poked his card back into his wallet and lifted out the scrambler card that would erase the lock code set by the hotel. The third and final card, the initializer, would program and seal the new key codings into the reading system. It would be blind to everything except his card. The hotel would be unable to alter the card code. If a guest was sent up, his or her card would not function. The staff would assume the lock was broken and contact the maintenance company responsible. That wouldn't occur for at least a few days. In the meantime, the hotel would simply list the room as unusable. They would never know he was in the room. To be doubly safe, he would use the HeatWave Sentry to make certain no one was in the hallway whenever leaving the room.

Tossing his black overnight bag onto one of the double beds, he switched on the television and keyed up the channel featuring the events and meetings in the hotel for that day. The trade show was listed— Canadian Police Chiefs' Convention and Trade Show. He turned and zipped open the bag, shoving aside the video camera to pull out his blue shirt and grey pants.

There would be no problem acquiring a visitor's badge for the trade show. They would tell him that the show did not commence until the following day, but he would point out his video camera and explain that he was recording the event for the police union. Once he told them who he was with, there would be no problem. He had the credentials should they be needed. He could become one of any number of people.

There would be a great commotion on the convention centre floor. Crates coming and going, people milling around, everyone needing something, seeking something. He had attended these events before.

He always arrived early to discover how they worked, what went into putting them together. Most of the related shows he had attended offered few surprises. He had already envisioned the coming of most new products and services. Electronic shows were his favourites, the surveillance sections. He would chat with exhibitors about the breakthroughs in his field, explaining the features of the new products he had been working on and having the luxury of choosing which company he would sell his new inventions to, which outfit would market them with the most success, who was best respected in the field. He lived well from his inventions.

"Seemingly so normal," he whispered, thinking ahead to images of Yvonne, the way she had slapped herself last night, the way she was punishing herself. It was all coming back. She was getting sicker by the moment.

Unzipping the side compartment of the bag, he extracted a small brown envelope. He opened the flap and slid out the photographs he had processed from the Stillshot X11 attached to the video player. Polaroid-like images of Yvonne having sex. Still-lifes that gave way to more fluid imaginings. He heard the audio in his head. Images refreshed memory, even possessed the power to recall linked audio. She so much resembled the woman in his thoughts.

He laid out the photographs on the bed, studying them. Too involved, he warned himself. Too close to her. Just do the job and be done with it. Again, he thought of the woman and a queasiness came over his stomach, a sinking sensation in his genitals. Retraction. But a lust for her as well. All those years ago. Ten years, but the sting was still there.

He argued with himself, his eyes flickering across the frozen images of Yvonne gasping, straining, her facial expressions blending: anger to extreme pleasure, cruelty to release. Frozen facial expressions that could easily be misinterpreted as a woman in the throes of death, strangulation. Sexual images bearing such uncanny resemblance to acts of brutality.

The ordered photographs giving the serial impression of movement, but taken alone, blown up larger, they could imply another scale of emotions entirely.

The man turned and glanced at the movie card beside the television, scanned a few of the offered features. The latest releases attracted him in no way whatsoever.

He tugged shut the drapes and flicked on the television on his way to switching off the lamplight. He stood by the bed and watched over the photographs of Yvonne, a young woman so much like her mother, so much like her mother that the man's jaw tightened. The flicker of the television giving Yvonne's features shifting dimension, bringing them to jittery life.

Sergeant Uriah Cooper was early for his morning meeting with Lieutenant Johnston. In an effort not to be late for meetings he usually wound up arriving well ahead of schedule and found himself with time on his hands. He sat in the padded chair in front of the lieutenant's desk and went over his notes. His call to Higgins in England had proven next to fruitless. They had chatted for some time about similar cases, but relating to gay men and cross-dressers.

Maybe there was a connection. A gender possibility. Higgins had enquired as to whether Cooper had finished his paper for the *Journal of Forensic Psychiatry*. Cooper admitted that he kept getting side-tracked. He informed Higgins that perhaps he would wait and see what turned out with the case he was presently involved with. A paper on a serial killer of lesbians would receive prominent attention. Higgins agreed and wished him success.

"What's new?" Johnston came in his door, moving quickly to take his position behind his desk. He was a man in a perpetual hurry, a man who demanded brisk, precise answers, to gain an overview of the situation, focus, and subsequently, to have control. In this respect, he was much like Cooper, only Cooper was more meditative.

"We've determined this is no simple stranger-to-stranger crime," Cooper began. "The absence of clothing on the victims implies a sexual preface. We've discovered another long black hair. We sent it along to Halifax to see if it's a match with the one found on the other body."

"Matching hairs at both locations."

"Yes." Cooper glanced up from his notes, citing Johnston's displeased expression as he shifted papers around on his desk and shook his head. "Psycholinguistic analysis tells us that the caller's voice was a male's disguised as a woman's."

Johnston stared at Cooper, his mind seemingly stuck. He gave a dazed shake of his head. "What've we got here, Cooper?"

"I have a feeling this isn't your usual chronic criminal we're dealing with. We've got someone with a personality disorder, probably a psychopath. That's not so unusual for killers. But there's a degree of intelligence with this one and that's rare, as you know. The ligatures were telephone cord. Maybe someone with the telephone company. A disgruntled employee."

"So you've got long black hairs. Female?"

"I don't know. Long implies female. *Implies*."

"But a male caller who knows where the bodies are, disguising his voice like a woman's." Johnston stood and went to his window overlooking the rubble of the Church Lad's Brigade Armoury, a devastating fire having levelled it the year before, almost taking out Fort Townshend as well. He surveyed the rubble and then glanced toward the harbour down the hill, the gleaming blue water, a white vessel drifting in through the narrows. He paced back to his desk and poked his large wire-rimmed glasses back up on his nose, sucked on his bottom lip.

Cooper swivelled in his chair to follow Johnston, watching him stand while he raised his coffee cup and drained it.

"Well, fuck this," Johnston announced. "Fuck this, outright."

Cooper was taken aback by the force of the lieutenant's outburst. He was not a man who usually swore.

"We've got to get this under control, Cooper. The place is going to turn into a zoo. Reporters are calling me from across the island; a few came in from

Halifax. I got a call last night at my home from CBC Toronto. The media's been talking to friends and relatives of the victims. They've put two and two together and discovered that both of the victims were lesbians. Have you seen the news this morning?"

"No."

"It's only a matter of time before this goes national. I send them over to media relations, but I've got to talk, too. We're going to need a full media relations unit."

"We talked to a..." Cooper flipped over his notes "... Lawrence Prouse at 64 LeMarchant Road. Prouse's name came up on the digitized mapping system. Prior for stalking. But I don't think he's guilty of this mess. We have others with priors, but two are locked up, and the other's been out of province, on holidays."

"Why's this Prouse guy not guilty?" Johnston sat in his seat and set both elbows on his desk. "A stalker. It connects."

"Stalking his ex-wife. If he was stalking strangers, then I'd be more concerned, more sexual implication. But stalking a loved one is more common. Not as invasive."

Johnston raised his eyebrows.

"You know what I mean."

"You better watch your words these days. Tread carefully."

"Yes, sir."

"Who else in the house? Jealous neighbours? Someone doesn't like this guy?"

"We're checking."

"They could be leading us to them. Do a door-to-door."

"Pendegast is doing one this morning."

"Pendegast?" Again Johnston's eyebrows shot up.

"He can handle it."

"I wasn't questioning that," Johnston said defensively, and then gave Cooper a faint conspiratory smile. "Christ!" He rifled through his desk drawer. "I had those passes. You know." He shuffled the paper to one side. "Passes to the convention. Just what we need. Canadian Police Chiefs' annual convention in the middle of this. Wonder what the topic of conversation'll be down there?"

"Two guesses."

"You want theories, there's the place for you."

"You think?"

"Of course, I'm serious. Lots of brain power down there."

"It won't help with this."

"Check your arrogance at the door, Cooper. Not in here."

Cooper frowned and scratched his goatee. He slipped off his glasses and briefly rubbed his eyes, waited for the lieutenant to speak again.

"Call your friend in England?"

"Yes." Cooper fitted his glasses back on.

"Anything?"

"He's checking."

"We know the victims were lesbians, but what about the killer? A lesbian killing lesbians?"

"Maybe, or just set up to look that way. No semen samples. No condoms. But that doesn't mean anything. It could be a man. Not interested in sex. Or death is the sex for him."

"No signs of struggle, right?"

"No."

"What you said earlier. I don't agree with dismissing the stranger-to-stranger possibility."

"Why?"

"We both know why. Use your head, Cooper. Stimulation doesn't mean it had to be natural. The woman could've been forced to masturbate at gunpoint."

"Sure, a possibility, but the lesbian preference suggests—"

"In my mind, for whatever that's worth, we're talking about a man, someone with access to the property."

"Landlord, family member, friend, locksmith—"

"Or a police officer."

"Right."

"You go that route?"

"Yeah, could be a police officer with an electronics background."

"So why would they have a man in their room?"

"Could be a bisexual element."

"I don't know, Cooper."

"Human nature."

"We're going to scare the hell out of the gay community. Lesbian witch hunt." Johnston gave another dazed shake of his head; his phone buzzed. "This is shaping up to be nasty." He snatched up the receiver and watched Cooper while he spoke. "We're working day and night. Forty officers are doing door-to-doors. We've got our best officers on it. I can't say any more without compromising the case. Okay. You're welcome." He hung up, his expression unchanged.

"People want the TV-show solution," Johnston said. "They're watching *NYPD Blue* and *Homicide* and expecting to see the murder solved in half an hour, or..." Johnston leaned across the desk, "... there's the absolute maximum, right."

"What's that?" Cooper asked.

"The ninety-minute movie. Two hours tops. Can you solve this one in two hours?"

Cooper smiled contemplatively, unhooked the earpieces of his glasses, took them off and studied the smudges on the lens. He glanced around for a tissue, then— finding none— tugged the end of his orange shirt out from his pants and cleaned them that way.

"One more call from our concerned citizen and I might get a trace."

"No more calls," Johnston raised his voice. "Another call means another body. Right?"

"Maybe."

"I don't want another body. Another body would turn this city into the scumbag journalism capital of the world. It's all bad enough now. No more bodies. No more volume on this."

"I know." Cooper imagined the scene— reporters from all across Canada and around the world, swarming the Fort Townshend parking lot.

Johnston stood from his desk. "Talk to everyone in that house where the stalker lives. Everyone. Look for someone with a relationship. The long black hair, for instance."

"Sure." Cooper stood, flipped shut his notepad and slid it into the front pocket of his orange cotton shirt.

"I want you to be there. Connect with Pendegast. You talk to them. You see in. That's priority."

"Okay."

"And one other thing."

"What's that?"

"If this thing blasts off, if it gets out of hand the way I suspect it will, when you sell the movie rights, I want Clint Eastwood playing my part."

"Do you have any extension cords?" The man was large and sweating, the sleeves of his white shirt sloppily rolled up, hair matted along his oval pink face. He asked in an almost pleading way. "Please say that you do."

"No problem," Yvonne smiled, flipping the length of black hair back over one shoulder. She jotted a note on her clipboard. "I'll send one down. Your booth number?"

"TNH Services." The man pointed across the large convention floor, waving his hand back and forth, "In the corner there."

Yvonne checked the alphabetical exhibitor list and found their booth number— 334.

"I'll send someone over with it right away." She scribbled the number beside the order and stabbed the pen tip against the paper, making a period. "As good as done." She glanced at his badge, "Mr. Dyke."

"Great." The man turned around, almost tripping over a wooden pallet blocking one of the isles.

Yvonne raised her walkie-talkie. "Tim?"

A moment later: "Yes."

"I need an extension chord delivered to TNH Services, booth 334. Please?"

"Right away." The sound of the young man's voice through the walkie-talkie: a memory of static, of voices coming to her through the wires. She squinted the memory away, pursed her lips in concentration on what was needed to be done here and now.

She studied the wooden pallet, her tired mind wandering, her ears hearing voices amid the buzz of confusion on the trade-show floor. She heard a female voice, snarling, staticky, "Come and see me. I've got something for you. Something good to eat." She shut her eyes, the room filling her head, the luscious red-drenched room with the naked bodies. She opened her eyes and took a deep breath. Refocusing on the wooden pallet, she thumbed the walkie-talkie button. "John?" She waited, walked amid the exhibitors assembling their booths. "John?"

"Yes."

Yvonne spotted Terri further up the aisle. She spoke into the walkie-talkie while watching her boss conversing with one of the exhibitors. "Start moving the empty boxes to storage," she said. "Pallets, boxes, anything that's served its purpose."

"Sure."

She ticked the extension cord note off her clipboard, wrote Tim's name beside the tick, and flipped over to her move-in list. As usual, most of the companies had arrived early in the morning, ignoring their placement on the carefully conceived schedule. But the major problems had been overcome. The loading doors had finally been unchained at 7:10 a.m. That seemed like days ago now, even though it was merely a few hours. She glanced at her watch, saw Terri Lawton standing only a few feet from her, pointing one of the boys toward the stage at the other end of the exhibit area. Finished with her directive, she stepped up to Yvonne.

"How goes it?" Terri was wearing a smart turquoise-coloured suit with a white blouse that showed off her tan. Her long black hair was combed back over her forehead, gathered back with the length of it swirled up into a bun twisted and pinned so tightly that it seemed to draw taut the skin on her face. She was a woman in her forties who took extremely good care of herself, passing for someone in her mid-thirties. There was an exuberance about her; everything seemed to be going well in her life, always.

"Not bad." Again, Yvonne flicked the sheet over to the move-in schedule. "Almost everyone here. A few arriving tonight. Three companies. They wanted late slots. After shop closes."

"Excellent," Terri beamed. "Everything's going fabulously."

One of the young male workers wandered up to Terri, seemingly not knowing what to do with himself.

Terri watched him with alert curious eyes.

"What should we do once the stage area is filled?" he asked Yvonne.

"Use the foyer until we see if there's another meeting room we can use. We'll move the stuff from there."

"Okay." He smiled and tilted off, glancing back at Yvonne, his eyes flashing down at her revealing line of cleavage before he turned away.

"Beasts of burden." Terri scoffed, shaking her head at Yvonne. "The only thing they're good for is carting things around."

Yvonne was going to add one other thing, but thought the comment inappropriate, considering the situation. Her mind flashed on Zack and she had to halt the progression, refocus out of her daze. Her mind was exhausted and alert at once, in a state that easily provoked and nurtured fantasy. She had to hold tightly to the present, to carry out her job. Regardless, she felt a slight twinge of arousal at the memories of last night.

"You look very nice. A touch of cleavage. That works well." Terri stared at the cut of her neck-line. "Don't worry. I approve." She smiled, broadly. "Sucker the exhibitors in. Keep them happy. At least, they pay my bills. These ones. The ex Mr. Lawton couldn't claim as much."

Yvonne smiled in compliance.

"Keep up the great work." Terri placed her hand on Yvonne's bare arm, squeezed tenderly and kept her hand there, rubbing the skin slightly, warmly. "You're doing just great."

"Thanks." Yvonne felt shivers race up her spine, goosebumps break out across her flesh. She turned her thoughts to Zack again, tried to imagine him naked, but instead saw only his eyes, the hint of blue eye shadow as he blinked, close to her, on top of her as he moved inside, whispering her name, sounding so gentle and tender, the voice of a woman enticing her nearer.

"I'm having a little get-together after the show." Terri removed her hand from Yvonne's arm and crossed her fingers. "If it's a success."

"I'm sure it'll be. The weather's great and..."

"We'll see tomorrow, if the numbers are there." She winked at Yvonne and turned away, only to pause and add admiringly, her eyes dipping again toward the slant of Yvonne's cleavage, "Great job."

Yvonne nodded in thanks and turned away, grateful to be free from the woman's eyes. She heard the voice through the telephone, sounding in her head, "I'll lick those fingers. Smell them. Where they've been." She stepped slowly, hesitantly, as if treading away from the certain clutch of those words, walking on a tenuous substance. A few more steps and she was forced to stop. Someone was blocking her progress in the aisle, a man in a blue shirt and grey pants, a video camera raised to his eye, the lens pointing directly at her, obstructing his face.

SIX

A knock on her door jostled Mrs. Kieley from her nap. Finding herself sitting in her rocking chair, she reached for the television remote and pressed the mute button, cutting off the volume on the soap opera.

She waited for the sound of the knock.

The knuckles rapped three times.

She would not dare move from her chair. Gregory had advised her to never answer the door unless she had buzzed someone in, and to never buzz anyone in unless she was absolutely certain who it was. And there had been no buzz on her intercom. Who could it be? She thought of those two murders, her jaw slackening. The murderer coming after her. No, coming after her son; the officer investigating the murders. That happened. She had seen it on television.

Listening intently, her muscles on the alert, she decided that if the knocking continued, she would phone Gregory. Was this an emergency? He had given her his pager number. She waited, feeling as if she might burst into tears from the fear. But the knocking did not persist. She stood from her chair, groaning at the pain in her knees, steadying herself before pulling at the material of her housedress where it was stuck to her belly. Blowing out breath, she went over to the door and pressed her ear against it. She heard two men talking briefly and then the sound of them knocking on the door across from hers.

"Thank God," she whispered, blessing herself. She heard the young artist calling out from across the hall. One of the men identified himself as a police officer. She recalled Gregory's words: "Not even someone who says they're a police officer. That's a tactic sometimes used by criminals to gain entry."

Mrs. Kieley heard the sound of the young man's door opening, then dull words of conversation, muted slightly through the barrier.

"Yes?"

"Thanks for buzzing us in. I'm Constable Pendegast and this is Sergeant Cooper. We'd like to ask you a few questions."

"About what?"

"Do you have a free moment?" the man's voice sterner, becoming more authoritative.

"I don't..."

"It's nothing too heavy," a different voice, butting in, younger, more casual. "It's just about some people in the building. Basic info. Really. Just take a sec. We'd appreciate it."

A pause, then: "Okay."

"Thanks."

Mrs. Kieley heard them enter the apartment, the door shut. She could not make out any of the other words. Stepping back from her door, she noticed something on the floor and bent to pick it up, groaning as she went down and slowly came up again. It was a business card, black ink on white, the crest of the Royal Newfoundland Constabulary up in the left corner, the name— *Uriah Cooper, MSc, PhD. Criminal Behaviour Analysis Unit*— printed across the centre. Then there was the address, the telephone number and fax number.

Mrs. Kieley carried the card over to her chair and laid it on the table beside the phone. Business cards could easily be printed, she told herself, having learned from her son to trust absolutely no one. Not in this day and age of what he called "desktop publishing." The consequences of one simple gesture of trust, such as opening a door, could prove deadly.

"This is really none of our business, you know." Cooper casually leaned forward on the worn beige tweed couch in Zack Brett's apartment. He glanced up at Constable Pendegast, who refused to sit. Instead, the big man stood, glancing around the apartment, carefully taking in each detail, a technique that was absolutely unnecessary, more for show than anything else. Such intrusive tactics accomplished little other than to make the person defensive. That could be helpful in certain cases. But not now.

Cooper could take one glance over the living room and know exactly what Zack Brett was like. And even a glance wasn't necessary. He could simply observe details in his periphery while speaking with Zack, take in the brash colours of the paintings on the walls, the reds and yellows mingled with black, the twig stand in the corner where the telephone was set, weavings hanging down from the twig braces, the knickknacks on the mantelpiece from Mediterranean countries, a plastic bull from Spain, a colourful rooster— the symbol of Portugal— wooden candlesticks, an empty wine bottle (obviously from some special occasion), and above the mantel a dark mahogany mask, more than likely from Africa— Morocco by the looks of it. Tangiers.

No doubt, Zack was the type of guy who hung out with Natasha's crowd. In fact, Cooper thought he looked familiar. Maybe he had met him at one of the parties that Natasha had dragged him to. But it would be unprofessional to mention the social meeting, to shift the tone of the conversation toward a friendlier context. Besides, he did not want to mention Natasha, just in case.

"It's kind of bizarre, actually." Cooper smiled, knowing the exact tone of conversation to adopt, the mind link with the bohemian lifestyle that Zack Brett no doubt lived. "Someone coming into your apartment, the place where you live. Your sanctuary. Strangers with badges, pieces of tin. You think about it, it's surreal." Cooper frowned and shook his head slightly, rubbed his palm over the short bristles of his hair. The haircut would win points for him. It was a common cut among the renegade types.

When Cooper glanced up, he saw that Pendegast was looking down at him, a confused expression making his face seem even rougher and more unpleasant.

Cooper winked up at Pendegast, but in an almost mocking way. It was for Zack's benefit.

Zack sat in the burgundy wicker chair across the room, over toward the mantelpiece.

"But someone's killing women, just like in the movies. The big screen coming down to invade our lives here, in small-town St. John's. Reality, hey?"

Zack stared at Cooper, leaned back in his chair, set his hands on the curved armrests and crossed his legs at the ankles. "Why do you want to talk to me?"

"We can't let you know that," Pendegast adamantly professed, more for Cooper's benefit, it seemed, thinking that Cooper might reveal information about the caller which would find its way to the general public.

Cooper gave Pendegast an irritated look. By openly displaying his displeasure with Pendegast, Cooper would bond with Zack Brett: dissension against the confines of the police force. That sort of thing. And it was somewhat accurate anyway. He simply played it up a touch.

"What're you working on now?" Cooper asked.

"Working, what?"

"You're a painter, right?" He motioned to Zack's paint-stained white t-shirt. "A lot of paint on that piece of cotton. It's a regular thing, right? You're not just painting the rooms blue, red, yellow, teal, grey..." Cooper named the colours streaked and dotted across the t-shirt. "That'd be some wall."

Zack hesitantly smiled.

"Anyway." Cooper sighed and stood, purposefully eyeing a huge painting to the right of the doorway leading into the hallway. The canvas was almost entirely black with only vague slits of deep blue here and there. And eyes: bulging, depthless bird's eyes.

"That's a series," Zack offered.

"Oh, yeah." Cooper glanced over at him, then turned to see that Pendegast had sat on the couch, either finally catching on to what Cooper was doing, or giving up. He poked at the overflowing ashtray on the glass coffee table, shifting the butts around, searching.

"What's it called?" Uncapping a stick of lip balm, Cooper stroked it on, then rubbed his lips together, dropping the stick back into his pocket.

"*Niggers.*"

"Ooow. Controversial." His eyes beamed at Zack, his lips sheening. "That's what art's all about."

"It's not a racist thing."

"Yeah, I know. It's a statement. Shock value. Black things. People fear them.

Black is ugly. Black is death. Night is death. We have to overcome our fear of darkness in order to eradicate prejudice towards black people." Cooper shifted back to studying the painting, knowing by the look on Zack's face that he had hit a home run. A few more words and Cooper would have Zack's complete trust.

"It's all image now," Cooper observed, turning to face Zack, "our society. Nothing inside. Fashion. Image. Fashion versus God. Society's obsession with image. Gloss, worship supermodels and special effects in movies. No plot any more. Plot, what's that?! Gimme flash, gimme style. Fuck contents, right?"

Zack nodded uncertainly, then glanced at Pendegast, who kept his expression fixed.

Cooper was on a roll. He spoke quickly, using his hands to emphasize certain points. "People unwilling to look inside, to study the depth, because they'd be frightened by their own sense of mortality. Because society is losing its spirituality, its faith in some kind of god. It's the fault of the electronic age, where the video of real life becomes more important than real life itself."

Zack seemed puzzled. "Just what're you getting at?"

Cooper wondered if he had gone too far, complicated things in a way that Zack could not understand. That would be counterproductive.

"Not the thoughts of a cop, right?" He smirked down at the carpet. "That's just image, too. I'm a cop. But I'm something else. I'm also a doctor." He glanced at Pendegast, but Pendegast wasn't anywhere near getting it.

"We're all something else," Zack agreed, sitting forward in his wicker chair, joining his hands and letting them hang between his knees.

"Anyway, this woman-killing thing." Cooper spotted a large flat Indian pillow on the floor in front of the mantel. He sat down on it and crossed his legs. "Been a while since I sat on the floor. Good for perspective." Cooper tilted his head and looked up at the ornate plaster ring in the centre of the ceiling surrounding the dangling light fixture.

Zack took another look at Pendegast, obviously needing reassurance that these two men were actually cops.

"You don't think I killed any..."

"No, don't even say it, man." Cooper raised his hand.

"Let's cut to the chase here," Pendegast's voice boomed out across the living room. He pulled out his pad and flipped it open.

Cooper realized that he was going to start reading out dates of the murders, asking where Brett had been on those nights, all the standard shit.

Sighing, Cooper set his hand to his chin, gently massaging his goatee with his index finger. "Le voila," he whispered, pointing his fingers at Pendegast, hoping Zack would catch the humour. Pendegast read out the dates in a severe fashion, just the dates, no questions, no set-up, then dramatically flipped the pad shut.

Cooper regarded Zack. "So?" he said, standing, "There you have it. You want to confess now or should we beat it out of you?"

"You're kidding, right?"

"What d'you think?" Cooper asked. "I mean, really."

Zack glanced back and forth between the two police officers. "Two nights ago," he said, "I was here and then I was with friends down on Victoria Street. 144 Victoria. Gord Rodgers' place."

Gord Rodgers. Cooper repeated the name in his head. That's where the connection was. Gord Rodgers was Natasha's roommate. They lived together in an apartment that Natasha was just about to move out of. Cooper wanted her to move in with him and she had finally agreed. She was spending most of her time at his place anyway. Just as well to make the big leap; plus, Cooper didn't like the idea of Natasha having a male roommate. He was old-fashioned that way.

"'Til what time?" Pendegast asked sternly.

"Two, three, I don't know."

"Okay, that's fine," Cooper indicated, turning to offer a censuring look so intense that even Pendegast understood the gist of it.

"Thanks," Cooper said. He extended his hand. Zack stood and shook it. "You have an exhibit coming up or anything hanging?"

"A few pieces at Pollyanna."

"Down on Water Street?"

"Yeah."

"Good. I'll have a look."

Pendegast nodded sternly at Zack and opened the door. Moving toward it, Cooper paused, facing the shut panelled door across the hallway.

"Who lives there?" Cooper asked in a hushed voice.

"An old woman and some guy. Her son, I guess. I don't know if he lives there, or just visits. I don't see him much. Either of them."

"Oh," Cooper said. "Thanks, again."

Cooper and Pendegast headed down over the carpeted stairs, hearing Zack's door closing behind them. Cooper hoped Pendegast would not question his tactics, would not mention it at all. He was not in the mood to explain.

"He seemed okay," Pendegast said, lifting a stick of chewing gum out of his pocket. Pulling the wrapper off, he let it drop onto the stairs while he folded the gum into his mouth.

"You drop something?" Cooper asked, slowing, eyeing the wrappers.

Pendegast turned up a lip at the wrapper. "That's what they've got cleaners for."

"You think?"

"Yeah, that's where they get their name from. Cleaners. They clean."

"Brilliant!"

"Don't want to put them out of a job." He chewed and gave a big toothy smirk.

"Right." Cooper took the final stairs down to the first floor. "They might turn into lawyers or doctors. Heaven forbid, right?"

"You want to try that one again?" Pendegast asked, nodding toward the door across from Prouse's.

"Sure."

Pendegast knocked.

They waited in silence, listening for an answer that did not come. Pendegast turned and stared at Mr. Prouse's door. "Want to do him again?"

"What for?"

"We didn't get a complete rundown on who's who in the building. He's the landlord."

"True." Cooper approached the door. "Good point," he said, giving Pendegast his due. Pendegast, sensing Cooper's approval, leaned forward and knocked, more loudly than Cooper's original tapping.

"No one home by the sounds of it."

"Are we outta here, then?" Pendegast asked. "I'm starving. How about you?"

"You're always starving." Cooper took the short flight of stairs down to the porch door and pushed it open with Pendegast close behind. "You should lay off those steroid injections."

Pendegast laughed and punched Cooper in the arm.

They left the house and headed around back, along the path between maple trees and the flower beds set beneath the narrow clapboarding.

"You think I'm into steroids?" Pendegast asked, pausing by the side of his red sports car.

"No, just kidding." Cooper said. He heard a hammering sound and glanced toward the yards skirting the shallow parking lot, trying to determine where it was coming from. Unable to locate the source, he refocused on Pendegast.

"I can get you some if you want."

"What?"

"Steroids."

"No, thanks all the same."

"I'm going for a sub."

"Subs are good," Cooper said, saliva pooling in his mouth.

"You're fasting, right?" Pendegast said, nodding seriously, trying to understand. He opened the driver's door of his car and leaned in, settled behind the wheel, then spoke with Cooper through his opened window. "You gotta get tests done or something?"

"No."

Pendegast squinted, fitted on his mirror shades, "Then what're you doing it for?" He turned the ignition key, revved the engine, smiling proudly up at Cooper.

"It sharpens the mind." Cooper unlocked the door of his VW, but didn't get in. Instead, he leaned on the metal-hot roof and stared up at the blue sky, the air enclosing him. He felt the heat of the roof through the sleeves of his shirt, wondering whether he'd have to lift his arms away. "Man, this is a beautiful day," he mumbled.

"Opposite with me," Pendegast called out. "If I don't eat, I can't think straight."

Cooper regarded him, drawing his eyes away from the luscious blue sky. He had to raise his arms after all. Much too hot. "You know what, Pendegast?"

"What?"

"You watch too many cop movies."

Pendegast glanced back over his shoulder, then shifted into reverse. "You ask me," he said, "you're the one watching too many movies. Those weird fucking foreign ones." He floored the accelerator, his tires spitting dust and gravel into the air.

Cooper stood perfectly still, the sun on his face. Two crows swooped overhead, one after the other. He could hear their wing feathers rustling. "Control" was the key word here. Cooper hoped himself a better man for not speaking out further.

SEVEN

Mr. Prouse opened his door and peeked out. He caught sight of Mrs. Kieley's son, the policeman, making his way up the second flight of stairs. Luckily, the policeman had not caught sight of Larry. He quickly shut the door, not wanting to be spotted as his tenant took the corner for the next flight. He did not want to be perceived as some sort of paranoid criminal, peering out through a crack in his doorway. That would only bring more unwanted attention.

Regardless, he stayed close to his door, hoping to hear Yvonne coming in through the main entranceway. He thought of the flowers he had delivered in the presence of Zack Brett. Zack and Yvonne seemed like such an unlikely pair. He was the lazy artist type and she was so mannerly, practical, a businesswoman, her feet planted firmly on the ground. Larry liked the idea of a woman in command of her life. He admired the strong image. His mother had been practical and kept everything in order, taking control of all the family matters when Larry's father died when he was ten years old. His mother had been dead for four years now. He was surprised by how long she had actually been absent from his life.

He cracked the door again when he heard the sound of the policeman's voice upstairs. "Mom! What's the matter?"

"Policemen were here."

"When?" Gregory Kieley sounded alarmed.

"A few hours ago. Someone named Sergeant Cooper. He left a card."

The voices faded, then became muddled as they moved into the apartment and shut the door. "More police," Mr. Prouse whispered, quietly closing his own door. He had heard them out there earlier, refused to open for them. They had been here once already. What did they want with him again? He turned toward the closet door and opened it. He hadn't checked his garden today, to see if the slug pellets he'd sprinkled on his flower beds last night had done their job. The image of Yvonne's naked body filled his thoughts. He had been sprinkling slug pellets in her flower box when she stepped up, her skin so white in the soft lamplight from the street. The memory brought tears of yearning to his eyes. He ached to be a younger man, ached so desperately.

He'd gather another bunch of flowers for her. Persistence was the key, his mother had always professed. To hesitate means death. She had never stopped, never rested, was always on the go, planning something or carrying out her daily chores at the properties around town. She was quite a handyman. He always helped as best he could, considered it his duty, his obligation to his dead father. He was the man of the house and had to prove himself as such. He loved his mother dearly and was sensitive to her emotions. He protected her and did always as she expected of him, even accepted the job at Newfoundland Telephone that she had secured for him, a favour from a friend, all those years ago. He had taken the job without argument, despite the fact that he had wanted to open a flower shop instead.

His mother was a wonderful, strong, good-humoured, attractive woman who avoided men, considering it inappropriate to marry again after the death of her husband. It just wasn't the thing to do; it showed lack of respect. So she had devoted all of her attention to Larry, her precious little boy.

Thinking of his mother, Larry Prouse was visited by an image of Mrs. Kieley. He went to the kitchen and lifted the cellophane wrap from the plate of date squares, raised one and took a large bite. Chewing vigorously, he glanced at the kitchen chair where Mrs. Kieley had sat. Something about her appealed to him. He felt comforted by her. Not only did she remind him of his mother but also of his wife, Gail. He corrected himself: his ex-wife. Gail, he mustn't think of Gail. He had been ordered to stay away from her. He had been treated like a common criminal. Charged with stalking. He loved her. He loved her deeply. Was that stalking? There was no one else in the world for him. Why was he fooling himself with ideas regarding Yvonne? He swiped the tears from his eyes. He was just an old man. A worn-out old man. What would someone like Yvonne want with him?

Taking the final bite of date square, he wondered if flowers were really accepted any more, or were they an old-fashioned gesture, more to be frowned upon, to pity the giver as someone from an out-dated generation? It was so difficult to present oneself to a woman, so very frustrating. But he would be careful, take his time, be conscious of every movement and word. There was hope. Any sort of hope, however faint, would get him through.

He thought of his videotapes. Women that were so easy. The images were his. They were so accommodating, the way a woman was supposed to be. They didn't judge him. They didn't require romancing. There was no need to weigh every word spoken. They were simply naked and beautiful. To be adored. And he adored them all. (There were his favourites, of course.) It wasn't just their naked bodies that he adored. It was much more. He adored the way they spoke, their distinctive mannerisms. He watched their beautiful faces with the weight of adolescent longing mounting in his chest. Their smiles, their gasps of pleasure as their bodies accommodated the fingers and tongues of other women. So willing to please, living for pleasure only, such a gratifying life.

Thinking on the subject, he decided he would have a little peek at a video, a viewing of the beautiful female flowers as they opened for each other, before going out to check for the slimy gatherings of slugs that had been recently troubling the stalks and petals of his splendid flowers.

Yvonne's feet were killing her. She had forgotten to bring along the second pair of shoes recommended by Terri Lawton. It was a trade secret to change shoes a couple of times a day. It kept the soles of her feet from becoming accustomed to the shape of the shoe and subsequently becoming sore and tired. She made a mental note (how many mental notes, she frustratingly asked herself, can a mind hold?) to make certain to pack an extra pair of shoes in her tote bag as she fit her key into the porch lock.

Pushing it open, she glanced at her mail slot and saw the white of envelopes. Letters seemed like a faint consolation to her hard day. Perhaps there was some good word in one of the envelopes. Removing them, she shuffled through the bills and requests from charities. Nothing of interest. She unlocked the inside door and entered, glancing at her apartment just ahead and to the left, up over the three carpeted steps. She felt the relief in her muscles already. Home sweet home, she told herself. She sighed and fitted the key into the deadbolt lock, her movements halted by the sound of her telephone ringing on the other side of the door.

She twisted the deadbolt, then hurried to unlock the doorknob, turning it and throwing open the door, leaving it wide open as she ran toward the phone.

She watched the caller ID, waited to see the silent blink of UNKNOWN NAME, UNKNOWN NUMBER, wondered if the telephone company had connected her service yet. She had called earlier, during the mayhem of move-in, and had been assured that the service would be in order by the end of the day. Out of breath, she grabbed up the receiver and gave a stern, "Hello?"

"Yvonne?" A scratchy woman's voice.

She gave no reply.

"Yvonne?"

"Yes?" she asked.

"It's Terri."

"Terri, hi." She hooked the length of black hair back behind her ear. Her heart was racing anxiously, and it was not from the run to the telephone. She had been genuinely frightened by the voice.

"You okay?"

"Yeah, I just got in, had to run..."

"Catch your breath."

"I'm okay." She laid down her mail beside the answering machine, swiped at the sweat on her forehead while casting her eyes up at the ceiling in frustration. "You still down there?"

"Yes, believe it or not I'm still at the hotel."

"No rest for the weary." Yvonne glanced back at her apartment door, noticing her keys dangling in the doorknob. She watched the opening, waiting for an image to appear there. She had a premonition. Someone was coming for her. Her pulse quickened. She thought of closing the door, but the thought was not as exciting as the alternative. She was thirsty. She needed a drink. A glass of wine, no, ten glasses of wine, to be lost in the boozy lull of alcohol and submerge herself in dark sexual escapades. That was the plan for the evening. And she was looking forward to it. Complete abandonment of all responsibilities.

"Just wanted to call and tell you what a great job you did today." As usual, Terri's voice was brimming with enthusiasm.

"Sounds like you're losing your voice."

"Always go a little hoarse. You know me, talking too much."

Yvonne heard the words as if through the years, the gravelly texture, the generosity, the enthusiasm. The woman's voice would ask for something now. In compliance with the pattern from the past, she would request something of Yvonne.

"I wanted to remind you about the shoes."

"Yes."

"Gotta have the extra shoes." Terri's laugh was tired and genuine.

"My feet are killing me." Yvonne gazed down at her shoes, kicked them off. She peeled off her nylons and tossed them at the television.

"I know the feeling, believe me."

There was a moment of silence. Yvonne could not determine the true purpose of the conversation. It seemed to be leading nowhere in particular, as if Terri's motive for calling was something other than what she had stated.

"I'm just finishing up. Hang on a sec." Terri's voice moved away from the receiver, calling out to someone, "Is it locked?" A distant reply. "You have the keys?" Her voice closer again, "Sorry about that. Locking up."

Yvonne's eyes still on her open door, a man in black silently stepping up, pausing for a moment to smile in a sinister way, then crossing the threshold. Yvonne flinched slightly, but then smiled at him, tilting her head in apology, seeing his made-up eyes, seeing the way those made-up eyes were watching her.

Sergeant Cooper had a headache, nasty pressure behind his temples, rocks popping to life in his brain, growing larger. Shoving all the good sensation out his ears. Spew. Chew and spew out your ears. Thoughts in, thoughts out. In with the good air, out with the bad air.

The first two days of a fast usually hurt the most; after that it was colourful euphoria, a sense of limitless well-being and an astuteness of mind that separated details in a way that often astounded him. But for now he was troubled with a vicious headache and then unexpected lightheadedness a moment later.

He had returned to his suburban bungalow on regal Prince Charles Place. Such a noble name for a suburb, Natasha had commented when he first took her home. He agreed. People were always trying to make things sound better than they actually were. Words. Descriptions. Adjectives. That's what it was. Adjectives were the great deceivers in this world. There should be a special jail for adjectives. Gross generalizations. Lock them away— Regal and Colourful and Vicious...

Pulling into his driveway, he saw three neighbourhood kids racing off the curb on their skateboards, the wood slamming the concrete. He heard the hiss of a water sprinkler in the neighbours' back yard— the man with the lawnmower fetish. The sprinkler had been on all last night and was still running. What a waste, Cooper told himself as he stepped up his stairs and opened the front door. Inside the porch, a daddy-long-legs was fluttering against a corner. Cooper reached down, lifted it by one of its brittle legs and let it loose out the door.

He smiled to himself, wondering where the insect was now, what the insect saw, wanting to see with its eyes, that string of flight. How far had it travelled in those brief moments? He often found himself wondering about the lives of bugs and insects. Millions of them everywhere and everyone despising them. Insects always the evil beings in cartoons. Wicked, nattering, unwholesome bugs conspiring against the fluffy creatures. But they each held a secret life and precious life force. They were alive and— undoubtedly— that life was just as singular as any human life. It was a creation. Why would anyone so thoughtlessly destroy it? He gently laid his keys on the old-fashioned washstand just beyond the porch door. The action of laying the keys in place greatly intrigued him. He was conscious of each inclination, slight shift in mood.

"Hello?" he called, hearing Natasha's reply from the dining room just beyond the living-room archway at the back of the house. No doubt, she was studying. He stepped quietly in, measuring his steps, seeing her sitting at the table, her head propped on one hand, her other hand writing on a lined sheet in a binder. Several books were opened in front of her.

"Studying?" he asked, adding immediately, "Stupid question, right."

She gave him a tired smile that warmed his heart. She was wearing a black body suit, her short blonde hair highlighted by it. He stood there staring at her face.

"What?" she asked, her smile growing. She scratched her nose. "My nose has been driving me crazy."

"The heat, I guess. It's dry. Put some cream on it." He gently touched his chin with his fingers, pulling on the uneven hairs of his goatee.

"When are you going to shave that thing off?"

"When you let your hair grow long."

"It stings my face."

"Long hair?" Cooper smiled.

"No, that hair on your face."

"Your words offend me."

"You're such a jerk," she said. "Bug off."

He stepped over and kissed the top of her head, then went to the fridge and pulled open the door to lift out a bottle of mineral water. Doing so, he caught sight of the leftover curried chicken and his stomach grumbled in a punishing way.

"Why don't you have a little bite?" Natasha stood from her chair, coming up behind him and slipping her arms around him, hugging his chest.

He was bothered by the light in the kitchen, aware of the hum of the fluorescent tubes overhead. He uncapped the bottle of water and held it against his face, then drank from it, the coldness paining his front teeth.

"Have some fruit," she said, her low tender words in his ears. "That won't hurt."

He wanted to drink and drink until the bottle was empty, but the coldness began to stab knives behind his forehead and so he squinted, one eye fully shut, and laid the hollow plastic container on the counter. Doing so, as if a connection had been sparked, the telephone rang. Magic. The thought amused Cooper as he reached for the switch for the overhead light and flicked it off. He was drawn to the ringing, drawn to the peal of bells in a way that others were drawn to ceremony in ancient cultures, stepping to take it in his hand, to learn the secret, the mystery. A simple telephone call. Simple, but filled with folktales and fire: the possibility of anyone materializing on the other end.

"I was going for a drink," Terri Lawton explained in a tone that vied for casualness, "to unwind. Wanted to talk with someone about the day. You doing anything? Care to join me?"

"I'd love to," Yvonne lied, "but I'm exhausted."

"I understand," Terri said, her tone vaguely dejected. Recovering at once, her voice regained its spriteness, "Well, another time. There's that get-together after the show. Dinner at the Cellar. Don't forget."

"No, I won't."

"Okay, great. What've you got on your agenda for this eve?"

"I'm going right to bed." Yvonne emphasized the last word for some reason, spoke it in an almost teasing way.

Zack was creeping close to her, grinning mischievously, moving across the living room as if he were a beast stalking prey. Quietly dropping to his knees, he delicately lifted the hem of her dress, peeked under, then glanced up at her with a demonic expression, flashing his teeth and clicking them together as if to bite.

Reaching down, Yvonne let her hand rest against his dark hair. They were like a pair of sinister crows, she imagined, both of them with their dark thoughts and black hair. Black Irish. She had read about their sort. How the Spanish had invaded Ireland centuries ago and the Spanish had bred with the locals. Yvonne studied Zack's hair as he pressed his cheek against the front of her thighs and gave a sweet groan of longing.

"Sorry," Yvonne said, into the receiver, but intending it for Zack as well.

"No, that's okay," Terri assured her. "I'll probably just head home. You have my number there just in case?"

"I don't think so."

"In case you need me for anything. I thought I gave it to you during the last show."

The raspiness of her voice, the almost huskiness of it, the feel of Zack's stubble against her thighs. His tongue dabbing here and there.

"Probably wrote it on a scrap of paper. You know me. I'll write it down again." Lifting a pen from her desk, Yvonne searched out a piece of paper among the clutter, then awkwardly leaned forward, allowing Zack to continue his thrilling exploration. She flipped over the envelope of her electric bill and scribbled down the number, then wrote "Terri" and a question mark after the name.

"Okay, I'll see you tomorrow," Terri's voice was lulled and melodious, a singsong. "Sweet dreams, sweetie."

"Thanks. Bright and early." She hung up, tightened her hold on Zack's hair, squeezing a fistful and yanking his head back. "Fuck. It's so hard being nice."

"Try not to break my neck, okay?"

"Why not?"

"Because, I'd probably die."

Yvonne shrugged, "Big deal." Then she smiled and winked at him.

"Who was it?" he asked, casting a glance at the phone.

"My boss." Yvonne relaxed her grip on Zack's hair.

"Is he after your body?" Zack reached around behind and firmly squeezed her buttocks, delighted with the feel of her smooth pantyless bottom. Looking up at her, he appreciated the view— Yvonne's breasts two perfect mounds beneath her dress.

"She. And yes, I believe *she* is."

"Ooooh, it's like that, is it?" He moaned loudly.

"Stop it." She stared down into Zack's eyes. "A new twist on the sexual harassment thing, hey? Maybe I can get on *Oprah*."

"A lovely one." He grinned, raising his eyebrows. "Much lovelier if I get to watch. Why didn't you invite her over?"

"You're such a twisted bastard," she spoke the words meanly, as if genuinely repulsed, but her actions defied words. She tightened her grip on his hair and pushed his face into her groin, then threw back her head when she felt his warm wiggling tongue find its mark. She kneeled down on the carpet, face to face with him. Draping her arms over his shoulders, she kissed him. "Let's be tender," she whispered, consciously changing her tone. "I feel like making love."

"Dangerous," he said. "Making love's more dangerous than any sort of nasty stuff. It means so much more, so much depth, commitment. I don't know if I can handle it." He quietly pecked her cheeks again and again.

"My bum's still stinging from the last time. Blistering hot." She took hold of his face and held it firmly, kissed him fully, her warm tongue probing his mouth, her eyes staring at his eyes, studying the eye shadow in a searching way. The sight of it heightened her arousal, a slight rise, pleasant ascension in her groin.

She heard faint footsteps above her head and glanced up, withdrawing from the kiss.

"Noisy neighbours," Zack complained, mock hostility cutting his voice. "Let's go up and butcher the bastards."

"I wouldn't try that."

"Why not?"

"I saw him today. The guy's a cop. He was down at the show."

"A cop?" Zack leaned away from Yvonne, one hand braced on the cushion of the couch beside them.

"Yeah. It's a cop show. Equipment and stuff they use. Canadian Police Chiefs' Convention. It's a big thing."

"Just what I need. Fuck." He sat back on his haunches, his mood souring. "More cops. Cops fucking everywhere, man."

"What d'ya mean, more?"

"Two were in my place today, but..." he paused, his brow furrowing. "They were asking who lived next door to me. Wouldn't they know?"

"I don't know." Yvonne straightened, quickly easing away from him, thinking of a drink, a glass of wine. She went into the kitchen, calling out, "What'd they want?" When she returned, she held an opened bottle in one hand, two glasses in the fingers of her other.

"Questions about those two women, the ones who were killed."

"Asking you?"

"It's fucking weird, eh? But why would they ask me about the guy across the hall if he was a cop?"

"They can't know where every policeman lives in the city. Must be hundreds of them." Yvonne handed Zack a glass and poured them both large amounts. "You like white? It's chilled."

"Yeah, it's okay."

She drank immediately, chugging half the contents of her glass.

"Maybe it was some kind of trick," Yvonne suggested, ignoring Zack's look of dismay at the briskness of her consumption. "Using what you knew about the cop across the hall as some way of getting information out of you."

"Could've been," Zack admitted.

Zack sipped from his glass, watching her.

"You like your wine," he said.

"It makes me feel sexy," she whispered girlishly. Then she shut her eyes. "It's so nice to be home."

"That's cute. You're a regular Barbie doll."

"And you're my charming Ken." She went over to the CD player and selected a disk by Transvision Vamp. A few moments later a sugary female voice began listlessly singing, her voice one steady sexy breath.

Yvonne sang along while she danced, seductively swaying her body for Zack, "I'm a bad valentine, such a bad valentine. I'm a baa-ah-hah-ah-d valentine. I'm so bad, bad, bad." She pouted and tilted her head, reached around back to unzip her dress. She let the material slip away from her shoulders but did not take the dress off as she continued swaying. She emptied her glass and danced over to allow Zack to pour her another. Downing it, she let her eyes fall shut while she danced seductively and ran her fingers through her long black hair, gathering the strands around front and rubbing the length of it against her face with both palms, so that Zack lost sight of her, having no idea who she really was.

Uriah Cooper reached for the receiver hanging on the wall. It seemed smaller, lighter than usual in his hand, not the proper size at all. The texture of the hard plastic was coarse against his fingertips, not smooth as expected. He could actually feel the pores.

"Hello," his word.

"Uriah?"

"Yes." He recognized the voice at once. "Richard, how are you?"

"Fine. I gathered the information you requested. I've faxed the hard copy and downloaded the electronic into your e-mail."

"Fantastic, thanks. I really appreciate it." Cooper felt the rush of adrenaline coursing through his body at hearing Richard Higgins' voice. They had engaged in so many inspiring and thought-provoking conversations in England while Uriah was a student of Richard's.

"How's things going at your end?" Higgins enquired evenly.

"Heatwave. Two bodies. I'm fasting."

"Keep the water to your system."

"I'm trying."

"Extremely dangerous to fast in heat of any consequence. What temperature?"

"Still mid-thirties."

"Extremely dangerous. Do you hear me, young man?"

"Don't be so dramatic," Cooper said, smiling at his mentor's wryly severe tone.

"I have warned you, my friend."

Cooper glanced over at Natasha. He covered the receiver and mouthed, "Richard." She nodded and gave an understanding smile before returning to sit at the dining-room table where she resumed her studies.

Richard Higgins was recommending daily doses of fluids. "At least eight eight-ounce glasses. At the very least. Stay away from tap water. The fluoride and chlorine traces can be quite offensive. Strictly mineral water."

Cooper was already familiar with this information, but he remained patient, respectful.

"Definitely," he said. "I'll watch out."

"Do you have anyone in mind? Our lady-killer."

"Someone in mind. Yes and no."

"Exactly." Richard Higgins laughed brightly on the other end. "A ghost of what's— in fact— real. Like attempting to catch sight of someone through a fog. You must squint harder."

"Or wait for the fog to lift."

"Fog lifts, there's more bodies uncovered. Haven't you seen the classic films?"

"True." Cooper went on to carefully explain the details he had gathered up to that point, taking his time to perfectly articulate each piece of information and what it implied, one way or the other.

"Fascinating. The telephone wire is something new as well. And— of course— the lesbian twist is quite charming on its own. If that's what we're actually dealing with here. It has quite a bit of depth to it. The caller with the disguised voice. Quite complex. Theatrical. I almost envy you."

"Don't." Cooper felt goosebumps rise to his skin at the mention of Richard Higgins envying him. "It's an amazing case. Have the British press picked up on it yet?" he asked.

"Nothing yet. Only a matter of time, though. It can only enlarge itself.

Strangulation is a pet peeve with us Brits, you know. And— again— the lesbian angle is quite winsome."

Cooper laughed, then checked himself, "I shouldn't be laughing."

"Who should be, then?"

"I don't know."

"Never start pretending that you are something other than a human being."

"Who said that?"

"I did."

"That's a fine one. I'll keep that in mind. How's Barbara?"

"Hanging in there. They've taken off one breast. The cancer is terrified of them now, gone into hiding."

"Give her my best."

"Yes, I will. When can we expect to see you again? Are you flying over for the Investigative Psychology Conference?"

"Yes, I'm presenting a paper."

"On what subject?"

"Maybe on this."

"Intriguing case. You could come out of this an expert in the field. There's no other case of its sort on record, and no known database compiled on female serial killers. What's most important, and you know this, Uriah, is right there in the information that you've just told me. There's some gender confusion, it seems. Be it male or female."

Cooper was lost in the British flow and rhythms of Richard Higgins' voice, memories of afternoons spent in the local pub. Tall pints of creamy, bitter Guinness. He waited a moment, allowing the silence to settle between them.

"Uriah?"

"Yes."

"How long have you been fasting?"

"A day and a half."

"You're not going to collapse on me, are you?"

"No, not at all. I'm chipper." He was taking on the vocal inflections of the British. Hearing Richard, being in the presence of anyone from England, sometimes led him back to the times when he'd studied over there, and he would pick up a trace of a British accent, as he had hanging around the pubs. It was not put on at all, or intended— simply the product of some sort of complex adaptation mechanism.

"If you need anything at all."

"I will."

"Call."

"Yes."

"Good to hear your voice, young man."

"The same for me, old fellow. It really is. Thanks for the information."

"Not a problem. Not in the slightest. I look forward to raising a pint."

"You're making me thirsty."

"Too bad you're fasting," Higgins said in a devilish tone. "Guinness is not on your menu. Cheers." Richard hung up.

Cooper reluctantly laid the receiver to rest, stood staring down, Richard Higgins' face large in his mind. He idolized the man, and was remarkably comfortable in his company. Higgins was a father-figure and Cooper longed for that relationship now. Someone to sit down with and talk through the details and proposed solutions. Cooper was looking at the kitchen linoleum, the subtle gold strokes against the beige squares. Subtlety.

"What did he say?" Natasha's voice, in his ears, in the hollow of the kitchen, inside his head.

"There's nothing to say," Cooper told her, shifting his eyes and stepping out into the dining room. "Everything I need is right here."

Natasha smiled, pleased with the proposition. "You mean in this house?"

"That depends."

"On what?"

"Do you have a taste for ladies?"

"I've thought of it," she shyly admitted, leaning back in her chair and biting on the pencil eraser.

"I bet you have." Cooper pulled out a chair and sat, his legs wobbly. "I'm going to rest..."

Natasha laughed lightly. "You need a rest. You're pasty-faced."

"...then go back in to check over the info that Richard just sent along. E-mail."

"Don't you want to hear more on my lesbian views?"

"Love to." Cooper leaned forward and lifted off his glasses, smearing the sweat from between his eyes.

"Women can be so much gentler than men," Natasha admitted. "Women's bodies are much more erotic."

"So, you've partaken?" he asked evenly. He recognized the non-judgemental tone, the one he'd mastered during his studies in psychology.

"Maybe."

"You're teasing me, right?" He hooked his glasses back on and sat up.

Natasha's eyes gleamed.

"Secrets," Uriah said, unable to sustain the emotionless tone. "Tell me."

"No." She retracted from his request, pretending to return to her studies. "I can't."

"Go on, you can't do that to me. It'll drive me crazy. And besides, I'm a doctor."

"You're not that kind of doctor."

"I'm a certified sex therapist."

"You wish. Certified, maybe."

"Tell me. I need to know." She watched him as he nodded encouragingly. "Come on, come on, little lady. Spill the beans. It'll drive me crazy if you don't tell."

"Okay." She pressed her lips together, then clicked her tongue off her teeth. "I was just a teenager."

"And..." Cooper stared at Natasha, sensing the nip of arousal.

"It was with Jackie."

"Jackie?"

"My best friend from years ago."

"Okay, go on. Take your time."

"We were sitting on the couch in her basement and it just happened."

"What'd you do? Did you kiss?"

"No, it wasn't like that. It was just something that happened. The timing." Natasha shook her head. "I don't know. It was a lot of things."

"So, did you get naked?"

"No, we didn't get naked, pervert."

"No?"

"No. We just masturbated each other."

"Really?" The nip of arousal suddenly strengthened, mounting toward a full bite. "Sitting on a couch."

"Yes."

"With all your clothes on."

"Yes." Natasha glanced at his pants. "I can see you're enjoying this."

"And then what? Did it happen again?"

"No. We never even mentioned it. We never talked about it."

"That's something. I bet it was a thrill you never matched since."

"Something like that."

"I mean the illicitness of it. The newness of the act. You enjoyed it, right?"

"Of course, why wouldn't I? We were gentle. A woman can be so gentle. And she knows exactly where to touch."

"I'm not gentle enough for you?" Cooper asked, trying to sound reasonable, but coming off too defensively, his cheeks flushed.

"No. It's not that. I mean a woman knows a woman's body because she has one the same." Natasha laid down her pencil, placed both hands on her notebook, glanced down at her spread fingertips. "It's that simple. What amazes me is why more women aren't lesbians."

"It's self-love," Cooper ventured. "Masturbation in a three-dimensional mirror. The ultimate act of self-adoration. Homosexuality adds up that way."

"Is that a homophobic statement, Doctor Sergeant?"

"No, not at all. You know better than that. And what's with this doctor sergeant stuff?"

Natasha rolled her eyes toward the television. "I've seen the news."

"Please don't watch that crap. It'll change me."

"No, it won't. Besides, you look cute on television."

"Cute?"

"Yeah, you're not the tough-guy type that you're trying to be. You're cute. Little baby face. Well." Natasha glanced at the clock above the television. "I'm going down to the apartment to pack up some stuff."

"You're going to give me the woody and then scoot outta here?"

"You asked for it." She began shutting her books, laying her pencils and pens aside.

Cooper watched her delicate actions. "Oh. By the way, darling, I questioned one of your friends today."

"Really." She leaned forward in her chair. "Tell me."

"Secrets. I don't know if I can."

"Come on." She made an impatient gesture with her hands, beckoning the information nearer. "I told you mine."

"You know the rules. Don't mention this to anyone. Promise?"

"I promise."

"Zack Brett."

"What'd Zack do?"

"He didn't do anything."

"You questioned him about the murders?"

"Yes."

"Get outta here! Why?"

"He's the dangerous type. Looks the part, I mean. Mostly a poser, though."

"You think?" Natasha straightened in her chair, joined her hands and let them rest against the edge of the dining room table. She stared off, distracted for a moment. "Zack."

"What's he to you?"

"Nothing. He's a friend of Gord's."

"I thought that was the connection."

She pressed her lips together and nodded firmly. "You got it."

"You ever... You know."

"With Zack?" She laughed in a way that told Cooper she had thought of it. "Not my type."

"Too smart for him?" he asked.

"Thanks for the vote of confidence." Natasha hooked a length of her short blonde hair behind her ear, then leaned forward on the table. "You're staring."

"Things come to life. Colours. I love this feeling. When I'm fasting. Strength through restraint, through refusing, like you can almost control the elements. Squeeze them in my mighty fist." Cooper laughed.

"Let's fast together," Natasha suggested.

"If you want."

"I read somewhere that it's great for sex. Heightens the feelings, the sensations, orgasm."

"I wouldn't know about that. I'm not getting any."

"No, I'm sure!" Natasha burst out laughing and chewed on the end of her pencil. "We'll need a crate of mineral water between us."

"I'll pick it up on my way home." He stood and Natasha rose as well, stretching and groaning.

"I need sleep."

"How about it?" he asked, his eyes on her breasts hugged by her black bodysuit.

"Just like that?" Natasha laughed again, then dipped her eyes toward the paper she was working on. "I've got to finish this. Then go down to Victoria Street."

"They work you like pigs in that program."

Natasha frowned and shrugged her shoulders. "It's all about job security."

"Yeah." Cooper stared at the carpet, the deep green pile soft beneath his socks. "When will you be done?"

"With this? Late tonight."

"No video?"

"Not tonight." She followed him to the door where he laced his sneakers. Outside, on the top landing of the concrete stairs, he noticed the mailbox and his mail from the day poking out from the lid. "I didn't even notice," he said.

"Because it's not important." Natasha leaned out the doorway and pecked him on the cheek. "You're preoccupied."

"It doesn't matter. Mail." He blew out a breath. "Who fucking cares, right? I'm high on starvation. What could mail possibly mean to me?"

"You could eat it," she suggested, leaning further out, her arm braced against the aluminum storm door.

"Right on, baby." Cooper gazed out over the street; kids on skateboards flipped up and down over the curb. Another pair of youngsters lumbered past on roller blades. A young girl on a tricycle drove along a freshly paved driveway. A mosquito buzzed fiercely into his ear, then out, away from him, its sound receding.

"Quick visit, Doc."

"I'm just wandering."

"Well, wander on."

"I needed to see you. But I need to drive." He watched the child pedal up and down over the still-soft asphalt, her wheels leaving faint indentations. "Going to be a nice night," he said, enthralled by the sight of the child.

"When you come home we'll go for a walk." She stepped out on the landing in her bare feet and kissed him on the lips, watched as he walked down the concrete stairs and bent into his car. She heard the sound of him starting the engine and then the sound of him trying again, the horrible grinding.

"You shouldn't be driving," Natasha called, but she knew he hadn't heard her. She could hear the music from his tape deck blasting out through the open windows. Uriah played his music loud. It was Airto, the Brazilian percussionist, his voice popping the jungle rhythm out into the suburban neighbourhood, an angelic voice rising in the background, beneath the chaotic beat, chanting melodiously.

Cooper turned up the music, his mind flashing on an image of Natasha and Jackie masturbating each other on a couch when they were teenagers. It was enthralling, almost spiritual. He felt invigorated by the knowledge. He wished that he had been there to witness it. The intriguing purity of the act. Uninhibited nature at work.

Yvonne was on her third glass of white wine. Kneeling next to Zack, she was staring at him in a mischievous, devoted way. The material of her dress had dropped away from her shoulders and hung loose to uncover the lacy trim of her white bra and her smooth cleavage.

"You wanna get a bite, baby?" Zack asked. "I'm starving."

"No."

"You don't like to eat?"

"I'm too fat."

Zack laughed, glanced at her breasts. "Fucking right. Those tits are monsters."

Tears glossed Yvonne's eyes as if she had been slapped. She watched him incredulously, then sank back on her haunches.

"What? I didn't mean it. Come on, I was joking. Jesus, you're so sensitive."

"Look who's talking."

"Fuck." He stood, sat on the couch, and wouldn't look at her. He heard her sighing.

"Did they ask about me?" she asked, out of the blue.

"Who?"

"The police."

"No." He blew out a disgusted breath. "Fucking pigs."

"Don't be so predictable."

"What..."

"My father was a cop."

"So what?"

Reaching forward, she slapped his arm, too hard to be playful? She snorted hot breath and stared at him, wanting to be friends again, but uncertain.

"Actually," Zack confessed, "one of the cops was pretty cool."

"My father was a cop and he was an art lover, a book lover." She counted on her fingers, her speech slurring slightly from the wine. "All of that. Opera. Ballet. He loved it all. Drank good wine."

"I believe you. An aristocratic cop."

"He was." Her usually pale cheeks were flushed, burning red. She stared at Zack with a look he had never seen before, loyalty battling something very close to revulsion. "He was a great man."

"I'm sure he was."

"You're living in the sixties. Police aren't like that any more. They're educated and... Christ, you can be so stupid." She stood away from him, stumbled slightly at her sudden rise, touched her forehead as if to steady herself, then tugged up the shoulders of her dress and reached around back to zip it up.

A silence clotted between them. They waited, watching each other, the hurt in Zack's eyes.

"Look," she said, "I'm really tired."

"I'm not stupid," Zack said plainly. "You think I could do what I do if I was stupid?"

"I know." She shook her head and looked away, staring at the huge painting that Zack had given her. "I know. I know. I'm sorry. My father was such a sweet man."

"You keep saying." Zack shifted uncomfortably on the couch. "So what happened to him?"

"Nothing. Why?"

"You said 'was.' I thought..."

"No, he's alive. He's just retired."

"Oh." Zack glanced around the apartment, his mood dampened, distracted by hurtful thoughts. "And what about your mother?"

"What about my mother?" Yvonne asked, her voice so stony it prompted Zack to look at her.

"What does she do?"

"She's dead."

"Oh, shit, I'm sorry."

"My mother," Yvonne spit out the word, paced around the room, then headed for the hallway.

Zack waited, then heard Yvonne rummaging through things in what he suspected to be the storage closet toward the end of the hall. She grunted and cursed as she tore through boxes, then returned with a scrapbook held over her head.

"My mother," she said, hurling the scrapbook toward him. It thudded against the back of the couch and fell onto the floor. "She was a vicious bitch." She teetered slightly, her words slurring. She wiped at her lips, then at her entire face. "I hate this fucking heat."

"Are you drunk?" Zack stared at the book, wondering if he should reach for it. Glancing back at the doorway, he saw that Yvonne had disappeared again, was out in the kitchen, poking around in the cupboards, banging them and searching the drawer beneath the stove. He heard the rattle of the silverware drawer. A few long moments of silence, and then what he thought to be a sharp gasp.

"You want something to eat?" Yvonne called, her voice normal again, calm and even, as if no argument had occurred between them.

"Okay, thanks," he called back.

"I'll give you something to eat."

Zack picked up the scrapbook and set it in his lap, opening the thick cover to see the yellowed newspaper clippings, the date from ten years ago, August 15th, the same month as the present.

The headline: "Double Female Murder." He read the story. The names of the women. Patricia Unwin and Doris Potter. Further along in the progression of clippings, the arrest of a police officer, Gregory Potter, for the double murder. The policeman's face covered in each photograph, a coat over his head, hands raised to block the camera's view of him.

"Fuck," he whispered, turning over the stiff, plastic-covered page. "Fuck." Looking up, he saw Yvonne standing in the doorway, completely naked, blood dribbling from one breast, a lit candle in one hand, her other hand holding something in her fist. She slapped off the light switch and there was only her wavering image in the flickering candlelight as she stepped toward Zack. She held up what had been concealed in her fist, a tube of lipstick.

"You're bleeding," he said.

"Yeah," she said, smearing the blood across her breasts. "It feels *good*."

The man had explained his occupation to Yvonne and so his presence at the trade show had been nothing out of the ordinary. She had read his name tag, saying, "So, that's your name." She did not recognize it, but why would she?

He smiled at the live sounds of Yvonne's crying. Zack had been gone for at least ten minutes, unwilling to withstand her violent insults as part of sexual play. Any talk of her mother or father was certain to do that, to set her off. She had reached the point where she was mutilating herself. That was fine with him. The more emotionally upset she was, the greater her instability.

He watched the black video screen. He had switched it off, merely listened to the audio. One component. Audio was much like early radio, but even more natural. The pauses not implicitly for dramatic effect, every word not necessarily counting. Use the imagination. The elaborate playing field, where long silences and erratic— often misunderstood— lines were perfectly natural. Nothing scripted. Nothing according to plan. So much detected from this one single component of life.

The man listened to Yvonne's sobs, having no idea what would happen next, but guessing. Betting on the certainty of his judgement. Gestures rising from sound, a pleasurable grunt suggesting further abandon, a violent curse implying forthcoming movement.

The proliferation of the video image had crucified the imagination, had made it concrete, actual, instead of keeping its essence abstract, in the mind of the beholder.

The man shut his eyes, then pushed the digits on the fabricated telephone panel before him, knowing them by heart, his fingertips speeding over the memorized pattern.

The sound came almost instantaneously into his headset, one ear filled with the sound of the intimate ringing at his end, the other ear hearing the more removed sound ringing in Yvonne's apartment. An electronic balance that made him feel perfectly rooted, wired straight into her.

The sound of her quick footsteps across the rug, then over hardwood toward the edge of the living room, closer to the door. Her footsteps slowed. She was angry. He pictured her paused by the door. She was thinking of her mother. Perhaps, she was bargaining with her reflection in the mirror, but the urge would do away with all that.

It was the strongest, most vital, energy, the rash, clarifying surge that sped the body toward bloody epiphany.

She would not answer the phone, but he knew the sound was tormenting her, ripping her insides to pieces.

Her hand on the old tarnished brass doorknob, the rattling of it as it was twisted. The faint squeak of the hinges as the door was hesitantly opened.

"Sweetheart," he whispered. "Darling... it's Mommy." He smirked at his own reflection in the curve of the black monitor.

The sound of her door shutting against the drill of the telephone and the intentions of his unheard words.

Constable Pendegast sat in his car outside 64 LeMarchant Road. The car was parked under the shade of a red maple tree with branches that stretched out over the street, and the heat was almost bearable. He had seen the black-haired woman enter the premises at 6:14 p.m. He wondered whether he should go right in and question her, or if he should call Cooper first. No, Cooper didn't need to get in on this. The sight of the long black hair had made Pendegast's heart speed in anticipation, as if he had just undertaken a short jog.

"This is her," he'd whispered, remembering how Cooper had suggested that the killer might be a woman. A woman killing women. A lesbian strangling lesbians. And the concerned-citizen caller had told them that the killer lived at 64 LeMarchant Road. Bingo! "This is the dyke we're after," he'd muttered under his breath. "That dyke face. She looks the part."

Reaching for the door handle, Pendegast paused to lift a stick of spearmint chewing gum from the pocket of his white shirt. His mind weighed the scenarios. Go in there and ask the questions, alert Miss Long Black Hair to the fact that they were watching her, or wait it out, follow her and see what came of that? If she was guilty, then he'd bust in and catch the dyke in the act. He would crack the case himself. He let go the door handle and lit a cigarette, admiring the taste of the gum and the fullness of the smoke being pulled into his lungs. He thought of going for a sub, of drinking coffee from a styrofoam cup while he waited it out, doing time on the stakeout. He raised his mini-recorder to his lips and gave the snappy details, clicking it off and on as the info struck him.

Something kept nagging at him. What? He should call Cooper, but he knew that Cooper would then suck up all the credit. No doubt about it. "Fuck him," Pendegast whispered. He'd wait. At the end of the day, if Miss Black-Haired Dyke didn't leave, then he'd reconsider letting Cooper in on the info. But for now he'd hang onto the possibility of solving this thing in a matter of hours. He'd be the hero. The hero. The press, who were only interested in catching a word with Cooper, would want to talk to Pendegast, on television. The story had made the national news last night. He'd seen it and sneered at the shot of Cooper climbing into his car, not willing to comment on the case.

His stomach grumbled. He thought he caught a whiff of onions drifting from somewhere, but there were no sub shops close by; must be wafting from one of the houses. He picked up his radio and called the station, requesting a pizza delivery to 64 LeMarchant Rd. A half hour later he intercepted the delivery boy and gave him a nice tip for his troubles. Then he carried the pizza back to his car across the street. He ate the pizza and popped the cap on the icy-cold cola. The first gulp stung his eyes in a pleasurably punishing way.

When he was done, he lit a smoke and folded a piece of chewing gum into his mouth. No time to work out tonight. He'd miss the ladies at Divine's Gym. There was this one blonde-haired number with nice small hard tits who always wore a skin-tight outfit and lifted weights. Sometimes, he'd spot her on the barbell. She had big biceps, a firm, toned body. He liked a woman with a strong physique; a bit of muscle did something to him. A woman who could hold him tightly, a woman who could put up a bit of resistance, wrestling and meaning it while he was having sex.

At 7:46 p.m. Miss Black-Haired Dyke left the apartment. Pendegast caught sight of her going around back of the house and then pulling out of the driveway in a red Escort. She turned east, heading toward Harvey Road. At the lights, she curved down Long's Hill toward downtown. Pendegast's heart sped. She was moving toward the locations of the two previous murders. He followed a car-length behind as she cruised downtown, turned along the harbourfront and slowly drove up and down, looking at the ships tied up. Then she headed back up onto Water, travelling east, up to Duckworth, straight to the Newfoundland Hotel, then out King's Bridge Road connecting to Logy Bay Road. She was going for the ocean. When she reached there, she parked on the side of the road, the edge of a cliff almost directly beneath her, and stared out over the calm Atlantic.

Pendegast didn't know what to do from there. He needed back-up. Other vehicles to pass the chain. He was about to radio the station and relay the information. Other ghost cars would be sent out immediately. But on his second pass, near the spot where she was parked, Miss Black-Haired Dyke cut out ahead of him, not even seeing him, seeming lost in thought, or drunk. Had she been drinking? He could pull her over and check it out, even have a little fun with her, order her into the back of his car and give her a good cock lesson. Get her down between his knees and make the dyke bitch swallow. As enticing as his imagination made it out to be, he knew he couldn't pull that and get away with it. This time. He'd have to find another drunk female driver. Maybe later in the night. They'd do anything to avoid being charged, particularly with the new stiffer drunk-driving laws. The last woman, the one he'd taken out to the woods, had stripped for him and stood naked in the headlights of his car, shivering. He'd told her to kneel down. When she did, he grabbed a solid handful of her jet-black hair, unzipped himself, and took a good long piss on her face. She'd started crying, but that even made it better. Then he'd jerked off in her hair.

Thinking back on the episode, Pendegast rubbed his palm over the stiffness pushing behind his trousers. He'd love to pull her over. He was tempted and came close to slapping on the blue light on his dashboard a few times as he followed her back into the city, down Torbay Road where the woods soon thinned and were replaced by apartment buildings and duplexes. They passed K-Mart and two strip malls, heading down over the hill that took them beside Hillview Terrace apartments. She turned onto Elizabeth Avenue. He glanced at the Tim Hortons. He could use a doughnut or two. A pack of bits. No time to stop. This chase was making him hungry.

Black-Haired Dyke made all the green lights on Elizabeth, took a turn at Carpasian and made it back onto LeMarchant Road.

Grossly disappointed, Pendegast watched her pull into her driveway. He turned into a driveway a few houses past hers, spun around, and was back on the other side of the street, under the maple tree shade, in time to see her head into the house.

Pendegast watched her body moving. Nice ass. Could use a little toning. She walked like a man, strutted a little. Didn't know how to move her ass properly, make herself attractive. He was disappointed by her big tits. He didn't like big tits. The smaller the better. He liked flat-chested babes.

Snatching hold of the rearview, he tilted it his way to check his reflection. Smoothing down his hair, he then licked his finger and traced it along his eyebrows, straightening out the hairs. When he was through, he glanced back at the house. Maybe Miss Dyke would go out again later. He'd hang on. Good old-fashioned police work. Maybe pay her a little visit and fuck the truth out of her, fuck her until her jaw rattled out a confession. She needed a good screwing to set her straight. He'd solve the case the way it was meant to be solved, while Cooper was off tinkering with his faggy computers and books.

EIGHT

Sergeant Kieley had explicitly reiterated his instructions. "Make certain you do not open the door for anyone." When his mother looked somewhat taken aback by his harsh insistence, he added, "I'm worried about you." He informed her that he would take care of the matter himself. A simple telephone call would determine what was up with Sergeant Cooper. They were probably doing door-to-doors in the area, leaving no stone unturned to solve the murders.

"Don't they know you live here?" his mother asked.

"Why would they?"

"Don't the RCMP keep in touch with the local police about—"

"Not on this case. And where I live is none of Cooper's business."

"I see."

"Just make sure you don't open the door," he said, avoiding her eyes, "I know what happens to people who open their doors to strangers." He flicked through a copy of *People*, "I've seen the bodies. Believe me. I'm not trying to frighten you," a calculated glance at her, "but it's better to be safe than sorry."

"Of course, I understand, Gregory." His mother rocked tentatively in her chair. Reaching for the fan, she clicked the button down from "high" to "low."

"Good." Kieley stood and went into the kitchen for a drink of water, calling back, "I'll connect with Cooper and explain what's what so he doesn't bother you again."

Tuesday morning Kieley left the apartment to go directly to Fort Townshend to give Cooper the information first-hand, to tell him a thing or two more about how he was carrying out the investigation. He'd had enough of Cooper's inadequacies.

Stepping out of his apartment, he slid on his sunglasses and faced another brilliant summer morning, still heat hanging punishingly around him. The heatwave dulled a person's spirits. The outdoors had become a place to be avoided rather than enjoyed.

In his car, Kieley winced at the hot damp air and quickly rolled down both windows. Pulling out, he switched on the radio in the middle of a report by an exuberant announcer that the temperature would hit 32 degrees. What was that in Fahrenheit? He could never get used to metric. He was taught the metric system in school, but its introduction had been too late, and it wasn't just his generation, either. In a mall a few weeks ago, he had overheard a group of teenaged boys stepping away from a mystic weight scale, one of them asking the other, "So, what's that in pounds?" The other, shrugging, "I don't know."

Fort Townshend was only a few minutes from his apartment, heading east on LeMarchant Road. A left turn directly onto Parade Street was prohibited and so he was forced to turn up shortly before the intersection, to the right of the island with the small bus depot, and then up Cook, east on Merrymeeting and then down Parade and into the station. The edges of the parking lot were occupied by a few stray media vans. He recognized the logos for CTV and CBC, but there was another van, a rented one a cameraman and a reporter stood beside. The logo on the camera was one Kieley could not place. Something foreign. The media were becoming more and more interested. One more murder and the floodgates would open. Several residents from the neighbourhood were lingering near, anxious to catch a first-hand piece of information regarding the killings.

Kieley cruised past the uniformed officer stationed there to watch over the media and pulled into a space with a sign marked for police personnel only. He reasoned that they would realize the car was a rental and put two and two together. He got out, casting a look back at the vans. Uncharacteristically, he grinned to himself. What a show! What a spectacle! The attention that such crimes attracted. The hyper-real mania focused this way. The possibilities that opened up.

Kieley made his way toward the rows of tinted doors. Inside the low brick building, he stepped past the exhibit featuring old weapons and uniforms, a history of the Constabulary, and paused to take a closer look. Moving from one display case to the other, he glanced at the wall of dark grey tinted glass behind which police personnel milled about. He nodded at the friendly receptionist in her wheelchair, who gave him a warm smile.

"What am I doing here?" he muttered to himself, realizing he did not want to face Sergeant Uriah Cooper. An utter waste of time. He had better things to do. He decided to leave the building and visit the police convention again, see if any of his old friends recognized him. He left the building and returned to his car, cruising out of the lot and heading down LeMarchant Road. Passing in front of his mother's apartment, he caught a glimpse of her profile in the upstairs window. All those soap operas she watched in the daytime. They sometimes seemed to blur what she thought was real and fantasy.

The soap opera was one shock after another. There was so much going on, so much confusion. It sometimes unnerved her, interfered with her sleep, scrambling the plot lines with her own life, and she would wake up, calling out to one of the characters in a panicky tone, warning him or her of the danger. "Watch out, Crystal! Watch out! Run!" The danger. That's what they used to call it when she was a young woman, sitting in the St. Pat's theatre watching the serials. The danger. They'd ask each other, *What was the danger this week?* But with the soap operas, there was so much danger she couldn't keep track of it all.

She had that feeling now as she dozed, the pulse of the television screen and the whir of the fan seeming to lull her to sleep, but also penetrating her thoughts, barbing them with suspicion. In her daydream, she was questioning her son.

"Gregory," she said.

"Yes, mother." Gregory appeared transformed, taller, with thicker hair. Refined thinner features. He had dyed his hair. He was dressed in a tuxedo, a slim champagne glass in his hand. The room was luxurious, dark mahogany panelling hung with exquisite works of art. A billiards table was off to one side, the green cloth unmarked, a buttery-smooth burgundy leather chair slightly to his right. Gregory's face was very different, but definitely Gregory's. He watched his mother with handsome severity, anticipation, as if his mood was darkening. Tense music heightened the scene.

"Those years I was in the St. Agnes Home, and you were in the Yukon."

"Yes." Gregory's facial muscles flinched in an almost imperceptible manner as he raised his glass and carefully sipped it, his intense eyes measuring her.

"You were on a special assignment."

"Yes." Stern, almost disagreeable, but then the smile. Charming, trying to warm her heart.

"How come you never wrote?"

"I'd telephone instead, mother."

"Not even a postcard."

"You know me. I hate to write." A casual step nearer, glancing away to shift attention from the certainty of his calculated advance. "I have trouble with it."

"Yes." Her muscles tensing against the shadows creeping into his eyes, his hands clutching the glass so tightly.

"And Doris?" She touched the string of pearls at her neck. They were so smooth, so cold against her fingertips. "She left you."

"She did." The glass exploding in his grip. He allowed the thin shards to shatter and drop away, ignoring them.

"Where is she?" She glanced at his hand, saw that it was, remarkably, uncut. "You never talk about her. A man talks about his ex-wife."

"Why?" So close to her now, so near.

"Don't," she whispered.

"I have to." His hands reaching, thumbs pressing firmly into her wrinkled throat, savagely intruding upon her windpipe. "You see, I killed Doris."

Mrs. Kieley woke with a start, gasping for breath, her heart beating in a troubling way, her hand darting up to touch her wet neck. Was it blood there? Whimpering, she looked at her fingertips. No, it was sweat. Shifting her eyes toward the window, she realized where she was and let out a sigh of relief, shutting her eyes and touching the pearls at her throat, finding her St. Christopher medal, taking hold of the medallion, its comforting smoothness between her fingers.

"Foolishness," she muttered. "These dreams." But her thoughts continued to sweep her beyond the apartment, back into the past, photographs of Gregory as a child, at nursery school, his cap and gown in his graduating snapshot, through high school, in uniform after graduating from the RCMP academy. His wedding photograph. The one she kept on her white side table in the St. Agnes Home. Doris. She was a lovely woman with a fine figure, although a bit of a loudmouth. Strong-willed, they called it these days.

It did her no good to think of Doris. Gregory was her only child, her only blood relative. Practically everyone else had died off and she had no friends. If there were any out there, they would have a hard time finding her, having reclaimed her maiden name after her husband's death. She preferred it that way. Didn't want to see anyone from the past. She liked to keep to herself, always had. She cherished her privacy.

She thought of Mr. Prouse. His charisma. He was a real charmer from the old school, steel grey hair slicked back, solid features and excellent manners. It would be nice to enjoy some male company in her final years. But Gregory didn't care much for him. She could tell that. She thought of Peter, her husband dead all these years. The dream of Gregory had made her long for Peter, made her feel slightly guilty for thinking of Mr. Prouse. She hadn't even thought of Peter for so long, but now she longed for him in a heartbreaking way that encouraged the need for some sort of companionship.

Forlornly, she shifted her thoughts away, concentrating instead on the loveliness of her new home, saying a short prayer to St. Christopher, patron saint of protection in travel, thanking him for making Gregory's move back to Newfoundland after all these years such a safe and prosperous one, thanking all of the saints in heaven for bringing her wonderful son back to her.

One of the computer registration systems was down. First the printer had gone on the blink, feeding the labels through out of line, and then the program had crashed and wouldn't allow itself to be re-booted.

Just what I need, Yvonne told herself, then swiftly explained to the line-up that the terminal was down and directed the visitors in front of that station over to the left registration desk. Those in the line did not appreciate being shifted, several of them groaning or rolling their eyes at having to tag onto the back of the parallel line-up.

Yvonne thanked them with a congenial smile, then hurried off to call the Xerox office. Rushing, she was made aware of the pain in her breast, the material of her bra catching in the slit she had inflicted on herself last night. Revelling in the doing of the deed, she desperately wanted to gash herself again. There was a bathroom down a secluded corridor around back of the office. What could she use? Hurrying into the office, her eyes scanned the draped tables, the makeshift desks. Pens. Pencils. A stapler. Imagining punching staples into her breasts, she almost whited out, her knees wobbling with dread and violent excitement as she checked the yellow pages and found the Xerox number. She glanced at Sally and Len, the two office workers. Len was typing a badge for an exhibitor, and Sally was jotting down notes of some sort. The Xerox office was next door, in the Cabot Place tower. "Printer's down," she said to Len and Sally. Catching her breath, she dialled the number. They told her that they'd have someone there in a few minutes. The technician was out on a call, but they'd make certain she was dealt with immediately following the completion of that job. Fifteen minutes, tops, they assured her. When she protested that she was running a trade show and required immediate attention, they told her they would page the service technician at once.

"Is the manager in?" she asked, eyeing the stapler, her fingers reaching for it.

"Yes. But she's on another call right now."

"I'll hold." She picked up the stapler, felt the weight of it in her sweaty palm and licked a few droplets of sweat from above her top lip.

When Yvonne was finally put through, the manager, a female, Yvonne gladly discovered, assured her that she would be down personally to lend a hand.

She hung up, taking a deep breath.

"Everything okay?" she asked Len and Sally, tightening her grip on the stapler, checking their eyes to see if they had noticed it.

"Yup," Sally said confidently. Maybe a touch too self-assured, too upbeat, Yvonne noted, something like the woman on the reception desk of the hotel. Len had simply nodded and smiled, more natural, easy-going. Genuine. No problem here, his smile seemed to say, and even if there was then he'd look after it. Not to worry. No false assurances.

Her mind was racing as she left the office in the Schooner Room. She heard the buzz from the convention floor across the foyer, noting by the volume of the sound that there must be a reasonable number of visitors, enough to keep the exhibitors happy, she hoped. Terri was in there chatting up the clients.

Turning in the wide foyer, stapler firmly in hand, Yvonne faced the lengthening single line-up in front of the registration centre toward the front. Escape, she told herself. I have a few minutes before the Xerox manager arrives. Compelled, she turned away from the line-up, and rushed down the secluded corridor, heading for the washroom. Charging in through the door, she was further aroused by the polished, dimly lit ambience of the haven. She stepped toward the stall farthest in the back. Its door was open and she moved in, paused to listen, then turned to face the mirror. Not a sound in the room. She unzipped her mauve dress and briskly pulled down the front, exposing her mauve bra and the deep cleavage of her white breasts. She lifted her breasts out, aware of the tender slit above her left nipple, the gash pronounced. She dabbed it with her fingertip, pressed harder, and shut her eyes.

If anyone came in, she would simply close the door to her stall. It was safe. She pressed the stapler to the sore edge of the slit, sensing the arousing coolness of the steel. Watching her reflection in the mirror, she slammed the stapler with her palm and buckled over with pain. Genuinely flabbergasted by the unsuspected intensity of the hurt, she straightened in disbelief, lifted the stapler away and stared in a stupor at where the staple had dug firmly into her flesh. She traced the thin silver edge with her fingertip and then pinched it, tugged it out and glanced at herself in the mirror. No blood that she could see, only the whiteness of her face, her expression making her nauseous, her breakfast beginning to burn in her throat. She swallowed and slammed a staple into her right breast.

Grimacing in pain, she repeated the procedure, two more in each breast, circling her nipples. Then she madly shoved shut the door to her stall, left the staples inserted and kneeled, the smooth tile thrilling her knees. Leaning over the toilet bowl, she manically sucked her fingers, wetting them, making certain they could go down her throat easily. She pushed them in, until feeling resistance, the first retch, the relief, the arousing urge in her groin while she groaned. She forced her fingers deeper, the vomit surging up, clunking into the toilet bowl and then gushing out. Water flickered against her face and she lowered the hand that had been in her mouth to the elastic waist-line of her panties, slipping her fingers down over her pubis, shifting her knees apart, she frantically thrust her fingers in and out.

Back out in the foyer, having cleaned herself up, plucked the staples free, stuffed toilet paper in her bra to staunch the blood and checked herself in the mirror, Yvonne stood back in the world of responsibility. The registration problem remained unsolved, but she shied away from instructing Pamela, the woman sitting at the downed terminal to fill out the registration badges by hand. It was unprofessional and Yvonne despised the look of it. However, if the line-up became much longer, she would have to resort to that. It was the only way of keeping things flowing smoothly. Dropping the stapler back in the office, she paged one of the "beasts of burden" (as Terri called them) to bring an IBM typewriter up from the office. At least, the badges would be typed.

She walked briskly toward the front tables to watch over the registration, helping Pamela fit badges into their plastic holders, glancing at the names and then handing them to the specific visitor, "Enjoy the show, Mr. Power." With each movement of her arms, the lingering thrill of pain in her breasts stirred and repulsed her. It had been exciting at the time but now she hated herself for being so weak and perverse.

She reached for another tag, slid it into the plastic, glanced at the name, "Enjoy the show, Mr. Prouse." She looked up as she handed over the tag and saw her neighbour standing there, his casual likeable smile.

"Hello," she said, slightly overdone, perky, she realized, but she was in her trade-show-greeting mode now. Facing someone familiar like this, someone she knew, turned the scene startlingly surreal.

"Hello, Yvonne." Lawrence Prouse slipped the string around his canvas safari hat, and then around his neck and let his badge drop down against the front of his floral silk shirt.

Yvonne was handed another badge by Pamela. She slipped it in and reached behind Mr. Prouse, passing it over without reading the name. The procedure was getting sloppy. She had to move Mr. Prouse so she could keep the pattern flowing.

"Well, I hope you enjoy the show," she said to Mr. Prouse, trusting he would take it as a dismissal. He stepped forward a few feet and paused behind her back, lifting his badge and reading it, obviously pleased with his presence in the convention centre.

Yvonne tried her best to ignore him, but as the line-up began to shorten, she asked Pamela if she could handle it alone. Pamela said, "No problem," supplying a badge to the next registrant and smiling warmly, but with professional tact.

Good help is a real bonus, Yvonne told herself as she turned to face Mr. Prouse, no way of avoiding him. He'd wait there forever.

"What're you doing down here?" she had to ask.

"My brother works with ElectroDam. He gave me a pass."

"So you're checking out all the police toys."

"I have an interest in electronics. Dabble in it."

"Really?"

"Really." His eyes sparkled and he gave her a secretive smile and a wink. "Surveillance, counter-surveillance, that sort of thing. Always wanted to be a private detective. Since I was a kid."

"I see." She began walking. "Well, I'd better get back to work." It was essential that she make the rounds, move from booth to booth asking the exhibitors if everything was in order, if they required anything at all. It was a nice touch and a great way of keeping on top of any problem that might arise, deal with it immediately, thus limiting its impact on memory.

Mr. Prouse followed her in through the open double doors that led into the buzz of the high-ceilinged convention centre.

"I've got a few things I'm trying to peddle." He raised his black hard-plastic briefcase and patted the side.

"That's great," said Yvonne, distracted, feeling the pain more now, the throbbing in both of her tender breasts.

"Wish me luck."

"Good luck," she said. "See you around." She signalled with her arms the width of the layout. "Have a good time."

"Okay." He watched her walking off. She glanced at him as she took a turn down E Aisle.

"Small town," she muttered, halting her step at the Lapdog Services booth, glancing down at a brochure featuring a glossy colour photograph of a German Shepherd, a police officer crouched beside the door of a police cruiser, arm draped around the dog in a friendly manner. Then she smiled up at the exhibitor who was standing by one of the royal blue display panels, hands joined casually behind his back. He was wearing a dark blue suit and white shirt, maroon tie. He watched her with interest, glancing at the cut of her dress and then looking into her eyes, smiling as he stepped toward her.

"How's it going?" she asked, the man's lustful leer giving her the creeps.

"You like our doggies?" the man enquired, his eyes flicking to her breasts. He came closer and slid his arm around her shoulders, waving to one of his associates who was bent beside a box, lifting out a stack of brochures.

"Come meet Yvonne," the man said. "She's our lovely little hostess." He grinned at her, again glancing at her breasts, his brow furrowing. "You spill a little something on yourself?" he asked, pointing toward her chest. "Pizza or something?"

Yvonne peeked down, saw the spray of tiny red dots staining the fabric of her dress, seeping from her breasts. "Christ!" she said, apologizing immediately for her careless appearance. "Sorry."

"That's okay. It's okay, sweetie."

"I had pizza for lunch... Must've splattered on me."

"Don't worry your pretty little head about it."

Yvonne felt his hand release from her shoulders and drop lower to gently rub her behind.

"We won't hold that against you."

NINE

Sergeant Cooper realized that the key to everything lay in who had called alerting him to the LeMarchant Road location. "The Concerned Citizen In Drag," as the man had been labelled by officers on the force.

Cooper sat in his office, the mini-recorder on his desk. He pressed the play button, activating a copy of the original tape. "I can't control who's dead next." The caller wanted Cooper to believe he was a woman. Who were the women suspects on LeMarchant Road? One woman had come up on his digital mapping system, but she was in Florida on vacation. Her whereabouts had been confirmed by one of the officers on the task force. Then there were the two males, one for robbery, the other break and entry. Both serving time at Her Majesty's.

Cooper's mind shifted back to 64 LeMarchant Road. Lawrence Prouse. Stalking. Cooper flipped through his notes. He saw the names of the women living in the old house. Yvonne Unwin and Sarah Kieley, the two names he had received from Lawrence Prouse via a telephone call. Sarah Kieley was in her seventies or eighties. She could not be responsible. There was no point interviewing her, upsetting her. Her son was a police officer from Toronto, just moved down. Was he transferred? He made a note to check on him with Johnston. He hadn't recalled hearing anything about him. Maybe he was with the feds. That left Yvonne Unwin, the young woman in 1B with the long black hair.

Pendegast was watching the house, waiting for Unwin's appearance. He'd conduct an interview and if there was anything worth following up, then Cooper would pay a visit. He pulled off his wire-rimmed glasses, cleaned them with the tail of his shirt. The heat made it necessary to clean them three or four times a day. There was always that uneven line of film toward the top of the lenses. He drew a deep breath and stared ahead at the bulletin board across from his desk, the photocopies of the newspaper clippings— the crimes he had recently solved, including a serial rapist.

The media had recently dug up the rapist's past and highlighted the depth of Cooper's efficiency, his mastery of the field of criminal-behaviour analysis. They were making him out to be some sort of whiz-kid when— in fact— that case had been solved without much effort on his part. A prostitute who had been assaulted years before by the rapist— but never reported the attack— had memorized the man's licence plate and held it in her head. A mind for numbers.

Cooper broke his line of thought, disconnecting from that case. He wrote out Yvonne Unwin's name again. Wrote out 1B, circled it, then crossed it out, drew a picture of an apartment door, wrote 1B on it. Following procedure, Cooper had already checked Unwin out on both systems, Police Information Retrieval Centre and Canadian Police Information Centre. Local and national. Nothing on either. She wasn't a habitual.

From what he knew of Yvonne Unwin, she did not fit the profile, did not even come close. He wrote down the words "mother" and "father," circled them. There had been hundreds of Unwins on both police computer systems and he knew each should be searched. He had turned that over to one of the crime analysts, Constable Butler. That number of Unwins would take time.

He glanced at his watch: 7:14 p.m. He hadn't called Natasha. It was what day? Tuesday, he guessed. The pages of a calendar flipped over in his mind. One month, then another... Years passing. Sheafs of paper months blowing in the wind, tossed here and there in a blizzard of lost years. An image of him with a long white beard, sitting in a rocking chair on a country veranda, watching pretty young women walking past while he licked his lips and farted.

What day?

Picking up the telephone, he called home to discover there was no answer. Natasha was probably down on Victoria Street, packing up, or out with friends. When was the Folk Festival she had mentioned? Not 'til the weekend. What else was on the go? What had she mentioned? Catching caplin down in Middle Cove, a bonfire on the beach. He cursed his bad fortune for not being able to join her. He adored a good bonfire. No doubt Ed would take along his guitar and there would be Phil's accordion, a real lively night of Newfoundland tunes.

"Forget it," he muttered, drawing his thoughts back to Yvonne Unwin, scribbling out the beach scene he had begun drawing. Unwin was twenty-seven years old. Cooper had the basics on her from her driver's licence info requested from the DOT in Ontario. No speeding infractions. Recently returned to St. John's— her birthplace.

Why would she be killing people? It didn't make sense. But there was the long black hair. He gave a slight shake of his head, feeling as if he was being played for a fool. Whoever was calling wanted him to believe that Yvonne Unwin had committed these murders. He was wasting his time. But what about the black hairs found at the crime scenes?

"A sample," he muttered to himself. If she refused there was nothing they could do. They had no corroborating evidence to back up laying charges.

Why the house on LeMarchant Road? Why the misdirection? Was that what it was? A complete misdirection to tip the focus away from the actual area were the murderer lived? The murders had been committed at locations in the core of the downtown area, not far from the gay dance bar— the Zone. Undercover men and women officers were already doing duty in that bar at night.

Cooper had taken care of that. They were interviewing known lesbians in the area. This was turning out to be a real witch hunt, just as Johnston had suspected. A real lesbian witch hunt. It wouldn't be long before the gay community would be screaming human rights violations.

He made a note to contact the Gay Rights Association and try to develop a rapport with someone there, to acquire information that would make him appear well-versed in lesbian relationships. He had already taken it upon himself to thumb through one of the books he'd bought yesterday at the downtown bookstore. A book on lesbian lives. But there was nothing out of the ordinary to be found there.

Studies indicated that there was a high rate of previous sexual assault by males among lesbians. But then there were other studies that suggested lesbians were simply more inclined to seek therapy and thus the higher rate. They were more willing to come out of the abuse closet, so to speak. Three of his courses in his masters program had been centred on sexual behaviour.

Regardless, this lesbian angle didn't ring true to him. Why? He wrote "why" on his cluttered notepad. He was seeing the faces of the dead women. He was seeing them in his mind and then he realized he was sketching them in detail, their faces, their eyes, noses, lips... The victims were— indeed— lesbians. Their backgrounds had been checked. What was troubling him, then?

He slapped down his pen and called Constable Butler to see how she was progressing with the Unwin search.

"Nothing yet."

"Okay, thanks." He hung up and decided to take a run home; the office was beginning to shrink around him, an empty box in an empty world with him sitting in the middle of it. He imagined a view from above, the roof torn off his office, the camera zooming back, city, province, country, continent, earth, space, stars, aliens watching him from far away, giggling.

"What're you giggling at?" he muttered, shaking his head at the utter absurdity of what he was engaged in. What pathetic creatures we are, he told himself, so incapable of seeing things as they are. We invent a realm of science that attempts to set things in order, but it's only our tenuous perception of order that keeps the balance. In reality, it's all just chaos.

He was doodling again. The name: Unwin.

Patience, old chap, he told himself, adopting the voice of Richard Higgins. Patience was needed, but patience would undoubtedly lead to another death.

While they were watching Unwin, someone else might strangle another woman. Another death would make it next to impossible for him to move freely through the city. The media were already pestering him. Johnston had called earlier to let Cooper know that NBC and ABC had both called for basic details. Soon they would have to post police vehicles at the entrance to Fort Townshend to keep the media out, to pull them over, to simply allow Cooper to drive clear of them.

Sighing, Cooper stood from behind his desk. He turned toward his computer screen and bent to switch off the info he had been reading about Lucy Kellogg, the serial killer who had murdered all those men in England. A disturbed woman. Greatly disturbed. No semblance of normality in her life: a history of severe abuse, and convictions for violent offenses.

He pressed the power button and the screen blinked off. Leaving his office, he was surprised at the long shadows in the evening parking lot, seeing the rented vans. The count had risen from three to five. Reporters stepped from the vans, pointing cameramen toward Cooper seventy feet away. Zoom in. They were kept at bay by orange barricades and had been given explicit instructions not to cross them. Two uniformed officers were posted there in blue short-sleeved shirts and hats to make certain the press was contained.

The journalists would soon be multiplying at a greater speed, breeding amongst themselves, Cooper mused. Like earthworms, leaving a silver slimy trail. Cut them in half and you couldn't even kill them.

He moved toward his parked car. He had seen a few of the newscasts on television. Lead story on local stations, fourth or fifth from the top on national television. One more body and the entire world would be tapped into this. His name was being tossed around, the term "investigative psychologist" always tagged on. They had even brought up clips of popular movies, movie stars playing the kind of role they thought he actually lived. What a sensational farce!

His mouth was sticky and foul. He was thirsty, hungry, tired and alert at once, his bones ached, yet he could have run a mile if he chose to, if he pushed himself. He needed a trace, another call from the caller and a trace. That was the next step, but that would mean another body, another announcement that a body was waiting for them at a given address.

A psychological profile of the killer. That was in development. The idea of a disgruntled telephone employee was being checked out, with a leaning toward females. All employees and ex-employees. It was a chance, be it however slim.

Cooper put no faith in it, but it had to be explored. Every possible angle touched upon.

Long black hair— another key. Was Unwin the next victim, or was she the killer trying to destroy images of herself? All of this info had been in the preliminary profile that he'd put together yesterday.

Futility throbbed in his bones, making him feel vicious. He focused his hunger on this sense of futility, this urgency to solve the crime. His jaw ached with vacuous longing, his nerves sparking. He was staring toward the media vans.

Unlocking his car door, he continued watching the reporters while his thoughts wandered. The reporters had caught sight of him and were bobbing and waving like a bunch of lunatics. He bent into his car and engaged the engine. There would have to be another body to progress any further. He needed to trace the call. The first call to the station had come up UNKNOWN NAME, UNKNOWN NUMBER on the master panel in the communications department. With a trace they could get by that. The next call. The next body.

Cooper flicked on the radio, disgusted with himself. He drove from the parking lot, slowing as the reporters came near his vehicle, held back by the uniformed officers.

"It's just a big movie," he mumbled to himself. "A tragedy. Those dead women are just actresses." He wanted to roll down his window and say a few words to the reporters, but that would be totally unprofessional. It would give them what they wanted, the up-to-the-minute footage of him to open the news story with. The colourful starring role that must be filled. The cop with pizazz, with character. The cop-pop-psychologist. They had already picked up on the doctor sergeant name the boys had tagged him with. Soon, his "in" box would be filled with messages from publishers in Toronto and New York, agents, movie people. He would have a list to choose from. They would want an exclusive. His story. Some would go so far as to leave ballpark dollar figures with the receptionist.

Cooper's car passed through the opening in the line of reporters. He glanced at them in his rearview as they chased after him on foot. He sped up, as if to outrun his thoughts. Two vans pulled out of the lot to follow, but a cruiser tailed them, immediately flashing its lights in warning, and the vans pulled over, allowing Cooper to escape. Fortunately, his home number was unlisted. But that wouldn't stop these vultures. A good hacker could get the number from the telephone system and turn it over to whoever was willing to pay the price.

He took a turn on Merrymeeting, heading east toward his home in the quiet suburbs. He thought of the beach party in Middle Cove, wondered if he should go along. No, it would be a waste of time. He was too caught up in these murders. He'd be thinking about them. Best to be alone.

Or maybe it would be a good thing. Get his mind directly off the murders and allow his subconscious to operate on its own, sublimate the facts and sift through them like an abstract sleuth unto itself.

Rationalizing that it was only a fifteen-minute run out to the ocean, he decided to have a look regardless. He drove out and parked close to the edge of the high cliff overlooking the arc of beach.

The sun was close to the water, a ball of mute round orange that bathed everything in its lovely light.

Gazing through his window, down over the granite and brown rock cliff, spotted with rugged crevices of grass here and there, he saw a crowd far below, standing out in the water, scooping up caplin in their hands or nets, others casting fishing lines. He rolled down his window and heard the sounds of laughter and merriment drifting up to him. He thought he heard Natasha's distinct laugh and it touched him deeply. He spotted her in her jean cut-offs and white tank top, wobbling in the water, her feet on the slippery beach rocks that rolled beneath her bare-footed grip, being supported by two male friends.

Cooper rolled up his window and fiercely scratched at his goatee, then shifted into drive and headed down the steep road, past the opening to the gravel parking lot for the beach, feeling dejected and bothered, feeling so alone and useless, his mind occupied by the shifting male and female faces of a killer.

Mr. Prouse had spent the entire afternoon at the trade show. Yvonne had caught sight of his bright floral shirt and canvas safari hat in the various booths along her continued treks through the aisles, his briefcase opened on a draped table as he passionately explained complex details, his hands in the air, shaping invisible circuitry.

Fortunately, she had taken along a second dress, as she always did for trade shows, just in case she happened to spill something on herself. Never thinking that the stains might be blood. After enduring the harassment from the obnoxious exhibitors, she hurried off and retrieved her dress from one of the spare meeting rooms and hurriedly changed in the bathroom.

Exiting the bathroom, she came face to face with Mr. Prouse. He pointed towards the men's door. Excusing herself, Yvonne indicated that she had to make her rounds. Mr. Prouse trailed after her. Whenever she glanced behind, down the crowded aisles, she glimpsed him. Sometimes he would be looking directly at her and his eyes would flinch away, feigning interest in a nearby booth.

Then, she saw him again.

Parking her fiery red Escort at the back of the house on LeMarchant Road, Yvonne locked the car doors (the area was bad for break-ins) and moved along the side of the house toward the front entrance way, the grass beaten down into a path between the clapboarding and the thick trunks of the maple and chestnut trees. In the shade, she studied the jolly jokers and the lobellia in the flower beds trimming the house; a black and white cat scurried out of the tall grass, startling her. She heard a large house fly whiz past her left ear as she stalled in front of her own window, checking out the white window boxes beneath her bedroom window. That's where she had seen Mr. Prouse the other night. Was it last night? No, the night before. Had he been tending to the flowers, or watching her? It had been suspiciously late in the night. Either way, he could not have helped but see her. Naked.

Unlocking and twisting the warm brass knob on the old door, she stepped into the merciful cool of the porch and checked her mailbox. She was made aware of the throbbing in her breasts as she reached for her mail. The throb had become duller, but it was still there, as much as she tried to sublimate it. She flicked through the envelopes: a few bills, a letter from her father.

Her father! She had instructed him never to write to her in St. John's before she left Toronto. She had sent him a letter with her specific instructions, sent it by registered mail, but had obviously included her return address by accident, or had she on purpose? Did she really want to reconcile with him?

No, she hated him.

Moving into her apartment, she heard the unlocking of a door behind her, but paid it no attention. It was Mr. Prouse. She closed her eyes for an instant, then turned to shut her door, seeing Mr. Prouse standing directly behind her, a forlorn expression on his face.

Yvonne nodded, smiling briefly in a manner that implied she was tired and not really interested.

"Working late," he said. "How was your day after?"

"Exhausting." Yvonne gave another brief noncommittal smile, holding on to the edge of the door with one hand while she hung her keys on one of the small wooden pegs protruding from the piece of horse-shaped folk art. Again, reaching, an awareness of the pinprick wounds in her breasts.

"This heat! Have you ever seen anything like it?"

"No, not really." In reality she had— in Toronto, but she didn't want to encourage the conversation.

"The show went well for me. Lots of connections." His charming smile. Everything about him so charming in an old-fashioned good-natured way. He shrugged his shoulders. What was it about him? Was he like her father? Was that it? "Maybe something'll come of it."

"That's great. Good luck."

"It was a wonderful surprise to see you there."

"Small world, hey."

Mr. Prouse stared at her, thinking of what she had said. "Yeah, it is," his tone almost passionate. "It's a very small world." His thoughts seemed to catch on a consideration, something that was bothering him. "Oh, I meant to ask you. When I was at the telephone company, there was a woman. Someone Unwin. I can't recall the first name. You have anyone working there?"

"Which department?"

"Marketing."

"That'd be Muriel—"

"Yes." Mr. Prouse raised a bent finger, "Yes, that's it. Muriel. Muriel Unwin. What's she to you, if you don't mind me asking."

"My aunt."

"You see, a small world again."

"Sure is. Well, good night." She began closing the door and Mr. Prouse made a brief movement to step forward, to impose with another statement. It was a jittery action, like a flinch, a nervous reaction to Yvonne's impending withdrawal.

Yvonne stared at him, but he held himself back, nodding politely instead as her door continued closing.

"Listen," he said, his voice calm, almost sad. "I was wondering if you wanted to get together for a bite some time. I can cook. I love cooking."

"I..." Yvonne was not interested, but she needed to remain civil, after all. He was her landlord, and she loved where she lived. It was so convenient and comfortable.

"My speciality's fettucini with garlic sausage. Home made. I get them from Auntie Crae's. You ever try them?"

"No." She offered another weak smile.

"You're tired, I know. Just think about it." He stepped back into his apartment and gave her a caring smile that seemed genuine, then shut his door.

Yvonne shut hers, staying behind the barrier for a few moments, leaning, her eyes shut, asking herself, Do men have any idea what it's like getting hit on all the time? It's not arousing, it's just numbing. She heard Mr. Prouse's door open and hoped he would not knock on her door. She waited, and detected sounds of him moving around in the apartment, so he must have just left the door open to facilitate air circulation. The stagnant hot air had the dour weight of some old permanence in the Victorian building. Her apartment certainly held the heat. One thing she was thankful for was that she was not on the second floor. It would be totally unbearable up there. She pitied Zack. But maybe the sweat made him work better, the stress stirring up all those angry artistic sentiments.

Drifting into the kitchen, she kicked off her shoes, watching them clunk on the linoleum. She sighed when she opened the refrigerator door and saw its pathetic contents: bottled spaghetti sauce, catsup, a blue carton of milk soon to go bad, and a white styrofoam take-out container with her leftover chicken-avocado salad from Zapata's. Three days old. Not worth the risk of food poisoning. Although sometimes she enjoyed food poisoning. Mother Nature's super laxative.

She decided on tea and then a visit to Zack's. She had been unreasonably mean to him last night, abusing him, spitting on him, and even hitting him. But he had seemed to enjoy it, had revelled in how she had cut herself, had even tasted her blood. It was like he was always trying to provoke her, as if he knew more about her than he was letting on. He could push her buttons like no one else she had ever known. Her behaviour never bothered him in the slightest.

Talk of her father always upset her. And now the letter from him. She imagined the tone of the letter, the pleading questions, the same requests that she had heard and/or read for almost ten years, since the death of her mother. She had to get away from him. She had moved here to escape him. What he was doing to her? The only recourse had been withdrawal from his life. She couldn't report her own father to the police. Who would believe her, anyway? He was a policeman for all those years. He was respected.

Her stomach was bothering her. She patted it and reached to slide the kettle onto the burner, finding that there was not enough water. She held it under the tap, filled it with a short furious blast, set it in place then returned to the fridge and popped open the styrofoam container, sniffed at the leftovers, and ate a piece of brown-edged avocado from between her fingers, the creamy garlic dressing refreshing her taste buds. Who cares about food poisoning, anyway, she joked with herself. Just another excuse to puke.

Chewing, she glanced at the letter from her father sitting on the kitchen table. She read his handwritten name: Fred Walsh. Yvonne's mother had kept her maiden name and made certain that it was passed on to Yvonne. Her stomach tightened, her shoulder muscles cramping from the day's tension.

Her father. He still continued to seek her understanding, her assurances that everything would be okay. He continued to explain the past away, sort it out, make it believable to her. His version.

Staring at the letter, she felt like a teenager again, rebellious and powered by unchallengeable knowledge. She felt the need to constantly defend her father, as she had always done to her friends and acquaintances, explaining how different he was from the stereotypical brutal cop. He was a gentle man, a refined man, who appreciated the cultured life. He read books, not trashy detective novels or thrillers, but literature. Books written by authors whose names she could not even pronounce. He had tried to get her to read these novels, but they were so difficult to make her way through, so dense and filled with overly involved plots. She had tried, tried so intensely to please him, to belong, tried so hard to be like him, like her mother.

She stared at her father's envelope, his handwriting, remembering how he would read to her, read from books that described ideas she could not grasp, could not understand, no matter how much she tried. Her father had turned her off reading. She could not even go into a bookstore without flashing on his face. She could not pick up a book without feeling a twinge of revulsion.

Lifting a piece of tortilla shell and shredded cheese between her fingers, she dropped it into her mouth. She was hungry. Maybe that's what the problem was. When was the last time she had eaten anything substantial? Chewing, she closed her eyes as the telephone began ringing.

"God," she hissed through her teeth, hurrying nonetheless to bend over the caller ID, the digits she identified as belonging to her Aunt Muriel. She let the phone ring until the answering machine picked up.

She didn't need a conversation with her aunt this late in the day. She decided that she was definitely hungry now. Irritable. That little snack had convinced her. She wanted a glass of wine. The kettle began to whistle as she heard the message, "Hi, Yvonne, this is your Auntie Muriel, just checking in to make sure you're okay. I haven't heard from you in a while. [a pause] I was speaking with Dr. Healey on the telephone [another pause] Give me a call when you get a chance. Bye, sweetheart."

Yvonne folded her arms across her chest while listening to the message. She gave a bitter little laugh. Muriel liked to keep her eye on Yvonne. That was one of the drawbacks about returning to Newfoundland; her mother's sister was still living here. Aunt Muriel had taken it upon herself to act as her mother, to try to fill her mother's shoes, and Yvonne avoided her for that very reason. They even resembled each other, and this unnerved Yvonne to no end. Also, Aunt Muriel kept in touch with Dr. Healey about Yvonne's progress. Even though the doctor refused to divulge information relating to Yvonne's case, Muriel was always certain to call anyway and stick her nose where it didn't belong.

"I'm busy," Yvonne muttered to the machine as she shut it off, the kettle shrieking steadily. She turned for the kitchen and slid the kettle off the burner, took down a cup, unwrapped a camomile teabag and dropped it in, poured the water. She paused while pouring, laid down the kettle, left the cup where it was and whisked a glass from the shelf, pulled her last half-filled bottle of red wine from the bottom cupboard and yanked out the cork. Her movements froze.

The telephone again.

In the living room, she saw the readout: UNKNOWN NAME, UNKNOWN NUMBER, and waited for it to stop ringing.

It wouldn't, continuing for a count of twelve before Yvonne delicately lifted it from the cradle and held the receiver to her ear without saying a word. She could play the game just as well as whoever was on the other end, she confidently told herself, listening, not saying a word, waiting, hearing the low even hint of breathing, aware of her own breathing, making it obvious that this was a showdown of some sort. After a few moments, she felt a smile growing on her lips, so pleased with herself, challenging the fear, so able to take things into her own hands, to meet the invitation.

What was the person on the other end thinking now? What was she thinking?

"Hello, Mommy," Yvonne said, kissing the receiver. "I love you, Mommy." Silence from the other end. She hung up and downed her glass of wine. Grinning, she went for another.

After finishing off two more quick glasses of wine, she stripped down, unhooked her bra and checked the cuts on her breasts, running her fingers over them, thrillingly unsettled by the sparks of pain. She stepped out of her panties, feeling revived just getting out of her clothes. She pulled on a sleeveless black tube dress, carefully fitting it down along her sore breasts, flicked her long black hair out over her back and left the undergarments on the floor where they had fallen.

Again, she thought of Zack and the look that she was after, how she wanted to portray herself to him. She went into her bedroom and rummaged through the small wicker basket on her dresser, found the black nail polish and the black lipstick, returned to the living room to sit on the couch and place the nail polish on the coffee table, stroking her nails with the tiny brush, studying the blackness, the sweat rising to her pale skin, her hand trembling slightly. The soggy tortilla and browned avocado were sitting heavy in her stomach. Or was it just a nervous stomach? She felt that urge, the urge that warned her anything might happen.

The air in her apartment was stuffy, even though the sun was almost at the horizon. The still heat hung in the apartment like an oppressive force all unto itself. She was accustomed to this sort of heat from Toronto, but there were plenty of air conditioners to give some relief. That was one of the things she did not miss about Toronto. The summer heatwaves. The metal and concrete heat that made it difficult to breathe.

"I need a fan," she said aloud. "Beg, borrow or steal." She thought of trying the malls again. Maybe a new shipment had arrived. It was impossible to get a breeze going in her apartment. She had opened the old windows (they'd been opened for days now), but there were no windows on the other side of the apartment, so no draft could filter through.

A fan. She blew a few strands of black hair away from her lips and stroked the black polish onto her pinky.

With a little luck Zack would have a fan for her. Maybe even something more than that, she hoped, picturing the sheen of his skin, the unyielding stiffness of him going in and out of her. There was something truly hedonistic about having sex in this kind of heat, something so consumptive and overpowering about letting loose.

Pleased with herself, she finished her other hand, then blew on her nails, going into the bathroom to gingerly stroke the black lipstick on. Satisfied with the effect in the mirror, she downed another glass of wine then moved toward her door in her bare feet, opened it and stepped out into the hallway. Slowly swishing her fingers in the air, to dry her nails, she paused, catching the sounds of a whirring fan, her ears pricking up. It was coming from Mr. Prouse's apartment. She quietly drifted over to the crack in his door, moving closer to peer in, holding the door frame, the wine setting a dull mischievous glint in her eyes, an unsubstantial wavering that seemed to darken her very blood-line.

Mr. Prouse was in profile to her. He was sitting shirtless in a recliner, the curly silver hair on his shoulders and chest thicker than she expected. He was watching a video of two naked women. At first, she darted back, not wanting him to see her. But then she was entranced by the sight of it. Leaning back in, she trained her eye on her neighbour's hand, steadied between his legs, stroking himself larger. He wasn't wearing shorts. Why had he left the door ajar? Had he been expecting her? Or was he an exhibitionist? Her eyes drifted back toward the television screen.

The loveliness of the two naked bodies, her heart aching, her hand reaching forward to soundlessly push the door open slightly wider, the movement catching Mr. Prouse's eye. At first, he showed concern, his expression stiffening, uncertain of her presence, but then— seeing the sexually devious look in her eyes as she stepped in— he hesitantly smiled in welcome.

Without uttering a word, Yvonne prowled near the screen, calculating each bold step. Teetering before him, staring down, further intoxicated by her position above him, her position of control, she quietly kneeled, ignoring Prouse as she sat on her haunches, the material of her dress catching in the nicks on her breasts, and glanced back at the screen, watching the women move atop each other, wearing nothing but white garters and nylons. The blonde woman held the brown hair of the slighter woman, a tangle of hair in her fist as she pressed the woman's face between her legs. Pleasure lifting her features, her eyes shutting, lips parting to take a luscious breath.

Yvonne knelt up and faced Mr. Prouse. The size of his penis was intriguing. Unexpectedly, it was thick and long and rock-hard. She reached out and took hold of it.

"You want me to suck you off?"

Prouse, eyes glazing over, nodded quietly.

Yvonne teasingly lowered her mouth, dabbing the tip with her tongue before working up and down, savouring, performing the show for him. She pushed his cock down her throat, burying it deeper until she felt the first urge. She breathed through her nostrils, the sucking sound turning wetter. Again, she deep-throated him, feeling the soggy tortilla and brown avocado coming up in her throat. She heaved, but swallowed, water rushing to her eyes while she tried to hold that sexy look.

Without glancing at Prouse, she turned and dropped forward, on all fours, waiting, anticipating, sensing the illicit thrill of what might happen. Bravely, impetuously, she reached behind to coax up the hem of her tube dress. She felt the television images flicker across her face, the women displaying such erotic care in their loving, such grace and faultless passion.

She felt Mr. Prouse kneeling behind her, his fingers brushing her skin, alerting her to the coming entry. The touching between her legs, the gentle stroking that found her wet. And then the entry, the thrust that made one of the women dead. One of the women dead. Her mind replaying the treacherous scenario as she wet her fingers, then pushed them down her throat.

Vomiting, she neared climax, retching and groaning, the water in her eyes resembling tears, the retching tears she had cried since that day she stood in the warm moist air of the red-shadowed room, watching what had happened so many years ago but seeming like only yesterday. Crying as she vomited onto her landlord's rug, her cunt clamping desperately tighter around Prouse's cock with each violent contraction of her stomach.

Zack took great pains to sustain his image as an intriguing and prodigious young artist with a dangerous edge. Dangerous. He wanted to be dangerous and last night he had gone there, had delved deeply into that chasm. Yvonne and her blood, the violence, the carnal disorder that burned a flush into his cheeks. Yes, he was dangerous. If only the critics knew how menacing he truly could be. One of the local critics had called him: "An emerging artist with dark austere vision." His work was described as "raw and powerful." Weak sloppy words that said nothing, Zack assured himself condemningly. And now this critic. This stupid critic from Toronto. Zack fantasized about ripping his throat out.

How many times had he read the word "powerful" in reviews of movies, books, music? The word simply wandered around the guts of the matter, the description missing the mark entirely. But critics were mostly a pathetic bunch of losers. Flush the toilet and they disappeared. Zack's favourite quote. He had come up with it himself and tossed it out at his favourite bars whenever anyone was willing to listen, usually younger women. He could go on and on about critics and often did to his friends and acquaintances that he spoke with at the Ship Inn while downing glasses of Southern Comfort.

"A critic is .1% artist and 99.9% failure," he'd often say. "They have no vision. If they had vision, they'd be artists, not miserable ditherers who get off on slashing other people's work to bits. Jealous fucks."

He'd been interviewed a few times, mostly by student newspapers. The alternative newspaper— NOW— and a few underground magazines had interviewed him while he was in Toronto for the opening of an exhibit of young artists that featured his work.

The generic question had been: "Why is your work always so dark?" and he had responded with "Why are you here interviewing me?" This particular interviewer— a girl with a shaved head and a stud in her left nostril— had simply nodded and smiled in camaraderie, although he felt she hadn't gotten the point at all, was merely trying to act hip, nodding her head like that and agreeing with such vigour. So Zack was forced to add, "Because people have a fascination with darkness, attraction-repulsion." The young woman had approved and— after countless drinks at a black-walled graffiti-covered club on Queen Street West and much forgotten conversation— they had ended up in her bed together in a dump with a mattress on the floor and books and magazines littering the place. She had been a wretched lay, not adventurous, as he had hoped. The major papers, the *Toronto Star* and the *Globe & Mail* were obviously afraid of his vision. They refused to interview him. The commercial press was terrified of artists who might offend someone.

A few months back, a woman producer from CBC's *Midday* had called, saying that they wanted to interview him in his apartment (after he had returned from the Toronto opening) and he had reluctantly agreed, telling his friends that he would show them a thing or two. He was only doing interviews now because he needed to gain a footing; once he was established he would refuse all interviews. No time for them. He would be a recluse and avoid the media. Maybe come out of hiding once every ten years for a major television interview with Connie Chung or something like that.

When the female producer, a woman named Delia Butkin, called to do the pre-interview, he had tried to contain himself, but had gotten out of hand, fired up, his cheeks burning as he explained his vision, to disrupt the complacency of the hordes who had become numbed by the televised nipple. His purpose was to violate them visually, to slash up their petty thoughts. He had gone on and on and had realized, after hanging up the phone, that he had done the number on himself. The next day Delia Butkin called back to say that the St. John's crew was occupied with other things, extremely busy and wouldn't be able to get to him. "We'll just have to postpone it," she told him.

Zack had painted his apartment, arranged his studio for perfect presentation. "Until when?" he'd asked.

"Indefinitely," she had said.

Fuck *Midday*. Fuck CBC, for that matter. So cozy and complacent, so upper-middle class. So highbrow. Great for professors, yuppies and old ladies. And that Malerie what's her name, the redhead, Christ, how much of her sugary shit could a person take? The only one worth her salary had been Pamela Rawlins. She had it together. She had the guts. She wouldn't take the crap. She dug for the truth, wouldn't be put off by rhetoric and formula answers, and so they'd fired her. Just their style.

Zack was on a rant, pacing his apartment, after having just come in and opened his mail. "Fucking press," he cursed aloud, you have to spell everything out for them. They're the worst kind of vultures, making a secondhand living off the original work of others. He'd like to break their fucking necks.

He had received a review in the mail, reading it again for the fifteenth time. It was about the exhibit in Toronto featuring his work and a few other young less gifted Newfoundlander painters. The reviewer had written: "Zack Brett's vision is of the basest quality. Darkness simply to be dark. Offensiveness for its own sake. There is little here to suggest endurance. However, one finds a flash of competence here and there that might suggest that with a great deal of work and application, he might someday amount to a minor artist."

"What's the matter with people?" he muttered, "Unhappy. Petty lives." He went over to the kitchen table and picked up the review from where he had thrown it down. He scanned it and dropped it again, let it settle on the table and picked up his pack of cigarettes, ferociously dug one out and lit it with a vengeance, slamming the lighter down on the table with such force that he was not certain if there had been a knock on his door or if it was the sound of his fury, echoing, rebounding, striking the door.

He paused, swiped a trickle of sweat from his temple and listened, his glance darting toward the hallway. He picked up the review and stepped into the living room. Who was it now? Who would dare visit him at a time like this?

The knock, a low delicate tapping. A woman's knocking. Yvonne? If he opened the door he would not be held responsible for his actions. He knew that things could go very badly for her. They would argue, or worse. His nerves sparked beneath his skin. And this fucking heat. Fucking, fucking heat. He dragged the back of his arm across his lips. Yvonne must have heard him slam down the lighter. She knew that he was in there.

"Yes," he called, gruffly. He snatched a draw from his cigarette, harshly blew the smoke out of his flared nostrils, licked sweat from above his top lip.

"It's Yvonne," her sweet voice dulled by the thickness of the door.

"Hang on." He laid the photocopy of the review on the centre cushion of his worn couch. She would see it there. At least he might be able to get a bit of sympathy from her. That would be reassuring. After all, she admired his work. He would be able to talk about it with someone. Whatever good that would do!

Zack made certain the photocopy could be seen as he backed away from it, crossing the living room for the door. When he opened it, he saw that Yvonne was leaning on the doorway casing, her eyes closed, her expression completely relaxed, as if she was drugged up. She opened her eyes to see his face, his eyes intensely watching her.

She's tired, Zack thought angrily, or drunk. Great! She needs comforting, too. What good is that to me?

"Hi," she said, reaching for his t-shirt.

"Hi." He was curt with her, his eyes mean and uncaring. He knew the look, had practised it often enough. He stared at her chest. "How's your tit?"

"So," Yvonne said in an enchanting, dripping tone, ignoring his anger, "do you still objectify me?"

TEN

Wednesday morning Gregory Kieley was sitting on the couch beside his mother's empty rocker. He heard the toilet flushing down the hallway, the sound of the door unlocking.

"Are you not working today?" Mrs. Kieley asked him as she stepped into the living room. She went over and sat in her chair, watching him with a worried expression. "Are you sick, Gregory?"

"No. Time off." He glanced toward the window, seeing the trees stirring in the slight morning breeze. The day had not yet heated up. It was almost bearable in the apartment. He had switched off the fan his mother had taken from the St. Agnes Home. He didn't like the sound it made and— besides— the air was breathable.

"You turned off the fan. Are you chilled?"

"I'm fine." He sighed, stood from the couch, and went out into the kitchen to pour himself a bowl of cinnamon-flavoured cereal. He leaned into the fridge, admiring the rush of the air on his face, lifted out the milk. Pouring it into his bowl, he was startled by his mother coming up behind him. He spilled a small splash and immediately went to the sink to snatch up the cloth, wipe it up.

"Sorry," his mother said.

"It's okay."

"Are you okay, Gregory?" She sat at the kitchen table, her soft face cramped with worry.

Stop following me, he wanted to say. Just let me be, leave me alone.

"Didn't sleep well," he confessed, turning to give her a brief kind smile as he wiped up the counter.

"I know. Me, too, my love."

He tossed the washcloth into the sink.

"Is this murder case bothering you?"

"I don't know." He lifted a spoon from the drawer and sat at the table. "Maybe."

"You're always like this when you're working on something." She pulled out a chair across from him and sat. "When you're close to shutting someone down."

"Shutting someone down?" The statement made him smile.

"That's right."

"You're watching too much TV, Mom." He spooned the cereal into his mouth and chewed.

"What're you thinking about, Greg?"

"Nothing." He raised the spoon dismissively, slipped it in his mouth. Discovering that it was empty, the cool steel against his teeth, he dipped it back toward his bowl.

"Always thinking, off somewhere, always so distant, ever since you were a little boy. But worse since the Yukon."

His expression remained unchanged as he scraped the cereal down from the sides of the bowl.

"The Yukon," his mother said, a hint of genuine uncertainty in her shaky voice. "Is that where you changed so much?" She leaned ahead slightly to look into his eyes.

"I'm not in the mood to talk about that," he indicated, unwilling to meet his mother's eyes. Instead, his eyes skimmed over the headlines of yesterday's *Evening Telegram*. He lifted a spoonful of sugary milk and read about charges of government patronage, an earthquake in Mexico and the murders...

Mrs. Kieley watched him in a daze, as if she were somewhere between a dream and waking. She studied his lips for a moment, her soft eyes growing sad, her wrinkled eyelids drooping.

"You weren't in the Yukon," she said, needing so desperately to speak the words.

"Sure I was." Gregory Kieley had read several books about the Yukon. The days of the Gold Rush. The history of Dawson City. All the touristy info that he had found in the small library where he had spent all his free time.

A few moments later, he glanced at his mother's eyes, drawn there, but this time it was she who averted his look. She stared away, toward the stove, frowning, her lips trembling, as if she were about to cry.

Zack's image had appeared fleetingly in Yvonne's mind over the course of the trade show. All of her thoughts shifted quickly as new concerns, requests, and preoccupations moved into place, but today was the final day of the two-day event and it seemed to be a great success. Terri was ecstatic; all the comments from exhibitors had been very positive. And so Yvonne focused on the celebration, her mind invariably drifting toward an image of Zack. Zack knew how to celebrate, was the type to say something out of the ordinary, something special that she had not heard before, but he wasn't too far out there, too weird.

She tried not to think of Mr. Prouse, what she had done with him, what she had let him do to her. Her stomach shrank in fear. Mr. Prouse and then Zack. She felt a cringing in her groin when she thought of AIDS. No protection. It always made the thrill more extreme while caught in the heat of it. No protection. She seriously doubted that Mr. Prouse had AIDS. An old man. But Zack— he was a different story.

Hate and love. One of those real relationships, those artistic relationships where they tortured each other and thus intensified the emotion, forged the deep-rooted bond.

Sitting in one of the comfortable armchairs in the Delta lobby, Yvonne gazed down the wide foyer toward the draped tables that acted as registration desks. They signalled the beginning of the convention centre. The mid-afternoon line-ups had dwindled down to a few stray visitors. She could hear the distant buzz occasionally pouring out from the two sets of open double doors. There was nothing more she could do.

Resting as she was, she made plans for after work, her mind always returning to Zack, drawn to the thick smell of paint in his apartment, the paint on his work clothes. The way he spoke, the hidden meanings and innuendos.

Last night, she had insisted that he take her around on a tour of his place.

"See what the freak eats, how it sleeps," he had said in reply, blowing smoke up at the ceiling, obviously displeased with something, in a sour, threatening mood. She could tell just by looking at him. He was seething hatred. His movements said it all as he crushed out his cigarette.

She had wandered toward the hallway, ignoring him. That's what she figured was the best thing to do. He was temperamental, no doubt about it, artists were like that. But they were generally harmless. She hadn't heard of any artists who were criminally insane or anything. She searched through her memory, quickly passing over the image of her mother in her studio back in Toronto, across the street from their apartment on St. Nicholas. Yvonne had often dropped in after school to watch her mother work; Patricia Unwin's gentle hand dabbing the brush against canvas, making colours come to life, so much in her hands, capable of so much. The images. The bodies. The naked female forms.

But that was not what she wanted to recall. Attempting to produce the name of a crazy artist, she came up with Van Gogh. He'd cut off his ear and sent it to his girlfriend. Mutilation. That was true love. That's as much as she remembered about Van Gogh, except his colours, of course, the brilliant strokes of yellows and blues, and then there had been Picasso. He was out of control, but not dangerous. Artists were generally fiery, self-obsessed, but harmless. They harmed people with their ideas, with their minds. That's how they got rid of their anger. They abused people that way. Just as dangerous, but not a crime. Not in this country, anyway. Fucking people over mentally.

"Are you as tragic as Van Gogh?" she'd asked back at him, seeing him down the hallway, keeping a distance from her as she moved toward the open bedroom doorway at the end of the hall. Zack's jaw was fixed, his body wound tight.

"Just as I expected," she said, peeking in, "a mattress on the floor."

"It's a futon," he barked.

"Oh." She moved in through the doorway, glancing up at the ceilings. "You should paint the place, brighten it up."

"I painted it already."

"White. Not very original for a painter," she was being playful, teasing. Zack was not in the mood, but she kept it up regardless, pushing him to see what he would do, how he would react, just how out of control he could be with her. How out of control she could make him.

"Where does an artist get money to live in a place like this?"

"I make money." He leaned in the doorway, picking at one of his thumbnails, then chewing at it.

"Selling art?"

"And other things." He stared at her, spit out the skin he had pulled away from the corner of his thumb.

"Oh. Waiter. Dishwasher. That sort of artist-waiting-to-happen thing?"

The look he gave her could not be more volatile. "What would you know about it?"

"You having fun yet?" she asked when he moved in closer, sucking in his cheeks in a dramatic fashion and glancing around at the mess on the floor. He did not smile, merely stepped past her closely, and went over to where a sketch pad was opened at the far side of his bed. He bent and flipped it shut.

"Secrets?" she asked.

"Yeah. Things you wouldn't understand."

"Oh, yeah." She stepped out through the doorway, his mood souring hers. She paused in front of the second bedroom, the door closed. The design of the house was fairly symmetrical, the layout of his apartment matched hers. This room must be a fairly big one, the high-ceilinged bedrooms generally being twenty by twenty.

"What's in here?" she asked, turning to see Zack's body positioned riskily near her.

"Nothing," he snapped, checking the knob with a rattling twist.

"Touchy," she said, all traces of playfulness shot from her tone.

"It's my studio," Zack said, almost embarrassed. His reaction was peculiar. She had never seen this side of him. He was always so strong and steady, in control.

Yvonne studied his features, the faint blush in his cheeks. She searched his glassy eyes.

"I don't want you going in there," he said. "It's private."

"I want to see."

"No."

She continued watching him, her eyes narrowing, her jaw clenching. "What do you have in there?"

"Nothing."

"It's about me, isn't it?"

"It's a surprise," he admitted, trying to lighten up, to pass it off. "You'll see it, eventually."

"Oh, yeah, is that a fact." She flicked her hair back over her shoulders.

Zack licked his full top lip and turned away.

Yvonne watched him as he paused by the opening to the living room, waiting, staring into the living room, watching her in his peripheral vision, keeping an eye on her. She waited until he finally turned toward her, then tried the knob again, smiling at him, taunting him.

"If you keep doing that," he said.

"What? What're you going to do?"

"Don't tempt me." He squinted, his nostrils flaring.

"No. Let's see it. You gonna hurt me, Mr. Artist?" She held up her hands, flashing her black-polished nails. "You gonna beat me up?"

"That's what you're here for, right? To be hurt, again? You're fucking sick, you know."

"Yeah, well what does that make you?" She snorted a laugh. "You can't hurt me, and besides I've already been fucked once tonight. You don't mind, do you?"

Zack's expression remained fixed on her.

"Just being the slut you want me to be."

Zack stepped toward her, was near in an instant, raging, raising a hand, wanting to strike out. He held his anger in check. "The slut you want to be," he snarled.

"I'm dirty now. Do you like that?" She snatched hold of Zack's hand and slipped it under the hem of her black tube dress. "I'm dirty. You like the feel of that?" She tossed his hand back and slapped him across the face so violently it brought tears to his eyes.

"Don't look to me for sympathy," she said. "I'm not your mommy."

Zack grabbed her and threw her onto the floor.

"Don't hurt me," she said, her face struck with terror, but then laughing, crawling away from him, the hem of her dress up over her waist. He stepped on her foot and she flinched.

"Stay put."

He reached down and forcefully rolled her over, dropped down on her back.

"Nice and sloppy," she grunted, feeling him slip inside her, flinching at the pain in her breasts, but turning it to her favour, devouring it. She struggled away. "Just get it wet," she snorted, "that's all." She clawed at the hallway carpet and slid away from him. Scrambling over the living room threshold, she scooted ahead, up on her feet, and turned to see Zack back in the hallway, his black denims kicked off one foot.

"A little taste," she said, gripping the knob. "See you tomorrow." And she pulled the door open and was out, expecting Zack to follow her, but he didn't. She ran down over the stairs, excited by what she had done, her heart beating violently, the air thinning slightly as she descended.

On her landing, she noticed that Mr. Prouse's door was open. She also noticed that he was not standing in wait, hoping to catch a glimpse of her as she passed. Why wasn't he standing there, desiring her? Why?

She paused, trying to remember if she had locked her apartment. If she did, she had forgotten to take her key and was locked out.

"Great," she whispered, sweat creeping along the creases in the backs of her legs. She blew hair away from her eyes, then ran the back of her hand across her forehead. Glancing at Mr. Prouse's door, she reached for her own knob and found that it was unlocked. She was about to step in when she stopped herself, again glancing back at Prouse's open door, then staring above toward Zack's apartment, a whirlwind of sexual desire sweeping her thoughts away from a daring unbalanced centre.

Letting her knob alone, she crossed the hallway and pushed Prouse's door open slightly; immediately she looked toward the television. It was blank, Prouse's chair empty.

She called out, "Hello," but there was no reply. She stepped in, through the living room, the layout identical to Zack's. The sound of something hitting the floor above her head. She peeked at the ceiling, imagined Zack stomping around in anger, throwing something, smashing something, slashing artwork to pieces. She was delighted that she had inspired such emotion in him. Let him destroy his apartment, let him sit amid the rubble and look around to think of her. From destruction, a deeper love.

She blew breath up at her perpetually sweaty forehead and whispered, "Mr. Prouse," realizing she did not even remember his first name. She moved closer to the blank television, saw the wet spot where she had thrown up only an hour ago. All cleaned up. Turning, she made her way toward the open door, crossed the hallway.

She twisted the knob to her apartment and opened the door.

"Jesus!" she gasped, jutting back two steps.

Mr. Prouse was bent over the coffee table, equally startled by her entry. The vase of flowers he had been arranging toppled over, landing with a dull thud on the Navajo rug, water spilling out, darkening the shades of cream in the jagged lines, deepening the burgundy and the forest-green.

"What're you doing?" she demanded, pointing back at her open door.

"Please," he said, coming toward her, his hands extended, palms raised, exposed in a desperate signal of negotiation. "Please."

She could not believe it. Outraged and confused, her face contorted with shock and vicious disbelief. "What're... Get out."

"Please," he said, racing past her and shutting her door, throwing his body against it so she could not pass.

"Get out," Yvonne yelled, "or I'll..." She glanced around for a weapon, something to throw or strike out with. Her eyes flicked toward the mantelpiece, spotted a ceramic angel sitting on its pedestal, blowing a kiss, a wreath of dried flowers around its head. She took hold of it with one hand and raised it.

"I'll kill you," she roared, her voice scratchy and bullying.

Despite his attempt to confine her, she knew by the pleading look in his eyes that he was terrified.

She was the one in command.

"I love you," Mr. Prouse blurted out. "God, I love you so much." He threw himself at her knees, clutched on. "The way you are. The things you do."

Yvonne could not suppress the disobedient exasperated laugh. Hearing it, Larry Prouse gazed up at her face and laughed outright, too, a blast of relieved air.

"Yes," he said, "I love you. You're just the woman I've been longing for."

"Get out," Yvonne said, her laugh turning hot again, lowering the angel. "Get out."

Mr. Prouse scrambled back on his knees. Standing, he turned and dejectedly opened the door. He paused and faced her again. "Sorry," he said, pointing at the flowers. "I hope you like them." Yvonne stepped nearer and kicked shut the door in his face.

An image of herself in the full-length mirror, the black lipstick, the black nail polish on her raised fingernails, the ceramic angel clutched in her hand. Mr. Prouse was hers now. Her little puppet, a fuck whenever she wanted one. Free rent, maybe. A shiver coursed up her spine as she watched her reflection wavering.

Unbalanced, she cautiously turned away, made her way to the bedroom, detecting a peculiar sound, a mechanized whirring that rose and ebbed. In the bedroom, she glanced around and spotted it almost instantly. There, by the window, plugged in— the fan blasting a wave of cool air across her body. She shut her eyes and thrilled at the relief.

"Another gift from Mr. Loverboy," she said, smiling and then collapsing onto the unmade bed, her fingers on her lips, desperately rubbing them, her knees trembling, her heart beating faster as a wave of dislocation attempted to push her out of her own body. She was fading, drifting into the black abstract, sweating with fear as the panic attack took hold.

The air conditioning in the Delta lobby alerted Yvonne to just how hot it was outside. She glanced through the floor-to-ceiling glass pane, out at the limousine parked in front of the pillars across from the main entrance of the hotel, the sun gleaming off the black paint. Panic attacks usually stayed away from her in daylight. They visited mostly at night.

She had been hoping that Mr. Prouse would not attend the show today and— respectfully— he had not. Then there was Zack, that frightening look in his eyes, his eyelids dusted with powder, his features changing, becoming softer, highlighted by...

"Yvonne," the female voice of someone stepping nearer.

Focusing out of her fantasy, she saw Terri standing before her and was slightly embarrassed to be in a state of arousal with her boss so close by.

"Almost closing time." Terri tapped her watch facing, then folded her arms and bunched her shoulders together, making a cute pleased face.

"You need me?"

Terri's smile broadened. "No, you're on break, right? That's okay."

"It went well, hey." She sat forward in her chair to give the impression of alertness.

"Excellent." Terri offered a broad smile that made her face seem attractive, almost pretty. If she would only smile more, learn how to hold the smile longer before more serious thoughts interfered with it. The smile was a rare thing and it gave her face such vitality. Was it the smile, Yvonne wondered, or the thought of the money that powered the smile? Success.

"We're having a celebratory dinner at the Cellar. Remember?"

"Tonight, right."

"I can count on you to raise a glass?"

Without pause, Yvonne agreed, "Yes, sure. I wouldn't miss it."

"Great." The smile again. "Should be a good time. I'd better head back in." That smile, what it hinted at. A thought struck Yvonne as she watched Terri Lawton walk away. Tingles sparking through her limbs. The telephone calls. The sound of breathing on the other end. It was delicate breathing. Terri Lawton's smile, the knowing look in her eyes, her voice. Was it the voice that she recognized?

The telephone calls. Yvonne straightened in her seat. It made perfect sense. Why hadn't she seen it before? The calls were coming from Terri Lawton.

Cooper circulated a memo among the officers. It requested that if anyone possessed information regarding a violent offender in the area with an electronics background then would they please notify Sergeant Uriah Cooper. There had been two leads, but one of them was already serving time in Kingston and the other had a solid alibi, working on electrical jobs at St. Clare's hospital the nights of both murders.

Cooper called the Spy Depot in Toronto, requesting a list of clients in Newfoundland who had recently purchased surveillance equipment from their mail-order division. He specified anything relating to voice-modification devices. The client list was forthcoming. In a similar vein, he had requested a list of officers who had worked in surveillance in Newfoundland. One of the analysts was working on that.

Cooper was sitting behind his desk in his stark pale blue office, writing out pages and pages of notes, circling items and drawing lines connecting them.

Unwin. He circled the name. Wrote it again. The past. Toronto. He called Butler.

"I told you about Toronto, right?" he asked. "To focus there?"

"Yeah, that's what I'm doing."

"Anything?"

"Not yet. There's hundreds of Unwins, but I'm almost done."

"Is Fahey there?"

"Yes."

"Put him on. Thanks."

There was a silence as the line clicked to hold.

"Constable Fahey."

"Hello, John. This is Uriah Cooper."

"No matching crimes anywhere in Canada yet. Nothing's turned up there. But I was down at the Police Chiefs' convention and I mentioned it to Inspector Craig from Toronto, don't remember the division, but he says the murders sound familiar. He meant to give you a call after he read it in the papers."

"I've got a message from him." Cooper riffled through the five messages on his desk, finding the one in question. "He's at the hotel. I called but couldn't connect."

"He said he was thinking on it. Going to make a few calls back to Toronto. He has recollections."

"That's good." Cooper wrote the word "good" on the message slip, beneath the inspector's name and underlined it. "Thanks, John."

"If there's anything matching, murder-wise, that happened up there, I'll hit it soon."

"Great, thanks." Cooper hung up and stared at the wall across from his desk, the powder blue bulletproof vest hanging on the otherwise empty wooden coat tree.

The coat tree seemed to be stretching, becoming elongated. He took a long pull on a plastic bottle of mineral water, holding the liquid in his mouth, savouring the purity of it before swallowing.

He glanced around, staring at the four walls that made up his small box of an office, again intrigued by what he was doing sitting here, back in the office, back in the same place again. A man in a room trying to stop someone from killing other people. He imagined his exact location flashing on the digitized map in his computer. He had been so many places in the past few hours, but here he was again, as if he had never left his office.

Why here? Why killings?

There had already been a few murders in June, three— in fact— making St. John's (for the first time in history) the murder capital of eastern Canada. But those other murders had been solved in no time. The two down on Casey Street and the other involving Dunkin, from the family of Dunkins noted for their brutality. The police knew who was who in a city. They just had to go and pick the killers up. Simple as that.

But these murders. These female murders were different. Female murders spooked a city. You could kill as many men as you wanted and life went on. But when women died, there was heart-gripping panic.

He turned to his computer screen. It was crowded with text. Words detailing sexual assaults and murders. He read the descriptions, sensing himself becoming aroused. Just a physiological reaction, he assured himself. Get past it. His senses were operating full speed ahead and so he could brilliantly visualize the action behind the words he was reading.

He had to pause, veer away, clear his thoughts by thinking of Natasha, of making love with her in the shower as they had last night. Again, he focused on the words. A woman bashing a man's skull with a hammer while she had sex with him. He imagined Natasha's lips kissing his chest. A woman who had sliced off her lover's scrotum and boiled his testicles. How could anyone do these things? Reading such cases intrigued him. He could not possibly get into their minds, even though this was meant to be his job. How could he possibly understand them, unless he was like them?

To get into their minds would mean becoming insane.

"This is fucking useless." He wondered if fasting produced a state of mind similar to insanity. Sensitization, acute attention to specific details, derailing of conventional thought. The frontal lobe shrinking.

The telephone rang.

Cooper patiently lifted the receiver and listened.

It was Butler. "I found an Unwin in Toronto wrapped up in a murder. A double murder, as a matter of fact, almost ten years ago to the day. Patricia Unwin and another woman— Donna Potter— murdered in bed together."

"Oh, yeah." Cooper doodled, then threw down his pen and sat back in his chair, rubbed his palm along the short bristles on his head. "And?"

"There's a problem we can't seem to figure out."

"What's that?"

"The name of the accused and all information relating to him or her has been stricken from the database."

"What d'you mean?" He leaned forward, picking up his pen again.

"Someone must've been tampering with our system."

"Tampering? How could they tamper?"

"A hacker."

"What about next of kin, for Patricia Unwin?"

"Let me see... She had a husband and a daughter."

"What was the daughter's name?"

"Yvonne."

PART THREE: ANSWERING

ONE

Before leaving the trade show, Yvonne informed Terri that she had to run home first and change for supper. She would've preferred not to join the dinner party. She felt totally burnt out, exhausted from work and from the draining, lingering shadow of her sexual exploits of the previous night.

However, she knew it would be a terrible mistake to not show up for dinner. Some of the staff would be there, maybe even a few choice exhibitors, the ones who had contracted four or more booths. Terri sometimes invited them along for celebrations. They were costly affairs, gourmet meals, countless Scotches, and bottles on top of bottles of aged wine.

Yvonne decided that she would join the group for an hour or so and then excuse herself, claiming exhaustion, sickness, whatever.

Back at her apartment, she noticed the tiny red light flashing on the answering machine and went over to the phone. She pressed the recall button on the caller ID and saw that six calls had been received.

UNKNOWN NAME, UNKNOWN NUMBER flashed up with two repeats, plus another UNKNOWN NAME, UNKNOWN NUMBER with an L in front of it, informing her that it was long distance. Perhaps a credit-card company looking for payment. She went over her bills in her head. Visa, just paid. MasterCard, a few weeks late. Car loan, paid on time, always. She would take no risk with her car. Then who was the long-distance call from? She doubted that her father would have had the nerve to call.

The two remaining calls were from Aunt Muriel and Dr. Healey. In place of his name, the words PRIVATE NAME were displayed, but beneath those words the digits of his home number were plainly listed. He had told her that he rarely gave out his home phone number, but— in her case— it was necessary. She was in an extremely precarious condition. He did not say those exact words, but that was what Yvonne surmised from his mannerisms and expressions, the careful look in his eyes as he watched her. Even though he always seemed mildly distracted, he would focus on her in a stunning way as if she and the distraction both existed in the same place.

"You're obviously a very intelligent woman," he had told her on their first meeting. It had taken him no time to come to this conclusion, besieged by an instant and peculiar sense of interest, hanging on to her every word.

"You're well ahead of most patients. You're aware of your problem. That's the first big step."

Yvonne had taken to Dr. Healey. They shared something intuitive. Despite the doctor-patient relationship, they had bonded in a way that put them both at perfect ease during their informal meetings. Friends, nothing more.

It had been a while since she had visited with him. Lately, the trade show had occupied most of her time. She should make an appointment. She should, but also felt that she shouldn't. Sometimes the appointments seemed like a waste of time, talking and talking and nothing happening. They wore her down.

The telephone rang just as she turned away from the desk with the thought of getting a popsicle, changing her clothes, and sitting for a moment. She turned back and glanced at the listing. UNKNOWN NAME, UNKNOWN NUMBER. She picked up the receiver and listened. Silence. The moist click of her lips about to speak.

"Hello, hello," she said in a child's voice that brought goosebumps to her flesh. She briskly detached herself from her own voice, shutting her eyes and seeing herself as a young teenager.

Utter silence at the other end, and then, "Yes, honey. It's me."

The voice exact. The calls as an adolescent that her father had handed to her with that warning expression on his face, the continued calls from her mother that he allowed her to take. He didn't want to drive a gap between them, he said. Her father, leaving her to talk in private, going into his den and locking the door.

"Hello," she whispered, playing the part, twirling the wire with her finger and bending at the hip. "Is this my mommy? Mommy, is that you?"

"Yes, sweetheart. It's time to go back in."

Zack unlocked the door to the spare bedroom and stepped inside. He left the light off, not wanting anyone to see in from the street. He was naked, as he always was when he came into this room to work and enjoy the intimate presence of what he was creating. The project he had been struggling with was almost finished. Bending down beside his work table, he picked up one of the Polaroids from the floor next to the cushions he had laid out there.

Photo in hand, he moved toward the window and tilted the photo back so that its glossy finish caught the streetlight. He studied the image of Yvonne, her face, the shape of her body from a distance. Sensing a faint rumbling in the wall he was leaned against, he peered down into the dim front yard to see Yvonne hurrying out. Pressing close to the glass, he could see the black top of her head. He glanced back to where the Polaroid camera was resting on his bench, but the flash would give him away. He watched her briskly stride toward the corner that led around back of the house. While she rounded the corner, Zack caught a glimpse of what she was wearing— a white blouse and a short navy blue skirt, more conservative than the black sleeveless tube dress she had worn last night.

He waited for her headlights to appear. Watching the driveway, he noticed a car starting up across the street, headlights off, a man behind the wheel taking a bite from something, the position of his head suggesting that he was watching the driveway.

Just a coincidence, Zack told himself, don't start getting paranoid. It was all bad enough, with Yvonne spiting him this way. She could be so nasty, vicious. She was just the type to head down to George Street— the strip of singles' bars where men and women dressed fashionably and were excessive with money. All flashy sports cars and perfect hair styles. Tight pastel-coloured tank-tops and shorts, the men in white shirts (to show off their spiffy tans) and creased summer slacks, the women tanned beyond belief from lying in solariums. No doubt, Yvonne would go down there and drag someone home just to make him jealous. His guts tightened. Beneath his window, Yvonne's red Escort pulled out into the street, heading east. The car across the street switched on its lights and drove off. Was Yvonne being followed? And by whom? Whom had she pissed off enough to want to follow her? Was she in danger? Zack calmed his thoughts. Yes, just a coincidence.

He shifted his focus to where Yvonne was going. The singles' bar. Again, he felt the aching in that place connecting heart to gut. The singles' bars were rife with superficiality. He despised them. All so frivolous. The thinning of the soul, the breakdown of belief. People becoming more and more frightened to search inside, opting for fashion instead of substance, image only. So afraid to look inside because they might face their own loneliness, their own emptiness.

As a remedy, always keep moving, plenty of action, wild laughter, kicks without pause.

Zack preferred seclusion and the clenching of his soul, working it like a muscle, reading and thinking through the endeavours of the world. North American idealism. How much did he detest it? The soap-opera values. American imperialism. Paganism seemed the way for him, at one with the elements of the earth. But he knew he must first lose the hatred and bitterness he felt toward the common man. Common. The value of intellect was diminishing year by year. The populace despising artists. Painters, writers, dancers were looked upon as lazy bums who should grow up and get real jobs. Where was the admiration that people once held for artists? They were once revered, considered the most powerful of people, sculptors of the soul, voices of the times, priests of the invisible. That sentiment had been quashed. By what? The proliferation of the empty image, the living out of other people's lives as seen on television. Never your own life. It must resemble someone else's. And you must make money. Piles of it.

Zack was certain that Yvonne was heading downtown to get drunk, to celebrate the completion of her trade show (and celebrate without him). Maybe the man in the car was meeting her somewhere and had waited outside to make certain she was coming. It took all sorts. Two of them arriving home drunk, sexual play. Another man with Yvonne, or maybe a woman. Was she bisexual? She was just that type, too. Anything goes. He had experienced her "anything goes" on a first-hand basis.

The knot in his stomach tightened, the agonizing want of her, the brutal taste in his mouth. She was doing all of this to him. She was doing it to drive him out of his mind, to torment him in this stretch of staggering humidity. How could he stop himself from thinking of her? It was not possible.

He glanced at what he was planning, turning to study the progression of the project. He stepped towards it and wondered what Yvonne would think when she discovered the true depth of his obsession.

Yvonne's assumptions had been incorrect. When she arrived at the Cellar, she was led through the restaurant into the private eating area with books recessed in the walls and muted lighting. There she saw Terri sitting alone at a table for two. Terri had been watching the entranceway for Yvonne's approach and smiled congenially.

"I ordered some wine," she said, her smile widening. She stood and kissed Yvonne on the cheek.

Flustered slightly by the kiss, Yvonne nodded thanks to the maitre d' for pulling out her chair. She sat, trying to mask her confusion, as the maitre d' lifted the bottle of wine from the brown stoneware cooler, pausing for Yvonne's okay.

"Yes, thanks," she said, glancing at his handsome composed face. She held the stem of her glass as he poured, and then she raised it to drink. Done with his service, the maitre d' dipped his head and left them to enjoy each other's company.

"Congrats," said Terri, raising her glass high.

Yvonne joined in the salutation, the glasses clinking, and they both drank to the toast, Terri smiling behind the rim.

"I was expecting to see Carol and Pamela," Yvonne commented in an off-handed way, dabbing her lips with the white napkin.

"They had other plans." With these words, Terri glanced away, and Yvonne knew immediately that her boss was lying. Regardless, she accepted the explanation. She would try to enjoy herself. A free meal and good wine. Why not? "Were you happy with the attendance?"

Terri, done with cheerfully surveying the other tables, returned her attention to Yvonne. "Yes. Couldn't have been better."

"It's great when everything goes well."

"It's all such a gamble." Terri indulged in another sip of wine. "With the consumer shows, if I don't get the attendance, I can lose twenty thousand dollars, just like that." She snapped her fingers, smartly.

"Must be hard on the nerves." Lifting a bun from the basket, Yvonne set it on her plate, cut it and slathered it with great heaps of butter. She didn't usually eat butter at home, but when she was out there was something tasty about it.

"The business shows are a little more stable. The booth costs are higher, so the attendance isn't a major economic factor. Everything's paid for if you have a full floor plan."

Yvonne had surmised as much. She had figured out the business the first few weeks working there. It was relatively easy to run such an operation. She had even thought of getting into the business herself. With the knowledge she picked up from Terri, she would be able to go out on her own. But there was more that she needed to learn, particular things about marketing that Terri would never share openly with her.

"It's not as easy as a person might think," Terri said, as if sensing Yvonne's thoughts. "You need connections, and a strong background in marketing. A young slave who worked for me a few years back thought he could compete against me." Terri smiled and snorted contemptuously, glancing at Yvonne's lips as she took a nibble of bun. "He had to file for personal bankruptcy. Twenty-three years old." She raised her hands in exasperation. "Didn't even have the sense to get incorporated. He lost everything. Car. All his belongings. Serves him right."

"People think everything is easy, especially the ones who have no idea at all." Yvonne smiled at Terri, the wine beginning to settle her nerves, to encourage social graces. Yvonne knew the wine could have leaned her either way, drawing her into a deeper sense of moroseness or easing her thoughts. She was pleased that whatever governed her disposition had opted for an easing. After all, she was supposed to be celebrating.

"Everything's a gamble." A glint in Terri's eyes as she glanced at Yvonne's fingers. "We all gamble every day, hoping the odds will switch in our favour."

"I guess."

"Look at politicians, for instance. They're the worst gamblers of all. Bad addiction, gambling with our lives." Terri paused, giving her head a slight shake. "Don't let me get into that. Politicians." She gave a mock giddy shiver and sipped more wine, glanced at Yvonne's white blouse. "Always fighting with the government. Business."

"Cheers," Yvonne said to change the topic.

"To success."

They clinked glasses and Terri's face beamed with brighter pleasure. Again, she glanced at Yvonne's gold ring with its red garnet.

"That's a lovely ring," Terri said, holding out her hand for Yvonne to present her fingers. Complying, Yvonne leaned forward, her breasts brushing the edge of the table, setting off a flurry of pain. She gently laid her palm against Terri's. "It's old. Was it your mother's?"

"Yes," she said, carefully prying it off and handing it to Terri. "You want to try it on?"

Terri accepted the offer, slipping it onto her finger and holding up her hand, admiring it, then turning her hand so that Yvonne could have a look.

"What d'you think?"

"Thanks for inviting me," she said, her tone saucier than expected.

Terri stared into her eyes and gave an abrupt, knowing laugh as if everything had been determined for her. She slipped off the ring and watched her fingers as she gently laid it in Yvonne's opened palm.

"We are alike, aren't we," she said, as the waiter approached to enquire if they were ready to order.

Hesitantly, Yvonne nodded.

The two women left the restaurant at 8:17 p.m. It was a humid, sticky night. All movement seemed slowed; even the passing cars appeared sluggish. The two women strolled leisurely toward the Atlantic Place parking garage directly behind the restaurant, chatting about something.

The man waited for Terri Lawton's mini-van to arrive on the exit ramp and then pulled out of his parking space across from the dimly lighted entrance to the Cellar.

He knew all about Terri Lawton and her sexual preferences. He was surprised to see that Yvonne had left with the woman, had left her own car parked a few spaces over from his to join Terri in her mini-van. But— perhaps— not so surprised at all. He followed them to Terri Lawton's house on Gower Street, a three-minute drive from the parking garage, up the steep grade of Prescott Street and then right, along the long strip of heritage homes. When he was a boy, Gower Street had been a slum, one of the worst areas in town, high crime rate, white trash, but then the heritage craze hit and the yuppies bought up the houses. Renovation became all the rage. Everything done over and painted with the utmost care, the eves and window trims highlighted with aristocratic colours— burgundy and cream, clapboards painted olive, slate blue, burnt orange...

The van parked in front of Terri Lawton's house. Terri stepped out and moved around back, to the passenger side. She slid open the wide door, saying a few words to Yvonne while lifting out a box. Yvonne stepped up beside her and grabbed one.

An acceptable ploy, the man thought, tell Yvonne that she needed help unloading boxes from the show site, then ask her in for a drink and close in for the kill.

They made two more trips. On the final trip in, Terri pulled shut the front door of the salmon-coloured row house with white trim and lovely flower boxes beneath the windows a mere few feet back from the sidewalk.

The man waited patiently, knowing the women would not be in each other's company for very much longer. Some time later, he checked his watch as the front door opened. Twenty-three minutes had passed and Yvonne Unwin hurried out, alone, slammed the door, her arms hugging her chest.

The white blouse and navy blue skirt she wore were not enough to make her body feel warm, even in this heat. Furiously, she walked off, heading east along the gentle slopes and rises of Gower Street toward the distant grey Hotel Newfoundland. There she could easily get a cab from the line of taxis parked out front.

The man stepped out of his car and wandered over to Terri Lawton's house. Testing the doorknob to find it unlocked, he knew better than to glance around the street, to check doorways and windows. He paused for a moment, taking a deep breath.

Constable Pendegast started awake. He was having a wonderful dream about three pumped-up blondes lifting him over their heads. But suddenly there were lights shining in his eyes, two bright lights blinding him for a moment before arcing away. The sensation of his dream was soon erased as he realized— with mounting dread— that he had fallen asleep on the job. Classic surveillance fuck-up.

Cursing himself, he slammed the steering wheel and jumped out of his car, racing toward the Cellar. He threw open the door, ran around from table to table with his badge held in the air, knowing in his gut that it was too late, knowing that Unwin had left with the woman she had met there. He had already been in once, glancing around as if searching out a dinner guest, and had found Unwin neatly nestled away with her dyke friend in the private eating area.

Pendegast accosted the manager, speaking quickly, erratically, wanting answers.

"The two women sitting together in the private area. Younger woman, older woman. How long ago? How'd she pay?" He made them dig out the credit card receipt to get her name, threw open the telephone book and found one Lawton listed on Gower Street.

"Out of my way," he shouted, turning for the doorway, wanting to push people from his path, but— unfortunately— no one was standing in his way.

The man had just gripped the knob to Terri Lawton's house when he noticed the faint headlights from an approaching car. Testing the knob, he found that it was unlocked and regretted having to stroll on, drift away from the door, just to be safe. Twenty feet down the street, he ducked into a doorway, watching the car screech to a stop. A muscular man with a fancy hair-do sprang from the vehicle and raced toward Lawton's door. He crashed it open with his shoulder, not even bothering to test the knob.

A few seconds later, the shrill pitch of a woman's scream sounded from within Lawton's house.

The telephone rang and Sergeant Uriah Cooper, pausing from typing an e-mail message to Richard Higgins in Oxford, grabbed for the receiver. He glanced at his watch, slightly after midnight.

"Sergeant Cooper, CID."

"Doctor Sergeant." The woman's voice? The man's?

Cooper straightened in his chair, switched on his mini recorder.

"Yes?"

"What're you waiting for? Another cunt-loving-cunt to be killed? Shoved in the closet where she belongs? Haven't you checked the file?"

"What file?" Cooper asked, exasperated.

"I sent you a file when I saw that story about you in the paper. The one where you shut down that serial rapist."

Silence from Cooper, trying to keep the caller on the phone.

The voice tittered, "Someone must be stealing your mail."

"I doubt that."

"You know what to do. Don't act stupid."

"Tell me what to do."

"Clear it up."

"Clear what up?"

"The past."

"How would I do that?"

"Find out who's really guilty. Find that out."

"Tell me."

"Don't you know who I am?"

"How can I know, if you don't tell me? You're the one who knows. You're the one with the power here."

"I'm Patricia Unwin. Want me to spell it for you? I live at 64 LeMarchant Road, and I'm almost dead again, this time for good."

"Patricia?"

"I meant Yvonne." The line went dead.

Immediately, Cooper telephoned the switchboard in the main building and requested the number on the incoming call he had just received.

While he was waiting, he switched to another line and contacted the communications centre. He was told by the communications officer that the number was from a cellular owned by William Gaston. He was given the address— 1262 St. Clair Avenue. He switched back to the first line and was informed that the reading had come up UNKNOWN NAME, UNKNOWN NUMBER. Cooper stood and lifted his suit jacket from the back of the chair, shoved his arms into the sleeves. He knew that something was very wrong about this. Something was way off about the idea of a cellular.

Yvonne was dreaming about her mother.

Her mother was painting, and softly speaking. "Did you ever notice how many people there are on the sidewalks, so close together, almost on top of each other? They just pass by without even looking at the eyes of these strangers, who could be friends or enemies. Why aren't they harming each other, or touching each other, so close... Millions of people. Just flowing by." She was painting what she was saying, her words somehow translating perfectly into images. Yvonne was young, a girl, and her mother was stroking the canvas that turned out to be Yvonne's body. Stroking it with her fingers that were tipped with the fine soft horse hairs of paint brushes.

Then there was the sound of chopping. She was in her childhood house in the place they called The Gut, a small fishing inlet on the east side of St. John's where she had lived before her family moved to Toronto. The house was dark and there was a chopping sound. She imagined her mother cutting the heads from codfish on a splitting table in the back yard. The smell of fish. A rotting fish head beneath the hem of a dress.

Disturbed by the prospect of witnessing the decapitation, she believed that she was somehow involved in the operation, that it was really her holding the blade. But when she arrived at the dark back door, she opened it to see that it was not the back door at all, but a deep closet, with clothes she pawed through, fabrics of various colours and textures, silks and cottons, velvets, until she saw the flesh ahead, the body of the woman, the naked body in the closet.

The smell of fish. No, of something else. A head between a woman's legs. Her own head, eyeless, rotting.

She awoke in a sweat and quickly sat up in her bed, focusing out of the dream. Her mother had never cut the heads from codfish. There was no splitting table in her back yard. They were not involved in any way in the fishery. These discrepancies unnerved her. She could not make sense of any of it. The lingering image of rotten fish made her panicky, her ears still hearing the sound of chopping, then, vaguely, ringing.

A knocking on her door. She threw her legs over the side of her bed and hurried for the door, her knees weak, sweat trickling down the insides of her legs, her voice even weaker, scratchy, when she called, "Yes."

"It's Mommy, Yvonne." The chilling voice behind the door, bathing her in hot and cool sweat.

"Yes," she said with dread, swallowing hard, believing that she might be still dreaming, the tingling beneath her skin convincing her that she was— only now— slowly drifting into startling realization or away from it. She was having trouble breathing in this world, this real world, her heart racing, hammering in the back of her neck. She was guilty of something, her dream had been implying as much.

A moment passed and she was reaching for the doorknob, clutching the smooth metal and trying to turn it, but someone was holding it firmly on the other side. A solid grip.

She was not dreaming, although it felt as if she was, the brash colliding unrealness of the scene. This real world. This too-real world.

"Yvonne? Baby? You're finding me."

"Please don't hurt me," she whimpered, backing away from the door. "Please, please, please..." She heard footsteps lightly moving away, out in the hallway.

"Mommy?" she pleaded, rushing for the door, trying the knob again. This time, it turned easily in her hand. And when she opened the door, she saw that no one was standing there. She listened carefully, beyond the pounding of her heartbeat, hearing the faint sound of what she believed to be a door quietly shutting, up on the second floor.

TWO

"I have to say that I'm really pleased to see you," Dr. Healey evenly allowed, his tone implying inherent concern. Leaned forward in his leather chair across from Yvonne, he gave her a consoling smile. "It's been a while since our last visit. How did the show go?"

"Very well." Yvonne was seated in an identical leather chair no more than three feet away from Dr. Healey; the chairs were situated in front of the doctor's desk. Yvonne knew that they were arranged this way for some specific reason. To keep the doctor and client (as doctor Healey referred to his patients) on equal terms or something psychological like that, to develop a comfortable relationship so the client would be at peace, speak freely of what was troubling her, expose herself to this complete stranger with a diploma that allowed him knowledge of the most intimate details of her life. This mental voodoo man at whom she now stared with questionable eyes.

"How are you feeling today?"

"Fine." Over the years, Yvonne had read countless psychology books, trying to figure herself out, to delve to the root of her problem. She had searched for some recognition, some glimmer of hope that she was not as deviant as she suspected. She particularly identified with Freud's theories and took comfort in his focus on sexuality. She too believed that a great deal of behaviour sprouted from the urge.

Dr. Healey watched her searchingly, his small blue eyes seemingly set too far apart on his broad face, making him appear like some sort of inquisitive insect. "I've been concerned about you because of these murders."

"Really." Yvonne shifted in her chair, yanked down the hem of the skirt, where it had hiked up slightly, and smoothed the fabric. She had felt the chill from the air conditioning in the doctor's office gently touching her along her warm thighs. The pain in her breasts had made its presence known when she tugged at her dress. The throbbing was not so bad today, the wounds beginning to heal, become slightly itchy.

Healey straightened in his chair. "Yes," he said, joining his hands in his lap. He had rolled up the sleeves of his turquoise shirt and Yvonne saw— for the first time— the small tattoo on the pale skin of his forearm. A rose. She had never seen this before. A peculiar tattoo for a man. She studied his features, his pale complexion, his thinning brown hair-line, his narrow lips. He was attractive in an original sort of way, his intelligence, his sensitive, almost feminine, features, the sculpted shape of his head giving him a look of quiet refinement, of delicate yet unyielding contentment.

"These murders. Do you want to talk about them?"

"I don't know," was the only reply she could come up with. She felt dazed, detached in a drug-like way as she mentally recounted last night's episode with Terri Lawton. The pale yellow of the office walls further subdued her. She stared at the artwork. Picasso's disjointed faces. Fractured landscapes by another painter, everything broken into cubes.

"Are you worried for your safety?"

"I don't know."

"You can tell me anything," Healey kindly suggested, blinking, but holding the blink a moment too long, one of his idiosyncrasies. "Speaking things aloud is the first step to getting a better perspective on our lives, admitting our fears and inadequacies to ourselves. To hear them spoken makes them real."

"I can't tell if I'm worried."

Healey nodded consolingly, then rested his head against his spread thumb and index finger, his elbow propped against the armrest of the chair. "It's okay. Just take your time."

"I can't tell."

"Do you think these murders might be committed by the same man who killed your mother? The method of murder was strangulation with telephone wire. And the way they were discovered— the bodies in the closets— mirrors... A coincidence perhaps." Again, the extended blink.

Yvonne remained silent, uncertain in her thoughts, uncertain what Dr. Healey was trying to get at.

"This is why I'm concerned. Even though you were there when your mother was murdered and you identified Gregory Potter in court, your mind suffered such a trauma..."

"...that I've blocked out any sort of image of him," Yvonne finished the sentence for him. "Believe me, I've thought of that."

"Not remembering what he looks like is perfectly natural. Post-traumatic stress accounts for a great many things. But the problem is you wouldn't recognize him."

"I don't know. I might," she said distraughtly, her thoughts struggling through images of faces, men's faces flashing through her mind. Different eyes, different lips, different noses, all shifting, instant by instant.

"We can't count on that." Healey searched Yvonne's features, as if attempting to divine the danger she might be in. "Let's move on to other things."

"I'm taking laxatives again," she said matter-of-factly. She thought of how she had cut herself, but would not say a word about it. She did not want to be hospitalized. Healey could do that to her if he thought she was harming herself. But she wasn't harming herself. It was a game with Zack. They were playing a dark violent game that was exciting.

"Why do you think that is?"

"I don't know."

"Possibly it has something to do with these dead women? The anxiety."

Yvonne's expression hardened as she thought of Terri Lawton's sexual advance.

"These killings might be re-enacting what happened with your mother."

Yvonne gave a slight shake of her head.

"We talked about the laxatives in relation to your mother's sexuality; how you might have feared, and perhaps continue to fear, being like her. This element of control over your body."

Remaining still, Yvonne stared at the cubist's face of a woman in the painting directly across from her.

"And so you go about trying to control your desires, your body, by taking laxatives. Denying your body its sustenance." The statement was spoken as a suggestion, almost a question, followed by the blink. "You remember this conversation?"

"Yes."

"And now these murders, and the laxatives. A relation could be gleaned, I believe."

Yvonne observed the features of the painting beginning to shift, to merge toward an image she recognized. Terri Lawton's face appeared to her in the disjointed painting, the woman's face merging with the careful details of her mother's features. The coal-black hair hanging straight and loose.

"Are you aware that both of these murdered women had long black hair?"

"Yes."

"Are you concerned that you might be in danger?"

"Yes."

"Have you contacted the police?"

"No."

Dr. Healey paused, weighing her last response. "All of this must be terribly unsettling for you."

Yvonne said nothing, stared at the eyes shifting, her mother's becoming her own.

"Does it give you a feeling of powerlessness?"

"Yes."

"This could be related to the laxatives as well. You feel out of control. You want control, you want to change. The way to do this is through realigning your body. Making it the way it's expected. So you take laxatives to control your body, to alter the image. Perhaps you're afraid and this is how it manifests itself."

"Yes."

"I really think you should contact the police."

Mention of the police penetrated her stupor. "The police can't help me."

"You don't think?" Healey raised his head from where it was resting against his spread index finger and thumb. He lightly touched his chin.

"Someone has been calling." Yvonne's eyes shot a look at the doctor. He leaned forward, hands joined between his knees, keenly watching her pale face framed by the blackest hair.

"Who?"

"A woman. She keeps calling."

"A friend?" The prolonged blink.

Yvonne squinted, "I don't know."

"What does she want, this woman?"

"She says she's my mother."

"Your mother," Healey whispered softly, glancing at the tape running in the recorder on his desk, checking to make certain the record button had been activated.

Yvonne nodded in a detached way. "Yes." She stared beyond Healey, out the window, the leaves of green trees fluttering, her vision blurring.

"Did you love your mother, Yvonne?"

"Yes." Tears in her eyes, her lips trembling.

"She's on your mind."

"Yes." Yvonne burst into confused tears. Her head tipped forward as if to hide her eyes, yet she made no attempt to cover her face.

Healey tugged a tissue from the box on his desk and leaned forward to hand it to her. He straightened in his chair, tolerantly allowing time for release. He quietly chewed on the inside of his mouth and blinked patiently while studying Yvonne's weeping face.

"Tears are good," he said, in his most calming, reassuring voice. "Tears work wonders."

Yvonne sniffled and wiped at her eyes. She shook her head and stared down at the carpet.

"Could it be possible that Potter followed you from Toronto?"

"I don't know." Again, she sobbed. "I've thought..."

"This man killed your mother. He could be viewing you as your mother. You look very much alike. Seeking revenge for what your mother did. Needing to take revenge on you for identifying him."

Yvonne adamantly shook her head twice, denying it.

"I'm sorry. But I have to say these things. I want you to know the danger that's possible." His words spoken evenly. "Will you please contact the police?"

She wiped at her eyes with the tissue and then crumpled it in her fist, turned her eyes to look up at the ceiling. "Yes."

Healey smiled. "That's great."

"Are we done now?" she asked, her red-rimmed eyes peeking at him.

"I don't know. Is there anything else you'd like to discuss?"

"No." She laid the mangled tissue on the edge of Healey's desk.

"Can we talk briefly about your father?" he discreetly proposed, a speculative uncertainty in his eyes.

"No." Yvonne swiped at her eyes with the butt of her palm.

"You should try."

"There was nothing the matter with him."

"I'm not saying that. But your feelings for him are quite intense."

Yvonne turned her eyes back toward the painting against the sunny yellow wall, disjointed features, eyes out of place, mouth moving, lips growing moist...

"Who do *you* think is killing these women?" Dr. Healey's mouth remained vaguely open, as if anticipating a revelation.

Yvonne was transfixed by the painting. Dr. Healey didn't have to look to see what held his client's interest. He knew what was there, how often Yvonne stared at it.

"A man?"

"I don't know."

"Why do you think these women were killed?"

"Because I'm innocent." Her thoughts elsewhere. Yvonne tilted her head slightly as if recognizing something through the blur. "Because I loved."

"Loved your mother?"

"Yes."

"The way a child loves her mother."

"I don't know what that is."

Dr. Healey glimpsed back at his desk, again checking the tape in his recorder. Finding that there was plenty of time remaining, he faced Yvonne, "Can you tell me who killed your mother?"

"I keep telling you."

"I need to know again, please, Yvonne."

"That man."

"Gregory Potter?" Healey took a quick look at his watch. He hated having to do so, but others were waiting.

Yvonne's brow tightened and she had trouble with the word, "Yes."

The phone on his desk buzzed, signalling the next appointment. Healey leaned back in his chair, blinking, allowing a moment of silence to clear the air between them.

"That woman is very much like your mother," he finally commented, turning to observe the painting, to be a part of what she was feeling, to let her know that he was with her on this. "Apart from herself. Not herself at all. Is that what you believe? Your mother was a very talented painter, wasn't she? Did you know I have a few of her paintings?"

Yvonne stared at the Picasso. The features had aligned perfectly to shape the face of the woman she had once loved more than anyone. The woman who had hurt Yvonne so badly. The woman who had been hurt so badly by love, murdered by love.

THREE

The man slid the SystemsCrasher CD into his terminal and punched up the dial window. He typed in the telephone number for the main terminal at Fort Townshend, hit the enter key, and the disk immediately whirred, working to unscramble the code, flashing through thousands of number and letter combinations.

The man waited and switched on the monitor that gave him a view of Yvonne Unwin's living room. No one there. He clicked on the audio and heard the faint ticking of her wall clock. The computer screen continued to flash, white letters against hunter green, "searching."

Seventeen minutes later, the gold symbol for the Newfoundland Constabulary, the ornate oval with the letter "C" in the centre and the crown atop the oval, appeared against a royal blue background. He typed in the name "Yvonne Unwin" and was surprised to see that she had not been booked. He called up the names of other criminals and studied their colour photographs, read their profiles, scanned their fingerprints. All very interesting. He typed in his own name out of curiosity, and found that it was not there. Maybe again, some day. No, he didn't think so. They would be powerless to bring any serious charge against him for what he was doing. No law could be applied. He had already researched the possibilities.

Cooper hung up the telephone after speaking with the Toronto inspector in his downtown St. John's hotel room. Inspector Craig was familiar with Unwin. It had been a sensational case. The lesbian angle, plus the fact that a police officer with the RCMP had been charged with the double murder. The policeman's name was Gregory Potter. And the women were involved in a lesbian relationship. One of the women was Potter's wife.

Cooper contacted the Toronto RCMP headquarters himself, requesting a sheet on Potter. The clerk put him on hold and then came back on the line to inform Cooper that there was no listing for Gregory Potter in the RCMP's employment database.

"I've just been speaking with Inspector Craig of 48 Division, Metro Police. He's familiar with the case. Gregory Potter was stationed with your RCMP office."

"I'll try again." A few moments later: "No, I'm sorry. Nothing coming up."

"Is it possible the information's in there, just lost?"

"I wouldn't think so."

"Could you try CPIC?"

"For a police officer?"

"Yes, he was convicted."

A moment later, "No, no, nothing there."

Cooper ran his palm over the short bristles of his hair, his eyes shifting searchingly.

"Okay," he said. "Could you check the paper files for his work history?"

"I could. But that'll take quite some time."

"This is in relation to a series of murders in St. John's." Cooper felt like crossing his fingers. "The lesbian killings?"

"Oh, really. Right. That was on the National last night. You must be the famous doctor sergeant." She laughed in a knowing, sympathetic way.

"Yes."

"No problem. I'll get back to you as soon as I can."

"Thanks." Cooper gave the clerk his number, momentarily thankful for the fringe benefits his minor fame allowed. He asked the female officer to fax along the file once it had been cleared by the necessary officer.

Standing from his desk, he shut down his system and clipped on his beeper. Things were going somewhere. He had paths to follow. He felt slightly relieved that the dead end was giving way to a slight footpath.

But then an image of Pendegast made him pause and shake his head. Pendegast, the idiot, had busted in on Terri Lawton, Yvonne Unwin's boss, last night, admitting that he was looking for Unwin. Word would travel back to Yvonne Unwin.

Pendegast! How could he have fallen asleep? It was so characteristic. It was just the kind of thing that would happen to him, like something straight out of a ridiculous cop movie.

"Why so surprised?" he said aloud.

He thought of... It took him— frighteningly— a moment to come up with her name. Natasha. His girlfriend. Natasha. Time to get some sleep, he cautioned himself, can't even remember your girlfriend's name. She hadn't come home last night. After checking out the wire-tap lead at 1262 St. Clair Avenue and discovering— just as he had suspected— that the man was unquestionably innocent (William Gaston had turned out to be a small elderly man with a severe hearing problem and a heart condition, thus the need for a cellular), Cooper had retired home and waited for Natasha's return.

As a distraction, he had taken notes on the case, worked things through regarding the cellular deception, all the while glancing at the clock. The cellular must have been cloned, he told himself. If you had the proper equipment, you could stand by the side of a road and monitor cellular transmissions, steal the necessary info— the ID number and electronic serial number— and then burn it into your own cellular. When the call was traced, the original owner's name and address were identified. Only someone with an extensive electronics background would possess such information. Or a police officer.

He wrote out the name Gregory Potter and glanced at the clock again. He had already issued a Canada-wide warrant for Potter's arrest.

Again, he thought of Natasha. She had probably been down at her place on Victoria Street. He decided that calling her would be the wrong thing to do. He had to trust her. But was he suspicious, or simply worried? Or jealous? She was probably packing things up. The bonfire party had— no doubt— gone on well into the night. Maybe she stayed at a friend's house. Maybe she was with another man. Or a woman.

"Detective Cooper," his name called by several dull muted voices. Cooper paused, realizing he had wandered out of his office and was standing in the parking lot beside his car. He stared toward the reporters. The story had caught on and been sensationalized beyond belief. He counted five vans and three cars beyond the barricade.

He shuddered at the feeling of deja vu as he climbed into his car.

At the barricade, facing the reporters, he waited for the officers to clear a path for his vehicle.

"Detective Cooper," they clamoured, waving pads and recorders as if they were weak-kneed fans craving a few precious words or a coveted autograph. He imagined himself as one of the Beatles, a black wig, British invasion bob, black suit. Who would he be, John Lennon? Ringo Starr? He had to wipe the smile from his lips.

"It's Sergeant, not Detective," he said, rolling down his window. "Detective is American." He imagined how he looked to them. The cameras all pointed his way, like electronic leeches sucking up a shallow representation of his body that they could manipulate later. Freeze frame and wrap words around him until their point was made. Regardless, he was attracted to what might be said, how he could respond out of the ordinary, make a mockery of their game.

Cooper straightened his glasses and felt the plastic edge of the clip-on shades. Cool, he told himself. I'm so fucking cool, man. He watched the crowd of journalists struggling behind the orange barricades, their static in his ears as they shouted to outdo one another. Why were they so anxious, as if they were solving the crime themselves by abstracting information from him?

He scanned the small crowd, the disorder, not saying a word, enjoying the view, the mayhem, so much interest. He thought of the volunteer work he had done at the Grace Hospital, visiting elderly patients and those from out of town. Bringing them in their snacks and having a chat. He recalled one man— Mr. McCoubrey— who hadn't had a visitor in four years. He had been in the same room for four years, no family, no friends. No one cared the slightest about him. He was totally alone. Cooper had asked him if he needed anything and the man had asked for a tin of Orange Crush. Of all things.

Returning from the gift shop, Cooper had popped the tin and set the straw between the man's lips. Mr. McCoubrey had drunk slowly, carefully, his throat slowly constricting and releasing, his doughy eyes searching Cooper's face. When the man was through, he tilted his head away from the straw, releasing it from his lips.

"My God, that was fine," Mr. McCoubrey whispered, "Thank you." His eyes glossing, "God bless you." The image stuck with Cooper. All those lonely people hidden away in institutions. He thought of the work he had done with mentally challenged children. The explicit joy of their ways. If only such causes could get the press lavished on murders.

Cooper straightened his glasses again, the grips slipping on his sweaty nose, the dry heat of the sun full on his face as he watched the cameras and faces beckoning to him. He was no longer amused, no longer smiling. He imagined more and more media. A monstrous crowd. The electronic eye of the entire world.

He opened his door and stepped out to a hush from the reporters. They had not expected such compliance on his behalf. He was aware of his body drifting through the heat, blending with the purifying silence of the crowd. They watched him with reverence. Again, he became amused. His slow smile seemed to raise the volume, the buzz of questions rising before him, as if he was enjoying himself, possessed by movie-star charisma. The questions soon turned to manic shouts as his smile broadened.

"I knew a man named McCoubrey," Cooper began, his voice a murmur. He gently pushed his glasses up tight against the bridge of his nose. "The skin on his hands was soft and transparent. You could count the veins and bones..."

"What?" several reporters shouted. "Could you speak up, what...?"

FOUR

"How is it?" Zack Brett called out. He was seated on the floor, his back against the front of Yvonne's dark green couch. He was eating noddles with chopsticks from a cobalt-blue pottery bowl.

"It's great," Yvonne said from the kitchen.

Zack stood and turned off the television. He hated television. It was so intrusive, so much of a distraction, especially when he was eating. It even seemed to affect his digestion. He had brought down a pot of Thai noodles, having cooked them with Yvonne in mind. A peace offering. He knew when it was time to settle things. Both of them had contributed to the confrontational mood in his apartment the other night. He realized that. He was reasonable, willing to share the blame, if only because he was compulsively attracted to her. He was willing to make concessions to continue being party to her derelict sexual favours that were so hard to find in a city the size of St. John's. The mere thought of what they might do next sped his pulse and turned his breathing hot. There were no limits. He recalled the sweet metallic taste of Yvonne's blood, sucking the gash in her breast while he fucked her.

Yvonne returned to the living room with a bowl balanced in both her hands and set it on the pine coffee table. She kneeled and glanced at the door.

"You're looking good," he said, raising a small shrimp clamped between his chopsticks.

Yvonne smiled morosely. "Sure," arranging her chopsticks between her fingers. "So, which painting was it that sold?"

"One from the *Niggers* series, like the ones in my apartment. It was hanging at Pollyanna. You should drop down and have a look at the others."

Again, Yvonne glanced at the door.

"I love galleries," she said, distracted. "The quiet respect. They're almost like churches, sacred places." Noticing her agitation, Zack looked where she was looking.

"You expecting someone?" he asked, slightly put off by her lack of attention to his success.

"No."

"Just a fascination with doors," he said shortly.

"I'm sorry. I'm expecting a visit."

"From who?" Zack tipped the bowl to scoop up the last bits of noodle stuck to the sides.

"I don't know."

"Well, then, how do you know—"

"I just know." Yvonne said firmly. "I'm sorry, I'm just... I had to quit my job today."

"Why'd you do that?" Leaning forward, Zack set his bowl on coffee table.

"My boss made a pass at me."

"Sexist pig. You should report him."

"You're the sexist pig. My boss was a woman, remember? I already told you that? She made a pass at me last night."

"That's where you went."

"I was out to dinner. It was supposed to be..."

"I saw you going out... Ohhhhh, I get it. With this lesbian killer thing. She's got you spooked."

Yvonne stared at her bowl on the coffee table, barely touched, her chopsticks poised over it.

"You think she's the one doing those women?" He thought of the man in the car who had seemed to be following Yvonne, began to tell her, but stopped himself. She seemed troubled enough. And— besides— Zack was relieved that she wasn't with another man, hadn't been secretly meeting with the man in the car. Or— for that matter— the car just might've been a coincidence. He didn't want to buy into paranoia.

"I don't know."

"Just because she made a pass at you?" He glanced at her breasts.

"Why? Couldn't she be?"

"Those murders have got everyone spooked out. It's all people talk about. All that's on the news. That cop who was in my place. He was on there. He's a strange crime doctor, mind doctor or something. He was just on TV, said something about an old man. They had histories of those dead women on, too, going right back into their pasts. Way back, like they're the ones guilty."

"Guilty of something."

"Yeah, of being lesbians. It's fucking sick."

Yvonne shrugged. "If they weren't that way, then..."

"What? You don't actually believe it was their fault, do you?"

"Forget it." She sighed, picked up her bowl and poked at her noodles.

"So why didn't you have a little roll?" Zack asked, his tone more reasonable, "with your boss."

"Ex-boss," Yvonne corrected, "Mr. Mind In The Gutter," standing and drifting over to the window. She bent back the Venetian slat and peeked out. "So, you've forgiven me," she said with her back to him.

"What for?"

"Leaving you with your dick in your hands." Yvonne laughed at her own humour, turning to smile at him.

"Figuratively speaking, of course."

"Yeah, sure. I meant literally."

It was the first time Zack had seen her kind smile. It touched him deeply, although he would not have admitted it.

Yvonne came over, picked up his empty bowl, and went out into the hallway. Zack heard her scraping the contents of her bowl in the garbage and then putting both bowls in the kitchen sink.

"I wouldn't worry about getting another job," he called out. "You've got the brains and the beauty." He murmured to himself, "And the animal magnetism."

Yvonne returned just as the telephone rang. She frowned and wandered over to the desk to watch the caller ID. It was a local number with PRIVATE NAME printed above it. She recognized the digits as belonging to Terri Lawton; they matched with the ones she had written on the back of the envelope two nights ago. It was still there on the desk. The answering machine beeped, but no message was left.

Sighing, she scanned through the list of digits on her ID machine. There was another call from Muriel Unwin, Aunt Muriel, another L-UNKNOWN NAME, UNKNOWN NUMBER, a long-distance call. The credit-card company? Her father? She'd torn his letter to shreds and thrown it out, unread. Maybe it was something urgent. Maybe he was dying. She didn't want to know. If he was dying she only wanted to know after he was dead. And a closed coffin. She didn't want to see his face ever again.

"I need a job," she said, staring at the caller ID.

"If you need a few bucks," Zack offered.

Something changed in her face, her expression darkening. "You're in better spirits than the other night." Yvonne looked at Zack, almost regretting having spoken the words, bringing up the other night. What was she trying to do?

Couldn't she leave well enough alone? She stepped over and sat on the floor next to him, staring into his eyes, unable to contain her almost taunting smile.

Zack shrugged it off, reaching to brush her long black hair behind her ears. "I'm successful now. I was a failure the other night." He stood, his hips level with the top of her head. He stayed that way for a moment, staring down at her large hazel eyes, her full lips decorated with luscious brownish-red lipstick, his hands in her warm black hair.

"How are you?" he asked, studying the hair at her white temples as he brushed the sleek strands back with his fingertips.

"I've been a bad girl."

"Really? You can't always be a bad girl."

"Yes, I can."

"Why's that?"

"I did some naughty things."

"What?"

"I let Mr. Prouse fuck me."

"Is this fantasy, now?" Zack asked, mildly amused.

"No," she insisted, her eyes eclipsing with sinister intention. "I let him fuck me because I was a bad girl and needed to be punished." She unzipped his denims and kneeled up. "Are you going to punish me?"

"Yes," Zack said, his voice shivering.

"Tell me." She took him in her mouth and shut her eyes to listen.

"I'm going to punish you," he said, his hands tightening their hold on her hair, making two fists as he coaxed his groin forward.

The man switched off the video monitor, bored with the scene. How quickly it turned to sex with her. The slightest twinge of anxiety and she needed to be distracted, abused, filled, made to feel whole.

He shut his eyes, wondering what time of day it was. Equally bored with the silence, he switched on audio only, wondering if the movements he was hearing in his headset were live sound or recorded. Incidents, of late, were confusing him. He was beginning to shy from the part that he was playing, beginning to lose his sense of authority, knowing now that everything would soon be coming to a close. Yvonne was being watched. He had spotted undercover cars outside her apartment. He cast himself off, adrift in the auditory pleasures of Yvonne's sweet voice.

Strangely enough, the sex scene was quieter than expected, calmer, more loving than the previous encounters. They were beginning to care for each other, to take comfort in each other. Once the auditory level dropped during sex, then passion was making way for love, for progressive, enchanted love.

And he knew that once that happened, trouble was soon to develop. Love was the great divider. When those sentiments were stirred, became obvious, when the roots began to pierce the heart, tangling emotion, then it was easier for someone to die. Crimes of passion were— by far— the most common.

"What happened here?" Zack's low voice.

"Mmmm, staples," Yvonne said, dreamily. Her ebbing moans, the uncharacteristic purr in her tone, the tender need, the whispers— what was she saying? The man turned up the volume on the panel, watching the glowing green digit ascend from four to seven.

Yvonne was whispering words, then moaning, the moan leaning toward aggression. Her emotions shifting. The loving sentiment too profound, too unnerving. "Please," she quietly pleaded. "Don't tell my mother."

"What?"

"Don't tell Mommy," she said, groaning, abandoning the words as Zack continued making love to her.

"I want you to see me crying," she whispered, her voice wavering to the momentum of Zack's efforts, the sound crackling sharply in the man's ears.

The sound of kissing, Yvonne's moan. She was the one kissing, exerting herself, the strain. She had risen from beneath Zack, a relieved murmur of pleasure, as she lay back down, flat to the rug.

She whispered something too low for the man to hear, into Zack's ear.

"I don't think so." Zack's voice.

No sound. An impregnated silence. The utter absence of sound implying a revelation that had caused pause.

"What's the matter?" Yvonne asked. "Don't stop."

"I can't."

"Why?" Yvonne kissing him, "Come on, please. Just imagine." Kissing more, not his lips now, a different texture of kissing as she moved along his skin, the unmistakable sloppy sound of fellatio, the needy grunts with her mouth full.

Another telling pause.

"You like that?" Yvonne's smiling words.

No reply.

The man clicked the button up. Eight, nine...

The staticky crackling whisper: "Now, come on, honey. Sweetie." The loud wet sizzle of kissing. "Give it to your momma." Her voice abruptly louder, "Your momma wants it like it should be," forcing the man to squint from the outburst, the harsh auditory violation, his hand snatching for the dial, shutting it down to three. Yvonne's voice lowered as if in sync: "Stick it in deeper, baby. Oh, yeah. Does that feel good, honey? Make your momma come."

I know better than that, Pendegast told himself as he grunted, bench-pressing three hundred pounds. Just because he'd found Terri Lawton alive and ticking didn't mean Yvonne Unwin wasn't doing the killings. She was guilty. He could smell it. He had a built-in shit-detector that told him, but try convincing the wishy-washy crew down at Fort Townshend.

Just wait until the DNA results of those hair samples came back from Halifax, he told himself, straining to lower the barbell, his facial muscles shivering. He had picked up a few of Yvonne's hairs from outside her door, found them embedded in the carpet and taken them as evidence, sent them off for a match against the hairs found in the hands of those two dead women. As soon as they came back, they'd see all about it. But that would take two weeks. Too long. He had to do something to shut her down before that.

Grunting, he pushed furiously, then set the barbell on its stand and blew out a breath, wishing he was watching Unwin's place right now. It was his day off. Nothing he could do about it. Someone else was staking out 64 LeMarchant Road. Johnston had warned him about the case after the incident with Terri Lawton. She'd called the station and complained about him that same night. That wasn't enough to do much. But her words, coupled with the complaints from those jerks down at the Cellar, had got him a reprimand.

"Too delicate a situation," Johnston had told him. "Take it easy." But even what he'd done hadn't been enough to get him hauled off the case. A cop had to do a lot before his crew turned on him.

Fuck them all. And fuck Cooper, too. Freaky faggot weirdo.

Pendegast lay there sweating, enjoying the solid feel of his heartbeat, the sheen coating his skin. He sat up on the bench, grabbed for his towel hung on the edge of the barbells. He always hung his towel there. It was like one of his personality traits. Always had things in mind, do little things that made him special. Done swiping the towel over his face, he saw how that muscular little blonde on the rowing machine, sliding ahead, then back, pulling, was glancing at him as she rowed.

He gave her his best closed-lipped smile and wink, and draped the towel over the back of his thick neck, allowing the ends to hang down. He held each end with a tight fist and sat there watching her, deciding the time was right to make his move.

"Looking good," he said as he came up to her and crouched near. "You could handle a little more tension."

"You think?" She smiled at him, her long lashes blinking.

"Yeah." He stared at her taut glossy arms. "Great biceps."

"Thanks." She beamed, blushing in a way that made her tanned skin splotch slightly red high in her cheeks.

"I've got a few great videos," Pendegast said, watching her slowly begin to slide again, the muscles in her calves tightening as she pushed back. "Body-shapers. I tape the show. They've got great tips for women."

"Those women are in the most excellent shape."

"Hey, I've seen better," he said, touching his chest with his fingertips, then pointing at the woman, smiling again and giving a short laugh.

The woman laughed lightly and stopped rowing, eyed her towel. Pendegast handed it to her.

"I'm Rhodie," he said.

"You're a cop, right?"

"How'd you tell?" he proudly asked, puffing out his chest and pushing out his chin, tightening the skin along his jaw-line.

"You look like one." She dabbed at her face. "I'm Barbie." She held out her hand. "Like the doll."

"No kidding. Nice to meet you." He gave her another sexy wink and pointed toward the showers. "I'm going in. How about a drink after."

"Of what?" She seemed confused.

"A beer or something."

"Oh, sure, yeah. Okay."

They took separate cars and parked on Water Street, then strolled together up George Street past the huge black decorative gumps, used for tying up ships, past the tall black old-fashioned streetlights and colourful frontings of the various pubs and bars.

"How about Greensleeves?" he asked.

"That's hot," Barbie said, her pink high heels clicking along the sidewalk. "My friends hang out there."

"Great."

Four drinks later they were back at Pendegast's apartment. A few seconds after shutting the door, Pendegast had Barbie up against the wall and was kissing her, laughing and moaning.

"Hey!" she protested, pushing him away. "Not so fast."

"Sorry." He held up his hands, then reached for his waist, pulled his white tank top off over his head and struck a pose for her.

She laughed, crinkling her nose and touching her lips with her long pink fingernails.

"What're you doing?" she asked.

"Showing off."

"You're nuts."

"No, I'm not." He briskly pulled his t-shirt back on. "I was just messing around."

Barbie watched Pendegast's sturdy, smiling face. "Okay, *I'm* nuts, then."

"Let's have another drink." He went to the kitchen to pour rum and cokes.

Later, drunk and in bed, Pendegast smirked at his accomplishment. Barbie on top of him. He liked his women on top, so he could look up at them. "Nice," he said, his hands squeezing each of her arms. "Make a muscle for me."

Barbie played along, laughing as she sloppily flexed her arm. Pendegast squeezed it. "Nice and hard," he said.

"You like that?"

"Like what?"

"Nice and hard," she giggled.

Pendegast's mood darkened. "What d'you mean?"

"Nothing, just, you know..."

"Know what?"

"Nice and hard," she giggled again and winked, made an oval with her lips.

Pendegast shoved her off him. "What'd'ya mean by that?"

Rolling onto the bed, Barbie shot a shocked look at him. "Hey, what's the matter?"

"You saying I'm a fag or something?"

"A fag!" She burst out laughing, her head lolling drunkenly. "No. You're not a fag."

"I'm no fag. I was just fucking you, wasn't I?"

"Yeah," she said, "you were. You were fucking me..." She made a wobbly movement to get off the bed. "I think you were..."

Pendegast made a grab for her, but held back.

"Hey." She stared at his hand, made a motion to pull free even though he was not holding her, then tried to stand.

"Go on, then."

She fell back onto the bed, managed to stand, picked up her shorts and top and swayed out of the room. "You got a little dick," she called back into the bedroom. "Can't even get it all the way hard."

"You're fucking brutal," he shouted, his voice booming out into the living room of his small apartment. "You got a face like a man. Should wear a bag over your head." Listening, he heard the door slam.

"Bitch," he said, enraged, his thoughts trailing Barbie, leading down over the stairs and out into the street. He thought of his next move. All of a sudden, he was wide awake, stone-cold sober, his mind on Yvonne Unwin. She was the one really occupying his thoughts, keeping him from properly fucking that Barbie bitch. Yvonne Unwin. Dyke. Cunt. Whore.

When he had calmed down, he lay back on the bed and closed his eyes, picturing Yvonne Unwin and Barbie having sex, seeing Yvonne—with engorged manly biceps—strangling Barbie. "Yeah, that's good," he whispered pleasurably, stroking himself. "Yeah, give the cunt what she deserves."

FIVE

Employment prospects were pretty grim. It was a hard way to start a Monday morning, but there was no way Yvonne could continue working with Terri Lawton. She thought of suing for sexual harassment. That sort of action would draw unwanted attention and make it next to impossible to get another job.

Yvonne had just finished checking the board at the employment office and was back out in the heat of Water Street, wandering up toward Atlantic Place. The downtown area certainly had changed a great deal in the years she had been away. When she was eight, a year before they had moved to Toronto, the employment building had been a store called Bowring's, the place where well-off people shopped for quality clothing, women's hats and gloves, men's brand-name suits, leather shoes, perfume, lovely gift ornaments...

She glanced at the Scotia Tower, the sun glinting off the towering steel, the summer-blue sky looming above the highest floor. Dick's & Co occupied the ground floor, the entranceway recessed thirty feet along the grey brick walkway. Dick's had been the main bookstore, the oldest in St. John's, with books stacked from floor to ceiling in their old building further west on Water Street. It was the place where her father had shopped for his literary books. And now it was reduced to a stationery store in an office tower. The big bookstore chains in the malls had stolen all the business. In fact, the Avalon and Village malls had practically wiped out commerce in the downtown area.

The downtown merchants had developed a Downtown Development Corporation, but that hadn't helped much. Parking was the huge problem, everything clumped together, the old stores in rows, back from a time when everyone walked or took the now defunct streetcar.

The Scotia Tower was a new addition. She stared up at it, her mind flashing back to Toronto. It was not near the height of the towers there. She remembered when her father first took her to downtown Toronto. She was nine years old and when she looked up at the towers, she had felt unnaturally dizzy, as if the towers were throwing her life off balance.

Yvonne caught a whiff of French fries and glanced at the Ziggy's chip truck. She would have loved a bag of fries, but it was too hot. She craved the air conditioning of Atlantic Place, another building that had not existed when she left Newfoundland as a child.

It was close to noon and she felt drained, her hunger intensifying to the point of nausea. She'd walked down from LeMarchant Road, wanting to save money on gasoline. She wouldn't be driving much for the next few weeks. In fact, if things didn't work out with a new job, she'd probably have to give up the lease on her Escort.

In the employment office, she'd filled out the required forms for collecting unemployment insurance. Or employment insurance, as it now was called. Why would anyone need employment insurance? The new name made no sense, but that was bureaucracy for you. UI. Pogey. EI. Whatever. The claim would take a few weeks to process and she'd receive her first cheque shortly thereafter. One thing about Newfoundland. It had a great social-security system.

She stopped to check around the street, suspecting that she was being followed, watching the cars pull up to drop their weekly slips in the slot outside the building that housed the federal government offices. She was amazed at the number of new vehicles that people drove. Shiny Chevy Blazers, gleaming compact cars. The economy in such a state, but everyone seemed to have so much money. Where was this recession everyone was talking about?

Wandering up the wide stairs of Atlantic Place, she entered through the smokey grey glass doors and glanced at the magazine kiosk before moving into the food court area. She took a quick peek at the Tim Hortons counter, then crossed the area of chairs and tables to stand in front of the Chinese-food booth. She ordered an egg roll and chicken fried rice. It was time that she ate something. She was dizzy and weak, her thoughts too hyper.

While she ate, her mind wandered over her history of jobs: trade-show floor manager, advertising sales rep for the Board of Trade's monthly magazine— a job that had given her many connections, propositions as well, from several businessmen in the St. John's area, sleazy people. They were still out there. Harassment charges and the general heightened awareness to the concept of sexual discrimination had little effect on some men. Or women, for that matter. It was pathetic. And before the advertising sales-rep job, a short stint as a waitress in Toronto and long before that— as a teenager— work in a record store in the Eaton Centre, the job that had been cut short by the death of her mother.

Splitting the egg roll with the plastic knife and pouring on the plum sauce, she shifted her thoughts back on track, making a mental note of some of the more honourable business people she had met while working with the Board of Trade. Other, sleazier men came to mind as well, but they would be a last resort. She could easily play up to them, wear a short, low-cut dress, sit slightly forward in her chair during the interview, whatever was required of her (short of outright sexual favours) and then once she got the job she could look after herself, make certain things clear. If her boss continued to trouble her with his lewdness, then she'd threaten to report him to the human rights board, sexual harassment, the whole show. She could handle a man. That would shut him up and she could work in peace, although under continual strain. Could she work in peace in that situation? She wasn't able to with Terri Lawton. What was the difference with a man?

She sighed at the injustice of having to resort to that sort of nonsense. Scooping up a forkful of rice and slipping it into her mouth, she reasoned that the legitimate people were the ones to contact; first, try the businesswomen. She shuddered at the thought of Terri Lawton. Barred the image of her face, advancing toward her, her fingers gently on Yvonne's face, then tenderly on the fabric of her blouse above her sore breasts...

All women bosses weren't lesbians. That's ridiculous. Don't even think it. Stupid and stereotypical. She scooped another forkful of fried rice into her mouth and glanced at the wall of windows that gave her a view of the harbour, the boats across Harbour Drive and the short tin steel-supply buildings that serviced the boats, the shipyard further off toward the west, a cargo carrier up in dry dock. She felt at peace with the ocean so near. In a city, and yet the ocean was at the edge of downtown. She glanced around the bright eating area and was startled to see Mr. Prouse walking toward her, a tray of food in his hands.

She made an instinctual flinching gesture to avoid him, but he had already seen her; their eyes had met directly in that fraction of a second and she smiled briefly at him.

"Hi," he said, charmingly, but slightly embarrassed as well. He motioned to the empty chair across from her.

"Sure." She thought of that night, of what she had let him do. He was an old man. What had she been thinking? She had been drunk. Then him, in her apartment, the rage she had unleashed at him, the fury. Her mind running through that evening, her stomach turning over. She hated and despised herself for letting him fuck her. Mr. Prouse's face as he left the apartment. So pathetic, just like her father. She had gone into the bedroom and found the fan. The one good thing that had come from that night. That had been thoughtful. And the flowers. Regardless, she felt a sickening shrinking in her groin.

"It's crowded here," he said shyly, settling across from her, the wrinkled skin around his nervous eyes making him seem so sad.

She was in a forgiving mood, the food reinstating her resiliency. The fan had been a gift. It did not look new, and so it must have been his own. He was enduring the heat to make certain that she was comfortable. And— besides— she needed to have a talk with him. She wanted to be left alone. Mr. Prouse was harmless, more like a stray puppy dog looking for someone to cuddle him. But her mind flashed on the videos he had been watching. Sickos. Why had she let him fuck her like that? She had to be more in control, had to learn to turn off the sex switch. Her mind flashed through the string of men she had brought home from downtown over the years, all faceless, all meaningless, simply there to do their job and then get out. Service her and go away.

Mr. Prouse was glancing at her in anticipation.

Yvonne said, "Are you following me?" A thought struck her. He might really be a cop. It was possible. This disguise. Undercover cops could be anyone. Something to do with her mother. These new murders. Was she a suspect?

Lawrence Prouse's eyes gradually lost their glimmer of ambiguous pleasure. Yvonne realized she was watching him with a look of mild disgust.

"I don't like people going into my apartment," she said harshly, knowing how to handle him.

Mr. Prouse glanced behind his back. Yvonne's words had been loud enough for others to hear. "I thought after... you know." He dipped his eyes away from her. "I thought flowers would be nice." He tilted his head slightly, as if begging her forgiveness. "We're friends, right."

"Are we?"

"The door was open. I heard you moving in there, but when I said your name no one answered. I heard you in there, footsteps."

"I was upstairs."

"Upstairs?" He squinted. "I heard you in there. My ears work perfectly well." He obviously prided himself on this fact.

"So you went into my bedroom."

"Yes, I called out, but there was no answer. I thought something might be the matter."

"Sure." She gave him a knowing smile, flicked the length of her long black hair over her shoulder and poked at her rice with her fork. "You were just looking for more, you old sleaze."

He blushed, "You're a very forthright young woman."

"You bet." She met his eyes, challenging him. "So you left the fan there and went off."

"Fan?"

"The fan, you know." She flapped her hand in front of her face. "Thanks for that. An exchange for services rendered, I guess. A little gift."

"Don't talk like that, please."

"Whatever."

"I left flowers."

"Yes, I know you left flowers. I was there, remember?"

"You really gave me a scare when you came in." He shovelled a forkful of chips, dressing and gravy into his mouth, chewed and shook his head, shifted the food over to one cheek. "I thought you were there already. But I couldn't find you."

A chilling shiver, seemingly liquid, scooted up her spine, blunting her cynical edge. "Are you sure about the fan?"

"No fan," he assured her, looking down at his plate. He tore open two small packets of ketchup and squirted them evenly around the snack.

"And my door was open?"

"That's right." He lifted a forkful of brown and red slop. "Every now and then I like to treat myself," he said, dipping his eyes toward his food. "I don't care if it kills me. I love it."

"Good for you," she said dismissively, focusing off, recalling the night when she had found the fan. Shortly thereafter, she had taken a shower, to be refreshed. Stepping out of the shower, she had heard a door closing and assumed it was someone else's in the building. Mr. Prouse's, more than likely, thinking no more of it because the telephone had began ringing. UNKNOWN NAME, UNKNOWN NUMBER. She had raised the receiver and spoken horrible words to the listener on the other end, outlining graphic details of what she would do if she discovered who it was. Violent and torturous. Fight fire with fire.

Watching Mr. Prouse shovel the chips and gravy into his mouth, she seriously thought of having her number changed. Give in and get the number changed. No, she couldn't give in. Again, she considered telling the police. Why hadn't she told the police about the calls? Because they might think that she was crazy. And she wasn't crazy. Even though— it seemed— the caller was trying to drive her out of her mind. She would not allow her mind to be overtaken. She was strong and totally in control. She would not let Dr. Healey or the police put her away.

The fan. Her thoughts hitched on the fan. Why the fan?

"Mr. Prouse," she said.

He was watching her while he chewed, entranced. He swallowed and anxiously wiped his lips with the paper napkin. "Call me Larry."

"Larry. We're friends, right?"

He laughed. "Yes, I'd say so." Again, he blushed, his eyes glazing over. "I want to be your friend."

She reached across the table and placed her hand over his. He stared down at her smooth fingers, at the ring with the scarlet stone. He looked across at her, his eyes squinting with emotion.

"You remind me of my ex-wife," he said. "You have long black hair like her. Such fair skin." Reaching out, his fingers stalled, as if afraid to touch.

"You wouldn't hurt me, would you?" Yvonne asked.

"No." Mr. Prouse said. "I would never hurt you, Yvonne." He searched her eyes, frowning, love-struck, then contemplated the brownish-red mash of gravy and catsup. "I'd never hurt anyone."

"And you're who you say you are?"

"Of course. Of course I am, Yvonne. Who would I be if not myself?"

Kieley hung back, trying to remain inconspicuous. The suspect hurried across Water Street, dodging the mid-afternoon traffic and moving into the shadows of the low buildings on the north side of the street. The suspect continued past the stone police station that faced Water Street, its back court entrances positioned up on the parallel Duckworth Street.

Kieley kept on the sunny side of the street, passing an optical store, a bank, then Baird's Cove, where he glanced down the short street that met with Harbour Drive. The grey hull of a naval ship filled his vision. He kept walking, staring down Water Street to see the suspect pass in front of a communications building with its red and white metal tower on the roof. He looked up, the sun reflecting brilliant white off one of the three satellite dishes.

Keeping to his side of the street, he followed the suspect's progress in his peripheral vision. The suspect passed TD Place and paused at the corner of Water and Prescott, waiting at the traffic light, but then became impatient and took a left turn up the steep hill.

A police cruiser came down from Duckworth Street, slowing along the hill before turning west on Water. Kieley waited, peered up at the flush red bricks of TD Place, then turned to see that the cruiser had disappeared.

The appearance of the blue patrol car prompted a memory of Toronto, cruising the streets with his fellow officers at the beginning of his career, the smell in those cars. Procedure. Everything procedure, until the lines blurred. Was he operating outside the boundaries of the law, now? He didn't care. This would be his last case.

Crossing Prescott, he trailed the suspect east on Duckworth, passing a secondhand bookstore, the long fronting of a restaurant, people watching out the windows from their tables. He studied the books displayed in one of the

Wordplay windows as the suspect paused to read a clutter of promotional flyers stapled onto a power pole.

Continuing on past a two-storey building housing law offices, he walked along the war memorial, where the kids with their backward baseball caps stood in a tight circle, kicking a tiny beanball around between them.

The suspect strayed in toward the side steps of the monument, reading the menu in the window of Stella's, a vegetarian restaurant.

Kieley kept his distance. He could not get too close. He didn't want to take any chances. If he was discovered, then the entire set-up would collapse. And now that he had the invaluable surveillance tape, the tape featuring the disturbing and brutal images of Terri Lawton, he knew everything would now fall flawlessly together.

SIX

Aunt Muriel was a persistent pain in the ass. Yvonne would not hear from her for months, and then something would trigger her, and the calls would not stop. Aunt Muriel was even more of a bother since Yvonne had returned to St. John's; just like her mother in that respect, she would not rest until she had accomplished what she set out to do. Her mother's calls had continued, tearing Yvonne apart when she was a child. Her parents' separation and then the accusations and her father's demands that she stay away from her mother. "Don't find out why," he would tell her. "You don't want to find out why." Yet he would always allow Yvonne to talk to her mother. "Just listen to the type of person she is."

"I'll leave *another* message," Aunt Muriel said on the tape machine. "I want to make certain you're safe. This city's so dangerous all of a sudden." But there was something more than concern in her aunt's voice. A probing quality that went deeper.

Muriel was one of those people fascinated by practically anything, who could see the possibilities in the most basic assumptions. Yvonne's mother had been the same. Her mother— like Muriel— could look at you and know what you were thinking, could sense if you were happy, if you were speaking the truth. She was sensitive in this way, but Muriel was more realistic than her mother, more hard-nosed, logical. Her mother had been a romantic, a dreamer, an artist, obsessive and passionate. Muriel knew the value of keeping one's feet planted firmly on the ground.

Yvonne heard the click at the end of Muriel's message and then the whir of the machine rewinding itself. She went to the kitchen and popped the metal clip on a diet cola, chugging it until her eyes stung.

The heat was relentless, persisting for two weeks now. She never thought she'd ever be wishing for fog, but now her body screamed out for it. The heat was utterly unbearable, the humidity seemingly pressuring her skin, her organs; every millimetre of her body was irritated by the swell of constraint.

Making her way toward the bedroom, she stopped in the hallway to straighten a print of Munsch's sketch, *The Scream*, the man on the bridge holding his wavering head, his mouth and eyes alert ovals. Her mother's sketches had something of that texture and mood to them, but they had been mostly nudes. Her mother had been so melancholy, so unhappy with her life, until she had changed it, admitted the truth about herself; then it had been so different, so very different...

Her mother's sketches and paintings— all packed away in cardboard tubes—stood upright in the back of the storage closet next to Yvonne's bedroom. She imagined the earlier grim sexual portraits of men and women engaged in painfully awkward sexual practices, the smear of the black paint, the thickness of the lines, the heaviness. And then her later paintings, so vibrant and delicate, the female nudes with such fine lines and voluptuous natural figures, willingly, compliantly posed beside each other.

Yvonne glanced at the closet where the paintings were stored before crossing the threshold into her bedroom, the carpet soft beneath her feet.

The fan was running, its caged circle tilting back and forth, evenly spreading the stirred-up air around the room.

"I turned that off this morning," she muttered, briskly revolving to look toward the bedroom doorway, expecting to see someone standing there. A shock of fright. Someone. A woman with a length of telephone cord wrapped around her fists, standing in deadly wait. But no. No one was standing in wait, but she could sense a presence in the impregnated air.

Darting into the kitchen, she angrily yanked open the drawer, grabbed up the scissors, opened them and clutched them slightly below the double loops.

She tiptoed out of the kitchen and crept back into her bedroom, nearing the bed, expecting to see a hand snatch out and grab her ankle, holding on, dragging her under. Carefully, she bent, silencing her breath, kneeling, lowering her head. She threw back the edge of the covering, almost screaming in anticipation. No one there.

Gasping, she glanced up, checked behind her, noticing the closet door, breathing carefully, standing, tiptoeing closer until, pausing, staring at the old Victorian door, its two panels, her fingers trembled forward for the glass doorknob. Drawing in a shivering breath, holding that breath, sensing her muscles tightening, her brow webbing, her eyes set in the half-squint of expectation, she yanked the door open, the scissors held high in the air, then coming down. She stifled a scream, lashing her arm forward, stabbing, stabbing and stabbing the naked woman, the woman's face obscured by the shadows, but her body there, her naked body.

Yvonne thrust and grunted out a whimper, the body remaining rigid as Yvonne strenuously tugged the scissors free, the body tilting forward, the eyes staring alertly, unblinking, her mother's eyes, her mother's face. She screamed, but covered her mouth, retching on the muted scream. She could not breathe. She was smothering herself.

Her mother's face.

Terri Lawton's face. She squeezed her hand more tightly over her mouth, muffling the shrill scream, and shoved the body back into the closet, weakly stabbing it again, one more time, the scissors barely penetrating the flesh, but sticking in. She left the weapon there and backed away, cast a look at the fan, raced toward it. It was lighter in her hands than she had anticipated. She hurled it against the wall and a piece of the grey plastic corner cracked off. Bending, she retrieved it from the floor and pried it apart with her bare hands, discovering the video lens behind the on/off light button. She grunted helplessly and flung the works onto the bed. Where to go? What to do? She spun around and faced the body, noticed for the first time the telephone receiver shoved up, into the woman. Yvonne's eyes fidgeted over the slashes she had made with the scissors. No blood from the wounds, strangely; no blood from either of the wounds. Wounds that did not bleed because Terri Lawton, standing rigid, eyes open as if in alert recognition of what had finished her, had already been dead for almost two days.

The image of Yvonne stabbing the dead body had delighted him. Now, the video image had been disconnected. It mattered not. He shut off the video monitor and listened to the audio, her breathing, imagined the pounding of her heart in her chest, the blood racing to supply the muscles, her complexion draining white. He had felt that intensity before. He knew the adrenalin that was rushing through her hot flesh, how her thoughts were scrambling to deal with the dilemma. The circuitry gone haywire.

The woman in the closet. How fitting! How ironic! He had the tapes, he knew what had happened. He smiled and reached for the telephone, dialled the number on his panel and flicked a button, the beeping of the pressed digits reverberating in his left ear, Yvonne's tearful breathing still coming through in his right. He heard the click of the connection, the four rings. When the woman at the switchboard answered, he asked to be put through to Sergeant Cooper, then flicked on the mauve button for the voice changer.

When Cooper answered, the man wasted no time explaining about the woman in the closet. "She's there now," the man dryly informed Cooper. A frustrated sob in his right ear as Yvonne tried to steady herself. "She has a body in her closet."

"Hold the line a second," Cooper requested. "Let me get a pen."

The man smirked. Cooper was stalling for time, attempting to trace the call again. But it would be impossible. The number they came up with would belong to someone in another part of town, the owner of yet another cellular he had cloned.

"Hello?" Cooper back on the line, his voice evenly sustained. "You said something about a body."

"Just go there and see what the cunts are up to. They're dancing."

"What about the address?"

Again, the man smirked. "You know where she lives, but just in case your memory's been erased— which seems to be a genuine concern with me— it's 64 LeMarchant Road."

"LeMarchant Road." Cooper was making a big production of spelling out the words. "Yvonne Unwin."

"That's right. That's where she is right now with the proverbial skeleton in her closet. Don't you fine fellows have at least one imagination between you?"

"Yvonne Unwin really did the number on you, didn't she?"

The man was silent.

"I can understand that she made you suffer, Potter, but is this all worth it?"

"Nice try, Cooper." The man hung up. Flicked the switch to reconnect

Yvonne's sounds of distress in both his ears. What would her oh-so-cultured father, the honoured policeman, think of her now?

The sound of Yvonne's breathing, so laborious and frantic, suddenly muted by the sound of knuckles rapping on a door. The man gave an inquisitive "hm," the unexpected sound so near him, so crisp and authentic. Listening like this, he often thought that a knock on Yvonne's door was one on his own. But there was never a knock on his door.

The knock had come from the headset, from Yvonne Unwin's apartment, a mystery at her door, waiting to show its face.

"What's the matter?" Zack asked as soon as the door was opened. Yvonne was pale and sweating, her eyes electrified.

"Nothing," she insisted, her lips pressed tightly together, brushing her black hair back away from her face and nervously searching over Zack's shoulder. She licked her numb lips and leaned out into the hallway, turning sideways to get by Zack.

Someone had been in her apartment; someone was trying to drive her insane, to set her up, have her put away. The fan and now the body in the closet. It was Terri Lawton. Naked. Her naked boss.

After the death of those other women, this was all the police needed. They would lock her away. Nothing she could say would get her out of this. A body in her bedroom closet. What more proof did they need? The scissors that had stabbed the body still lodged in the flesh. She could not get them free, would not touch them for fear that she would use them to slit her own throat.

She stared at Mr. Prouse's door. Had he been in there? Had his talk of his ex-wife set him off? A sex-crazed madman. A murderer. A lunatic living right next door to her. She thought of racing across the hallway and banging on his door, demanding that he confess. Or maybe he was a cop as she suspected, keeping an eye on her. In that case, she would confess, turn herself in. She made a movement to spring into action, but Zack grabbed her arm.

"Hey," he said, "where you going?"

"No," she said, yanking away. She glanced back into her apartment then stumbled a few steps, raced up over the stairs. "Let's go, quick."

"What's the matter?" Zack pulled shut her door, then followed, taking the stairs two at a time, catching hold of her on the second floor and spinning her around, squeezing both her arms tightly.

She looked at him, his dark threatening eyes, the sweat beading along his hair-line, trickling toward his eyebrows, his heavy breath rasping through his nostrils. She stared at his hands squeezing into her arms. Had she killed the woman? No, the woman had already been dead. The woman was her mother. There were marks along the bluish skin on the woman's throat as if she had been strangled. Strangled? By wire. Telephone wire.

"Oh, God," she cried. Wouldn't the police know that the scissors had not killed the woman? Why had she been stabbing the body? Why would she stab a dead body unless she was out of her mind? "Oh, God," she said again.

"Yvonne?"

She focused on Zack's face, seeing her father's eyes, her father's lips.

"It's okay." Her father in his uniform, holding her arms, then releasing her. "It's all right."

"We have to go," she said, the words barely audible through a tight throat. She coughed and touched the skin along her neck with her fingertips. "I was sleeping and..." She took a step back from him. "...I had a bad dream." She moved close to his doorway and tried the knob. "We have to hide."

"Jesus, what kind of dream?" Zack squinted at her, unlocking the door and pushing it open for her, watching her scoot in. "Man, oh, man. You look wrecked."

"I'm okay." She stared toward the high four-over-four window at the front of Zack's living room, expecting to witness the pulse of red and blue lights at any moment. Approaching the couch, she sat down, hunched forward, thinking.

"You sure you're all right?"

"Yes, yes," she insisted, dazed, unable to focus, clawing at the sides of her face, at her hair, pushing her black hair back, as if it was someone threatening her, crawling along her skin, eating at her flesh. She shut her eyes and saw the woman's pale face, the face of her mother. She imagined it smiling, a hand reaching out to touch her. Fingertips dabbed at her skin. She flinched and opened her eyes to see Zack sitting close to her, his hand recoiling from where he had touched her arm.

"Whoa."

"Zack!" She scooted back from him.

"Calm down."

"We have to go," she said, standing, her nerves further scrambling, incited by the sudden movement.

Zack's telephone rang. She watched it.

"Don't answer it."

"Why not?" Zack demanded. No reply from Yvonne. Regardless, he let the answering machine get it. The machine played its message, then beeped, the message coming through. A woman's voice: "It's me, honey. You know now. My body's dead. But it's just my body." The abrupt click. The tape in the machine shutting down.

"What the hell was that?"

"I don't know," Yvonne's voice was almost hysterical.

"What's going on, Yvonne?" Zack stared up at her.

"They'll be after me."

"Who?"

"The police."

"Why would—"

"We can't stay here." She grabbed his arm and pulled him up. "We have to go."

Zack glanced back at the machine. "What body?"

"I can't... I'll tell you. I'll explain."

"Go ahead."

"We have to go." She moved for the door. "The police—"

"Why are the—"

"—are coming." Yvonne spun around and slapped her hand over Zack's mouth, pushing her body hard against his. "Shhh, shhh, shhh. Don't say anything, Zack. Don't say anything." She shut her eyes and shook her head. "I can't take another word. Just help me. Please, help me. Please."

Zack reluctantly nodded.

"Can we hide here?" she asked. "Is it possible?"

"I don't know, Yvonne. I don't know."

"Our concerned citizen said there's a body in Yvonne Unwin's closet."

Pendegast held up his portable radio, listening to Cooper's voice. He thought for a moment, glancing at 64 LeMarchant Rd. He pressed the button and spoke. "You get a trace?"

"It's a number outside the city. Another clone."

"So this guy's an electronics freak." Pendegast watched the window of Yvonne Unwin's apartment.

"One of the officers is bringing in a lesbian with violent tendencies, picked her up at the Zone. S&M, strangulation fetish, auto-asphyxia. That sort of thing."

"Likes it rough with her women." Pendegast laughed outright.

"Seems that way."

"Big bad bull dyke?"

"I don't know about that."

"Should I bust in to Unwin's now?"

"You know better. We can't act on the merit of an unidentified caller. I'll try for a search warrant, but we're only going on the strength of a phone call. I don't know if any judge would hand it over."

"What about Riche? Our concerned citizen's been batting .500. I think we should go in."

"I'll try Judge Riche. See if she'll go for it. I've got this interview coming in, too."

"I could drop by for a social visit, something relating to the other night that needed clearing up. Have her invite me in."

"Worth a try. But no TV stuff. No splintering doors."

"No problem. I'm gone." Pendegast threw down his portable radio and hurried from his car, checking both ways before crossing. He stepped up into the porch and buzzed 1B, waited. No answer. He studied the glass in the centre of the inner porch door, bending slightly to get a view through. So easy to smash. So easy. He stared at the glass and rubbed his lips, his body wanting in. He rattled the knob. Nothing. He pressed Mr. Prouse's buzzer and was hesitantly admitted.

Prouse came out to meet him, watched while Pendegast knocked on Unwin's door, waited. He glanced at Mr. Prouse, took in his floral shirt and peach-coloured rugby pants. No answer.

"I need to get in there," he said, pacing back from Unwin's apartment door.

"Don't you need a search warrant?"

Pendegast stared at Prouse. "I need to get in there."

"I think you need a search warrant. I'm sorry."

"Listen, stalker boy. How would you like to spend some time in prison for obstructing justice?"

Prouse backed toward his apartment. "I'm going to call my lawyer."

"No, listen." Pendegast smiled, changing his tone. Holding up his hands in surrender. "That's okay. I'll wait. No problem. I was just concerned for..." He pointed toward the door.

"No, I think I'd better call my lawyer."

"I'll wait." Pendegast quickly turned away. "I'll see her later. Relax, really. Everything's okay."

Prouse watched Pendegast with a look of uncertainty.

Pendegast waved and gave Prouse a big smile. "See you." Out in the street, he cursed, wishing he could have smashed Prouse in the head.

"What do these fucking people know?" Pendegast muttered as he bent into his car and banged shut the door. He glared at Prouse's window, saw the man peeking out. "They don't know fuck-all. They're just scared shitless of everything."

SEVEN

Muriel Unwin was the eldest of the two sisters. She had just celebrated her fortieth birthday when her sister Patricia was murdered, leaving Yvonne motherless and Fred Walsh without a wife.

It had been a tragedy, a sad case of a family turning its back on one of its members; that disconnection had led to Patricia's withdrawal, despair and eventual death at the hands of a vengeful police officer.

And Muriel felt that she had been partly to blame. She hadn't done enough to discourage Patricia from moving to Toronto. It was a dangerous city, in her mind. Anything could happen. The city had created a familial distance between her and her sister. They communicated only occasionally— birthdays, Christmas, anniversaries...

Then Patricia had announced she was leaving Fred to live with a woman. Muriel hadn't treated her sister the same after that. She had had no idea how to deal with the news, her mind thinking back to the bedroom they had shared, the bed they had slept in together.

She blamed Patricia— for being irresponsible, allowing herself to do such a thing to Fred and Yvonne. She told her sister as much, being the big sister, the preachy one. Five years the senior, she was privileged with much more knowledge and experience, or so she had thought at the time.

Muriel's gaze flitted across the map of Canada that was pinned to one of the short grey dividers in her cubicle. The promotional poster showed arching lines shooting out from Newfoundland and landing in various communities and cities across Canada. It was something she remembered seeing in airplane magazines.

The airline companies had utilized the design first, the flight lines, the connections.

Glancing toward her cubicle opening, she saw that no one was near. She opened her drawer and lifted out her sister's diary. The sounds of people chatting and milling about in the wide open area faded from her ears as she turned the small pages and began reading.

She had been so heartbreakingly wrong about her sister. Times were so different now. People were more understanding about sexual preference. And the arrival of Patricia's diary had made Muriel weep for the tragedy of misunderstanding that had taken place.

The diary had come to her three days before. Muriel received a box and a letter from her brother Luke. The letter explained how he had finally mustered up the courage to deal with Patricia's things, donating the clothes to charity, having to throw out other items because of mould and mildew, but he had found the diary in a false bottom of an old dresser Patricia had owned. He had been refinishing the dresser for the new baby's room and came across the diary. He had tried reading some of it, but it was too painful. He had written in his letter that it hurt too much to hear Patricia's voice in his head. Luke was sensitive like that. A bit of an old-school hippy. It had taken him all those years to deal with Patricia's things. He was living in the same small house with his girlfriend, both of them sweater-wearing potters. Probably hadn't painted the house since Muriel's last visit eleven years before. He took life easy, dealt with things at his own pace. Nothing seemed to faze him, generally.

Each of them so different. Patricia— anxious and delicate, so intelligent and fragile. Luke— calm and laid-back. And Muriel— the go-getter, the practical, aggressive one.

Muriel had read passages from the diary, touched by her sister's quiet thoughts, the terribly sensitive writing. She missed her sister so much that her heart ached longingly each time an image of Patricia came to mind. Patricia was such a caring person— wouldn't harm a fly. As a child she was a loner, although always involved in some sort of charitable concern, raising money for Oxfam, collecting used clothes, old eyeglass frames. She cared for every living thing and chastised anyone who even played cruel games with insects.

Yvonne needed to know about the diary. The police might find its pages interesting as well. They contained crucial information. She had been following the newspaper reports over the past two weeks, the women who had been murdered, the fact that they were lesbians. She prayed that there was no relationship between her sister's murder and these new ones. That policeman had been convicted. Gregory Potter. She would never forget his name or his face. But was he out of prison now? And was he really the murderer? The diary made her believe otherwise. It changed the shape of her thoughts in a cruel taunting way.

Then again Muriel wondered if the diary might cause more harm than good. Yvonne didn't need more prodding from her mother's past. Yet the diary could also— quite possibly— set Yvonne's mind at ease, to see what Patricia thought of her daughter.

Muriel was of two minds as to what to do.

After Patricia's death, and the sensational truth that caused the shock, Muriel vowed that she would look after Yvonne, swore that she would move up to Toronto and step into Patricia's shoes, be there for Yvonne. She had had several offers to leave the province over the past ten years, better jobs in larger marketing departments, with much larger telephone companies. There had been a chance to move to Maritime Tel in Halifax, a city she adored because— not only did it have the feel of Atlantic Canada like St. John's— but it was connected to other provinces. You didn't have to drive ten hours to board a ferry or take an airplane to connect with other parts of Canada. You could simply drive from one province to the next, exploring the small country towns. As an island, Newfoundland was notorious for its isolation; even in the age of instant communication, that feeling of isolation could not be vanquished. Muriel believed that inherent feeling of detachment was greatly responsible for Newfoundland's rich culture, and the hearty resourcefulness of its people. Newfoundland people could withstand anything, live through any sort of torment. They were the most durable creatures on God's given earth.

But not Patricia. She had never seemed to belong. Born in the wrong place and the wrong time, she sometimes told Muriel. She had to pack up and move to experience life, instead of stagnating on a rock in the middle of the Atlantic Ocean. But she could not withstand what life in Toronto could do to her either. She had left Newfoundland and been corrupted in the big city, had lost all sense of what was normal.

Muriel's eyes drew away from the hypnotic flow of her sister's handwriting. Again, she glanced at the map, steadied her eyes on Nova Scotia, the word Halifax. She could easily live in Halifax. And there had also been the opportunity in Toronto, to join her sister, but she knew she would never be at peace in a place like Toronto, with all that concrete and steel heat in the summer. She had been so uncomfortable that one time she went up to visit her sister and Luke during summer holidays. It was noisy and unbearable.

Patricia had taken her down the chaos of Yonge Street, the continual stream of people, colours and shapes, giving her an uneasy feeling, and there had been all those black people as well. A group of them hanging around the Eaton Centre who had come out and asked harshly for spare change. She refused, but Patricia complied, not because she was frightened, but because Patricia was the type who gave out spare change, digging in the pockets of her jeans until all her change was gone. Patricia was also the type who stopped and talked with drunks as if they were normal. She spoke with homeless people (so many of them in Toronto, Muriel noticed) asking them how they were doing. She had some sort of attachment to the down and out. Muriel recalled their times together at Memorial University. Patricia had been involved in the student newspaper— *The Muse*, the radio station— CHMR, the student council. She had been one of the main instigators of the Parkway Vigil, when a young female student had been killed crossing the freeway that ran through campus. The students had blocked the four-lane Parkway until they had reached an agreement with government to have two overpass walkways installed. Patricia always caring so deeply for other people.

Glancing across at the large square window panels that gave Muriel a view of the harbour narrows and Cabot Tower, far up on the rocky desolate Signal Hill, Muriel saw that the sky was brilliant blue, so clear.

Thank God the building was air-conditioned. She went through the appointments ahead for the day, but these times and faces were interrupted by an image of Yvonne. She wondered why Yvonne was not returning her calls. Was something the matter? She had a feeling that things were not well. That last time she had spoken to Yvonne, (she glanced at her calendar and flipped the page back to June) had been the 27th of June. At that time, she had not sounded like herself. Before that she had spoken to her niece practically every week, trying to renew ties. Yvonne was much like Patricia but she had a few of Muriel's qualities as well.

Muriel lifted the calendar and pinned it back, revealing the photo for July of the Harmony touchtone telephone. It was now August 15th.

It had been the longest time in years that Yvonne had not kept in touch, and there had been that call from Dr. Healey, wondering if Yvonne was okay, saying she had not been in for any of her weekly appointments.

Dr. Healey. Maybe she should notify him about Patricia's diary. No, Yvonne should be the first to see it, to know what its pages contained; then they would decide the next move. She would have to go over there. Yvonne was not returning her calls, because she chose not to or because she was in trouble. Either way, Muriel knew that things weren't right.

The buzzing of her telephone interrupted her thoughts. She pressed the button and raised the receiver, a call from her boss about targeted figures for the new Instacom 450—a cellular fax/phone combination. She swept Patricia's diary into her drawer and flipped through the files on her desk, opened one marked Instacom 450, doing her best to verbally summarize her scribblings, the numbers totally preoccupying her. Absentmindedly, she shut her top drawer, hiding Patricia's diary from sight.

The man knew they would return. Perhaps they had checked into a hotel for the night, or had gone to stay with friends of the artist. They would eventually find their way back to the apartment. There was nowhere else to go. People always followed the route back to their homes. No matter what. They were programmed to be most at ease in the places they had invented.

Zack's apartment was a mess. Artists had no understanding whatsoever of the pleasures of order. He was quite familiar with the argument—an uncluttered mind is an unimaginative mind. Absolute nonsense. There was nothing more imaginative than invention, and invention required a definite course of pre-digested information, statistical truths and proven theories, a logical trail of preceding facts that—when coupled with imagination—extended itself indefinitely in a forward pattern of limitless potential. Electronics was a prime example: a touch of imagination coupled with adherence to the basics led to significant breakthroughs.

Once he had finished setting listening devices in locations throughout the bedroom, living room and bathroom, (brushing away the dust, it stinging his eyes while he cursed, "filthy") he wrote down the telephone numbers scribbled on the top of Zack's two-year-old telephone book. Friends, no doubt. These numbers would come in handy to keep up his connections.

Done with securing a bug beneath the kitchen sink, he stood, brushed off his knees and then returned to the locked door of the spare bedroom, leaving this for last, knowing that important discoveries were always held behind locked doors. A simple cheap keyhole right in the centre of the knob. A toy lock that jiggled. He laughed at it. He could crack the whole thing off with a solid twist of his wrist, but it was necessary to not leave a trail of destruction. Altering the material make-up of an apartment was a dead giveaway. The exterior must remain untouched and no one would ever suspect entry of a more interior sort. Manipulate the invisible, that's how people were really changed, by the invisible, by electronics, microwaves, abstractions (including emotions), all so intrinsically linked.

The trick was to pass through space undetected, much like the microwaves powering televisions, cellulars, radios. Always present in the air, but undetected. This was how he preferred to think of himself, a complex system of impulses and retractions moving from one space to another and altering the elements as he deemed fit.

He lifted the key ring from his pocket and carefully, briskly selected one, fit it into the hole, jiggled it and turned the knob.

Opening the door, his hand clutched the knob, his heart beat in a manner that shot adrenaline through his bloodstream. He had been startled for a moment, for a fraction of an instant, before a smile freely spread on his lips. Never could he have expected as much as this. His eyes took in the treat before him. Was that Yvonne Unwin, naked and exposed to him, standing there motionless in the centre of the room, staring him straight in the eyes?

SEVEN

The room on Victoria Street was more or less a duplicate of Zack's bedroom: a futon on the floor, candles, a small black CD/cassette player with attached speakers. Colourful and morose art posters on the slate blue walls. The only noticeable difference was that there were countless stacks of books filed against the corners. The type of books her father had read. She recognized some of the names on the spines: de Maupassant, Tolstoy, Bowles, Hemingway, O'Connor... Reading the names, she grew feverish. Anything even mildly literary made her feel nauseous.

Yvonne shut her eyes and sat back on the futon, surprised at how comfortable it actually was. She had never been on one before. Her stomach began to calm when she looked at Zack, bent close to the futon, rummaging through a few pages of scribbled notes tossed on the floor.

"Whose is this again?" she asked, focusing on the foreignness of the room. The stimulating sense of voyeurism and adventure.

"Gord Rodgers'." Zack steadied himself, one hand against the futon. He picked up a page and settled next to Yvonne. "He's in Banff for two weeks, on a summer retreat."

"What's that?"

"Gord's stuff. He's a writer, but I can't make any of it out."

Tossing the page down, he leaned forward and picked up a book, turned it over, scanned the back cover. "He's a great guy. A real good-looking big guy. You'd like him." He looked at her, raised his eyebrows. "You feeling better now?"

"Better?"

"Yeah, the dream."

"What dream?"

"Ha, ha. Very funny." He studied the book again, squinted as if not reading the print but thinking on something unsolved.

"Banff's supposed to be beautiful." Yvonne was trying to reclaim her voice, a casual tone, but the energy still stirred in her bones. The telephone call to Zack's apartment had been real. He had heard it. It must be troubling him. Her smile was distressed, slightly nervous. She felt the smile fidgeting on her lips and so she licked them. The way Zack was holding the book bothered her even more. She felt like slapping it from his hands, exploding. Her mind still gravitated back to the body in the closet. The woman in the closet. The telephone receiver rammed between her legs. And that face. Was that why she had been attracted to Terri from the first day of her job interview? It was her mother's face. Was Yvonne going out of her mind? Had there been anyone in the closet at all? That tingling-white, creeping sense of dislocation and dissociation began to impress itself upon her. She checked her wrist, taking her pulse. It was popping fast. She needed to vomit. If she threw up, she would feel better.

Zack shut the book with a resounding snap. The butchering sound as the scissors cut through flesh and stuck, jarring Yvonne's wrist so that she was forced to hold the scissors tighter to thrust into the hard flesh, the flesh so incredibly hard, numb.

"Hey?"

Yvonne shifted her eyes toward Zack. He tossed down the book and raised a hand to brush her hair back away from her cheek. He was watching her in a way that compelled gooseflesh to her skin, in a way that made her feel almost precious. The tender look in his eyes working to further settle her stomach.

"I always end up with tragic women," he said lovingly.

"You think I'm so tragic?" She spoke the words with trepidation.

"I don't know."

"They say that means something."

"What?"

"Men who gravitate towards tragic women."

"What?"

"They're looking to be hurt. Secretly, or something. They really hate women and want an excuse to hate them even more."

"Yeah." He stroked the skin around her lips, circling it with two fingertips. "Who's they?"

"They, you know." It was refreshing to feel a smile. It helped. "Them."

"Oh, they. Them. Those ones."

"Right."

"We're all so fucked up, it doesn't matter. The trick is to find someone who's fucked up just like us. Match the sickness with the sickness, then you get married and pass your own personal sickness onto your children."

"Not me. That's just you. You're the sick artist." She tried to be tender, the emotions weakening her in a way that she both adored and dreaded.

"You want to tell me what's going on?" he asked, or did he ask? Had she imagined it; the shift in his tone? "That telephone call."

"If I tell you, then you'll be a part of it."

"That's what I want."

"It's dangerous." The cramped words were barely audible.

"Good."

"No, I don't mean fun dangerous. I mean prison dangerous."

"Really." He lowered his hand and dropped back on the futon, one arm resting across his eyes. He sighed. "That heavy, hey? Fucking crazy woman." He peeked out, lifting his arm slightly, "What'd you do? Rob a gas station or something?"

She pulled the elastic from her ponytail, defiantly shook her hair loose, then leaned down beside him, her cheek propped against her hand, her hazel eyes seeming larger the way she was watching him.

"You're not a murderer or anything like that, are you?" he asked, jokingly.

Yvonne remained quiet, staring.

"Who'd you kill?"

"No one." She poked him in the ribs. "Yet." The face of the woman in the closet flashing nearer, rudely cutting short any play at intimacy. She licked her troubled lips, scratched the tip of her nose. "I found a body in my closet."

"Is this the dream?"

"No, this is real."

"A body? Dead?"

"Yeah. A body is usually dead."

"Who was it?"

She could tell by his lackadaisical expression that he didn't believe her, that he thought it was some sort of joke. Zack turned on his side to face her, both of them lying on their sides. He grabbed for a pillow and doubled it over, jammed it beneath his head.

"So did you kill this person? Man or woman?"

"Woman." Her voice quavered.

"And she was naked, right?" Zack smirked a little.

"Yeah." Yvonne nodded. "How'd you guess?"

"Makes sense." A grin broadened on his lips.

"You don't believe me."

"Is this one of your fantasies?"

"No." Her jaw slackened. She stared at him with vague disgust. "I'm being set up. Someone's been in my apartment. A man or a woman. I don't know." She sighed in frustration, shook her head. "They keep calling and calling and hanging up."

"Why would anyone do that?"

"I don't know." She tilted her head back and gave a low moan. "God, I wish I only knew."

"Who would be setting you up?" Zack asked, playing along.

"I don't know. Someone's calling."

"And you killed this woman." Zack raised his eyebrows. Chuckling, he sat up, crossed his legs and set his hands on his knees.

"I don't know." She focused out of memory to see Zack's face, looking down at her, his eyes amused. "They're following me around."

Zack laughed. "I'm sorry." He searched her eyes.

"You're such a fucking jerk."

"Not as much as you think." He pinned her with a serious look, a darkness creeping in his eyes. "You have a gruesome imagination. I like that."

"I'm being followed. They probably followed us here."

"Followed you? You're joking, right?"

"No, no, no. I'm not."

Zack surveyed her features, divining for the truth. "If you didn't do it, then there's nothing to worry about."

"Maybe the police bugged my apartment, video equipment, too. They were watching us." She thought of the electric fan. Did the police leave the fan for her? Or was someone else involved in this, trying to drive her out of her mind, trying to break her down? It could be the police. They were famous for using peculiar psychological tactics, experimenting with new measures.

"How do you know they're watching you?"

"I found a tiny video camera in my fan."

"So, they could've seen us."

"Yes."

"Together."

"Yes."

"Everything."

"Everything."

Zack remained silent, giving the idea consideration. "You like being watched like that?" His mouth hung open, his expression boldly aroused.

Yvonne became aware of Zack's breathing as it turned harsher, coming from his nostrils. The slightest hint of stimulation changed him almost immediately.

"Maybe," she said, abandoning the fear, shifting it aside to be replaced by the urge. Reaching out, she let her fingers rest on his knee. She gave a smile of intimidating sexuality, bringing her eyes to secret life, a faultless escape attempt. She flicked her hair back over her shoulder and pressed the tip of her tongue against her top lip.

"They could bust in here any second." Zack said, teasing her. "Take off your clothes. I want to see those cut-up tits."

"See if they're out there. Pretend."

Standing from the bed, Zack stepped over to the red blanket that was pinned across the window. Lifting the corner, he peeked down into the street, recalling the man in the car, the car he had seen from his window. He searched for the same shape of car. No one. Regardless, he said, "They're out there, waiting." He stared back at her, holding his attention on her face.

"Take down the blanket so they can see in." Yvonne could feel her molars grinding against each other. She slackened her jaw as Zack uncovered the window, returned and lay down beside her.

"They have ladders."

"That look," she said.

"What?"

"That look on your face, like you're evil."

"You don't like that look?" He reached out and squeezed her right breast, enthralled by the sight of her flinching.

"You're trying to be mean."

"I'm just beginning to imagine it." He shut his eyes. "Tell me what you did to the body."

Yvonne watched his lips carefully, her eyes narrowing. "What d'ya mean?"

"Did you hurt it?"

"It was dead. I stabbed it with the scissors."

"Where?"

"In her... tits."

Giving attention to the emotion caught in Yvonne's words, Zack slowly smiled. "Then what'd you do to her?"

"I stuck a telephone receiver in her cunt." She knelt up, pulling her t-shirt over her head.

Zack studied her, his eyes on her breasts, the full sway of them as she sat back on her haunches, the markings of her wounds further exciting him. "What happened?" he asked, gingerly reaching forward to connect with the tiny reddish-black holes, the vague bruises that dotted her skin.

Yvonne glanced toward the window, imagined faces there, inspecting her. Faces always regarding her, wanting her.

"You like that," she said, leaning over him, then shifting one leg over his legs, brushing her breasts against his chest. She cringed slightly, the tender shards of pain deeply thrilling. She kissed him, guiding his hand to her breast. "Imagine they're cold. Hard. Do they feel cold?"

Zack nodded.

"I want you to do something."

"Fuck, name it. Anything."

She whispered to him and he slowly grinned in compliance. She rolled off, lay back, shut her eyes and did not move a muscle, even when she felt his hands on her breasts, freely moving them, squeezing them. She made not a sound as he yanked off her loose pants. He opened her legs, lifting the weight of them, one leg at a time, setting them apart. Not a muscle stirred in her face as he entered her, only her mind calling up images. The woman in the closet. Her boss. Her mother. The scissors going in. Her fingertips fingering the wounds. The telephone receiver entering the woman. No, entering her...

Under the pull of hypnotic eroticism, she matured into her mother, dead.

Pendegast watched the main doorway at 64 LeMarchant Road. It was growing dark. He believed that Yvonne might still be in her apartment, but after trying the door he was uncertain. He thought of calling Cooper through the portable radio, telling him that there was no answer. Cooper had already contacted him to pass on the info that Judge Riche would not grant them the warrant, despite the urgency of the case. The law!

No lights went on in Unwin's apartment as the darkness took hold. She could just be asleep. She could be gone, for that matter, snuck down the fire exit from the top floor, made it out the back while he was watching the front. He doubted that. She'd have had to climb a few high fences to get from one yard to the other and she wasn't the type for that, especially when she had no idea that she was being watched. How would she know?

She was probably up with that artist guy, the two of them talking about left-wing radical things. Gays and Afro-Americans and save the world. He could go up there and have a little visit with that scrawny artist guy again. He checked his notes. Zack Brett. Yeah. He opened his door and stepped out of the car, crossed the street.

In the porch, he buzzed Prouse's place and— again— was promptly admitted. No doubt, Prouse had been watching the car, knew what they were up to, hoping the car would drive off and leave him in peace. But, no.

Prouse came out to see him, a look of utter confusion on his face.

"Need to see Zack Brett," Pendegast commented without even glancing at Prouse, striding up the stairs and knocking harshly on the door. Immediately, the sound lent him the impression that no one was home. He had seen Zack Brett come in earlier. He knew that he was in there. He knocked again, three times, with conviction. No one.

Zack Brett had come in. Yvonne Unwin had come in. Was there some kind of secret exit? He turned toward the fire-escape door, directly at his right, shook his head. They had escaped together while he was trying to get into Yvonne's apartment earlier. They had made off on the fire escape.

"Fuckers," he mumbled and hurried down the stairs, taking them two at a time, his arms straight out at his sides, bracing the walls.

"Prouse," he shouted, banging on the landlord's door. He had heard Prouse going back in there after admitting him. "Prouse, Prouse," until it was opened by the terrified landlord.

"What?!"

"I need to get in."

"I'm sorry. I already said—" He moved to shut the door.

Pendegast stuck his foot in the crack. "Gimme the keys." Pendegast's big hand clutched in the air, snapping its fingers.

"I'll call..."

"Who? Gimme the fucking keys. I've had enough of you."

"The police. I'm calling."

"I am the police." Pendegast roared, shoving open the door so that it crashed against the wall. "I am the fucking police, you asshole."

Prouse backed away from the door.

"You resisting the demands of a police officer?" Pendegast raised his fist and struck Prouse in the face so that he immediately fell backwards, landing on his backside. Dazed, Prouse's hands slowly reached up to touch his nose, his astonished eyes cast toward Pendegast.

"Where're the keys?"

Prouse examined his hands, startled by the brightness of the dribbling red.

"Like a poppy." Pendegast said, furiously indicating the flowers on the walls. "One of your cute goddamn flowers, Prouse."

Prouse's eyes questioned Pendegast. This could not be happening. Who was this man? Not a police officer. Not in this day and age. He could not possibly be a police officer.

"This." Pendegast tossed his arm toward the walls. "Flowers. Blood's like a poppy." His breath was even, regulated. Punching Prouse had not exerted him in the slightest. "Where's the keys?" He watched the nervousness in Prouse's eyes as they glanced toward the couch.

"What're you looking at?" Pendegast asked, carefully drifting toward the couch then glancing back to see Prouse's eyes becoming anxious, frightened. Pendegast rifled through the cushions and toss pillows, his fingers searching down in the crevices until they struck something hard. He reached in, slightly deeper into the tight crease at the back and yanked out a videotape.

"Well, well, what's this, Mr. Prouse?"

"You have no right," Prouse whispered, blood on his lip, smearing across his top teeth. He rose to his knees, faltered, set his hand against the rocker to steady himself.

"What?" Pendegast laughed. "Right, sure. No right."

"Don't play that." Prouse came toward Pendegast and the officer hit him again, hardly giving him a glance as he struck him down. Pendegast bent and slid the tape into the machine, stabbed the buttons on the VCR and TV and watched the images fade to life. A woman was holding a candle above another woman who was tied to a bed, her arms and legs stretched away from her body, her eyes blindfolded, her mouth strained by a large red ball-gag. The unbound woman held the candle above the other's breasts, slowly tilted it, allowing the hot wax to find its mark. The bound woman winced, gasping behind her gag, a cry of pain, trying her best to turn it into a staged cry of pleasure.

"Well, well, well," Pendegast said, enthralled. He fast-forwarded the tape until the scene changed. He hit the play button and watched a woman dressed in leather hanging back on and bent forward, supported by chains from the ceiling. The other woman, also dressed in leather, was lightly whipping the bound woman's behind and calling her vulgar names.

"Well, well, well, well..." Pendegast laughed condemningly as he shot a scalding look back at Prouse. "Like the dykes, hey?"

Prouse leaned toward the couch, eased an elbow onto the cushion and pushed himself up until he was sitting. Settling, he held his face, and recoiled when he touched his swollen lip, groaning in pain.

"Like to see the dykes hurting each other." Pendegast nodded to himself, his jaw shifting in contemplation, his hands set firmly on his hips. "Yeah, I see it now," he admitted, thunderstruck by a revelation as he eyed Prouse. "Yeah, Mr. Prouse. I don't think I'll be needing those keys after all."

The telephone was ringing as Cooper entered his house. He knew who it would be and he knew what Johnston wanted as soon as he answered the telephone. Johnston was outraged by the media interview.

"What were you talking about?" Johnston wanted to know. "Who's this McCoubrey in relation to the case?"

"He was—"

"Pendegast out of control, like some sort of nutcase, and now you talking in your sleep to reporters. What you say is going right across the country, do you realize that?"

"Yes, sir."

"What was the point?"

"I don't know." Cooper rubbed the back of his neck. "I guess I was... just trying to be human for a second—"

"Human, Cooper? That's not your fucking job— humanitarian of the year. Get off it, now. You're only attracting more media with that sort of drama."

"I understand." He searched around the kitchen, through the archway. The dining-room table. Natasha's books open, but no Natasha. "It was a mistake."

"You came off like some psychic fucked-up fool."

This statement stabbed Cooper deeply. He pulled out a chair and sat down, glanced at the clock, took off his glasses and pinched the bridge of his nose. A silence settled between them.

"I apologize for that," Johnston said. "That was uncalled for. Those were the mayor's words. I was just repeating them... Cooper?"

"Yeah, I'm here." His stomach grumbled, his nerves shrinking in sync with the churnings in his gut. His head seemed heavier than humanly possible, yet packed with feathers. He fitted his glasses back on as if to catch a better glimpse of what might be bothering him.

"What's going on?"

"I'm taking a rest. I'm putting in all the time I possibly can. Twenty-four hours a day."

"I know. All right. But what is there? New, I mean."

"Nothing. A few calls on Gregory Potter amounting to zip. I'm still waiting for his file from the RCMP. Pictures to circulate. But I've got a feeling nothing's there. He's covered his tracks, has access, the electronic means to hack databases. He's deleting information all over the place."

"You try Canadian Press for a photo?"

"They dug through their files and e-mailed me what they had. Mostly covered-face shots. Sunglasses, dark beards, that sort of thing. Shaved head in one. Blonde hair in another. It's like he was planning this for a while. Had it in mind even while he was in court. I'm getting a composite drawn up from what can be seen."

"Court sketches?"

"They'd be in the file. I'm waiting."

"All right, keep me informed. Gotta go. Someone's on the other line."

"I'll keep my mouth shut."

"Good. No more theatrics." Johnston hung up.

Cooper reset the receiver on its cradle just as he heard noises at the front door. Natasha opened it. He caught sight of the leaves of a dogberry tree on his front lawn, stirring slightly behind her in the dusk. They reminded him of lettuce, a salad. Casesar salad, with French onion soup on the side. His stomach grumbled louder.

Again, the telephone rang. He snatched it up as he watched Natasha wave to him, her eyes tired, or stoned. He briefly returned the greeting without smiling. Sighting his fixed expression, Natasha drifted toward the living room.

"Hello."

"Cooper, this is Pendegast. Guess what?"

"What?" Cooper asked, his voice straining, exasperated, his stomach caving in, sucking him into its abyss. A plain slice of bread would be delicious. He'd bite off a piece and suck on it, whimpering like a baby at its mommy's boob.

"I've got Larry Prouse here. Caught him with a bunch of lesbo torture videos."

"Yeah." Cooper wondered if they might be eating dinner in the video. What they would be eating.

"I've got him at the station for interrogation. You coming down?"

"Why would I want to do that?" Whipped cream? Cherry pie? Edible panties?

"Tapes are nasty."

"Like what?" Cooper pulled his thoughts away from food, reset his focus on Pendegast's arrogant voice.

"Dungeon stuff. Torture."

"Simulated?"

"How should I know?"

"Is it acting?"

"Pretty convincing." Pendegast snickered. "If you ask me."

"Is it set up? Are they actresses or real people?"

"What's the difference?"

"What?"

"Who cares if they're real or not? It's a movie."

Cooper shook his head. "No, what I mean is, is the pain real? Is there screaming?"

Natasha poked her head in the kitchen, squinted at him. She mouthed the word "screaming."

Cooper ignored her while she opened the fridge door, bent to take out an apple, and bit into it. How could she, Cooper thought, hearing the squirting juicy crunch. How could she eat that sweet apple? He rubbed his forehead, prying his fingers into his skull.

"Who cares! Don't you get it? Remember what you told me about men hating women? Probably homosexual. So Prouse is probably some kinda homo dyke killer. Hates women."

"What?" Cooper's tone was utterly baffled.

"Remember you told me about misogynists."

"Pendegast," Cooper said tiredly, the sound of Natasha biting another piece of apple blasting in his eardrums.

"Yeah?"

Cooper sighed away what he was going to say. Instead, he opted for, "Okay. We have to be certain, right?"

"That's right, Doc."

"Every angle." A thought struck Cooper. He had been thinking of Natasha and then he found himself thinking of Yvonne Unwin. "By the way, who's watching Unwin?"

"Unwin?"

"Yvonne Unwin."

"She got away somewhere. Out the fire escape while I was attempting to gain entry to her apartment."

"Christ, Pendegast!"

"But I've got Prouse. Don't worry. Unwin can't be gone far. I put a call out. Patrol cars are keeping their eyes open. But she's not the key here. It's Prouse. There's something else we've got on him, and this is the clincher."

"What?"

"Get this: I found all kinds of electronic equipment at Prouse's place. A workroom full of it."

"What sort of equipment?"

"Panel boards. Crap like that. He's our guy, Doc. I got a feeling about him."

"Okay. I'll be down in ten or fifteen. In the meantime, ask him if he has any idea where Unwin is." Cooper hung up.

It was going to be another exhausting night. His body cried out for sleep; his shoulders and neck were painfully clotted with tension. Now there was the task of facing Natasha about last night, her disappearance. If he wasn't careful everything would be taken out on her, but didn't she deserve it anyway for not calling, for keeping him on pins and needles all night?

"Bad night?" Natasha asked. Finishing off the apple, she laid the stump on the counter and reached in the freezer for a tub of orange-pineapple ice cream. She popped the lid, grabbed a spoon from the drawer, and began eating it, sucking the spoon, savouring it.

"Yup," he said saucily, glancing at her jean cut-offs, her long beautiful legs, her slim body. She was stunning, her beauty was stunning and he wanted her desperately, but there was this concern, this anger in him that kept her at a distance, kept him from her.

"I thought we were supposed to be fasting together."

Natasha shrugged, then smiled. "I haven't got your discipline."

"You got that right." Cooper glanced toward the kitchen window. He hated the outdoors, the trees, the grass...

"Listen," Natasha said, "sorry about last night. I ended up at Jackie's. I needed a break from all this university stuff." She shook her head slightly. "I should've called, but I didn't want to wake you."

Cooper said nothing. He leaned against the counter and continued staring out the window above the kitchen sink. He could hear his neighbour with the lawnmower. Almost dark and he was mowing still. Cooper breathed. Hands were on his shoulders, delicate hands squeezing, making him melt with relief, with euphoria.

"How's that feel?" Natasha asked, her lips close to his ear.

But Cooper couldn't do it, couldn't submit, forgive her that easily. It would be wrong. What she had done was wrong in the context of their relationship.

"I was very worried," he said, turning to confront her, smelling the scent of orange-pineapple, the vague warmth of her perfume.

"I'm sorry." Natasha's eyes glossed over at once.

"Don't you think I've got enough on my mind right now without having to worry about you?"

Natasha cleared her throat and turned toward the counter, pressed the lid back on the tub of ice cream.

"I'm sorry," she said. "I've got a lot on my mind, too, you know."

"Try to be a little more considerate," he said distractedly, shaking his head at the ground. "Christ, Natasha! This is too much to handle."

She turned to look at him. He knew what was coming.

"Do you want me to leave?"

"Why do you always ask that every time we have an argument?"

"Do you want me to leave?" she asked again.

"Do you want to leave?"

"I don't know."

"I want a little relief."

"Why don't you eat something?" she suggested, trying a consoling smile.

"This isn't about food." His cheeks were burning, his mouth pasty. He licked his lips. "It's about caring, instead of thinking about only yourself."

"Is that right?" Natasha opened the freezer door and shoved the ice cream back in. She shut the door, briefly licked her fingers, then hooked a few strands of short blonde hair behind her ear. "I told you I was sorry. I don't know what else to do."

Cooper gazed away, through the kitchen window. Night closing in. The lawnmower from his neighbour's yard. If only he had a big stick, a great big stick to whack the fellow with.

When he looked at Natasha, he saw that she wasn't there. He heard the front door closing and thought of running after her, being reasonable. No. He'd had enough of reasonable. It was time for others to be reasonable.

"What am I doing?" Sighing heavily, he opened the refrigerator door and stared in at the contents, seeing nothing at first, drifting off, but then focusing—glass bottles of apple and cranberry juice, a blue and white carton of milk, the startling mixture of colours, labels... He took a chug of bottled water and then stood still, waiting to calm before moving, knowing that to move while so furious would lead to unwanted, uncalculated action.

What happened between him and Natasha was meant to happen. They were distancing themselves because of the case. He really didn't want to have her around, so he could devote all of his time to the murders. Maybe she could sense this, or maybe she was looking for attention, jealous of all the time he was spending away from her, neglecting her, or perhaps she was just aiming to stay out of his way, to let him carry on as she knew he should, consumed by the task. The anxiety was hard to take, but it also highlighted his ability to dredge the unseeable up from within, process it in a way that would be productive, sensitize him further.

"Bullshit," he said aloud. He took another chug of water and wondered what he had come home for? To be with Natasha or to purposely fight with her? He had seen her and now she was gone again. He checked his machine for messages, found nothing of interest (none of the media vultures had discovered his unlisted number yet) and left the house.

Sitting in the car, he switched on the radio, listened to a rocking fiddle tune by Figgy Duff and stared at his empty house. What was it for? he wondered. What was the use of his home lately? For that matter, what was the sense of having a life at all? It's all just death now, he told himself. Other people's deaths, eclipsing my life.

There was a green satiny pillow on the floor in front of Yvonne's figure. The man kneeled and looked up at her hard heavy breasts. He picked up the Polaroids from beside the pillow and studied them.

Image 1: A pleasant-faced Yvonne captured through a window coming up the walkway to her apartment. She was wearing dark sunglasses, blue shorts and a tight white button-up tank top.

Image 2: Yvonne standing on the sidewalk, her even expression in profile, dressed for work, watching something move up the street. A Metrobus passing in front of her. Blurred faces in the bus windows.

Image 3: Yvonne from behind, leaving, tight black shorts and a black t-shirt. Her hair in a ponytail. Out for a walk, or a run.

The man laid the Polaroids back down in their exact resting spaces. He knew that Zack— being an artist— would be conscious of specific detail.

So, this was Zack's shrine to Yvonne. He studied the polished toenails. Blackish-red, like the lipstick Yvonne always wore, the colour that showed up the startling fairness of her skin, the lines of veins in her breasts and thighs. The man's gaze roamed across Yvonne's naked feet, the sculpted lines between the toes. So realistic. The smooth shiny calves, the thighs, rising and forming the V, where hair had been expertly attached.

Reaching out, the man touched the hair, feeling the strands. They were softer than the real thing. He stood and slowly ran his hand across the soft-looking round of her hard pale abdomen, then turned his wrist, moved his hand across her breasts, admiring the slopes and rises.

He stared at her face, the glassy eyeballs reflecting light from the hallway, the wide dark eyebrows, the high amused cheekbones, a small nose above lips so full they appeared slightly swollen. They too were painted that luscious shade of black-red that adorned her toenails and fingernails. The foreboding colour, so striking.

The man took a step back to have a full look at her. Recalling Yvonne's naked body from the videos and juxtaposing it over this sculpture, he decided that she was identical to the real thing. The polyester resin sculpture an exact replica.

Strolling behind, he studied the rise of her breastplate, the sloping lines of her back rounding out into the shape of her high thick buttocks.

Yvonne Unwin, or rather the image of Yvonne Unwin in this room. How ironic. The resemblance was truly uncanny. It was entrancing. Here she was for him. Here she was, standing, to do with as he chose. But that was not what he wanted. He needed her breathing, alive, able to defend herself, to realize who he was. The look in her face as he spoke the words. Truth.

Her face. The colour of skin. This life-like image. With no life in it.

His mind flashed on a connection that would most certainly be the final stroke necessary to render Yvonne Unwin as helpless and confused as a lost little child.

Zack would have to become a part of the game now, whether he liked it or not. He would be forced to help.

EIGHT

Mrs. Kieley heard her son coming in. It was late at night and she was frightened. She had heard noises earlier down in Mr. Prouse's apartment, loud violent noises, and she had been terrified. She had been reciting the rosary.

Reaching to lay the smooth grey beads on the night table, she saw the red illuminated digits on her clock radio: 11:43 p.m.

Gregory's hours were becoming more and more erratic. There was no rhyme or reason to them. Or perhaps it was just her mind. She could not keep things straight. Lying in bed, she heard her son moving toward the kitchen, opening the refrigerator door. She heard a glass bottle of juice being pulled out along the wire racking, then a cupboard door opening.

Against Gregory's warnings, she had called down to St. John's RCMP headquarters. She had asked to speak with her son. The reply had shocked her: there was no one by the name of Gregory Potter working with the RCMP. She had even tried Gregory Kieley, assuming that her son might be using her maiden name. He had indicated some interest in this option some time ago, of changing his name again, as she had after her husband's death. But there had been no Potter or Kieley. She wondered if this might be part of his job. He worked undercover on extremely sensitive cases, so maybe his name was secret to anyone who called, maybe he went by another name down there. Or perhaps his work was so classified that only a few key operatives at the station knew of his existence at all.

Maybe he used a code name or something, like a spy in one of those movies that were around years ago. After all, she hadn't seen him on television, on the news. It was always that doctor sergeant fellow. Nothing about Gregory. Maybe he was like James Bond. *Diamonds Are Forever* had been on channel twelve only a few days ago. Sean Connery was such a real man. He was the real James Bond. All those other men since him had been pale imitations. Such a simple movie, enjoyable. Good guys were good guys and bad guys were bad guys. Not like the way things were now. The detective programs and police shows like *NYPD Blue.* That was a good one, but it was hard to keep track of who was who. Who was good, who was bad. Bad cops. That wasn't real at all. She wished things were real again, simple, easily divided up, no grey area to get lost in.

It was this sort of confusion that had made her call down to Fort Townshend, to check there as well. Gregory might be somehow hooked up with the local police. CID. But she had been told that there was no one working with them by that name. "Gregory Potter," she had repeated, then spelled it. They had even connected her with Inspector Johnston so that he could assure her of the truth. When she told him Gregory's name there was a slight pause, as if he did— in fact— know her boy, but then he had said, "No, I'm sorry. There's no officer working here by that name. Who's calling?" At that point, she had become flustered and hung up, terrified that they might trace her call, come to see her and take her to jail for deceiving them. She assured herself that she should not open her door. But it seemed as if Johnston had recognized something in the name. Had the head of CID been denying it, too, to cover up her son's identity?

It was impossible to sleep. Her mind would not let her be, her thoughts were jumbled with spy plots, soap opera deceits and police-show dramas, and she became anxious, shifting in her bed.

Finally, she decided to just get up and face the music, ask him outright. What would Gregory think? Would he think that she was a sick woman and suggest that she be put back in a nursing home? Gregory was her son. How could he possibly not be telling her the truth? "Sweet merciful God," she whispered, biting her bottom lip and pulling the lavender hankie out from the sleeve of her nightdress, dabbing the tears from her eyes.

Should she go out and ask him? He would explain to her the complexities of the case he was working on and— at the very least— she would be comforted by his reassurance.

Throwing back the covers, she fitted her feet into her slippers and stood, reaching for her night robe and pulling it on. Taking a deep breath, she opened her bedroom door and shrieked at the abrupt sight of Gregory standing there so near to her.

Yvonne opened her eyes at the sound of the telephone ringing. The dead awoken. Zack was above her, his face straining with the intensity of an orgasm. She felt him jerking inside of her, releasing his semen. He was not wearing protection. The sleek feel of him.

The telephone kept ringing.

"You should get that," she whispered, her eyes alertly watching his face.

Zack opened his eyes, strands of black hair matted to his forehead.

"It won't stop," Yvonne said, as if to herself, suddenly numb to sex, losing her concentration.

"It's not my place."

She waited, watching him, her eyes twitching toward the doorway. "Answer it," she demanded.

The ringing stopped.

"Jesus, man. What's with you and telephones?" Zack rolled away from her, resting on his back and staring up at the white ceiling, detecting the faint pinpoints of light, the glow-in-the-dark stars, the outline of the solar system that Gord had affixed to his ceiling. He was irritated. The sex over with, he had less tolerance of Yvonne.

"I hate telephones," she said, sitting on the edge of the futon, her back to him. "Doesn't everyone?"

Zack glanced at her, the cool pale skin along her back, then pointed up at the stars, "You see those?" he asked, trying to be civil, one hand still behind his head.

"Nice," Yvonne admitted, giving the stars a brief glance. "Let's look around," she suggested.

Zack kneeled up on the bed. "You're a real nosy one, eh?"

"I love having sex in other people's apartments. I love the feel of it. It's exciting. Mysterious. What could've been happening here. What kind of things."

"I like." His nervous system was settling. He even gave her a broad smile.

"Stay naked," she said to him. "Who's in the other bedroom?"

"That's Natasha's. She's moving out."

"Great." Yvonne sprinted from the room. She was bending back the flaps on one of the cardboard boxes when Zack came up behind her. Sensing him nearing, she hurried over to the multi-coloured dresser, began pulling open drawers.

"Having a good look?"

"You paint this thing?" she asked, still rummaging through the drawer.

"Maybe... You like?"

"Nice job." She smiled back at him, reaching out for his hand. "So you know this Natasha person?"

"Not really. That dresser was here before her."

Zack took her hand and she drew him closer.

She found the bra and panties, a silky red set, worn only once or twice, and took them out. Something for special occasions, no doubt. Turning to Zack, her eyes were glazed and wild. "This Natasha's got small boobs. What's she like?"

"Nice," he said, freezing, holding his breath, alertly listening, only his eyes shifting slightly. "Shhh," hearing movement beyond the room. Someone entering the house on the main landing downstairs.

"Shit." Yvonne's hands— clutching the fire-engine red undergarments— slapped against her chest. "My heart."

Someone unlocked a door and entered on the first floor directly beneath them.

They both sighed, their bodies relaxing.

Yvonne looked at Zack. Eyebrows raised, she laughed slightly.

"What a rush," Zack said. "Let's get out." He made for the door, but felt Yvonne gripping him from behind, bear hugging him, before she leapt onto his back so that he stumbled in reverse. "Hey!"

Hanging on around his shoulders, she leaned toward the bed, pulled him down. He fell on top of her and she shoved him off, kneeling, scooting forward until she was sitting on his chest, her eyes tempting his eyes as she laid the bra and panties over his face. "Put 'em on."

"Not likely," he said, snatching the undergarments and tossing them across the room.

"It's my turn, now. I need to get off," she said, grabbing them up from the floor, then returning to pounce on him, leaning forward to bite at his earlobe and whisper huskily. "Take a cold shower first."

"You're fucking perverse."

"Put these on," she shouted, pressing them hard against his chest with one hand and reaching back with the other, taking hold of his penis, jerking it quickly. "Please," she added, sweetly. "Honey bunch."

Reluctantly, he accepted them, held the bra up against his smooth chest. "They won't fit."

"I don't care," she said.

The telephone again.

Ringing.

She flinched, her eyes jolted.

"Forget the shower," she loudly stated, as if addressing whoever might be calling.

"What's—"

"Here," she scooted back, lifting Zack by the shoulders until he was sitting. "Put this on." She slipped his arms through the straps. Then knelt at his feet, tugging the panties on him, while swiping her hair away from her face.

The telephone. The peel of each intrusive ring sticking in her like a knife. She stood rigid, growled ferociously, then said, "I want to walk in on you. I'm going out in the hall."

The telephone.

The ringing telephone.

The telephone with a life all its own.

Gregory apologized for frightening his mother. He had been on his way to his room and had paused by his mother's door to listen for her sleeping breath, to check to make certain she was okay. That's when she had come out.

"I need a hot drink," she said, turning in the closeness of the hallway and moving for the kitchen. Gregory followed after her, his eyes on the carpet.

"You know," she said, sliding the kettle on the burner and switching it on, "I need to get in touch with you sometimes."

"My beeper. Anytime."

"But sometimes I need you quicker." She cast a glance at him while she took a cup down from the cupboard

"What?" Gregory sat straighter in his chair. "Why?"

"There was a lot of noise downstairs tonight. I was scared, Gregory." She broke down, holding the edge of the counter and touching her face. "I called the station," she sobbed.

"They don't know about me at the station."

"Why?" She wiped at her eyes with her tissue, blew her nose.

"Because I'm not working for the St. John's division."

"That's what I thought." She dropped a teabag into her cup and touched the kettle handle, as if prompting it to boil faster. The kettle began hissing. She pressed harder on the handle and the hissing grew louder.

"Don't do that." Gregory indicated. "That's too dangerous. You shouldn't force things."

"Who do you work for, then?"

"You know I can't say."

"Oh, I hate this secrecy, Gregory. I hate it." She slid the kettle off the burner and tore the top off the pouch of Neo-citrin, poured the powder into her china cup. Stirring in the hot water, she then tapped the teaspoon against the side of the cup.

"You put a teabag in there."

"What?" Mrs. Kieley stared into her drink. "Oh, no matter."

"Soon," he told her, "that'll be the end of it. I'm giving it up."

"Quitting the police?"

"Yes." Gregory checked the clock on the stove. "Once this case is through."

"And you know it'll be soon?"

"Two days, at the most." He watched her eyes, steadily, as if he could not be more certain of what he was telling her. "And it'll all be over."

Mrs. Kieley knew that look. She had come to trust it over the years. She raised her cup of tea and Neo-citrin and sipped the hot fluid.

Satisfied with his explanation, Gregory stood and warmly kissed his mother on the top of her grey-haired head. It was a long, almost-grieving kiss, as if saying goodbye to her. "How's it taste?"

"Like lemon tea."

"This is very important to me," he said quietly. "It needs to be over."

"Okay." She touched his cheek. "Go get some sleep now."

"Good night."

"Good night, sweetheart." Sipping her hot medicine, the warmth of it calming her stomach, she heard her son tinkering with something in his room. He had never let her down before.

Yvonne stared toward the hallway, as if working to keep the ringing of the telephone at bay with her threatening eyes.

"Close your eyes," she said to Zack, "like I'm surprising you. Just lie back. Go on." She leaned forward and yanked up the panties. "Lift your bum." Zack complied and she pulled the panties fully on, securing them snugly at his hips.

"Red's your colour," she said. "You look good in red."

He watched her as she backed out of the room, then slowly shut the door.

Yvonne turned and raced for the telephone. She snatched up the receiver and listened, pressing the moulded plastic against her ear, sealing the hole with the shallow dome of the listening device.

"Hello, honey," a man speaking like a woman, a woman speaking like a man. Which was it? She could not descramble the tones, isolate the dominant gender. Her mother? Her father? "Are you being naughty now? You're always so naughty. Such a mess I've made of you. Always trying to fuck me out of your memory."

Yvonne lips were trembling. A deep line creased between her dark brows. She hungered to reply, but the words— clutched by the distortion of past into present— clotted in her throat. She felt as if she had to spit. Sweat trickled between her breasts. She looked down at her hands and saw that she was twirling the telephone wire around her index finger. The cord rose from the back of the telephone, then dropped away from her fingertips, trailing along the floor toward the plug ten feet away.

"I'm in your closet," said the voice. "I'm still alive. Come and get me, sweetheart."

Wrapping the wire tighter around her hand, she jerked her arm, and the line went dead, the wire snapping free from the jack. Dumbstruck, she stared at the telephone, the grey line clipped into the jack at its base. Her fingertips nimbly unhooked it. Her heart was breaking all over again. It was swelling and shrinking and punching her at once, tearing her to pieces, punishing her; there was a metal clarity in her nostrils. She breathed deeply, remembering what she had discovered, the deed already done, only the scissors needed, the scissors she could not stop from coming down. She remembered her hands, the weakness in her hands and now that feeling, the rush of sexual arousal weakening her legs as she wound the telephone wire around both of her fists and stepped toward the bedroom.

PART FOUR: DISCONNECTION

ONE

The interview with Prouse had proven as fruitless as Cooper had expected.

Pendegast had been hot for a confession, so hot and demanding that Cooper had to suggest he leave the interview room. He would have ordered Pendegast to do so if necessary, but Pendegast had reluctantly complied.

Intimidation purged from the room, Cooper felt relieved, not only for Mr. Prouse but for himself. He took a moment to appreciate the calm, to attempt to diffuse the fear in Mr. Prouse's face, then went about asking brief and appropriate questions concerning the videotapes. He knew that Prouse harboured a hatred for his wife. She had left him and these videos were meant to be some sort of cerebral revenge on her, as if she was one of the women on the receiving end of the mock torture. Cooper suggested this bluntly to Prouse and the man broke down, crying.

"Do I need a lawyer?" Prouse had asked, his forlorn eyes staring at Cooper.

"No, not at all. But I do have the name of a good therapist if you're interested." Cooper gave him a friendly smile. He took out one of his cards, wrote a doctor's name and phone number on the back, and laid it on the table in front of Mr. Prouse. "You're free to go. Thanks for your time. I appreciate it."

"I'm not being charged?" Mr. Prouse stared at the card.

"I can't see why."

"The videotapes."

"There's nothing illegal about those tapes." Cooper straightened his glasses, raising his eyebrows slightly to adjust the fit. "They're therapeutic, actually. Produce a cathartic effect. Other people's fabricated violence diffusing your own."

Prouse rose and sniffed to clear his nose. Absentmindedly, but with embarrassment, he reached down and picked up the card, slipped it into his back pocket while glancing at the door.

"Go home and sleep," Cooper suggested, leaned back in his chair and chewed on the end of the pen he had been doodling with. "You need a run? I'll have an officer take you home."

"Not him." Prouse said, gingerly touching his nose.

Cooper frowned at Prouse's swollen nose, the speckled bruise around his eye. There would be no trouble because of that. Prouse was the sort of man who would keep quiet, not wanting the tapes brought up. Pendegast would get away with it, as he usually did. Rarely would he strike someone unless he had something on them— whether or not it related to the investigation in question was inconsequential. Such behaviour made Pendegast seem smarter than he let on, that the tough dumb cop image was just a role he was playing, that he was actually— deep down inside— someone else entirely.

Cooper shook off the thought. Prouse was standing there, waiting to be dismissed. Cooper was tempted to outline the procedure for filing a complaint, to get Pendegast kicked off the force, out of his hair. He was dangerous. But that would be unethical. Sighing, Cooper rose from his chair.

"What about the videos?" Prouse asked, his eyes fixed on the floor tiling.

"We need to hang onto them. Check them for possible authenticity."

"They're not real," Prouse promptly assured him. "I wouldn't..."

Cooper patted Prouse on the shoulder. "Just don't let it all get to you." He showed Prouse out, bringing him downstairs and asking one of the officers to run Prouse home.

"I'll walk," Prouse said. "It's just over there."

"You sure? It's dark outside."

"Yes." Prouse caught sight of Pendegast moving beyond one of the desks further in the reception area. "I can go?" he said to Cooper.

"Yes, of course. Think about seeing my friend. It's a better way. Cleaner."

Prouse nodded, backed away, then turned toward the row of smoky black glass doors, pushing one of them open and stepping out into the summer night.

The consoling smile melted from Cooper's lips. He searched through the reception area for Pendegast but saw that he was gone. Hiding, Cooper surmised. He thought of the time, the late hour, the day, and then he thought of Natasha. She was probably down at her place on Victoria Street, packing up, or unpacking. He assumed that she was heading there after storming out of his place.

There was nothing more that he could do. He decided to go down and visit her, talk things out. That was always the best way. Harbouring bitter feelings was no way to live your life. He would forgive her without an apology. Was it really worth it? Life was too short. He braced his hand against the reception counter, his body leaning away from him. He felt dizzy. He'd have to eat a little something. Grab a samosa at Fountain Spray on Military Road. No, eat nothing. He wouldn't give in that easily. Remaining faithful to his fast, to the course of action his resilient mind had chosen over his piggish body, he'd do without food for another day. No food until the case was solved. To keep distracted he'd head down through the maze of short streets to Victoria Street to see if Natasha was willing to let the past be forgotten and forgiven.

"I'll just press it here a little." Yvonne lowered the grey wire against Zack's throat. "Does that hurt?"

He shook his head, the backs of his eyes troubled slightly by the pressure.

"You like that?" she asked, sitting on his chest, stealing a glance down at the red bra tightly braced around Zack's chest. Yvonne released the wire from his throat, unwrapping it from one hand so she could reach down with her palm and feel the silk of the panties against Zack's erection.

"You really like that," she said, lowering her lips to his, kissing in a tauntingly erotic way. "Auto-asphyxiation. You get a great high."

"Do it then," he whispered, his Adam's apple panging.

"I'll do anything for you, dear, anything," she sang. She remembered how her mother had taken her to see *Oliver Twist*. A queasy feeling infected her genitals, a childhood sensation of reprimand. She saw her mother's face, tightly shut eyes, a gagged mouth trying to scream.

Coiling the wire around her fist again, she pulled it taut and watched Zack's eyes. The blood racing through her veins, the intense clarity in her nostrils. The precision of her sight.

"What about Natasha?" Zack asked, glancing at the open bedroom door. "If she comes?"

Yvonne shrugged, "All the better. Menage a trois."

"Like this." He strained to look down at how he was dressed.

"You're liberated." She kissed him. "You look so pretty. Good enough to eat. Red. Red. Red."

He laughed, bashfully.

Yvonne thrilled at the feel of the cool sheets, a stranger's bed in a room that she never knew existed until her entry, a stranger's bedroom to explore and violate.

"Stay put." She went over to the multi-coloured dresser, laid down the length of grey wire and pulled open the underwear drawer. Shifting the articles around, she lifted out a pair of black nylons, gave them a tug, and turned to Zack. "Roll over."

"Why?"

"I like it." She smiled at him, showing her teeth in an exaggerated way. "I don't want to see your face."

Zack rolled over, his cheek against the pillow. "I'm that ugly?" he said.

Yvonne pounced onto the bed and kneeled against the backs of his legs. Wrapping the nylons around his wrists, crossing and tightening the material, she tied a knot and firmly doubled it.

"Oww!" Zack said, loudly. "That hurts."

"Don't be such a wimp." She playfully slapped his silky backside, admiring the tight fit, the elastic of the leg holes cutting into his skin. She slid a finger in there, sensing the tautness, then leapt up and returned with a white brassiere, tied his ankles together. A long navy blue knee sock was wrapped around his eyes twice and tied at the back of his head. Done with her binding, Yvonne rolled him over to face her.

Everything was quiet as the bedsprings rose slightly, indicating that Yvonne had stepped from the bed.

"What're you doing?"

"Shut up."

Zack felt the bedsprings jerking as Yvonne threw her weight onto the mattress. He felt a forceful hand against his lips, pressing hard. "Don't talk, you cunt." Her hand lifted away and he felt the prickly cotton of a sock being shoved against his lips. Opening his mouth to protest, he felt the sock being rammed deeper into his mouth, so forcefully that tears sprang to his eyes, his throat muscles constricting, making him retch.

He waited, frustrated, pulled to test his restraints, felt the jarring sting of her hand snapping against his face. He never thought a slap could hurt so much.

"Stop that. You stay still."

Her weight off the bed once more. Her return with something that was zipped open. The clicking of tiny items off each other. Then the feel of something smooth and oily being traced over the shape of his lips. Fingertips carefully rubbing into his cheeks. The distinct smell of foundation makeup.

Yvonne's weight shuffled down and there was the cool feeling of a tiny brush being stroked onto his toenails, her breath gently blowing the liquid cooler.

Several moments of stillness, silence.

Zack breathed heavily through his nostrils. He listened, his senses intensified with anticipation, expecting another slap but hearing something from the outside hallway. No warning of footsteps, only the sound of someone entering the apartment, light footsteps out in the living room, the person clearing her throat— a gentle, feminine sound.

Zack tried to struggle, to get up, quiet footsteps down the hallway. Zack struggling to get free, pulling and rolling until he tumbled off the edge of the bed and hit the floor.

"Hiii," Yvonne said, her voice dripping with lecherous sensuality. "You must be Natasha."

"I... yes... Who're you? What're—"

Zack made no sound, hoped that Natasha had not heard him falling, the carpet had cushioned his tumble. He pressed closer to the bottom edge of the bed so that Natasha could not see him.

"I'm Yvonne. Zack said I could stay here." Yvonne's giggle was childlike, piercing. "I'm sorry if I scared you. I should get dressed. I spilled something on my clothes and I thought I could borrow something of yours, but you're so small." She spoke the word "small" almost lewdly.

"Zack told you..." Natasha's voice, receding, sounding slightly woozy, or was it tipsy. "But I'm still—"

"I guess I should be in Gord's room, right?"

"You're staying in Gord's room?"

"No, pleeeeeze, don't go away. This is your room. Come in." Yvonne following Natasha further out into the hallway, a silence as Zack remained perfectly still, his erection defying him, the terrifying arousing rush.

"I saw the way you were looking at me," Yvonne quietly said in the hallway. "Do you like my body? Someone hurt my breasts. Someone hurt me. A bad man." Silence from Natasha, a long stretch of silence, then a delicate protest, not words but a moan shaped like "no," then silence. Compliance. The sound that could not be mistaken: the tender moist click of kissing.

"Come on." Yvonne's voice louder, back in the room. The slow weight of a body sitting on the edge of the bed, then lying flat. "You're so beautiful." Whose words? Two bodies lying in rest above him, patiently moving in each other's arms, ignoring him completely.

Cooper pulled into the parking space in front of Natasha's three-storey row house on Victoria Street. Further down the street, something was happening at the LSPU Hall, a play or a concert. People were milling around outside, chatting casually or smoking cigarettes in the muggy night air.

Cooper wondered if he should be there at all. Would Natasha mistake his visit as him checking up on her? Stepping out of the car, he was surprised to sense a slight breeze, a letting up of the heat, a coolness beginning to breathe in and through everything. He glanced toward the harbour, between the two secluding cliffs that framed the narrows, the dark Atlantic beyond, but obscured tonight by a grey fog, creeping in, looming between the two cliffs. Only a matter of time before the city was cool again. He hoped this was a good sign, a signal of forthcoming relief.

A few of the people outside the LSPU Hall glanced Cooper's way as he headed for the entranceway of Natasha's building and found that the front door was open. A trusting bunch. He stepped into the downstairs hallway, glanced at the doorways of the first-floor apartments, then took the steep narrow flight of stairs to the second storey. Despite the slight chill in the air outside, the air in the building remained stuffy. He waited outside Natasha's door, listening, always pausing to listen before knocking. Something he had been taught to do. He thought he heard sounds, distant movements, voices, but the sounds could be coming from anywhere in the house. He carefully tried the knob. It was locked. He pressed against the door.

"Anything interesting?" a voice asked from the dim stairway leading up to the third storey. Looking there, Cooper saw a thin balding man smiling at him. He was sitting on the stairs, smoking a cigarette, holding it in an effeminate way, fingers pointing upward by the side of his head.

"I'm looking for Natasha."

"She's in there," he said, smiling, then taking a long draw. Tilting his head slightly back, he let the smoke cloud up into his nostrils. "I heard them." He laughed whimsically and stood, turned away, scooted up the stairs and around the stairway wall. "You should try knocking," he called out, shutting his door.

Cooper knocked, waited, his mind filled with possibilities. The man's laugh, *"She's in there,"* implying what? *"I heard them." "Them."*

No reply to his knock. He tried again, three times, each successive knock louder.

Nothing. He swallowed, hopelessly tried the knob, glanced at the stairway, expecting to see the man there again. His heart began to race. He forcefully twisted the knob. No giving in. Chewing on the insides of his mouth, he thought of kicking down the door. He shook his head at the idea. That was Pendegast's style. He wouldn't sink to that level. And besides— why would he want to bust in?

If Natasha was there, and didn't want to speak with him, then that was all he could do about it. He couldn't force matters. He knocked again, informing himself it would be his last attempt.

Nothing.

His heart ached miserably, his breath caught in his chest. Turning away, he started down the stairs, hearing the balding man calling from up above, "Ohhh, she's in there all right, Mr. Police Man." A laugh as the door shut again up on the third storey.

TWO

Dr. Boyd Healey buzzed his secretary to enquire if Yvonne Unwin had called to cancel her 3:00 appointment. His secretary, Mrs. Scott, informed him immediately, without having to look at the appointment book, that no, she had not. It was almost 5:00 p.m and the day had been blocked with patients, as usual. He had not even bothered to question Mrs. Scott at 3:00, the time Yvonne did not show, because another patient was quickly ushered in, a man fresh out of prison, agitated and in need of an Antabuse script. A steady show of faces from day to day, so few psychiatrists handling the workload in the city.

In the field, St. John's was noted for its shortage of psychiatrists and psychologists. Whenever Dr. Healey attended the AGM of the Canadian Psychiatric Association he was ribbed by his mainland associates about his plight in life, having to endure zillions of cases, plus the isolation. But it was a beautiful place, a few of them would profess, as if Newfoundland was some desolate mystical faraway island that few went to but those who did venture there came away changed and smitten.

"Terribly beautiful," Dr. Healey would say. "It's a terribly beautiful place."

And then his associates would start in with the latest Newfie jokes they had heard. There was always an abundance of them. In these politically correct times it was only permissible to make fun of your own. The Polish jokes no longer existed, the Jewish jokes were gone. But the Newfie jokes were endless. They were safe. Joking about counterfeit stupidity couldn't get anyone in trouble.

Dr. Healey endured the jokes.

"You know the recuperative value of humour," one of the doctors at the hotel bar would lightheartedly profess. Healey's associates would nod and wink whenever he might protest about the jokes being racist.

"You're not a race unto yourselves, are you?" they'd ask, "like Quebec, eh?" This statement would be uttered almost fearfully, under someone's breath, and only if there were no francophone psychiatrists present.

But generally these annual affairs were pleasant functions where he and his wife could visit another city. Where they could shop for the house at the specialty shops that the larger cities offered. Ottawa was great for this, Sussex Drive and the Byward Market and Montreal— St. Denis and Old Montreal. He had attended functions in both cities in recent years.

The conventions also gave him unlimited joy because he was able to discuss the latest in medication, and extraordinary cases. Psychiatrists were always attempting to outdo one another with their tales of patients. Dr. Healey had a passion for criminal behaviour. He devoured information regarding violent crime. He was fascinated by the prospect that one human being could take another's life with a sudden chaotic burst of energy. What type of mind could do that? To empty a person from their flesh, to make them no more. The power of that one action. Perhaps swift and precise, or clumsy and brutal. And then the life gone, completely.

Yvonne Unwin's file lay open on his desk. He was troubled by the fact that she had not called to cancel. At their last meeting, he had insisted that she return soon for another session, and the appointments had been bumped up to two a week. He had sensed agitation in her voice and gestures, an edge of anxiousness that signalled a forthcoming crisis. He thought that she had been doing so well. It had been ten years, but these things were known to recur, the suppressed anxiety resurfacing to cause various reactions: weight loss, panic attacks, chronic infections resulting from stress.

Yet Yvonne seemed to have avoided these symptoms. She held onto her standard weight. She had been diagnosed with bulimia several years before, but seemed to have had that under control, until recently. Dr. Healey recalled watching her in the past while she discussed her triumphs, but he had his doubts. She seemed too assured, too certain of her control over herself. Manic-depressive. Bi-polar. She should be medicated, but she refused traditional medication.

When questioned about sleeping patterns, she responded that she slept soundly.

Any shortness of breath, he had asked?

The reply was negative.

Any feelings of not being completely there? Of fading, becoming less than yourself?

No.

Bad dreams?

No.

All of these replies in the negative and yet there was a hint of sharpness, of above-normal speed to her expressions and gestures.

These deaths in the news. He had the clippings in her file, matched with the photocopy of the news stories relating to Yvonne's mother. Two dead women. Cause of death. Strangulation by telephone wire. Telephone wire. There it was again. And the bodies in the closets. Yvonne's mother and her lover, discovered stuffed in a closet.

Closing the file, he buzzed Mrs. Scott and asked that she try Yvonne Unwin's number. It was urgent that he speak with her. A few minutes later, Mrs. Scott informed him that there was no answer, but she had left a message on Miss Unwin's machine. Then she informed the doctor that she was leaving for the day.

Filing away the information on Yvonne Unwin, he stepped out of his office to see Mrs. Scott shutting the door to the reception area and walking toward the front of the old Victorian house that had been converted into doctors' offices.

He recalled from Yvonne's file that she lived on LeMarchant Road, number 64, three or four blocks east of his office. Slipping on his burgundy canvas jacket, he left it unzipped and stepped out into the foyer. It was recently painted, mustard with cream trim on the ornate mouldings and floorboards. He admired it on his way out.

Outside, the air was remarkably cool. The fog was moving up from the harbourfront.

"Hallelujah," he whispered, having forgotten that the heatwave was not so bad this morning when he came to work. But the air hadn't been as cool as it was now. He had been in his office all day. He was hungry; he had missed lunch.

The fog. It put a piercing nip in the air. Most times he was unhappy to see it, but today— after such a long stretch of humid heat (which— because of the discomfort— increased his appointments)— he was genuinely relieved to see it, hanging up around Cabot Tower.

Zipping up his jacket, he wandered along the sidewalk. He liked to walk, and despised automobiles for the pollution and unnecessary death. Behind the wheel, it was the same as having a loaded gun in your hands. How many patients had he treated for post-traumatic stress disorders after a loved-one had been killed in a car accident? Tragedy. Machinery. The Industrial Revolution. It was a curse. He jingled the change in his pocket as if in reply to his assumptions, confirming them. His thoughts preoccupied him as he continued on his journey, until he forgot where he was going, having to pause and familiarize himself with his surroundings.

He glanced back from where he had come, took a long blink, then turned to stare ahead. Yes, Yvonne Unwin. He hoped Yvonne would be at her apartment so that he could have a talk with her, try to help her deal with the trouble that he knew was mounting. The past always resurfaced. Such a strange concept, he mused, an intangible, an abstract thing, the past. It did not exist at all and yet it could do such damage to individuals and relationships. The past was like a gas, a toxin that seeped into the mind, seemingly harmless until the time when it was reactivated by another reaction, perhaps a chemical triggering another dormant chemical and the response being a physically or spiritually explosive one. He patted his shirt pocket for his notepad and sadly discovered that he had not taken it with him. He wished to write down a few thoughts on the topic for a paper he was working on for *The Sciences*.

Pausing, again he had to draw himself out of his thoughts, to take a moment to survey how far he had progressed. He searched the number of the house beside him. It was set back from the street, a concrete fence about three feet high edging the front lawn. The branches and green leaves from huge maple and dogberry trees hung in front, out over the sidewalk, so that he had to shift to catch the numbers. 76. He was on the right side of the road. Yvonne's was 64.

Just up ahead.

The police had not bothered to follow up on his tip. They had no intention of going to Yvonne's apartment. The man had been confounded as to why they had not visited her.

Perhaps the police were keeping their distance for another reason. They were not convinced that Yvonne Unwin was the killer. The man's calls to Cooper had shifted the attention. Police. He understood their thought patterns. He was disheartened that they had adopted such a predictable mental stance.

It was necessary to return to Unwin's apartment. The police would not bother him there. He would check outside the building first to see if any ghost cars were watching, walk around the house, survey the front and back for parked cars. He could spot surveillance officers a mile away. He seriously doubted that they would be there. If anything, they would be following Unwin or concentrating on patrolling the downtown area.

Outside 64 LeMarchant Road, his suspicions were confirmed; there were no unmarked police vehicles. He entered the building and stopped at Unwin's apartment, slipping the Entry-2000 from his pocket, pressing the trigger and turning it.

Inside, he immediately shut the door behind him and stepped for the closet in the bedroom. Crossing the threshold, he could not help but glance at where he had positioned the fan, in the far corner. No longer there. He found it on the bed, disassembled. Yvonne was on to the surveillance.

He saw the pinhole lens pulled free from where it had been set behind the round tab of red plastic, the tiny "on" lightbulb removed. He glanced overhead, unable to spot where the other lens had been concealed, where it was implanted in the ceiling.

The particular smell came to him as he neared the closet. It was a wonder Unwin had not detected it sooner. The faint whiff of rotting meat.

Opening the old panel door, he saw that the body had slipped to the right side of the closet, so he did not see the woman's face immediately as he had expected. Instead, he noticed her lower body, the dangling coiled cord of the telephone receiver almost reaching the floor, the receiver buried deep in the woman's vagina. Extracting plastic gloves from the pocket of his suit jacket, he snapped them on, then reached in, took hold of her arms just beneath the shoulders and straightened her. A few practically invisible fruit flies took to the air, fleeing from the woman's eyes, drinking there, laying eggs, the larvae hatching already. A pair of scissors was lodged in her right breast. He yanked them out and tossed them on the bed.

The man saw more tiny flies lift off and hang weightlessly in the air. He swatted at them and tilted the body forward until she fell against him. She was heavy and almost knocked him back while he stumbled and leaned into the weight to hold himself upright.

Awkwardly turning the body around, he dragged her out into the living room. Her heels were scuffing against the floor, bunching up the end of the Navajo rug. He blew breath at the tiny flies that hung near his face, then lay the body on the rug, beside the coffee table, within sight of the door that he would soon open and leave through once he was finished with her.

He studied the body with curiosity, seeing into it, knowing that ten trillion neurons would need to be connected to wire a human, all those connections. Ten trillion. It would take an eternity, and yet people were born that way. Now, the connections not working. Ten trillion. The thought was staggering.

He returned to the bedroom and lifted the scissors from the bed. Back at the body, he tried to imagine if Yvonne was left-handed or right-handed. His mind replayed visuals from the videotapes. She had reached for things with her left hand. He was almost certain of it.

Switching the scissors to his left hand, he knelt beside the woman. He held the blade tip against the flesh of her breast. The wounds that Unwin had made were void of pinkness, no reaction, the body's defence mechanisms shut down, only a blueish quality around the entry marks. The pink gone. Only the blue and blackness of old blood.

He had a better idea. One that would be less unpleasant. Rather than carving the word across the woman's breasts, he thought of another way that would be screamingly noticeable against the pallor of the woman's flesh.

Swatting at two tiny flies, he moved into the bathroom, rummaged through the medicine cabinet, then returned with the lipstick. Uncapping it, he switched it to his left hand. He was conscious of the feminine looping of his letters, the half loop at the beginning of the "M," the oval nature of the "O"...

The buzzer interrupted him, the buzzer to Yvonne's apartment, someone here to see her, obviously with no key. He finished his work and briskly stood to admire the harrowing effect. The buzzer again. Persistent. Whoever was there had no idea of what the man was doing, yet there was an urgency to the buzzing, as if the visitor knew something, was concerned, almost demanded entry. The police? Cooper? Finally.

He stood over the body for a fleeting moment. It was perfect. He peeked out to discover that the hallway was empty. Stepping out, he left the door ajar. Then he took the three stairs down to the main doorway, casually pushed out into the porch, as if he too was merely a visitor or was simply going out for a bite to eat or an engagement.

"Going in?" he asked the short man in the burgundy canvas jacket standing forlornly beside the mail box and buzzer panel.

"Yes," the visitor said, after a moment's hesitation, an extended blink. "Thanks." He reached for the door that the man held for him and distractedly moved up the stairs.

The man walked away from the house, turning along the sidewalk, not glancing back, not bothering to look in the window. He knew the Venetian blinds were shut. After a brief walk, he'd return to 64 LeMarchant Road to face the music.

He knew the police would be there. The time had come. His work was done. Or would they get the message? Yvonne's mother. Patricia Unwin. The resemblance was uncanny. And the man had gone so far as putting the credit cards and driver's license into the pockets of the woman's clothes tossed around Yvonne Unwin's bedroom. The ID cards were ten years old, yet they bore the name of Patricia Unwin, were— in fact— the actual articles that he had removed from the evidence bags all those years ago, wanting this woman's identification, wanting the intimacy of her, to try to understand the attraction. Unfortunately, he had been seen in the property room without authorization, not actually witnessed removing the articles, but later— when the articles were discovered missing and he was singled out as a suspect— his behaviour was questioned. He had had no explanation. This had only added to the suspicion of his guilt. The ID cards had been kept locked away in a security box in a bank in Toronto.

If that wasn't enough for the police now, then they did not deserve to be police officers. The body belonged to Terri Lawton, but would be identified as Patricia Unwin.

There should be no mistaking Yvonne Unwin's guilt.

THREE

Cooper received the call while he was scanning the faxed material on the Patricia Unwin case. He read about the young witness to the murders— the name withheld because the witness was a minor. Yvonne Unwin.

She had witnessed the murders, or so she had testified. She had identified Gregory Potter as the killer. She was there at the exact time Gregory Potter chose to murder his wife and Yvonne's mother. The murders had been committed at an address that was not the girl's home address.

The RCMP had yet to contact Cooper regarding the file on Gregory Potter. He was thinking about calling them again, when his telephone rang. It was Johnston.

"I don't know if this means anything to you, but a call came in last night from an elderly woman looking for her son, a police officer named Gregory Kieley or Gregory Potter. We know about Gregory Potter, but what about Kieley?"

Kieley. The name rang a bell. Cooper glanced across his notes. Sarah Kieley, one of the occupants at 64 LeMarchant Road. His breath constricted in his lungs. He closed his eyes, sinking deep into himself. A clown buzzer whirring off in the distance, the face of a cackling clown in a toy car zooming in to poke its over-sized tongue out at him. Pffft!

"I checked with communications, but it was an unknown name, unknown number. Unlisted. This morning I was able to contact the people at Newfoundland Tel needed to authorize a scan of unlisted numbers in relation to Potter and Kieley. Just got the call confirming two Kieleys, unlisted. Frank Kieley on Canada Drive and Sarah Kieley at..."

"... 64 LeMarchant Road."

"That's it. In the house with Unwin."

"Shit," Cooper muttered under his breath, rising from his chair.

"Get over there."

"I'm going." Cooper hung up, stood and lifted the bulletproof vest from the coat tree, slipped it on and secured it, then pulled on his windbreaker, hurried out and jumped into his car. Backing out, and turning, he caught sight of the anxious stirrings of the media crews in the distance.

"Fuck!" he winced, realizing he had tipped them off, his body language informing the predators that he was in a hurry. Reporters raced toward their cars and vans. The whirring, rumbling sound of engines being engaged. Cooper raced near, through the barricade, hitting his siren, switching on the blue dashboard light. The clown in his head. No, he was the clown, in his dinky little car with wobbly wheels, racing to the absurd scene of the crime.

The vans followed in a clumsy line, jerking and racing to get ahead of one another, nearly causing a dozen accidents in the opposite lane. Tires screeching. Horns blaring. There were not enough police cars to detain the mass exodus. Or so Cooper imagined.

The door open as it was, Dr. Healey suspected something was not right. Doors were not left open with no one at home. He had buzzed and there had been no answer. Stepping nearer, tilting his eyes into the gap, he was given a view of the naked body on the floor, the gash wounds and the long black hair that made him gasp, "Yvonne." Pushing open the door, he caught himself in mid-lurch, realizing it was not Yvonne at all. The woman was older. He carefully stepped to her and bent. There was no chance of him resuscitating the woman. By the colouration of her skin, she had been dead for quite some time. Healey breathed a nervous sigh. He darted a look around, wondering if Yvonne might still be in the apartment. No one. His eyes froze on the closet by the main door. It was open a crack. He stepped over to it and stood there, his hand reaching for the knob.

Yanking open the door, he discovered that it contained only clothes and shoes, but was intrigued to see a portrait pinned on the inside of the door. A self-portrait, it seemed. The signature at the bottom edge of the painting belonged to Patricia Unwin. The portrait featured an image of the artist in partial profile. She was staring at herself in a mirror, the reflection distorted, warped.

Healey turned back to face the body. Red moist letters were drawn across the slashed breasts, spelling: MOMMY. Other words were spelled across the backs of her hands. What looked like a name. He stepped nearer. Left hand: *Patricia.* Right hand: *Unwin.* The woman had the dark hair that matched Yvonne's. But this could not be Patricia Unwin. She had been murdered ten years before in Toronto.

Healey made no movement to touch the body. His presence might disturb evidence needed by the police. He had to use the telephone, to call the police department, but he would not use Yvonne's telephone. He remained perfectly still, aware that he might have already been somehow shedding fibres or hair or leaving prints. He glanced behind at the open apartment door. He recalled another apartment across the way. Stepping out on the exact line he had taken in, he knocked on the shut door. There was no answer. He knocked louder and waited, glancing back at the open apartment door.

Hearing the click of a lock, he faced forward to see a man in his early sixties, an apprehensive expression on his face.

"Yes?"

"There's been a murder," the doctor said matter-of-factly, pointing back to Yvonne Unwin's apartment. Healey sensed the sparkle of shock twinge in the man's body. Freud's dream coming to life. He could not stop the clinical nature of his thoughts. The most horrifying and shocking things in life set people in a dream-like state. Was that why nightmares were so real? Because they matched exactly the sensation of "real" terrifying encounters? He patted his pockets for a pen.

Lawrence Prouse's eyes shifted toward the door. "A murder," he said, dreadfully. "Yvonne."

"No."

"Who?"

"I don't know. Could I please use your telephone to call the police?"

"The police," Prouse said.

"Will you call them?"

"You can call them." He stepped back. "There," he indicated, pointing to the telephone resting on a table beside the couch.

Dr. Healey watched the man's actions. They were not stable. The man kept glancing toward the open doorway, toward Yvonne Unwin's apartment, as if fearful to venture out.

Dr. Healey studied the man as he gave the information to the 911 operator. There was no doubt in the doctor's mind that this man was already aware of the murder in the other apartment.

Prouse's buzzer sounded just as the doctor hung up. Hesitantly, Prouse pressed the button, "Yes?"

The staticky voice: "Mr. Prouse, this is Sergeant Cooper. Could you buzz me in, please?"

"That was fast," Healey commented dryly.

Prouse cast a paranoid look at the doctor. "I'm glad someone found her," he seemed to mutter, pressing the button to admit Cooper.

FOUR

Yvonne kept catching a glimpse of Zack watching her. Saying nothing when their eyes met, Zack simply went back to the magazine he was flipping through. She might have gone too far with him. The entire situation that morning had been painfully awkward. Natasha was the first to leave. Suffering from a terrible hangover and "needing air," she made excuses and dismissed herself from the apartment, suggesting that Zack lock up after they left. Taking a furtive glance at Yvonne, Natasha had offered an unsteady, almost apologetic, smile; then she was gone.

"She's such a beautiful woman," Yvonne said to Zack as they sat around the old chrome kitchen set. She spooned honey onto a piece of whole-wheat toast.

"Yuh." Zack stared at a photograph of a painting in *Canadian Art*. A luscious forest scene. Emily Carr.

Yvonne reached forward and touched Zack's bare arm. He was wearing his black t-shirt and black denims, always quick to get dressed, she noticed, as soon as he rose from bed. Yvonne, on the other hand, had simply put on her powder-blue bra and matching underwear, parading shamelessly around the apartment, as if rubbing Zack and Natasha's noses in what had happened the night before, the threesome that had gotten passionately out of hand.

Zack glanced at Yvonne's beaming smile.

"It's amazing what can happen if the circumstances are right," she said. "Anything... Wasn't that nice? Did you like Natasha?"

"I guess." Zack took a bite of his toast, ran his finger along the crust to catch a drop of honey.

"Too bad you didn't get to fuck her. Is that what's the matter?" Her wide hazel eyes watched him with genuine interest. She leaned toward him and mussed up his thick black hair. "You'd love to get your dick wet in her. She let me in, but she wouldn't let you. Staying faithful to her man, I guess."

"She passed out."

"So, why didn't you do her then?"

"I'm not like that." Zack laid down his toast, tossed the magazine aside and took a sip of apple juice.

"Jesus Christ," Yvonne exploded, bolting up from her chair and smashing her plate down against the table. The stoneware burst into shards, flying across the kitchen. "What the fuck's the matter with you? You're supposed to be an artist. Zack Brett, right? The dangerous artist! You're such an anal-retentive grandma." She turned from the kitchen and stomped out.

Zack watched her leave the room, the elastic of her panties rounding out the curves of her behind, the groove of her spine hidden by her long black hair, the straps of her pale blue bra over her shoulders faintly pressing into her pale skin. He saw her in profile as she turned down the hallway. Catching sight of her at that angle, he realized he was completely in love with her. So much in love with her that he denied the dark promise of tragedy that their relationship would doubtlessly deliver.

Rising from the table, he watched his step as he crouched to pick up the pieces of the shattered dish. Doing so, he heard Yvonne in the bathroom, the sounds of retching and gagging as the vomit clunked against the water in the toilet bowl.

"That man out there, the doctor. He knocked on my door." Mr. Prouse pointed toward his opened door, keeping his distance from Cooper, Pendegast and the uniformed officer standing behind them, glancing out at the activity across the hall, the ident officers and the coroner who had been called to the scene. "I told you already."

"What time was that?" Cooper asked. He was standing by the side table holding the telephone receiver in his hand, waiting to be put through. He had already seen the body, checked it over, made the required calls; but he had forgotten Johnston.

"Not long ago. Before you got here. Fifteen, twenty minutes. I'm not certain. How long have you been here?"

"Hello." Cooper turned to focus on his telephone conversation, giving the information to Johnston. He hung up and glanced at Prouse, then at Pendegast, who had taken a step nearer to where Prouse was seated on the edge of the couch.

Having sensed the uncertainty in Prouse's voice, Pendegast thought there might be some game worth playing here, a bit of fun with Prouse, even though he clearly wasn't the killer— that dyke Unwin was doing all those women, just as he'd thought— Prouse was still a pervert creep. He deserved it. Pendegast took another step toward the peach-coloured couch, so that Cooper raised his arm to halt his approach.

This tactic didn't bother Pendegast. In fact, he liked it— the implication that he was out of control and had to be restrained. "The doctor said you appeared anxious when he was in here, as soon as you opened the door, like you already knew about the murder."

Prouse's eyes flitted toward the open door, glimpsing the movements in the apartment across the corridor. He looked back at Pendegast, then at Cooper, joined his hands and let them dangle in front of him.

"Maybe you saw the body before the doctor discovered it?" Cooper asked.

"No." Prouse shook his head adamantly, repeated "No," in a calmer tone.

"Did you see anyone coming or going shortly before the doctor arrived?"

Prouse glanced at the television. "Yes," he said.

"Who was it?"

He pointed above his head. "Mr. Kieley, the policeman. His mother lives in 2B."

Cooper turned. "Okay, let's go."

Pendegast shot a scalding look at Prouse, then made for the door, passing the uniformed officer stationed there, but pausing long enough to lean back in, holding the door trim.

"Oh, one other thing," he said. He gave Prouse a manly smile and winked at him, folding a stick of chewing gum into his mouth. "How's your ex-wife doing?"

"I don't know," Prouse said, worriedly.

Pendegast glanced out in the hallway, then whispered confidentially, "You'll get her one day."

Gregory Kieley heard the commotion as he stepped out of his apartment. Sergeant Cooper was jogging up the stairs with Constable Pendegast following. Kieley had entered the building only minutes earlier, explaining to the uniformed officer standing guard that he lived there, and returned to his apartment to find his mother napping. He was on his way downstairs when he saw Cooper and Pendegast stopped on the stairs. They had caught sight of him. They both hesitated, but then advanced.

"Afternoon," Cooper said. "Gregory Kieley?"

Kieley nodded.

"On your way out?" Pendegast asked, nodding toward the door Kieley had just closed behind him. "We come in?"

"I don't think so," he said. "My mother's sleeping. Don't want her disturbed."

"I understand," Cooper said. "We have to look out for our mothers. Comes around, a full circle. They take care of us, then..." Cooper's speech was charged with energy. He smiled widely and licked his lips, a triumphant gleam in his eyes. "We take care of them."

Pendegast glanced at Cooper distractedly as if he made no sense of the point.

"We have a body downstairs," Cooper said. "Murder. I believe you're familiar with the MO. Nude female. Black hair. Ligature strangulation with telephone wire."

Kieley put his hands in the pocket of his grey raglan. "Maybe. I've come across all sorts of murders in my line of work."

"What work is that?" Pendegast asked forcefully. "You're not a cop any more."

Kieley gave him a stony stare. "What's it got to do with me?"

"You happen to see any suspicious-looking characters roaming the corridors?" Pendegast asked, chuckling.

"Who was killed?" he asked. "The young woman who lives there?"

"Yvonne is her name, although I believe you already know who she is. Quite well. "

"I know who she is. She's my mother's neighbour."

"No, I'm going back further than that, through the scrapbook. Ten years."

"Sergeant Kieley," Pendegast said, smirking. "Sergeant Potter. Gregory Potter."

A silence lingered between them. Kieley's expression remained unchanged.

"We'd like to ask you a few questions," Cooper said. He sniffed, seeming almost high on something. Reaching into his pocket, he uncapped the lip balm and traced his lips with it.

"What do you have to implicate me?" Kieley asked.

The smile dissolved from Cooper's lips. Seeing this, Pendegast lost his smile as well.

"I wouldn't mind going down and having a look, though." He started down the steps, confidently walking between Cooper and Pendegast, who stepped aside for him.

At the first level, Cooper ducked under the police tape, glanced back at Kieley and indicated that he follow.

"We should take him in," Pendegast whispered to Cooper. "He shouldn't see any of this..."

"Not yet. There's more to it." Cooper stepped near to where the body was laid out, avoiding the areas that had been shielded by the ident officers. He looked dwarfed, felt like an insecure teenager beside Kieley's large, emotionless body.

"There she is," Cooper said.

Kieley stared at the dead woman on the floor.

"We tend to have an attraction toward those who most resemble us," Cooper said. "Want to love someone, want to kill someone, might as well be yourself, or a close facsimile."

"You're getting at something," Kieley said, flatly.

Cooper stretched out his arm, stepping toward a stout man with blonde hair and burgundy zip-up canvas jacket who stood off in the corner speaking with a uniformed officer. "This man found the body."

Kieley followed Cooper over to the doctor, as if he was just another police officer on the scene.

Pendegast never took his eyes off Kieley. He hung close to the door, blocking it, just in case Kieley decided to make a run for it. And besides, he told himself, they didn't need any more people contaminating the crime scene. It was all bad enough. Didn't Cooper have any idea what he was doing?

"Dr. Healey."

The doctor looked at Cooper.

"I'd like you to meet someone. This is Mr. Kieley, once Sergeant Potter."

Dr. Healey automatically extended his hand. He stared at the man's face and his actions slowed. He blinked for an extended period, his face seemingly frozen in a stutter before recovering.

Kieley firmly shook the doctor's hand.

"Mr. Kieley's mother lives upstairs," Cooper explained.

"Yes," said Healey, "I remember. You let me in earlier, before I saw..." He glanced toward the body.

"My mother lives upstairs," Kieley interjected. "I was visiting."

"Mr. Kieley used to be stationed with the RCMP in Toronto."

"Oh." The doctor seemed perplexed.

When Kieley turned back he looked the doctor directly in the face, his stony eyes challenging him.

"He was involved in a very important case. Wrong end of the stick."

Kieley frowned, glancing at Cooper.

"Believe it or not, the woman who lives in this exact apartment was also involved."

Dr. Healey stared at Kieley. "Potter," he said. "Yes, I..."

"I'm sure Miss Unwin has told you all about him, Doctor."

"Yes."

"Only one problem. Why didn't she recognize him? He was just upstairs."

The doctor tried to speak, but he seemed unable, the words jammed behind his puckered lips before being forced out. "Post-traumatic affective disorder," he finally managed to blurt out.

"You think so?" Cooper said, "Maybe."

"If you did your homework," Kieley said, "you would've discovered that I was given a full pardon. You did your homework, didn't you, Cooper?"

"Yeah, actually, I did. Just read the file. Your guilt was questioned right from the start. Took ten years for the department of justice to release you. You came away with big bucks. A fine settlement, too. Wrongful conviction. Set you up for life. But ten years. How can you replace ten lost years?"

Kieley stared evenly at Cooper. "I know better than to let the past disturb me."

"Good thing," Cooper said, grinning at the absurdity of the statement. "Can we talk with you at the station? A few more questions?"

"Why not?"

Cooper instructed Pendegast to take Kieley down to headquarters for further questioning. "Hold him there until I can make it over." He gave Kieley a wink as the man was taken away. "I hope one of us sorts this out soon."

A few minutes later, Cooper— hearing a gasp from the doorway— turned to see a plump, middle-aged woman standing on the threshold of the apartment. The woman looked toward where the group of men was standing.

A uniformed officer was blocking her entry. He said, "She says she's related."

Cooper nodded and went over to her.

"Dr. Healey?" the woman quietly called out, staring past Cooper's shoulder, starting toward the doctor, but gently stopped by Cooper.

"You can't go in there."

The woman glanced at the body, a hand to her mouth. "Oh, my God! Oh, God! That's not... Yvonne. That's my..." She stumbled and dipped to the side, bracing a hand against the uniformed officer who caught her as she fainted.

"Lay her there, gently," Cooper indicated the carpeted hallway while Healey made his way toward the woman. "Get some water," he said to one of the uniformed officers.

When the water was delivered, Healey lowered the glass to the woman's lips, waited until she was revived, her eyes fluttering open.

"It's okay," Cooper assured her, bent near, beside the doctor. "It's not Yvonne."

"No," she said, her voice a weak shiver.

"You're Yvonne's aunt," said Dr. Healey.

"Yes, Muriel... Yvonne's aunt... Yvonne," she mumbled, turning her eyes toward the doorway. "Patricia."

Cooper assured her that the body belonged to neither.

"It's a woman named Terri Lawton," Pendegast called out, confidently adding that she was Yvonne's boss.

"Where's Yvonne?" Muriel wondered.

"We're not certain."

"My God. Is she—?"

"She'll be fine," Healey assured Cooper, standing slightly away from her. "Can you make it to your feet?"

Muriel nodded and Cooper and Healey helped her up.

"I'm Sergeant Cooper."

"The doctor sergeant?" Muriel turned her head to look at him. "From the news." She carefully tested her legs, studying his face. "I feared..." She uttered that she was about to be sick and was escorted to the landlord's washroom by one of the officers. When she returned, her complexion was pale and she appeared frail and older than her years. Although she stood near the threshold of Yvonne's apartment, her eyes purposefully avoided the body.

"Dr. Healey," she said knowingly, her legs still wobbly. "I came to see Yvonne."

He smiled consolingly, blinked and tried to speak, a sputtering sound in his mouth before the words flowed freely. "This is quite bizarre. We can only hope that Yvonne is well." He frowned at his use of the word "well."

"I was going to..." Her eyes fidgeted. She wanted to peek at the body.

"She resembles Yvonne's mother?" the doctor asked.

"It's my sister. How she was murdered..."

"Yes," said Dr. Healey.

"I called you earlier today," she said, her eyes finally peeking at the body, unable to draw them away, but repulsed and trying, slowly, eventually, to pull them from the mortifying vision of the telephone receiver lodged between the woman's legs. "This is so horrible."

"Yvonne's not responsible for this. They just took away the man. The man accused of killing Yvonne's mother. This man, Potter. Seems he'd followed Yvonne and..."

"What?" Muriel's face turned white as a sheet, her hand reaching at her side to brace herself against the uniformed officer one more time. She watched the man she assumed to be the coroner bend over the body for another inspection. A second uniformed officer came near them, lingering by the doorway.

"I wanted to bring you my sister's diary." Immediately Muriel burst into tears. "My God." Both hands to her face. The doctor tried to comfort her as she lowered one hand and reached into the wide pocket of her jacket. "I'm not too late." Extracting a slim brown journal, featuring an elaborate painting of angels on its cover, she held it up with trembling fingers. "I thought this might help you," Muriel cried, searching Dr. Healey's eyes for a compassionate response, assuming it would come from him. But Healey's eyes were shut as he stood there like a statue.

Cooper stepped in to gently slip the journal from Muriel's fingers.

Watching the journal leave her grip, she sobbed openly.

FIVE

"What are you—?" Mrs. Kieley demanded, her words cut off by what she suddenly saw as the police officers finished drilling the locks away on Gregory's bedroom door and pushed it open. Mrs. Kieley stared at the wall of equipment installed there, the electronics panels and screens, the headphones set neatly on a hook. All of this totally unknown to her; these police officers knew more about her son than she ever could. She glanced in bewilderment at the two officers who went about boxing and bagging the removable items.

"These articles are being seized as evidence in relation to a murder investigation," explained one of the uniformed female officers.

"Where is Gregory?" Mrs. Kieley demanded. She glanced up the hallway and saw other police officers moving from room to room, searching through the furniture and shelves. They had come pounding on her door. She was terrified, but she had to open. They had threatened to force the door. A crowd of media was outside her window, out in the street, in front of her house. She had switched on the news to see what was happening and there were live reports on several channels. Standing in her window, she saw herself on television, her head turned toward the screen, watching herself standing in the window. She was on television. And her son was on television. The doctor sergeant and Gregory, her son a murder suspect. A murderer. She felt dazed, unreal, adrift in woolly fantasy. Is this just a dream? she asked herself. One of my soap stories?

"Gregory Kieley's been taken to the police station," the uniformed female officer plainly said, giving Mrs. Kieley a sympathetic smile.

"Yes, that's where he works," she said, perplexed. "Did he send you here?"

A second uniformed officer, a man of average build with red hair and a long face, stopped flicking switches on the panel and patiently regarded her. "Is there anyone here looking after you?"

"Gregory looks after me," she said, gathering the fabric of her housecoat around her throat, her religious medal jangling mutely.

"We'll call someone to make other arrangements."

"What do you mean?" she asked, anxiously shuffling forward, tears bubbling up in her eyes.

"Your son has been arrested, Mrs. Kieley," the officer explained, trying to hold his tone level. "I'm sorry."

The female officer stepped away from a filing cabinet in the corner. "You see these?" She held Polaroids that she carefully showed to the officer speaking with Mrs. Kieley.

"What're those?" Mrs. Kieley demanded, rising from her daze, snatching the photographs away and looking at them. She stared at the images of the young woman from downstairs engaged in sex with a man.

The female officer delicately lifted them away from the stunned Mrs. Kieley.

"My son," she whispered. "What is... this... Is it... real?"

The female officer led her out of the room toward a chair in the kitchen and sat her down. "Can I get you something?" she asked, glancing toward an officer standing near the sink. "Could you get Mrs. Kieley some water, please?"

"I don't need water." She stared at the cupboards, all of them open and riffled through, boxes and jars out of place, scattered from their neat arrangement. She stood immediately and began straightening them.

"No." She would not look at the officers. "Where's my son?"

"He's been arrested."

"What for?" Mrs. Kieley took down a red box of round biscuits and opened it, her sad soft eyes filling with tears, blurring her vision. She already knew what for, but needed it confirmed, still attempting to determine if this was a dream, if there were any inconsistencies to the whole scenario as was the case with dreams.

"Murder."

"He's a policeman," she said, tears breaking loose to drip into the box of biscuits. "A detective sergeant."

"He was, Mrs. Kieley, but that was years ago. Before he went to prison."

"Prison," she muttered, shaking her head. There was no doubt, the tears were real. They were warm and wet. They clung to her face in a way particular only to the tangible.

"Yes."

"What's going to happen?" She braced both hands against the counter, giving in, sensing the realization further weakening her, and sobbed.

"I don't know, Mrs. Kieley. I wish I could tell you."

Detective Pendegast sat across from Gregory Kieley in the small interview room at Fort Townshend. The room was outfitted with the classic two-way mirror, only this one was square as opposed to rectangular. Kieley made a mental note of it. His eyes skimmed over the beige cinder-block walls.

"Tell me in your words what happened," Pendegast said, his deep voice carrying slightly, nothing on the walls to absorb the sound, not a print, not a photograph, only the brightness of the fluorescent light. Pendegast held a pen against the statement form. He followed Kieley's inquisitive gaze, looking at the telephone book on the table, a roll of paper towels.

Kieley glanced behind his chair while Pendegast filled out the preliminary info. Kieley noted the chair in the corner, no doubt where the guard sat after bringing prisoners or suspects in, the long black metal ashtray stand. He regarded Pendegast, then glanced at the black metal framing around the two-way mirror, graffiti scratched into it, obscenities and people's initials.

"Okay," Pendegast said, tapping his pen against the pad.

"Okay," Kieley commented.

Pendegast checked over his shoulder, examining the graffiti, "People couldn't care less."

Kieley scanned the form, the pen poised to trace out what he would say.

"You know how it works," Pendegast said, even giving the suspect a slight smile. He seemed at ease with Kieley, his mood lightened by a touch of admiration.

"Yes," Kieley said. "Where's Cooper?"

Sensing that the required information was not shortly forthcoming, Pendegast laid down his pen. "You want to talk to Cooper?"

"I think this is unnecessary."

"I'll tell you, Potter. Personally, I think you're as innocent as a newborn, but I've got to get this statement."

"Why do you think I'm innocent?"

"A feeling. A hunch." Pendegast smiled, glanced at the two-way mirror, leaned back against the wall and folded his arms. "You went through a lot of trouble to get here. A fellow officer."

Kieley eyed Pendegast, as if seeing some truth in the man that had previously gone unnoticed.

"Your wife's name was Doris, right? Doris and Patricia. You came home and found them together."

"That's not the truth."

"Which truth?"

"*The* truth."

"You know a lot about electronics. Cloned cellulars, surveillance equipment. Videotapes. We got it all from your apartment."

"Watch the videotapes."

"I don't need to watch those tapes. I know." Pendegast extended his hand and clasped Kieley's shoulder sympathetically. "Wrongful conviction's a nasty business. Especially for one of the boys in blue." He squeezed and then released. "Don't you sweat it. The system fucked you. You deserve to be cut a little slack." Again, Pendegast glanced at the two-way mirror, turning his profile slightly and tipping back his head as if admiring his reflection.

Kieley contemplated where he was looking. Cooper would be standing behind the glass.

Pendegast drew his eyes from the mirror. "Your mother tells us you spent some time in the Yukon."

"Why don't you just go watch those tapes."

"You were the one calling us, telling us about the murders."

"Sure. I admit that."

"To tell us who was actually killing those women."

"That's right."

"And we both know who that is, don't we?"

SIX

"You go in and check," Yvonne waited on the corner of Lime Street between the Irving Gas Station and the Lada and Volvo car dealership. The sun was behind her, having burned away the early morning fog that lingered from the previous night. No such relief now. She thought of Natasha. Sweet relief, her skin in the cool dampness of the fog chilling the air in the room. Female skin, so fair and sweet. But now, again, the sweltering heat that was driving her mad.

Yvonne could sense the sun's persistent heat through the back of her red sweatshirt, the humidity returning, thickening, making her uncomfortable, the sweatshirt too hot, almost woolly. Again, she thought of Natasha, borrowing something from the small blonde-haired girl, but nothing would fit. Natasha had been nervous, but willing, so willing, so gentle and giving freely. It didn't take long for her to give herself to Yvonne completely, so much uninhibited passion, the best orgasm she'd had in years.

"Lesbian chic," Zack had later said, dismissing it. "Being a lesbian's hip these days. Years ago the gay guys were hip. Now it's the gay women. Next it'll be hermaphrodites."

"Well, that explains it all," Yvonne had said, her voice dripping with sarcasm.

After that, Zack's mood had soured, and he suggested that he should return to his apartment. He had work to do. There were people who wanted his paintings. His time was valuable. Wasted hours away from his art.

Yvonne glanced behind, further down the hill, to see where Zack was stopped, watching the front of an old dilapidated warehouse.

"Never even noticed that before," he said when he made his way up to her.

From where Yvonne was standing, from that angle, she could see her house on a forty-five degree angle. No police cars parked out front. No warning signs. No police tape across the main doorway. No television cameras. It looked like a trap.

"Come back and tell me." Yvonne watched Zack finger a package of Export

"A"s from the pocket of his black t-shirt. Opening it, he nudged out a cigarette, then struck a match, the smoke lingering for a moment before languidly drifting upward in the still heat. Shoving the packet of matches back into the pocket of his black denims, he coughed and glanced at the house.

"Looks like nothing happened," he said impassively. "Maybe it was just a crazy dream." He flicked the burnt match away.

"If you don't come back," Yvonne said, ignoring his explanation, "I'll know they've got you and I'll go. I'll just go..."

"Where?" Zack asked bluntly.

"I don't know." She watched the street, no cars passing. Quiet. She heard birds chirping in a tree above her, the calls of youths from some unseen street beyond her field of vision. Children laughing, screaming, laughing...

"Back down to Victoria?"

"I'll call you. If you're not out in five minutes, I'll go, but I'll call you from where I am." Yvonne's voice was emphatic, assured, but her eyes appeared slightly bloodshot and agitated.

"Go back to Gord's," Zack suggested, taking a draw. "You and Natasha seemed to get along nicely."

"Right, like you didn't enjoy every second of it." Yvonne peeked at Zack's fingernails as he raised a hand to take another draw from his cigarette. The pink tint of nail polish. He had left it on to admire it. She had expected that he would strip it off immediately; most men would have, but he seemed to like it.

"Wait here." Without giving her another look, Zack walked off, then sprinted across the street. He opened the front door and entered without glancing back. He checked his mailbox slot, seeing the envelopes there. Had to get his mail. Could be good news. A cheque or another review. A good one for a change.

There were two envelopes in the slot, a bill and an envelope from Ikons—the gallery where he had shown his paintings in Toronto. He shoved the bill into his back pocket and tore open the gallery envelope as he went up the three steps, glancing at Yvonne's apartment door. He paused, listening, reading the review at the same time, his eyes skimming the lines until finding his name, seeing the words, "brilliant," "innovative," "one of the most promising." He smiled widely, feeling the rush pass through his body. There was even a large photograph of him standing with his arms folded in front of one of his paintings. While he was going up the stairs, he reread the article, paying little attention to anything else. It was from the *Globe and Mail*. He had actually made it into the *Globe and Mail!*

Outside his door, he glanced over at his neighbour's apartment; the old woman lived there with the policeman son. He waited, shoved the envelope into his back pocket and unlocked his apartment door. Inside, he couldn't contain himself, couldn't stop from pulling the review out of his back pocket. He glanced around the living room. All quiet. Stepping further through the living room, into the hallway, he was startled to see the door open to his studio, the door that he had always made certain was locked. Wide open.

Carefully, he moved toward it, review in one unsteady hand. Nearing, he caught a glimpse of the figure of a man standing in profile, studying the sculpture of Yvonne. The man turned and Zack saw who it was. He recognized the man. He had seen him before, many times.

"Hello," said the man.

Yvonne waited until she felt that danger was nearing. She thought of returning to Natasha's apartment, but— as much as everyone enjoyed the sex— she got the distinct impression that last night had been a one-shot deal, that Natasha was embarrassed in the morning, and perhaps had sworn to herself that she would never let herself go like that again.

Last night, shortly after the threesome had finished their sexual play, they were all sitting in the living room listening to a Tori Amos CD and drinking from their second bottle of wine. Yvonne remembered the punchy lyrics that Natasha had repeated once they were sung, "Just because you can make me come, it doesn't make you Jeee-heee-zus." She had a beautiful voice, a small figure, a pleasure to touch, the fashion-model smallness of her features, the innocent, slightly fearful look in her eyes when Yvonne had first kissed her. But then the shutting of those eyes, the letting go. The melting, magnetic passion.

She had enjoyed Natasha and wanted her again, like a mother wanting a child. It must be that same sort of feeling. Contentment. Natasha had mentioned something about university, that she was going there to work on a paper, the Queen Elizabeth Library, to get some books for her assignment, and then she was coming back for lunch. Was that a hint to stay?

So Natasha would be there. Alone. The idea aroused Yvonne immediately. Natasha's seduction. It was a safe place, a place where she could be comforted. But what after that? Where was she going to hide? She would have to flee the province. Catch an airplane later that day. Leave everything behind. But first she wanted to see Natasha. One more time. One last time. One final time.

She broke her gaze from where she was staring at the asphalt and pebbles beneath her feet. She took one last look at the doorway and saw Zack standing in the porch, waving her over, giving her the all-clear signal. Putting complete faith in Zack, she sprinted toward him, forgetting about Natasha for the time being.

SEVEN

Lawrence Prouse sat at his bench, unable to concentrate on the tiny workings he was attempting to construct. He had heard so many promising words at the trade show, so much hype, everyone functioning on an upbeat note. He glanced at the small stack of business cards and picked them up, recalling the commitments from the men and women he had spoken with, but when he contacted them later they would not return his calls, or they spoke briefly about how busy they were, and could they get back to him.

Nothing. Liars. Business.

He was trying to keep his mind off the murder in 1B, trying not to think of Yvonne Unwin and what she had allowed him to do to her. It would all end now. He had never had a woman like that before and the illicit attraction to her was heartbreaking. He wondered where she was. Was she gone? Would he have to put a new tenant in there? She'd paid the rent 'til the end of the month. Glancing around the apartment, he felt depressed at the thought that was troubling him. He would sell the house, sell off the other properties, to move away, to get away. It was a famous house now. Would that help the sale or hinder it? He glanced toward the window that gave him a view of the street. The police had cleared the media a while ago; not a car passed. It was like the town was deserted.

A new life, away from Yvonne, (or she might come with him), away from his ex-wife (and his compulsion for her).

There had been so much trouble. The police and then the reporters. All those questions. And then everyone leaving. They had all disappeared. Prouse had peeked out through his drapes to see police officers pointing and giving instructions to the media vans. They had driven off, and then the police cars had departed.

He stood and checked out the window, hearing the sound of someone entering the building at that exact moment. He heard the front door shut and then two sets of muddled footsteps moving past his door, the apartment door closing directly above his. Zack Brett had already returned, then come back downstairs. He had heard him a few minutes ago, talking with a man. Now, there was someone else up there. He had returned with someone. Yvonne?

Prouse's thoughts shifted across the upstairs hall. An image of Mrs. Kieley, her son arrested. Had Gregory Kieley murdered the woman in Yvonne's apartment? Murdered all those other women just as the TV reporters had implied? He should go up and speak with Mrs. Kieley, under the pretence of comforting her. He might also listen at Zack's door. He should demand to know what was happening. But he was fearful of where this sort of behaviour would land him.

Leaving his apartment, he first checked his image in the mirror, smoothed his grey hair with his hand, straightened a few stray hairs behind his ear and—using his pinky— nudged a few specks of sleep from the corner of his left eye.

At the top of the stairs, he stared at Zack Brett's door. Drifting near to it, he raised his hand to knock, but faltered. He clamped his teeth together and made another movement to knock. Again, he faltered, this time turning away to knock on Mrs. Kieley's door, thinking that she might not answer. He called out his name, "It's Lawrence Prouse, the landlord." He waited and there was a click and Mrs. Kieley peeked out, the soft skin around her eyes red and swollen from crying.

They had heard him calling out, "It's Lawrence Prouse, the landlord," and then the sounds of him entering the apartment across the hall. A few minutes later, they heard footsteps climbing to the second floor, and then someone knocked at Zack's door.

"Don't open it," Yvonne had commanded in a harsh whisper.

"I was talking with one of them," Zack said. "It's okay." He opened the door.

The silent beeper at Sergeant Cooper's belt began vibrating, interrupting him before he had the chance to say a word. He touched the device. "Vibrator," he said to Zack, then pressed the button, listened to the scratchy message to call Detective Pendegast immediately. "They don't make a sound. They vibrate, for undercover work. Which is fine as long as you don't lay them down."

Zack glanced at the beeper.

"Can I use your phone?" he asked.

"Sure." Zack stood rigid. He motioned stiffly toward the telephone.

"Interesting stand," Cooper said, admiring the piece of twig furniture, the legs bound together with strips of bark. Then he glanced at where Yvonne was sitting casually on the couch. "Hi," he said brightly. He raised the receiver and briskly pressed the digits, then stepped back to have a better look at the twig telephone stand, glancing at Zack. "Zero cost for materials, right?"

Zack tried a smile.

"Constable Pendegast, please."

"Come over," Yvonne said to Zack, patting the cushion beside her on the couch, but Zack remained standing.

"All right." Cooper spoke with his head down. "Okay." He hung up. "Seems this whole building is under investigation." He waved his finger toward the apartment door.

"I'm Uriah Cooper," Cooper said, stepping forward and offering his hand to Yvonne. "I've been trying to talk with you for a while, but we kept missing each other." Cooper was captivated by her dark beauty, her eyes. They seemed so suggestive, so sexual, and yet so clear, refreshing. He felt his breath catch in his chest and realized— with a distressing pang of longing— that he was horribly attracted to her.

Yvonne smiled and shook his hand. "The doctor sergeant," she said. "I saw you on TV."

Cooper blushed slightly and rubbed his palm over the bristly hair on the top of his head. "Yvonne?"

"Yes."

"Did you know that Gregory Kieley lives across the hallway?" He was staring, enthralled, couldn't help himself.

"I suppose," she shrugged.

"Think back. He wasn't Gregory Kieley, then... He was Potter. Gregory Potter."

Zack appraised Yvonne. She showed nothing, not a trace of emotion.

"Ten years ago, Toronto. You remember, right?"

Yvonne watched Sergeant Cooper, her eyes tracing the man's face, fixing on his goatee and the way he was delicately fingering it.

"You remember your mother?" he asked, lifting a stick of lip balm from his pocket and uncapping it. "This heat." He broke his almost hypnotic stare to glance at Zack, then back at Yvonne, to see her jaw-line shift, harden.

"We found a body down in your apartment." Recapping the lip balm, he dropped it back into his pocket. "Did you know anything about that?"

"No."

"Pardon me." He stepped around Zack and sat beside Yvonne on the couch. "You wouldn't know the name Kieley anyway."

Yvonne remained unaffected.

Zack shifted on his feet, startled by the blatant turn the conversation was taking.

"Kieley's his mother's maiden name. He used that here. He's an ex-cop who was masquerading as an undercover officer on assignment. But we had his paper file faxed down from RCMP headquarters and presto. It was our boy. Potter's wife was the woman who was murdered with your mother." He glanced at Zack, explaining mostly for his benefit. "She knows all this," he told Zack. "Don't you?"

"I guess I should've recognized him." Yvonne squinted at Cooper, uncertain of where she stood.

Cooper tossed another glance at Zack. "That was ten years ago. There were no photographs. He was kept away from the media. Police officer. He had some privileges not usually afforded most. We protect our own. Guilty or not."

"I identified him," she said, testing Cooper. "But I can't see him, his face. When I close my eyes, I can't picture him."

"Maybe you don't want to remember." Cooper pulled a photocopy of a newspaper clipping from his pocket and handed it to Yvonne. "Have a look."

Yvonne held the paper with hands that soon began trembling. There was the exact news story she remembered reading when she was seventeen. The photograph of Gregory Potter being led from the courtroom, hands over his face, large sunglasses blocking the upper portion of his face. The headline: COP CHARGED WITH DOUBLE MURDER.

Yvonne frowned and handed the newspaper back to Cooper. "I've tried to leave all that behind." She licked at her lips, Zack watching her through the corner of his eyes.

"What'd he want?" Zack asked, his voice suspiciously unsteady. "Here."

"We think he was trying to kill Yvonne. To work out some sort of complicated frame-up and revenge. Yvonne was responsible for identifying him in court. The women all resembled her. Even her boss—Terri Lawton. It's mainly the hair. The long black hair, like your mother's."

"Why would he want that?" Zack again, speaking flatly.

"Claims he was innocent." Cooper stood and held his hands away from his sides. "Who wouldn't, hey?"

Zack gave Yvonne a nervous look, and chuckled.

"But we have him now. You two okay here?" He glanced from Yvonne to Zack.

"Yeah," Zack said, his tone loosening, warming, coloured with slow relief. "Sure," almost over-confident. "We'll be okay."

"It's all under control now," Cooper assured them. "I have to get back to Fort Townshend. You need anything, call me. But in the meantime, don't worry about a thing."

"Why did he do it?" Mrs. Kieley wept, her flesh trembling where she sat on the couch. "Why? He couldn't have..." She kept surveying the apartment, the mess the officers had left behind. They had tried to put things back in place, but everything had become jumbled and recklessly arranged, not her life at all. She wanted to get up and busy herself with straightening things, but she felt so insufferably drained, her spirit crushed.

Mr. Prouse leaned close to her, wrapping one arm around her shoulders. "There, there..."

"What's going to happen to him?" Mrs. Kieley asked, allowing Mr. Prouse this friendly intimacy.

"He'll be fine." Mr. Prouse hugged his arm tighter. "I know he will. Nothing's over yet."

"What's going to happen to me?" Her tone so helpless when she regarded Mr. Prouse. "Lawrence."

"I'll look after you," he kindly professed. "You just stay right here in this house and I'll check up on you. Don't you worry about that. You've got enough on your mind."

Mrs. Kieley wiped at her eyes, watching Mr. Prouse with a tender, thankful expression. "You're such a sweet man."

"You can call me any time. I'll be here with you until everything works out and well after that, too."

"That's so kind of you." She dabbed at her nose, squeezing the base.

"It's my pleasure."

"Really? I can't expect..." Mrs. Kieley scanned the apartment again. Her personal things all touched by strangers. She began sobbing, her chest heaving as she dipped her head toward Mr. Prouse's arm.

"I'll look after you," said Mr. Prouse, holding her tighter, squeezing her. "I will. I promise."

PART FIVE: REDIAL

ONE

The man watched the image on the video screen— Yvonne shutting the door to Zack's bedroom. In her hand, she held a black-handled mirror. She raised it to her face, studying her darkened features in the fiendish red light cast from the red sweatshirt tossed over the small gooseneck lamp beside Zack's futon. She turned her face to observe her profile, her hair gathered and tied in a loose knot. She tilted the hand mirror down to study her breasts, washed in a bath of red, the cuts seeming to bleed again, then her waist, lower, the rubber phallus strapped in place.

"Daddy," she whispered, breathing deeply through her nostrils.

She lowered the mirror and watched Zack moving on the sheets, his face against the pillow, his hips thrusting as if grinding into an imaginary lover, the black length of the wig sweeping across the smoothness of Zack's skin, the hair gathered in a ponytail, the clip of the bra closure between his smooth shoulder blades, his shoulder blades rising as he raised himself on his hands, his arms straightening, as if lifting himself above a woman.

"You love her, don't you?" Yvonne whispered, moving close to the bed, reaching down to touch the silky back of Zack's panties. She slid her fingers beneath the line of soft elastic, pushing her fingertips searchingly into the crease of his buttocks.

Zack whimpered and lowered his head.

"Shut up," Yvonne said severely, then smiled, a slow menacing smile that set her harrowing eyes ablaze. She yanked his panties down and moved in behind him. "How can you love her?" she asked, kneeling up on the mattress, firmly taking hold of the base of the phallus. "Don't move," Yvonne's explicit words dropping to a hissing whisper. "Cunt loving bitch."

Zack flinched to move away, but Yvonne held firmly to his hips, clutching with incredible strength, as she thrust into him.

The man heard the staticky scratch of Yvonne's words in his headset. He lowered the volume and let the red-drenched scene play itself out. It would follow a pattern, the necessary pattern.

The time was nearing. A matter of minutes. All those days, weeks, months, years... and now only a matter of minutes.

TWO

The living room was illuminated by the dim flicker of a thick white candle on the glass coffee table. Zack sipped a cup of camomile tea and quietly watched Yvonne's eyes, as if stupefied by the lull of candlelight in the room.

"Did that hurt?"

Zack's nod was almost imperceptible.

"I didn't mean to hurt you." She leaned near him and stroked his hair. "How about your heart? Did I hurt that?"

"What heart?" he whispered.

"You liked it, though? You were moaning for more, squirming."

"I guess," he said, his eyes on the telephone in the corner.

Yvonne watched him with a searching look that ached for approval, "My mother was an artist, too," she confessed.

"Did you learn those things from her?"

Yvonne laughed sarcastically, a wet saucy laugh. "You're a real comedian."

Zack took another slow sip of tea, his eyes fixed on Yvonne's face. She was hopped up, her entire body wired.

"Stop staring." Playfully, she slapped at his knee. "It's like you're frightened or something."

Zack's eyes shifted toward the hallway that led to the bedroom as if expecting to see something step from there, some sort of lingering after-image of what they had done.

"It's not real," Yvonne chided, her pale cheeks flushed a smooth even pink, her eyes gleaming. "Fantasy doesn't hurt anyone. It just makes you feel great. Didn't that make you feel great?"

"It was okay."

"Okay?" she said spitefully, glaring at him. "It was more than that." Yvonne stood, paced over to the mantelpiece, her eyes studying the painting hung above it. The image of a woman, another piece like the one Zack had given to her, one of a series, the same woman, but the woman bleeding, her breasts slashed, her wide eyes staring. Children knelt at her feet, their mouths open, catching the drops of blood on their tongues.

"I never noticed this."

"It's new. I just hung it when you were in the bathroom."

"Am I supposed to be dead?"

"I don't know."

She stared for a while longer. "If a painter paints a dead body, is the painter guilty of killing that person, or a part of that person?" She shot an accusing look back at Zack. "How life-like do you have to get to make it real?"

Finishing off his tea, Zack leaned forward to set the mug on the glass top. "Are you saying that I've killed you?"

"You've violated me. My secrets. Privacy. That's like a death. That's me."

"I don't think so." Zack slouched back on the couch, drained. He was trying to stay awake. He had to. He must not fall asleep before Yvonne.

Yvonne reached back and pulled the knot from her ponytail, shook her hair free.

"People think I'm sick, dangerous," he admitted. "I'm sick because I create dark perverse paintings. They don't know anything. No one knows anything. I despise them."

"Live or Memorex?" Yvonne tried to smile, smirking weakly, growing tired of the conversation's direction. "The truth is stranger than fiction."

"The truth is a stranger to fiction." Zack's head turned to the sounds of two sets of footsteps coming up the stairs, making their way toward his apartment door, but then entering the apartment across from his. He glanced at Yvonne, saw that she was watching the door.

"Expecting someone?" she asked.

"No." He looked at her and there was a lie in his eyes. A lie so bold it seemed to change her heart, change her soul, reassemble her features.

"There's nothing to hide," she said, stepping toward him. Her legs opened around where he sat forward on the edge of the couch. He tried to get up, but Yvonne blocked his rise. She ran her fingers through his thick hair. "It's all just fantasy. Everything we live. One big abstraction that passes each instant."

"Is that so?" he said, nervously smiling at the carpet.

"Let's go back to bed. I'll show you there's no difference." A raunchy laugh deep in her throat as she pressed her groin against his chest. "I just can't get enough of you, darling."

"You can't get enough of yourself."

THREE

The electronic view of the bedroom was subdued, the monitor capturing a still image of the young couple asleep on Zack's futon. Or so it seemed. Carefully rising from the bed, Zack checked Yvonne's sleeping form. He waited a few moments, then stepped toward the closet and opened the door.

The man waited.

When Zack was done, and had returned to bed, the man then pressed the digits on his panel, hearing the ring in both earpieces. The connection would spark life. It was intrusive magic, sound waves activating body motion. Electronics, the new magic, controlling objects by exerting a minimal amount of force. Remote controls, power tools, computers, food processors. The press of a button. Force exerted over objects with the least amount of personal energy expended. Techno-magic. The new religion of the techno-society.

The line connected faithfully. It rang twice before Yvonne stirred slightly, an arm over the edge of the futon. On the third ring, she flinched to life, bolting upright and staring toward the sound. She alertly listened, shifting in the dark bed, then checking to see that Zack was still asleep. Tossing back the covers, she hurried down the hallway, not wanting to wake Zack. The streetlight from outside the living room window cast a wide bar of light toward the corner of the room.

Heart hammering in her chest, she picked up the receiver.

"Hello, honey," the voice, the woman, listening closely, the man. "Sweetheart, you couldn't kill me. You just couldn't. I love you too much."

"I kill you all the time," Yvonne blurted out.

"You didn't kill him. You don't know who he really is."

"Who?"

"Your little friend— Zack. Check the bed. See who it really is. It's me, baby. It's been me all along. I've been sleeping with you. Look in your bed, at what you've been touching."

Yvonne flung the receiver away, reached for the thin grey wire and yanked it from the wall. The telephone clattered onto the floor. She kicked it up in the hallway, the scraping of hard plastic against the hardwood until it met the bedroom door. She went toward it.

Carefully crossing the threshold into the bedroom, she saw that Zack was lying with his back toward her. Something was different about him; his black hair longer than she remembered. Had she noticed that it had grown? No, it was the wig. Not the same wig. Or was it? Was it real? She tightened the wire around her fists, tugged it and edged nearer to the mattress. Carefully kneeling on the futon, she drew the sheet back. No, it wasn't the hair that was different but the width of the shoulders. They were smaller, the slim slope of the pale back hairless, the hips and buttocks narrower. Not Zack's body at all, but something startlingly familiar about it. The body, exactly like hers. Exactly!

She touched the shoulder. Cold. She pulled the body toward her. It was heavy and rolled stiffly, the head sinking into the pillow where Yvonne's head had previously rested. She saw the face, the still open eyes. It was her. It was Yvonne. Her meticulous image. And then she blinked! Or did she? Had it been she who blinked? Flinching, she climbed on top of the body and pressed the grey wire down on her throat, her teeth gritting savagely. There was no struggle. No sound. She stared into her lifeless face.

"Die." She grabbed for the black hair and it came off in her hands, the bald head alarming her. In the darkness, she collapsed onto the statue, the polyester resin hard beneath her, like a corpse. She kissed the lips, tears in her eyes. "Who are you?" A hand on the hard breast while she wept, "Mommy, help me. Mommy, please, Mommy..." Her head wavered. She thought she might slip into unconsciousness. Then she heard a sound from behind her, a sound coming from the corner of the room, a voice. "Yes, Yvonne." Shocked, she checked over her shoulder, toward the closet, saw the door opening, slowly opening, another woman stepping out, long black hair, red bra and panties, stepping toward her. Another image of her, but not. The woman with manly features.

Yvonne leapt from the bed, knocked the woman to the ground, the wire thrust fiercely across the woman's throat, her elbows pressing down, increasing the killing weight.

There was a brightness in the room. Blinding lights flicked on. Squinting toward the doorway, Yvonne saw the man with close-cropped hair and a goatee standing there. The doctor sergeant, his hand on the light switch, his eyes watching her expectantly. Another man stepped in beside him, a big man wearing a suit and an outdated hair style. He quickly scanned Yvonne's body, smirking to himself as two female officers raced toward her, pulling her from the woman. No, the man. She saw it now. Zack. It was Zack lying there, holding his throat, rising up, sitting by the side of the bed.

Cooper took two steps into the room and waited until Yvonne was standing, naked and sobbing. "Put something on her." He tilted his head toward one of the female officers, then averted his eyes while the officer covered Yvonne with a bed sheet.

Cooper saw Yvonne's hands protruding from the creases of white sheet, noticed the grey wire where it was cutting deeply into the flesh along both her hands.

"It's not real," Yvonne said, snorting out wet breath. She stared at the polyester resin sculpture on the bed, held her hands over her mouth as if warming them. "Not real," she said into her cupped palms, bound by wire.

"Not this one," Pendegast countered.

Zack threw the wig off and hurried to pull a t-shirt and jeans on, then left the room, glancing back at Yvonne.

She looked to see what was holding her hands together. Telephone wire, wrapped around her tightly squeezed fists. "It's me." She was shivering, trembling. She turned away, the female officers holding her arms. She pulled one arm free and bent over, collapsed to her knees, shoved her fingers down her throat, vomit splattering on the floor. The female officers— having no idea how to react— stepped back from the display, avoiding the spray of vomit, watching while Yvonne heaved and gagged. When she was done, one of the female officers pulled Yvonne's hand away from her mouth and— grimacing— cuffed her.

Cooper stepped near to wipe Yvonne's mouth with a tissue lifted from his pocket. "You'll be okay," he assured her. "Dr. Healey will help you." He handed the tissue to Pendegast, who tossed it toward the corner.

"Help," Pendegast muttered in disgust.

Yvonne nodded, trembling so fiercely that her jaw rattled when she asked, "Where am I?"

"You're right here, Yvonne." Cooper glanced at Pendegast, saw the look of genuine revulsion on the big cop's face, as if he wanted to do serious harm to Yvonne.

"Help her get dressed," Cooper calmly instructed the female officer, leaving the room with Pendegast following close behind.

"Right, again," Pendegast announced in a brash voice.

Cooper ignored him.

"You don't solve murders sitting in front of a computer." Pendegast took hold of Cooper's shoulder, stopping him. Cooper simply stared at the hand while Pendegast stepped around front and gave his colleague a triumphant smile. "Guess I'm not needed here any more. My work is done." He wandered toward the open doorway. "See ya, Doctor... Sergeant. Whatever you're supposed to be."

Cooper watched the open doorway, thinking of all the things he could have said to Pendegast, all the things he should have said, but held back. A moment later, interrupting the litany of insults that raced through his mind, sounds issued from behind him. He turned to see Yvonne being led out of the bedroom. He licked his lips, then searched his pocket for the stick of balm, traced his chapped lips with it in a way that caught Yvonne's attention, making her stop dead in her tracks.

Yvonne shifted her eyes to see Zack lingering on the threshold of Kieley's apartment across the outer hallway. He was smoking a cigarette in a distracted way, frowning down at the hardwood floor, unwilling to meet her eyes, the lipstick and eye shadow still on his face. Behind him stood Mr. Prouse and Mrs. Kieley, watching Yvonne being escorted out. Mrs. Kieley wept and clutched Mr. Prouse's arm for support. And then there was Gregory Kieley, stepping ahead, a videotape in his hand. He raised it as she passed.

"Finally," he said. "The real story."

Yvonne gave no reply, knowing nothing of how that would be possible. All of the occupants of the house standing there, as if they had planned this against her, as if all of them had known and worked to make her insane.

She was led down over the stairs and out into the foggy night. The coolness breathing through everything once again. The stirring of the leaves. The freshness against the skin. The cleansing lusciousness of breath.

Sweet relief.

PART SIX: ANSWERING

ONE

The steam from the pad thai drifted up into Cooper's face as he stirred the bean sprouts, rice noodles, egg, green onions and sauce together to create one scrumptious pan of mush. He hadn't smelled anything so delicious in weeks. He was actually salivating and had to wipe at the corner of his mouth. Natasha had created the feast for him. pad thai with her secret sauce, and chocolate yogurt cheesecake for dessert.

Cooper laid down the wooden spoon and picked at a few noodles, hungrily gobbling and slurping them into his mouth. He shut his eyes and thrilled at the taste, savouring the flavours, the blandness of the bean sprouts, the freshness of the scallions, the dankness of the peanuts, the saltiness (but the inexplicable velvety other taste) of the shrimp paste... Opening his eyes, he secretively glanced around the kitchen. Natasha was in the bathroom. Again, he shifted his face over the steam, lower, savouring, lower, bending his knees, positioning his face until it was little more than a foot above the pan, then he stuck his fingers into the pad thai, first his fingertips, sensing the gooey warmth, then deeper into the meal, shoving his curled fingers fully into the mess. Scooping up the food, he raised handfuls to his mouth and stuffed them in.

"Hey!" Natasha standing in the doorway. "Get outta there, you pig!"

Cooper straightened, snapped out of his carnal revery. He stood with his curled fingers covered in sauce, rice noodles hanging from his lips and between his fingers. He sucked the noodles up and stared at his hands with a guilty shocked expression, as if he could not comprehend what he had just done. Or was it just an act?

"Wash your hands," Natasha said, "you rotten beast."

Silently, Cooper turned away, grumbling something under his breath as he moved to the sink and spun the taps, washing the traces away.

At the dining room table, Cooper popped open a tall tin of Guinness and poured it into his pint glass. He sipped at the thick creamy head and ate a careful forkful of pad thai. His zest for the meal had abated somewhat after he was caught in the throes of gluttony.

Natasha ate in silence, occasionally peeking at him over her fork.

When Cooper was done, he pushed his plate aside and yanked the silver platter of cheesecake toward him.

"You want a piece?" he asked.

Natasha shook her head, daintily wiped her lips with the red cloth napkin. "I'm watching my figure."

"Me too, you bet." Cooper sliced a thick piece of chocolate yogurt cheese-cake, realized the denseness of it as he slid it onto his plate, sensing how that denseness would feel in his stomach. When he laid it to rest, Natasha stood and smartly took the seat beside him, edging her chair nearer.

"Share?" she asked.

"I don't know." He gave her a skeptical once over.

Natasha lifted the fork from his fingers. She held it a moment, staring down at the cake, contemplating what she was about to say.

"Congratulations," she proposed, then dropped the fork to use her middle and index finger to scoop up the cake and raise a smeared hunk to Cooper's lips. Cooper opened his mouth for her, anticipating the overpowering sweetness and sourness coupled with the intoxicating richness of the chocolate. Natasha slid her fingers deep into his mouth. He sucked her fingers clean, then bit down on them, held them that way while he growled low in his throat.

Natasha watched his eyes, wondering, but then— once he released his grip— redirected her focus on scooping up more cake, patiently feeding him.

TWO

Sergeant Cooper entered the interview room at the Waterford Psychiatric Hospital to discover Yvonne already seated in place. Immediately, he noticed that she had cut her hair, the style excessively short, but not quite a brush-cut. He nodded to the orderly, excusing him, then pulled out a chair and sat with good-humoured ease. In his hand, he held a thick manilla envelope. He laid it gently on the desk and smiled.

"How are you?" he asked.

Yvonne nodded languidly. Medicated to the hilt, almost slow-motion, Cooper noted, not allowing this observation to dampen his spirit.

"I have something very important for you." He slid the manilla envelope across the table. "A copy of your mother's journal. We have to keep the original, but it's all there, her words that count."

"Words?" Yvonne Unwin hesitantly touched the envelope. Slowly, she reached for it with both hands, her fingers tightening, crumpling the edges. She gripped and pulled it against her chest, held it there while she stared toward the wire mesh window to the left of Cooper.

"It's very important that you know the truth about your mother."

"What's that?" Yvonne sluggishly asked.

"You read these." He pointed to the envelope. "This will help."

"No." She smiled feebly, her languid eyes shifting down to the package. "What's this, again?"

"A photocopy of your mother's diary."

"Oh." She carefully laid the envelope on the table and stared at it. A moment later she poked it with her fingertips. "The truth... just something..." Yvonne whispered at the envelope. She thickly licked her lips, then repeated the action, "... made up... like everything else..." Her voice faded off. "Are you really..."

"What?"

"Really... a policeman?"

"Yes, but I'm a doctor, too. A psychologist."

Yvonne's eyes traced the edge of the broad wooden table-top. "I remember."

"You've been through quite an ordeal. You've been put through..."

Yvonne shook her head, bluntly, back and forth, back and forth...

"Have you been watching the news?"

"Yes, I've seen the TV... The show... I'm on television... now..."

"Then you know about Gregory Potter?"

She nodded. "He's in it, too."

"He's still in our hands. But we'll be releasing him. The general consensus with the crown attorney's office is that he's innocent. They're ready to charge you with the killings. The tape of you and Terri Lawton."

"They show us..."

"Yes."

Yvonne curiously regarded the manilla envelope.

"And there's also the DNA results. Your hair matches hairs found on the bodies of the murder victims. That, combined with the videotape..." Cooper searched Yvonne's inert eyes.

"I did kill them?"

"I don't know. That depends."

"How?... How can it depend?"

Cooper glanced at the door, the guard posted outside, just beyond the small observation window.

"There was something bothering me about you identifying Gregory Potter in relation to your mother's murder. How you were there, alone with the two women. If you were so terrified of your mother, then what would you be doing there alone? Does that make sense?"

Yvonne numbly stared at Cooper.

"And you didn't recognize Potter, because the face you had in your mind was very different."

"Which face?"

"The face of the person who really killed your mother. This is the face you carried with you, that dominated your thoughts."

Yvonne stared, the numbness shifting toward vague helplessness.

"You told me about the telephone calls from your mother. Your father answering the phone always, making certain you took those calls. We have gone over the memories, each time going into his studio where there was another line. A private line. Remember?"

"My father..." her listless tongue shaping the words, "... was... sensitive. Classical music and... read books, important books. My mother, she was..."

"I'm a policeman, like your father, but I'm something else, too."

Yvonne stared at Cooper, squinting at what he had said.

"The diary told me what I needed to know. If you read this you'll know the truth."

"No."

"Your mother says in her diary that she tried to call you, tried and tried, but your father wouldn't let her speak to you."

"She spoke to me." Yvonne licked her lips, searched the very centres of Cooper's pupils, catching sight of herself, her pale face, her clipped black hair. "She spoke to me. Every day."

"I don't think so, Yvonne."

"She called me all the time." Yvonne's expression shifted, woodenly alert, as if she might be seeing something behind the fog of medication. "My father... answered. He gave me the..."

"I believe he was the one making the phone calls. He was the one calling and calling and pretending he was your mother."

"I can't see..."

"He said abusive things to you?"

"My mother?"

"Couldn't your father have been making the calls from the other line in his study? Just think. Two telephone lines. One in his study, his private line and the family line." Cooper slid the pages out of the envelope. "I photocopied the cover as well."

"No." She gave the empty envelope another look, as if speaking to it, "My father... was..." She studied the top page, a copy of a painting, the image of angels, great white-winged angels. Their eyes so content, their skin unmarked, robes of the purest white, wings of the softest down. Tears welled up in her eyes, slow tears that she did not even recognize because they rose from so deep. They broke and slid along her cheeks while she studied the painting.

"He wanted to turn you against her? He told you not to ever see her?"

Yvonne stared off at the pale blue wall of the hospital interview room, the wire mesh window, the grey sky beyond. Summer at its end. Summer losing its heat, the world cooling, soon to be frozen over.

"He warned you that she'd harm you, touch you. Do unspeakable things. That she was a lesbian and would try to assault you. This horrified you. You loved your mother. You loved her so much, didn't you?"

Yvonne set her fingertips against the photocopy, gently tracing the length of it. "The telephone would ring... at night..."

"Who really killed your mother, Yvonne? Whose face are you seeing in your mind?"

Her fingers moved along the edge of the manuscript, then pushed under, between the pages and the table-top, hiding her fingertips, retracting from the light.

"It wasn't Potter, was it? Even though it was his gun that fired the shots. It wasn't him."

Yvonne lifted her other hand, distraughtly running her fingers through her oily hair, startled by its shortness.

"My father read poetry to me, doctor. 'Down by the sea, Down by the sea, my Annabel Lee.'"

"It was your father."

Yvonne's head jittered slightly, her eyes shifting to the doctor's lips.

"Your father."

"No... My father would never... He was..."

"Your father was jealous of your mother. He visited your mother and found her in bed with Potter's wife. Yvonne? Did you see what happened? Was it planned?"

Yvonne stared, not seeing the doctor at all, not seeing what he was saying but viewing what she had actually witnessed. The doctor's words urging, compelling the link.

She was sitting in the dark blue LTD, parked on a street with rows of suburban bungalows. It was a busy street with cars steadily passing by. On the ride over, she had asked her father where they were going.

"A friend's house," her father had told her, glancing at her where she sat in the passenger seat. The smell of the leather seats, the hot air, the humidity in the car. No air conditioning. The air conditioning was broken. The humidity sticking to her, moistening her skin. She was wearing shorts, jean cut-offs, her legs sticking to the seat beneath her.

She waited outside, the car parked eight houses down from the house that her father had entered. She knew the houses, the colours. She remembered counting them, over and over, the sequence, pale blue, yellow, white... The window in the car had been rolled down, the heat so stifling, her sweaty legs adhered to the leather. The sounds of crickets, a lawnmower, sprinklers sweeping back and forth... She had to get out.

The car door was heavy. She was so tired from lack of sleep. The telephone waking her in the night, robbing her of her dreams. Plus the intense, punishing heat. It was impossible to sleep. There had been a heatwave and the telephone would not stop ringing. She had dreamed it, waking, or it had been real. The telephone ringing. All night long. Her mother calling. Her wicked mother saying that she would come to do things to her in her sleep. Her father had warned her to be careful, to watch out for her mother. Her mother was sick, insane. Her mother would rape her. "Do you know what rape is?" her father had calmly enquired, always calmly, reasonably, sitting on the wide cushion of the low oak-framed chair in his den, a small room lined with shelves and shelves of books, the place where they had their important talks, where they talked for hours and hours.

Yvonne had nodded, understanding what rape meant, but confused by the thought of how a woman would rape another woman. It was all the more disturbing because of her inability to imagine the act.

"She'll rape you," her father had assured her. "Your mother is extremely sick. Mentally ill. Be careful."

Yvonne shut the heavy car door and stood on the sidewalk, watching the driveway eight houses up, the heat wavering from the asphalt. She began walking toward the house, the day cut with such stunning clarity. She stood in front of the house's short banked lawn, looking around.

Behind her, cars passed. She didn't like the neighbourhood. It seemed fine on the surface, but there was something not right about it. It was old, vaguely run down. She moved up the driveway and heard a harsh muddled shout through the walls of the house, her father's voice. No mistaking it. She stopped in her tracks, almost stumbled. She had not heard him shout in quite some time. Only when her mother was still living with them, and— even then— only rarely.

Something was terribly wrong. She thought of going in the front door, but she was not supposed to be there. Not present at all. It was a secret, like something revealed in a nightmare that could never be repeated to anyone.

Another demanding shout, not as loud as before.

Why was he shouting? She walked around behind the house, noticed the lone tree growing between the two houses. A maple with bright green leaves reaching for the sky. A window in the neighbour's house, a woman doing something with her hands, preoccupied, perhaps the dishes, then glancing up, out, directly at Yvonne.

She continued along the concrete walk, stepping into a view of a rectangular back yard, mature trees and an old paint-worn picnic table, a round rusted barbecue on its three legs, a window adjacent to the narrow concrete walkway. She had to stand up on her tiptoes to peek in. There were drapes pulled across, red drapes, but there was a view through a tiny parting where the drapes were drawn.

Two women were lying on the bed, naked. They were both facing up, their legs bound with tape, their arms behind their backs so that their bodies were turned slightly. One was not moving; the other was struggling against her binds. The door was in the process of being shut, the lip of the door being yanked closed, an arm and the side of a man, a man in a police uniform, his face not looking back, but the sideburn and neck were unmistakably her father's.

Door completely shut. The struggling one, the one who looked remarkably like her mother, rolled off the bed and kneeled up beside the nightstand. She was side-on and sobbing while she shifted, her bound hands pushing against the knob, her cramped fingers scrambling to pull open the nightstand drawer. Awkwardly, she lifted out a pair of scissors by the handle-hole, but they dropped from her trembling fingertips, back into the drawer, (Yvonne twitching with fright), her mother almost buckling over in despair, in weakness, sobbing louder, her mouth opening wider against the gag. An instant only, before she regained strength, straightened, tried again, the scissors at her fingertips.

Yvonne watched intently, focused, a buzzing in her head that obliterated the sound of the back door opening, a man stepping out, striding toward her, nearer, until every nerve in Yvonne's body shrieked into action as a hand came down on her shoulder. She jerked back, screaming, her wide eyes fixed on her father.

"Yvonne," he whispered, "calm down. Your mother's in there."

"What're you doing?" she asked. "Mother's—" She pointed toward the window, uncertain if she should warn him.

"Come inside." Her father checked the grounds as he reached out and took her arm, gently, so very gentle with her, his touch, but his intentions, his thoughts...

She went with him, in through the back door that connected with the kitchen. Entering, she glanced at the stove, the hands of the clock, 3:15. The dials and settings for the auto timers, something cooking in the oven, a roast or chicken. The smell of it cooking, the odour turning her stomach.

"Wait here," he said, motioning to a kitchen chair with steel legs and a flower design on its vinyl-covered back-rest and cushions. His eyes on her as he began backing away, as if the mere sight of her was changing him. He lingered near the doorway.

Yvonne sat immediately, fretting about her mother, the scissors, wanting to say something, to warn her father. Her mother was crazy, insane...

"Don't move." Her father's head turned abruptly, hearing a sound from down the hallway, the sound changing him again, sparking his police instincts. "Stay there." And he had gone off, reaching with his right gloved hand to draw his police revolver from his holster.

Yvonne stood from her chair, peeked out of the kitchen doorway, staring to the right down the dim hallway. The house was strange to her, a stranger's house. Her mother in a stranger's house, living there in a way Yvonne could not understand. She inched out further, gasping for breath, her heart hammering, her skin tingling all over, out further into the hot hallway, down toward the bedroom. The bedroom door seemingly so far away. The door was shut. It had slammed. She only remembered it now. A slam, or was it a gunshot? The shut door barred sight, but she heard the sounds. Her father's voice, angry, whispering, grunting. A woman's whimpering.

The explicit words through the door, "You cunt. I fucking hate you. You're poison."

A woman's quiet sobbing, muffled and then clearer. A pretty voice, Yvonne thought, strangely. Such a pretty voice being hurt. Her hand automatically on the doorknob. She turned it, opened carefully, slowly, her father with a tight handful of her mother's hair, pushing her mother's face between the naked legs of the woman who was not moving, shoving it hard until her mother could not breathe. In his other hand, the revolver pressed against her mother's temple. And the hate in his face, the devilish red-shadowed hate that distracted him to such a degree that he seemed not to see Yvonne at all.

Her mother in profile, the left side of her face, the left eye turning to see Yvonne, her mother screeching behind the gag, the eye shutting, screeching higher as her father pushed with all his might, then released, her head coming up from the pain, her back arching, the telephone suddenly ringing, her father reaching back for it, his hand blindly searching on the nightstand, grabbing the telephone and yanking it from the wall. The bells of the telephone jangling as he tossed it onto the bed, the wire in his hands as he shoved away the revolver, the wire in the red-shadowed light of the stifling room.

A length of wire across her mother's throat.

Yvonne, tears in her eyes, bursting ahead, "Stop!" Her father finally seeing her, hearing her, looking toward the noise, almost as if expecting her, as if this was some sort of dark lesson that needed learning. "You won't be like her," he grunted, tossing the wire aside and snatching up the pistol.

Yvonne's eyes flinched toward the open drawer of the nightstand. She saw the gleam of steel, the blades of the scissors. She ran to the drawer, snatched hold of the scissors and held them clutched in both her trembling hands. She was shaking, violently. She sensed a wetness fan out against her jean shorts, warm running fluid quickly chilling along her legs.

"No," she said, stepping back, her father jumping off her mother, her mother gasping for breath through her sobs. Her father aiming the pistol at Yvonne, holding it level with his daughter's face, realizing what he was doing. Carefully, he released the cocked hammer and set the gun down on the edge of the mattress. Her mother's eyes fixed on the gun.

"Get away," Yvonne shrieked, her arms shaking violently, her eyes hurting from the strain. Something thumping onto the floor, her mother's feet having kicked the gun away. She saw it lying there and then her father's eyes as they anxiously shifted toward it.

"Don't touch that," he said. "Don't."

"Don't," she said, racing for it but kicking it under the bed by mistake.

"Move away," Yvonne said. She was so terrified: her legs practically convulsing, her arms shaking, the scissors jittering. Yvonne was weeping, her eyes blurring with tears, the image fogging over. She swiped at her eyes and steadied the scissors.

"Listen, if you touch that gun." He glanced toward the bottom edge of the bed. "It'll ruin everything. It'll be the end of us."

Yvonne shook her head.

"Your mother's sick."

Yvonne peeked at the other naked woman. The woman was staring at Yvonne, staring and staring, not blinking, and not moving, her breasts and hips, her legs and hair, her nude body bathed in the red light through the drapes pulled shut to the world.

"Get away," she screamed at her father, and he did as he was told, backing toward the corner as she inched nearer the bed where she reached and managed to cut the tape on her mother's hands and feet.

"Yvonne," her mother croaked, her voice barely recognizable, raspy and sputtering. She tried to swallow, tried to reach out to touch Yvonne, but Yvonne stepped back. Her mother sat on the bed, struggling to swallow, the muscles in her shoulders and neck working and working. Her mother turning on the bed, staring at the other woman. The loving tears, both hands on the woman's face as she sobbed, her mother's sweat-soaked face, her long black hair matted at her forehead and at her temples and cheeks.

"She's dead," her father barked.

"You bastard," her mother's voice hoarsely barking out as she rushed Yvonne's father. He grabbed her lashing hands, shoved her back onto the bed. Bouncing there, she caught sight of the scissors in Yvonne's hands. Snatching them away, she went for Yvonne's father.

"No," Yvonne screamed, her mother freezing, her father slapping the scissors away and tossing her back on the bed, her father on top of her mother again, the telephone wire against her mother's throat, her mother's eyes widening, revolving to watch Yvonne, the gasping of her swollen lips. It seemed to last forever. She remembered what her father had told her about how difficult it really was to kill a person. The body was very resilient.

"She won't hurt you," he frantically said over his shoulder, his forearms jerking as he yanked the wire tighter. "I won't let her—"

"Don't," Yvonne cried, dropping to her knees, reaching into the darkness under the bed for the gun.

"Don't touch it," her father said, kicking her back.

"Stop," she whimpered from the floor, "please, stop, stop..." She thought of going for the gun again. Grabbing it and squeezing the trigger, but she could not move. What would her mother do to her if Yvonne shot her father? They would be left alone. Alone, together in this bedroom. Her naked mother. What would happen? Shuddering, she ran from the room, out through the kitchen and into the back yard. She ran up the sloping yard, to the back fence, but it was too high to climb. A muffled boom from the house. She turned and watched the back door, saw her father coming after her, his form rising up the sloping back yard, his uniform, his hat, his gloved hands.

She faced the fence, frantically tried to scramble up the tall white slats. Minutes or hours later, she felt a hand on her shoulder and gasped in terror, turning to see her father standing there.

"She won't hurt you now," he kindly said, hugging her, soothing her. "She won't hurt you, sweetheart. You don't need to worry any more."

Yvonne watched her father's lips, her father's lips speaking silently. She was not listening. She focused hard to see the face, the whole. Not her father at all, but Dr. Cooper's lips. Or was it Sergeant Cooper's lips? He was speaking words that did not match what she was recalling.

"Is that the way it was?" he asked.

Yvonne stared at him, wondering why he would want to figure this out. Such a mystery to this man she did not even know.

"Potter didn't kill your mother, did he?"

No reply.

"He's being released tomorrow." Cooper straightened in his chair, pushed up the sleeves of his purple turtleneck. "Potter negotiated a plea bargain, pleaded guilty to a break and entry charge in relation to your apartment in exchange for testifying against you. He admitted knowing about the murders of the three women here in St. John's. He said that he followed you. I've read his statement. He admitted knowing and letting the murders build. But he can't be charged with that. There's no charge. He was aware of that at the time."

"I can't..." Yvonne said blankly, chewing on the corner of her bottom lip.

"Can't what?"

"... understand."

"Potter let the murders go on to have his name cleared in the most comprehensive way."

"I can't understand." Her fingers crept toward the diary, absentmindedly caressing the photocopied cover of the angels.

"He understands."

"No, no one."

"Listen, Yvonne." Cooper leaned across the desk, his hands very near hers. "Please listen to me. He has it all figured out. He believed you killed your mother. The woman next door to his house testified to seeing you through the window. You were visiting her, you told the court. You testified that you walked over to see your mother and found Gregory Potter there. Ultimately, it was Potter's revolver that killed your mother and Doreen Potter. Did your father steal it from Potter's holster, then replace it later?"

Yvonne turned up a corner of the angel cover and gently inched it back until seeing her mother's handwriting.

"He told me that he saw you in Toronto, the dead image of your mother. He assumed that you killed your mother and his wife. Because he knew that he didn't. And you were there; you admitted to being there in your testimony. He was dealing with the pain of losing his wife coupled with the pain of being wrongfully accused. He assumed that you were the killer. He couldn't believe his eyes. He couldn't believe that you didn't recognize him. You didn't."

"I don't know who... he is."

"He followed you and found out that you were moving to St. John's. He became infatuated with you. You reminded him of the woman who had been intimate with his wife. Intimacy. That shared sensation. He longed for you and loathed you. You were the connection to her. Then he set you up. He followed you. He made it seem as if you were killing those women. He planted hairs. The hairs between the fingers of the corpses were arranged so expertly. They had to be planted."

"Did he?"

"You tell me."

"I didn't kill my mother."

"I know. Neither did Potter."

"My mother."

"Your mother was a gentle woman," Cooper said. "An artist. I've read what she's written." He set his palm on the manuscript, searching Yvonne's eyes. "She didn't deserve what was done to her. She deserved to love you. For you to love her. Her memory must be honoured by bringing her real killer to justice."

"You don't... know."

"You were made to think this way, forced, abused mentally by your father. Isn't that right? You have to see this. Even if you did kill Terri Lawton, it wasn't really you. Your father's hate and bigotry made you kill, made you fear that you were like your mother, a lesbian, so you killed those women because you were attracted to them, craving for your mother, wanting her love, the violent horror of her death perverting that love, making it carnal, your desperation, but then your rejection of it."

Yvonne stared at Cooper, her lips parted, frozen, her tongue stirring, saying nothing.

"Is that what happened?"

"My mother..."

"You couldn't let her live, so you found her in other women, women who loved you or tried to love you, but it became sexual. It had to become sexual because they wanted you as a lover, not as a daughter. It was what you feared from your mother. You only wanted love. Motherly love. So you found the sexuality and killed it."

Yvonne numbly shook her head, her eyebrows twitching.

"If you killed those other women, it was fear that made you do it. Human fear and disgust. Implanted disgust."

The twitching travelled into her cheeks and then her lips. A moment later, her eyes flooded with tears. She wanted to tell him, to tell anyone, but what could she possibly gain?

"Yvonne, please."

"What?" Tears spilled from her eyes, the sudden sound of her name like a slap in the face.

"The truth."

"Why?"

"To make you better."

"You can do that..." Quiet silent tears. Squinting, her head tilted to the side. "...with the truth?"

"Yes, you can do that."

Yvonne gazed down at the journal, her tears puckering the paper in tiny rings. She thought of her father. Her father had been protecting her.

Cooper leaned back in his chair, sighed, then glanced at his watch.

"Will you please think about what I've said?" Slowly rising to his feet, he glanced at the journal. "Tell me if I'm wrong."

Yvonne stared up at him, her jaw slack.

"They've re-opened your mother's case."

"I killed her," she blurted out.

"Did you?"

"Yes."

"I don't believe that."

"No." Her pleading eyes drifting toward the door, as if to block the doctor's exit.

"Yvonne? I want to help you. Dr. Healey wants to help you, to open your memory so that you can see things as they were."

"Didn't I kill those women?" she said, trying to stand, but her arms weak. She dropped back into her seat.

"I don't know. Are you to blame for what your father made of you?"

"Please..."

"I can't tell you, Yvonne. You have to tell me."

Yvonne watched him. No words. There were no words for what she was feeling and would continue to feel regardless of what words she propped up. She watched Cooper be let out of the room. She saw a woman waiting there for him, a pretty blonde-haired woman who was familiar. The woman greeted Cooper, but her eyes watched Yvonne. Her name. It was a pretty name that suited her. Natasha. They turned and walked away. A man and a woman. Turned and walked away together.

The door remained open. Yvonne stood without paying attention to the guard. She slowly wandered down the corridor with the photocopy of her mother's diary in her arms. Crossing the threshold of her room, the door shut behind her, the lock harshly clicking in place, she sat at her bare desk in the corner and slipped the pages from the envelope, carefully began reading the sections Cooper had placed on top:

Thursday, August 10th

I wonder if I will ever see my beautiful daughter again. Fred is doing his best to make certain Yvonne does not see me. He has warned me again and again. I love her so much and I am in such pain, my stomach in constant knots. To take my beautiful child away from me.

I cherish the photographs that I took from the house. It's all that I have of her. My baby girl. I only wish that we could be together again in some way, that I could see her, talk with her, find out what is happening in her growing life. I'm missing so much, each passing day. Unforgivable.

I've thought it all through and decided that I cannot return to Fred, for Yvonne's sake. I don't love Fred. I love Doris. It has taken me all this time to admit it to myself. And I cannot go against these feelings any longer. These very real feelings that I have been keeping hidden for so many years.

Tuesday, August 14th

Received fantastic news today. Fred telephoned to tell me that he and Yvonne will come visit tomorrow. They want to talk to me. They want to meet Doris. I am walking on the clouds, a perpetual smile on my lips, but I am slightly nervous as well, hoping that everything will go well on their visit. I pray that this will be a new beginning for all of us.

Yvonne is coming to see me! My precious child. I love her so.

EPILOGUE

Natasha lay asleep in Cooper's bed. Cooper was standing naked by the window, the faint moonlight out over the yard finding its effortless way to the side of Natasha's pale face. Nothing would ever wake her. Cooper could come and go as he chose, any time of night, and she never so much as stirred. She would be sleeping in the exact same position as when he left. Late nights. The sort of work he did. He watched Natasha and then allowed his eyes to drift toward the closet. He wondered. Again, he studied Natasha.

Tiptoeing toward the closet, he reached for the knob and allowed himself to turn it, slowly, creating a mystery. He made a horror-show creaking sound. A faint grin softened his lips as the door opened and he was faced by the impression of his shirts hanging there. But what he was after could not be seen so obviously.

Kneeling on the carpet, he reached into the closet and pulled up the edge of carpet toward the back. Beneath the flap of pile were two strips of wood that were easily pulled loose. He reached down into the sub-floor and gripped something, carefully manoeuvered it out. As his hand shifted back toward him, the moonlight revealed the object to be a file folder.

Cooper stood and shut the closet door. He stepped over to the window and opened the file that had been sent to him weeks before the first murder. Kieley had sent it. The photographs of Patricia Unwin and Donna Potter. He grew excited looking at the photos, imagining what these two women had done to each other only moments before their brutal deaths. The detailed description of the double murder that had first aroused Cooper's curiosity, had given him the taste for lesbians, had allowed him to duplicate the original MO from that double murder twenty years ago. And so much intense stimulation in the process.

Turning his head, he glanced at the Mickey Mouse telephone, then shifted his attention to Natasha.

She's so beautiful, he thought. So perfect.

Shutting the folder, he scratched his goatee. Not a drop of sweat on him. A coolness in the room. Case closed. The murders neatly explained. Everyone happy. He was a celebrity now. The famous doctor sergeant. But more of a celebrity than people realized, considering what he had done.

He recalled his conversation with Kieley, how Kieley had said to him, "I don't care what you did. As long as they put Yvonne away." Kieley had doctored the videotape of Terri Lawton so that it appeared as if Yvonne— instead of Cooper— had killed the woman. Nothing mattered to Kieley as long as he exacted his revenge. And he had done that, pushed Yvonne over the edge. Yes, Yvonne had been with each of the murdered women, but only as a lover. Cooper had been following Yvonne from the start, had waited outside each location for Yvonne's departure, and then gone in to kill. Easy as pie. Simple as ABC.

Now, only to anticipate the next case, where he might have the information at hand to duplicate another series of murders, create another sensational case, and thus galvanize his fame. No doubt he would be consulted to help with murders all over the world now. What opportunity! On the talk shows he would speak of charity work, of esthetics and worthy causes. There was no limit to what he might accomplish. No borders. No boundaries. The media would listen and translate and cover the entire globe. He would become a murder authority. No, not "become." He already was one. From both sides. Killer and cop. A proven, murder authority.